About the Author

Brittany is a former middle grades science teacher, who graduated from UNC Chapel Hill with degrees in Education and Biology. She lives in North Carolina with her seven cats, who are really just small dragons. She spent over ten years committed to cat rescue before stepping back, allowing more time to write.

Sapphire

Brittany Leake

Sapphire

Enjoy this new adventure!

—Brittany Leake

Vanguard Press

VANGUARD PAPERBACK

© Copyright 2024
Brittany Leake

The right of Brittany Leake to be identified as author of
this work has been asserted by her in accordance with the
Copyright, Designs and Patents Act 1988.

A CIP catalogue record for this title is available from the British Library.

ISBN 978-1-83794-281-7

This is a work of fiction. Names, characters, businesses, places, events and
incidents are either the products of the author's imagination or used in a
fictitious manner. Any resemblance to actual persons, living or dead, or actual
events is purely coincidental.

Vanguard Press is an imprint of
Pegasus Elliot Mackenzie Publishers Ltd.
www.pegasuspublishers.com

First Published in 2024

Vanguard Press
Sheraton House Castle Park
Cambridge England

Printed & Bound in Great Britain

Dedication

To my mom, who was my first reader, and to Charlotte,
who kindled the spark.

the courtyard far below. The acrid scent of smoke burned her nostrils as she tried to stay calm and control her breathing.

The blue glow was coming from the Queen, lying on the floor near the bedroom and quickly fading.

She ran to her mother, her hands fluttering uselessly over her burnt and broken body. Her nightgown was stuck to her chest, blood soaking it and beginning to drip to the floor. Zhafaera pulled the cloth open slightly and could see a raw, gaping oval on her chest. The Sapphire was gone. Someone had ripped it from her. Zhafaera felt ill, the Sapphire's presence in her mind still grating and making her head pound. She looked back to her mother's face and jumped as she realized her eyes were open, bright, and staring at her. Her voice was the barest whisper as she struggled to get words out. Zhafaera leaned closer.

"*He has it. Run.*" Then her eyes closed, the glow faded, the mind-scream stopped, and Zhafaera was alone. She ran.

She ran through the royal quarters and hit the servants' stairs in the back, racing down the stairs and through the door. Down the hallway of the first floor, she stopped at the door to the throne room, hesitating. It was the shortest way out of the palace, but she could sense the Sapphire inside. Anything that made the Gem *scream* like that could not be good. On the other hand, she couldn't let anyone else take the Sapphire. She had to see.

Opening the door, Zhafaera crept silently through the room until she reached the large, polished silver throne.

She froze as she recognized the figure standing at the enormous window in the opposite wall, outlined in moonlight. Her uncle turned slowly, smiling oddly at Zhafaera as her heart pounded in her throat. His long black hair framed a pale, handsome face that was currently splattered in blood. In his hand was the Sapphire, about the size of her fist and flashing almost angrily.

"You can't," Zhafaera whispered.

"Oh, I can," Velexar assured her. "I can, and I *have*." He held the Sapphire up and Zhafaera scrambled to form a shield. Magic flowed to her, but she couldn't hold it without feeling like her head would explode. She ducked behind the throne instead, bracing for the impact. It never came. She felt the power of the Sapphire swell, but it was not under control. Peeking out quickly, she saw Velexar doubled over and knew the Sapphire was fighting back.

Zhafaera darted forward. Knives worked just as well as magic. She hadn't taken more than three steps before Velexar jerked up straight, the Sapphire gripped tight in both fists.

"I'll destroy us both if you make me," he hissed at her.

Zhafaera took a step back. "It will never be yours. A man will never wield the Sapphire."

"It will submit once you are dead, my dear. Now hold still while I kill you."

Zhafaera felt the Sapphire's power swell jerkily, and knew she had only moments. She made a split second decision. Flinging the knife in her hand towards Velexar, she turned and ran for the door. There was a flash of blue and a grunt, but Zhafaera didn't have time to risk a glance back. She could feel that the Sapphire had knocked the knife off course, but she thought she might have still hit him. Hopefully, it would slow him enough for her to make her escape.

Weaving her way through the back hallways, Zhafaera didn't stop until she reached the large, open entryway of the palace. Nothing stood between her and the exit but a wide open space. But crossing it meant she'd be an easy target for anyone who wanted to take a shot at her. In the end, speed won out, and she flew across the open space and out of the unlocked door.

She didn't have time to register her relief before she ran face first into something solid. No... some*one*. Large arms came around her shoulders and she fought to free herself or reach another knife.

"Princess? Princess Zhafaera, stop, it's Wren! I have a ship waiting in the harbor, we have to go *now*," the dark shape whispered. She stopped fighting and reassessed. Wren was her mother's most loyal commander – one of the few people she still met with besides Zhafaera – and Zhafaera knew if she could trust anyone, it would be him. As soon as she relaxed, Wren let go and stepped back. He pulled off his cloak and threw it around Zhafaera's shoulders.

"Pull the hood up," he said urgently, grabbing her arm and pulling her forward. Zhafaera hadn't registered until that point that there was a crowd gathered in the courtyard. Servants and nobles alike had abandoned the castle at the explosion, probably fearing the structure was unsound. Nervous babble rose from the crowd as they tried to figure out what had happened.

As she started to move through the crowd, an almighty shriek split the air and something huge swooped down on the center of the courtyard. Wren yanked her to the side and broke into a run with the rest of the screaming crowd. Zhafaera craned her neck, trying to see what it was against the dark sky.

There was just enough moonlight to outline the large shape as it came flying back over the palace walls for another pass. *Dragon,* Zhafaera thought in shock. *It's a dragon.* Flying behind it, flanking the dragon, were smaller shapes that she couldn't identify. At least it wasn't currently breathing fire down on them.

Tearing her eyes from the screaming dragon, Zhafaera ducked her head and let Wren pull her through the edge of the courtyard and into the night.

Chapter 1

Zhafaera had thought that when the keep at Crystal Point came into view, she would feel better, but somehow she was more nervous than she'd been since her flight from the city. She was torn – this was either brilliant or stupid, and at the moment, she wasn't sure which. But she still had hope that this was the right path.

Then a blast shook the ship and sent Zhafaera to her knees, splinters stabbing into her palms as she caught her fall on the rough planks. Her hope died as she braced herself and stood, looking behind them. She couldn't see anything yet, but she knew they were there. She *could* see her own ship, and what she saw wasn't good. Half of the aft of the ship was blown away, and they were listing sharply.

Working through the pain in her head, she drew power from the surrounding ocean and tried to *push* the ship forward. It helped a little, but she knew right away she wouldn't be able to keep it up long enough to make it to the shore.

Their ship was sinking. Fast. They were easy meat for the enormous black galleon coming up behind them. Their advantage had been in the head start their smaller ship had gotten, but now that was gone. The shore wasn't far, maybe a quarter mile, but Zhafaera doubted she could swim that far after over a week of little sleep and less food. She wanted to stamp her foot in frustration; to have come this far, only to be caught *now* was just too rich. But she had to give the appearance of calm for the sake of the crew scurrying across the deck like ants in a kicked anthill. She must be brave.

She jumped at a touch on her arm. Cursing silently, she turned to face Wren. He looked quite fearsome, a hardened man with a big, bushy beard and a distinct limp. After she'd run into him *that night,* he'd half dragged her through the Upper Market, avoiding the dragon circling the palace and weaving through side streets towards the docks. He had hurried her on board one of several ships that were almost underway. He was the reason they had avoided capture as long as they had. Without him, Zhafaera would almost certainly be dead by now.

"Princess," he said, "you have to get on a boat. We can send off all we have to draw their fire. You could shield yourself and make it to shore." He didn't say what she would do when she got to shore, when they had sunk her ship and her enemies decided to search the beach just to be certain.

She looked at the point of land jutting out into the sea. A castle—well, really a fort— made of dark grey rock sat atop the sheer cliff face, though all she could see from here were the dark walls and a few towers peeking over them. Its location on top of the cliff made it an ideal stronghold at the southernmost tip of Arenthia. At high tide, waves would crash directly on those cliffs, but for now a thin strip of sandy beach was barely visible. Not useful as a port, but excellent for a defensive position.

She was beginning to doubt her brilliant idea – sure, the family there had been their friends at one time, but who knew if they were still loyal? And even if they were, what was she bringing down on them? She had hoped to make it here before enemy forces caught up to her, but now...

"No, Captain," Zhafaera said, drawing herself up to her full height and shaking her head. "Even if I did make it to the beach, I wouldn't get far." She didn't mention that she was so tired she could barely see straight, let alone draw on her magic safely, or that when she did reach for her magic, she heard the echo of screaming. She glanced at the flag hanging limply at the base of the mast. "Raise the banner. We can at least go down with our pride." Assuming they let *her* go down at all. More likely, they would capture her and take her back to Arenthia for her uncle to deal with.

Wren grimaced, but bowed and limped off, barking orders as he went. He knew by now that it was no use arguing with her. She turned back to her study of the ruined stern of the ship, watching as the water climbed higher and higher up the deck. Soon it would be lapping at her feet, pulling at the hem of her loose blue gown. More than once she had considered ripping it off and burning it (just for good measure), but her mother had taught her that appearances must be maintained even – no, *especially* – in a crisis. Then again, maybe a crisis of this scale didn't

17

count. *I should ask mother to clarify that,* Zhafaera thought, before remembering that she could no longer ask her mother anything.

Zhafaera blinked back tears, looking up at the flag that was being hoisted into the air, watching as the wind caught it and unfurled it rapidly. The long shape of a dragon, blue on a field of silver, soared out over the deck. *This is it,* Zhafaera thought. *I failed.*

No sooner had the banner been lifted than the explosions started again. The mages must have finally come back in range. The first blast that started the sinking had probably been from their strongest mage posted at the top of the mast. And he had probably died, considering how much power it would have taken to hit them before they even saw the ship.

These blasts were targeted. The boats already in the water, filled with a few sailors each were first, the explosions sending founts of water ten meters into the air. They wanted to make sure no one escaped. Zhafaera grabbed hold of the railing as the waves crashed into the boat, rocking it back and forth and forcing it deeper into the water. She was beyond frustration – she knew she was stronger than all of them, but even if she could retaliate, she alone wouldn't be able to do much damage, weakened as she was. She decided she didn't care. Breathing deep and drawing on the very last of her strength, she took aim at the other ship's helm and sent a bolt of power straight for it, sending a spray of wood and men flying into the air. It was really quite satisfying.

That one strike was all she had time for before they hit again, hard. Several large pieces of wood flew towards her, and she threw up her arms to protect her face. She felt the wood scrape along her arms, and several small splinters flew through the cracks and struck her face. She only had a moment to feel the deck give under her feet, and then she was blown backwards and into the water. Her dress tugged her down deeper under the water, and she was dimly aware that the Sapphire was screaming in her mind again. Stunned as she was, she couldn't do much besides struggle weakly towards the light. As darkness closed around her, she somehow felt both sadness and relief.

***

Delan stood on the tower, looking out at the scene below. The dragon banner of the royal family burned at the tip of the mast, the only part of the ship still above water. Chunks of wood littered the sea around the ship, and the black ship circled the wreckage as if searching for something. It bore the banner of the royal family too, but with a strange change: the dragon on the flag was black and red, not the normal blue.

Word had come last week – a royal announcement through the message mirror – that Prince Velexar, brother to Queen Karaena, had assumed the throne after the "tragic" deaths of his sister and her daughter. Supposedly there was some kind of accident, but Delan wasn't clear on exactly what happened. The inquiries that his father had

19

made of other noble families in the lands surrounding them had been answered with nothing but praise for the Prince, despite the fact that he had always had a rather dark reputation. But no one seemed to think the deaths of the Queen and Princess suspicious – in fact, no one seemed to think much of them at all. Few people even mentioned them. His father hadn't seemed surprised exactly, more disappointed. Delan just knew that something was very, very wrong.

Delan wondered who had been on the ship. No one without a death wish would fly that banner now. A deserter? Someone who knew the truth and could expose Velexar? Maybe that's what they were searching the wreckage for: a body. If they were important enough to hunt down in the first place, no doubt they would look until they found it. A man as ambitious as Velexar wouldn't leave anyone alive to challenge him. That was why Delan's family had sent their tribute. If they were dead, there was nothing they could do to fight.

Some of the debris had reached the beach at the base of the cliff. It would be high tide soon, and no doubt by tomorrow the narrow path down the cliff would be completely blocked. They'd have to clear it out later.

"Delan, look!" a small voice beside him shouted. He forced himself to release the sword at his hip. He couldn't help being jumpy at a time like this, but he didn't have to show it in front of his little brother. Alec was only twelve and was a Fire mage, albeit an untrained one, as his father had refused to send him to the city. No one else in the family was a mage, unless you counted a great uncle somewhere, which was unusual. Sometimes it did come out spontaneously, although it usually ran in families. Now he was pointing down at the beach, a look of excitement on his face. Delan followed his finger and squinted. A larger piece of wood had washed up. But…what was that blue? It looked like cloth, but it was too far away to make out clearly. His heart skipped a beat. What if someone had lived?

"Stay here, I'm going down there," he said quickly.

He heard his father shift behind him, but he didn't say anything. Delan turned to face him. He was a tall man, and his eyes were the same blue as Delan's. "You would leave them?" Delan challenged.

"No," his father replied. "Just… be ready for what you might find. And be careful. If they don't find what they're looking for in the water, they'll start searching the beach." He looked back at the circling ship. "We'll prepare ourselves here."

Delan nodded and headed for the stairs in the middle of the tower. He circled down through the levels, taking the steps two at a time, running before he knew it.

He had met the royal family numerous times, mostly when they would make a circuit of their kingdom every year, although he could remember going to the capital when he was much younger. He remembered playing with the little Princess, who was about two years younger than him. He was always in charge of "showing her around," which he learned early on meant "keep her out of trouble."

21

Not that he was very good at it. Even though she was the younger of the two, she was a natural leader, and Delan was happy to follow her anywhere.

Their last visit had been over four years ago, when Delan was seventeen. They had stayed longer than usual because of an early spring hurricane, and during the weeks they stayed to help with repairs and healing, his friendship with Zhafaera had started to change. They no longer spent their time swimming and building sand castles or climbing the steep cliff and arguing over who was the bravest. Instead they spent days working together, helping with repairs to the castle and village and nursing the wounded. They had grown up together that summer, learning to accept the responsibility to care for the people that would one day be entrusted to their leadership.

Even though it had been years since they had last written to one another, he thought of her often. Then the news of her death came, and it had nearly broken him. Maybe that's why he ran. It was a foolish hope, but maybe, just maybe, she had lived through whatever "accident" had befallen the Queen. Maybe she was lying on his beach.

Delan finally reached the courtyard, where a few people were gathered at the gate, looking out at the wreckage. He forced himself to slow to a walk, and smile at them as he passed through the gate. They looked at him as though he was insane, and he let the smile fade. Several people twitched as if to stop him, but no one said anything.

He left through the small gate, and walked (fine, ran) down the short path along the outer wall until he reached the tiny crack in the cliff that marked the narrow path down to the beach. There he paused, looking down at the sandy shore. More debris from the wreckage had washed up, including a few oddly shaped bits that upon closer inspection were probably bodies, but he could still make out the big piece he had seen from the tower. From here, he could easily tell that the bit of blue poking out from under the wood *was* cloth, and there was something under the wood, pushing it up on one side.

The path was hidden in a fissure in the cliff, so it was hard to see out of, and nearly impossible to see the path from the beach. He climbed carefully down, making his way over the uneven rocks with the ease of long practice. He and his brother often came down to the beach at low tide. As he got farther down the path, the rocks grew smooth and slick, and he had to consciously slow himself so as not to lose his footing. At high tide, this part of the path was completely underwater, but he should have a couple of hours yet before that.

When he finally emerged from the crevice containing the path, he glanced quickly at the wreckage, where the galleon was still circling, but it would only be a matter of time until they made their way to the beach. With luck, the tide would come in before they could make a landing. He immediately made his way towards the wood with the blue cloth poking out from underneath, keeping low. He quickened his pace as he got closer, and when he saw a small white foot poking out from under the cloth he broke into a run again, trying not to trip in the soft sand. The foot never moved.

When he finally reached it, he grabbed the chunk of wood and heaved. It was thick and heavy, but he lifted it easily, though gently, and pushed it aside. Underneath was a young woman in an elaborate blue gown. His breath caught; it was her. There was no mistaking it, even after so long. Her long red hair was tangled in the wood around her, and she was so pale she looked almost blue. He dropped to his knees beside her and pressed his fingers to her neck, feeling for a pulse, but not expecting one. His eyebrows shot up as he felt her heartbeat, strong against his fingers. He shook her gently.

"Princess," he whispered. No response. "Zhafaera!"

She stirred feebly, her eyelids fluttering, but she soon fell still again. It was enough for Delan. He tried to lift her, but the gown was tangled in the wood, not to mention holding three times its weight in water. There was no way he would make it up that narrow path with this dress. He gently turned the Princess on her side, grabbed ahold of either side of the row of buttons up the back, and ripped the dress open. Trying hard not to look at her, and hoping that saving her life in this way didn't count as treason, he quickly pulled off the gown, leaving her clad only in a shift. At least this far south there was still a bit of warmth in the air, even in fall.

He carefully lifted the Princess into his arms, holding her limp form tightly to his chest and trying to pass some of his body heat to her. She was still and cold in his arms.

24

Delan checked the ship again. Still circling. He turned and made his way slowly across the narrow beach, into the fissure and up the path. Halfway up, the Princess started to shiver; he took this as a good sign – at least if she was shivering she was alive. He tried to force the heat filling him from his climb to flow into her, and to his surprise the shivering soon stopped; she looked so peaceful that he had a moment of panic before he saw she was still breathing. When he reached the top of the cliff, he could still see people standing at the gate, now pointing out to sea. He looked behind him and saw the black ship rapidly making its way to shore. Gritting his teeth, he quickened his pace to the side door. Several people ran forward to take his burden, but he only held her tighter. Some eyes widened as they recognized the girl who was supposed to be dead. Her fiery red hair was hard to miss, and she'd visited here often.

"Find a blanket," he said to them.

Some of the children ran, and their elders followed not much slower. As he crossed the courtyard, he saw his father coming down from the steps into the keep, Alec following close behind, practically bouncing on his toes despite the dark circles under his eyes. He must have done some magic, although Delan didn't see smoke or fire anywhere; without the control of a fully-trained mage, it often tired him to use it.

Seeing the Princess his father murmured, "It *was* her. There were whispers…"

"They're coming to shore now," Delan told him, jerking his head behind him to indicate the ship. Just in case there was even the slightest chance that he missed seeing it from the tower. "The tide might beat them to it and cover the beach, but we should hide her until we're sure."

His father nodded and led the way into the Keep. They had a secret chamber under the floor of the cells in the dungeon. Everyone expected secret compartments in studies, or pantries perhaps. But no one expected to find friends hidden away in the bowels of the keep. He just hoped the Princess didn't wake there.

***

Pain. Everywhere pain. Zhafaera woke in the dark feeling as if she'd been beaten over every inch of her body.

Pitch dark.

She couldn't see her hand when she waved it in front of her face. The ground under her was solid, not rocking as it would have if she had been on a ship. That meant she had to be in a dungeon somewhere. Perhaps they had taken her back on one of the flying beasts she'd heard whispers of in the weeks before the attack. Or maybe she'd just been drugged and kept asleep as they sailed back. She shook herself – now she was just letting her imagination run away with her. Her clothes were still wet from being thrown in the water, so she couldn't have been out long. That didn't change the fact that she was in serious trouble.

She felt something with too many legs crawl across her arm and flung her arm away from her, barely suppressing a scream. Now was not the time to be afraid of spiders. But she couldn't stop herself from running fingers through her hair, making sure there was nothing crawling around in there. Of course, any spider unlucky enough to find his way in would need weeks to find its way out of that mess.

Zhafaera stood carefully, a blanket she barely noticed falling away, expecting her head to hit the ceiling before she could reach more than a crouch, but surprisingly, it kept going. Once upright, she swayed, her head protesting loudly at the change in position. She quickly steadied herself, then stretched out her arms and walked sideways until she found a wall. Three steps. She followed the wall all the way around the cell, until she guessed she was about back to where she started. It was fairly big considering she was in the depths of a dungeon, but there was no door. The entrance must be on the ceiling, which was too far up for her to reach. She briefly considered using her magic to call a light, but quickly dismissed it as the dumbest thing she could possibly do; aside from the fact that the Sapphire's presence in her mind had settled into a distinctly uncomfortable ache, tripping her up when she reached for her magic, darkness would be her only advantage when they came for her. Well, darkness and the fact that she still had all of her knives... these people must be dumber than she thought to remove her dress but leave the knives strapped to her body.

She went back to where she thought the middle was and sat down. She would wait quietly until they came for her. She would not scream for help. Instead she meditated, trying to feel her magic, which was alarmingly low, and adjust to reaching for it with the feel of the Sapphire in her mind. Her headache started to fade, and when she started to shiver, she pulled the blanket back over herself.

Just when she was beginning to wonder if they would ever feed her or at least bring her water, she heard voices above her. Forcing herself back to calmness, she tried to listen. They were men's voices, and they didn't sound happy. Pushing aside the pain of the Sapphire, she sharpened her hearing with the barest trickle of magic.

"Are you satisfied now?" This voice sounded impatient.

"We have orders to bring the traitor back dead or alive." This from a gruff voice.

"We are loyal subjects of the King. If we see them, we'll be sure to let you know."

Zhafaera's breath caught. Could it be possible? Had she made it into the fort and, even harder to believe, were they still loyal? She had visited often when she and her mother Toured Arenthia; they always stayed here the longest. She had liked the whole family, but had always been friends with the older boy, Delan. No matter how long it was between visits, they always fell quickly back into an easy camaraderie. She felt heat rise into her face as she remembered how she had practically worshiped him, tagging along after him through every visit. She had come this way hoping that maybe she still had a friend here; she knew that her mother and his father had been friends too, and so of her choices, this seemed like the best at the time. Then again, most people were nice to your face, but would take any opportunity to betray you the moment your back was turned. She had too much experience with that of late.

So maybe she had some trust issues. Her plan had been to anchor in the cove and send some of her men to the tiny castle for supplies, and have them feel out the sentiments of its occupants. So much for that. No, it was much more likely that these people were holding her here so they could give her to her uncle themselves, and so gain favor with him. Why else was she stuck in a dark cell? She could trust no one.

The voices were moving off. There was nothing to do but wait. And hope that someone came to let her out.

***

"Princess?" Delan called down into the dark chamber. The light from his brother's small ball of light didn't reach the bottom.

No answer. *She must still be out,* he thought, *or dead,* but he ignored that small voice in his head.

He unhooked the wooden ladder attached to the underside of the ceiling next to the trapdoor and lowered it into the room. He told Alec to wait and keep the light steady, then began to climb down.

He realized something was wrong as soon as his feet touched the floor. She was gone from where he had left her. No sooner had this processed than he felt the cool kiss of steel at his throat. He froze, both hands out in front where she could see them, the light still flickering above.

"Did you think I was helpless?" Zhafaera hissed behind him. "Did you think I escaped just to sit down here like a good little princess and wait for you to come and haul me back to the city?"

Delan reminded himself to breathe. "Princess, it's me, it's Delan!" The blade didn't move. "We were trying to protect you. You washed up on the beach after they blew your ship to pieces and I brought you here while they were searching for you. We – we thought you were dead."

"Delan?" Alec called nervously from the top of the stairs.

"It's fine, just stay there," Delan said as loud as he could with the knife at his throat. To the princess behind him he whispered, "We're not going to turn you in. We were always loyal. We're still loyal, only to you. We can help."

There was a long pause. "Why?"

Delan was shocked. *Why?* "Because everyone knows what Velexar is. Or at least, they used to. He says it was an accident, and that you both died, but obviously *that's* not true. Something's wrong, and no one can *see* it. And... you and I... we're friends."

There was a long pause. Then he felt her relax, and the knife left his neck. "Are we friends still?" She sounded exhausted. "I don't know who to trust any more."

Delan turned to face the princess. Her face was like stone, showing no emotion, but was that a tiny waver in her voice he had heard? So unlike the bubbly girl he remembered, but he thought he recognized the spark in her eyes, even if it did seem to be dulled. It made him continue.

"Surely you knew you could trust us, or why would you have come so close? You were planning to stop here, weren't you?"

It was hard to tell in the dim light, but he thought her eyes were too bright. Definitely the lighting; the Zhafaera he knew never cried. "The thought crossed my mind. I had hoped you would be on my side, but I was afraid..." She took a deep breath and looked him straight in the eyes. "We needed supplies, and I thought you might –"she paused and looked down. "I'm sorry about the knife. I just woke up here and assumed..."

"Yeah, sorry about that, but it's the best hiding spot we have. No one ever thinks that we would put people we like in the dungeons." He tried a smile, and thought that maybe her lips twitched a little. Maybe not. Then he realized she was still wet, cold, and clad only in her shift, since he had ripped off her dress. He blushed and turned back to the stairs to hide it. "Come on, let's go up." He waited, reaching his hand behind him. She took it, and he closed his hand gently around her icy fingers. Already he

31

felt at ease with her, despite the knife incident. He'd missed her.

He let go of her hand at the ladder and let her climb up the rungs and into the dark dungeon. Alec's eyes looked like they were about to pop out of his head as the princess appeared through the opening. He'd still been fairly young when they'd last visited, and he was never as close to her as Delan was. Alec nervously handed her another dry blanket as she straightened out of the hole in the floor, and she smiled at him. At least, Delan thought it was supposed to be a smile, but it looked painful. She still looked like a drowned rat. That had been run over by a horse. And rolled in the sand.

"Thank you," she said as she wrapped the blanket around herself. Looking at Delan, she said, "I should go. They'll be back for me. I don't want to put you in any more danger than you already are."

Delan frowned at her. "Seriously? You've been on the run, you were nearly blown to pieces by mages, then almost drowned in those currents, *then* smashed against the rocks, and you want to *leave*?"

"Well what else can I do?" the princess said wearily. She sighed and seemed to deflate even further. "You don't understand; the longer he's unchallenged, the more powerful he will become. This is just the beginning. I have to figure out some way to fix this! I can't let him have the s—the throne."

"We'll help!" Alec jumped in. Delan and Zhafaera looked at him in unison and he shrunk a little. "Well, we will... " he muttered.

Zhafaera looked surprised, and Delan took advantage of her being momentarily off balance.

"Come on, at least come get cleaned up and eat with us, and then we'll figure out what to do, all right?" Delan said in what he hoped was a soothing voice, eyeing the scratches and splinters covering her face and arms.

Zhafaera suddenly looked exhausted, and Delan knew he had her. "All right."

Alec bounced and darted down the corridor, but Delan paused and made a split-second decision. He reached out and pulled her against him, wrapping both arms around her in a tight hug.

"I thought you were dead," he whispered.

"Not yet," she murmured tiredly, hugging him back.

"I'm sorry about your mother."

"Me too."

Chapter 2

Leaving her at the door, Delan promised to come get her in an hour for dinner. When Zhafaera entered the room she was greeted by the best sight she'd seen in her whole life. Not only had someone placed a tray of fruit, cheese, and a pot of what she hoped desperately was tea on a small table, there was a young servant girl standing next to the open door of a washroom, where Zhafaera could see a tub full of steaming water. Indoor plumbing was still relatively new, but it had caught on quickly.

The girl curtsied, balancing a stack of thick white towels. "Your Highness. I'm supposed to help you with anything you need."

Her inner voice screamed that she could wash and dress herself, but she knew it would be rude to send her away.

"Thank you. What's your name?" Zhafaera asked politely.

Another curtsy. "Mai, your Highness." A blush. "Would you like some tea before your bath?"

"Yes, please," Zhafaera said eagerly, thinking she might very well take it in the bath *with* her. She caught sight of herself in a mirror hanging over a small dresser.

Ugh. She was a mess. Holding up a dark red curl, she wondered if it would be better to simply cut it all off.

"You can't do that!" Mai looked horrified.

"Do what?"

"Cut off your hair! It's so beautiful!" *Talking out loud again. Lovely. I really have to stop doing that when I'm tired.*

"I suppose I won't, but it's going to be a nightmare."

"I'll take care of it!" Mai looked like she was going to start bouncing up and down any minute. Her smile faded as she got a closer look at Zhafaera. "But Princess... your face, your arms...some of those are deep! We don't have a healer, but I could call for someone to help tend to you..."

Zhafaera looked at the still-steaming water and grimaced. "I'll be all right. I have enough strength to heal myself I think; I'll just need help pulling out some of the splinters." Mai looked pale, but determined. Zhafaera sighed. "Maybe I should eat something first... "

***

An hour later, Delan knocked nervously on the princess' door. Mai quickly opened the door, and Delan could see the princess on the other side of the room, sprawled across the huge bed, wet red hair spread like a halo around her head, fast asleep. He told Mai not to wake her, but to stay nearby in case she woke up hungry. Alec pouted at dinner,

35

disappointed that the princess wasn't joining them, but his father agreed that it was best to let her sleep.

At least one of them could sleep. Delan tossed and turned all night, his mind racing with thoughts of the princess; how was she still alive? Would she be all right? *What* had happened that had led to her mother's death? She had come here, to him; he had to help her. What was she planning to do? What could *he* do? Round and round and round his thoughts went until he finally managed to catch a quick nap just as the sky was turning grey with the cold light of pre-dawn.

When he finally rose, it was all he could do not to pace outside her room until she woke up. He paced the library for an hour instead, until his father finally kicked him out, telling him, "go swing a sword until you feel better."

That helped distract him for a while, but then it reminded him of how he had stood out here with Zhafaera years ago, teaching her the proper way to throw knives. He remembered how she had stamped her foot in frustration when her throws fell short of the target. She didn't like failing, and she *certainly* didn't like being told she was too weak to throw properly. He smiled at the memory of the tongue-lashing he'd received for that comment. She couldn't have been more than ten when he started teaching her.

He was pacing his own room again when there was a small knock at his door. He opened it and found Zhafaera on the other side, staring up at him with those impossibly blue eyes of hers.

He couldn't believe how much better she looked. Her long red hair flowed loose curls down her back, shining in the light from the windows. She wore a simple white cotton dress that loosely outlined her figure (not that he was looking). He found it strange that he was now more than a head taller than her, and yet she had a commanding air about her that left no doubt as to who was in charge. She had matured into a woman since the last time he had seen her; her face slightly longer and more...regal. And more beautiful than ever. Her eyes were an electric blue that looked like they would start throwing sparks at any moment. All of his worry immediately faded away. She looked alive again. Although maybe that was just because she didn't have blood and splinters all over her face.

Finally, he managed to close his mouth, which was somehow hanging open slightly. He swallowed, then said, "You're finally awake. I was wondering if you'd sleep through the week!"

She made a face. "You try fighting for your life against the ocean and see how long *you* sleep."

Delan bowed low. "My apologies, Princess. I forgot how tiring a splash in the water can be." He tried to hide a grin as he straightened, catching Zhafaera mid eye-roll.

"Ha ha, very funny," she said, pushing him lightly.

"Are you hungry?" Delan asked. "It's about lunchtime."

"Starving," she said.

"Come on, I'll take you down to the kitchen. We can get something there and then I'll give you the grand tour."

"I've been here before, remember."

"Yeah, but I hear that memory is the first thing to go when you get old. Personally, I think my hearing is giving out first – too many fireworks from Alec." That earned him another eye-roll, but she was struggling with a smile.

As they left his room to head downstairs to the kitchen, Zhafaera spoke. "I'm sorry about the whole knife-to-the-throat thing yesterday," she said quietly, looking down. *Was that a blush?*

"Don't worry about it, I would have done the exact same thing in your position. It was stupid of me to walk down there without explaining first." Delan's smile faded. "You were so still when I carried you up, I was *not* expecting you to be able to sneak up on me, let alone pull a knife."

"Surely you of all people should know I practiced." She smiled slightly, moving closer and placing a hand on the arm he held out for her. "And Delan," she paused. "Thank you for rescuing me. Without you, I'd be worse than dead."

"You're welcome," Delan said, meaning it. "I can't tell you how happy I am – we are – to see you alive." *Get it together!*

"Well I intend to stay that way as long as I can." Zhafaera said as they left the room and turned left down the hallway.

The few servants they passed in the halls on the way to the kitchen stared wide-eyed at the princess, and many curtsied or bowed awkwardly. Though Zhafaera smiled and nodded at them, Delan thought she looked tense.

"Don't tell me you still preferred wandering around the castle in disguise to avoid all the bowing." Delan asked, half jokingly.

The princess looked surprised, but grinned. "I tried. I even succeeded sometimes. I'm just the same as everyone else." Her smile faded, and there was a bitterness in her words. "But, the last few years, my mother was... unwell. Most of the day-to-day tasks of managing Arenthia fell to me, and it was harder to sneak away." She sighed. "Mother always said you have to maintain dignity even when you least want to. Hence why you found me wearing that ridiculous dress."

Delan winced. Seeing as how she woke up without the dress, and Delan was the one that carried her up from the beach, she could probably guess who had removed it.

"You know, in any other circumstance, removing my dress without my permission would be considered treason and you would lose your head, but seeing as how you did it to save my life, I suppose I can let it slide." She flushed and started to ramble. "After all, if you had gotten halfway up that path and dropped me off the side because of that stupid dress, it would have defeated the whole purpose of rescuing me in the first place."

Delan struggled not to laugh. *Do not ask if it's treason if you removed her dress WITH her permission. Do NOT ask. DO NOT ASK.* "Glad to know I won't be losing my head any time soon." *That was almost as bad!* He shut up.

Once they reached the kitchens, Delan ducked in, leaving Zhafaera in the hall, and was immediately surrounded by the cook and his two assistants, all wanting to know what the princess liked to eat and if they should prepare a formal luncheon. He assured them that it wasn't formal, and that he and Zhafaera just wanted something they could take outside to the terrace off the dining room that overlooked the ocean. The cook refused to let Delan pack and carry the lunch himself, insisting that they should go sit and he would serve them himself.

It was a lovely day, with blue skies and a warm ocean breeze that made Zhafaera's hair flutter around her. Delan watched as she closed her eyes and breathed deeply, more relaxed than he'd seen her since she arrived. The sight made him smile.

As if she could sense his gaze, she opened one eye and looked directly at him. He blushed, having been caught watching her, but she just grinned.

"I've missed you," he said, smiling back.

Her eye closed again. "I missed you too," she said softly.

Delan hesitated. "I… I wrote to you."

Both of Zhafaera's eyes opened this time, and she frowned. "What?"

"I wrote to you. A few times. When you didn't write back, I just figured… " His voice trailed off. Why had he brought this up? She was the Princess, she didn't have to explain herself to anyone. It's not like he was *nearly* important enough to expect an answer, even if they had been close once.

But Zhafaera was sitting forward now, and her frown deepened. "I never got any letters." She paused, as if thinking. "None in the last four years, actually."

"I'm sorry, mine must have gone astray. Eventually... well, I stopped." He tried for a smile. "Didn't want to seem like a stalker, you know."

Zhafaera shook her head and met his eyes. "I would have liked to hear from you. And I don't think your letters went astray. At least, not by accident." She paused, and her eyes clouded. "He was isolating me."

"Who was?"

"Velexar." She looked out at the ocean. "A few years ago, my mother became completely withdrawn. She locked herself in her room and would let no one in except me and a couple of servants. I took over for her, but I lost my freedom." She shook her head. "My friends stopped calling on me, I had no letters, and I saw almost no one that wasn't a supplicant or a servant. And *him.*" She spat the word. "Velexar offered to help me during my mother's... illness. I didn't trust him – everyone knows his reputation – but he always... hovered. He was the only one I really saw regularly, whether I wanted to or not." She turned and met his eyes, and in them he saw a barely controlled rage. "I thought everyone else had abandoned me. But now I see it – I'd bet anything he intercepted your letters. He probably turned my friends away. He made it so that I was alone and vulnerable. Easy to control."

41

Delan reached out and placed his hand over hers. "You're not alone now." He gave her hand a squeeze and then let go as their food was brought out.

When the servants had left, with much bowing, Zhafaera shook her head and forced a smile. "So tell me, what did you write to me? What have I missed? How are things here?"

It was mid-afternoon by the time they left the balcony, having gotten caught up in catching up. Zhafaera had carefully avoided any further mention of her mother, and preferred to talk about Delan and his family, which was understandable. Having lost his own mother at a young age, he knew it was better to let her start that conversation. When they'd finished eating, Delan showed her around the castle, from the roof of the tallest tower down to the little vegetable garden behind the kitchen. It was just like old times, as if nothing had changed since her last visit, their easy companionship carrying them through the afternoon. As evening drew near, he escorted Zhafaera back to her room to dress for dinner, then retreated to his own room to at least change his shirt.

They met back out in the hallway fifteen minutes later, and Delan offered her his arm with a bow and a flourish. She delicately rested her hand on his elbow and he escorted her down to dinner.

They reached the dining room quickly, and if he hadn't known better, he would have said Zhafaera was nervous. He felt her relax slightly as she took in the small room where just his father and brother waited, but she was still more guarded than she'd been all day.

His small family stood and bowed, greeting Zhafaera as a princess, not a fugitive.

"Welcome, Your Highness," his father said seriously. "We are honored by your presence."

Alec gave a small wave from his father's left. He still looked tired, although he seemed to have recovered some. Zhafaera smiled at him.

She said quietly, "You all saved my life. There's no need for formalities."

There was a beat of dead silence before his father smiled and moved around the table towards Zhafaera. Finally releasing Delan's arm, Zhafaera stepped forward, giving his father a brief hug and saying, "It's good to see you, Lord Geon."

His father released her and smiled. "Come – eat with us." He gestured to the open seat at the head of the table closest to them, where he usually sat.

As they took their seats, servants came and set platters of food in the center of the table, then left through the main doors. Zhafaera relaxed as soon as they left.

Dinner passed quickly, as they all focused on eating while Alec chattered into the silence. Delan kept a wary eye on his brother, but thankfully even at his age, he knew to stay away from sensitive topics.

After a while, when everyone was finished, his father spoke. "Come, let's move into the library. We have a lot to talk about."

43

They all stood. Zhafaera automatically took the arm Delan offered; he was shocked to feel her trembling.

They reached the library, where a large fire was already taking off the evening chill. The room was cozy; thick rugs covered most of the stone floor. There was a loose half-circle of armchairs and a couch around the fire, with a tray of tea sitting off to one side of the fire, close enough that the fire was keeping it warm. The three other walls were covered top to bottom with books of all shapes and sizes. Off to the right was a long table covered in papers – mostly maps.

Delan led Zhafaera to the couch by the fire and she sat gratefully. He quickly busied himself with tea while Alec and his father sat down across from Zhafaera. She looked at Alec, seemingly surprised that he was still here. Her lips pressed in a tight line. "Alec, perhaps you should go to bed. This will be boring, and probably long."

"NO!" Alec yelled. Sparks flew from the fireplace, growing into tiny flames. Alec yelped with surprise, but the fires quickly vanished before they touched anything. Zhafaera rubbed her temples as if she had a headache.

"Please, don't do that again," she said calmly. "I'd rather not use my magic if I don't have to."

"Alec, she's right, it's time for bed," his father said.

Alec looked as if he would protest more, but he seemed to have been slightly shaken by his burst of magic, and how quickly she'd quelled it. He looked more tired than ever. He frowned, but left the room.

Zhafaera watched quietly. "He'll be a powerful Fire mage," she said once he'd left. "He's still learning control, though. This is a dangerous time for him."

"Yeah, we've learned to keep pitchers of water in every room," Delan replied, handing her a cup of tea and sitting next to her on the couch. "Thanks for that."

"Yes, of course, fire can be a danger," Zhafaera said with an absent wave of her hand. "But...you should know...my uncle – Velexar – can turn mages to his service against their will –"

"I'm sorry, *what?*" Delan interrupted. As if he didn't already worry about Alec enough, now she adds *this?*

"It's forbidden magic," she sighed. "But at this point, that means nothing to him. Some he can break in hours, others can take months, but eventually, most will break. I suspected he turned at least one court mage, and several students before the coup. I didn't know what to do. I tried to tell my mother, to make her act, but she..." She cut herself off, looking at Delan and his father, and Delan knew his face was pure shock. "I'm sorry, I don't mean to upset you. But as I said, this is a dangerous time for Alec. He's not yet secure in controlling his powers; that makes him an easy target. He has to be careful."

"I know," Geon said, voice steady and measured. "It's why I haven't sent him to the Cathedral in the city to be trained."

"You *know?*" Delan blurted. "*How* would you know?"

His father looked uncomfortable as Zhafaera pinned him with her stare. "Karaena and I – we were friends." He cleared his throat.

"She told you?" Zhafaera asked sharply. "She *knew*?"

"She knew Velexar was doing *something*." Geon answered. "But she couldn't prove it. She asked for my help."

"You spied for her?"

"I watched and listened," his father said steadily. "And I told her what I could. But he was gone so much, spent so little time in Arenthia, that it was difficult. But we knew he was using forbidden magic." He paused. "Karaena called him back to Arenthia four years ago, and then… nothing." He looked at Zhafaera.

Her face was still, but Delan could almost feel the anger rolling off of her. "Four years ago, my mother withdrew to her chambers and almost never left. I was the only one she would see regularly, and even then, she was different. You think Velexar did something to her." It wasn't a question.

"I'm sure he did. What, I don't know, but whatever it was, she cut off communication, and he stayed in the capital."

There was a long silence, and Delan could feel Zhafaera trying to rein in her temper. "Why didn't you warn me?" she hissed.

His father ran a hand through his salt and pepper hair. "For a long time, I didn't know what to think, why she'd pulled away. And then, when I heard you had taken over for Karaena in all but name, I—I was afraid."

Zhafaera's voice was quiet. "You thought Velexar was controlling me."

Geon raised his hands. "I didn't know what to think. You were young and impressionable. I thought it best to wait and see, and do what I could from here. I wanted to get her out," he whispered.

"You waited too long." Zhafaera's voice was cold, but Delan could hear the hurt in it. His father didn't respond. The room was silent.

Finally, Delan couldn't stand it. "Zhafaera, what happened? The official story is that there was an accident that killed you and your mother, but clearly that's not the case, so… "

Zhafaera stared into the fire for so long that Delan wasn't sure she'd answer. "Velexar killed my mother. Blew a good chunk out of the palace and set a fire. He meant to kill me too, but I escaped. Not something he planned for, I'm sure."

"But *why*?" Delan asked. "Why would *he* do it? What's the point? Power? As the Prince, couldn't he already pretty much do whatever he wanted?"

"I don't know, it didn't make sense to me either." Zhafaera snapped. "But he's the only one that had anything to gain from my mother's death." She took a breath. "Look, they may have left earlier, but without my body, he'll send those men back. I'm going to leave here as soon as possible, but he'll still come for you. There's no telling if he'll just search you again, or if he'll burn the place to the ground. You need to be prepared."

More silence. Delan didn't know what to say. How do you tell someone you're glad they came back – no matter what problems come with them – without sounding ridiculous?

Alec laughed from the hallway. Everyone jumped and turned to stare at him. "Let them come. We'll trick them just like we did today, and if that doesn't work, well, I'll fight them." Delan resisted the urge to smack his palm to his forehead.

But Zhafaera smiled. "Of course. I won't worry about you at all, then." She looked like she might cry.

"BED." Geon said firmly to his son. Alec pouted and disappeared again. This time they heard him stomping up the stairs.

***

It was some time before anyone spoke again. Zhafaera was trying to calm herself. Logically she knew it wasn't Geon's fault any more than it was her own, but still. She wrestled with the feeling.

"What are you going to do?" Geon asked finally.

Anger flared again. "*I* will go back to Arenthia, kill Velexar, and retake my mother's throne."

Geon held his hands up, palms forward. "I wasn't suggesting that you were doing nothing. But don't you think that the capital is the last place you should go?" He paused, thinking. "Your mother had good relationships with most of our neighbors, surely you could seek asylum somewhere."

She was quiet for a long time. There hadn't been a human war in over a thousand years. The four human nations had long ago decided that in order to survive, they had to stand united, and so all four participated in Gatherings. Laros, a string of volcanic islands covered in thick jungle across the sea to the East, was ruled by Fire Mages for the most part. They elected their leaders every ten years, usually men, and her mother had been... friends... with most of them. Technically, she had a grandfather there, but she'd never met him. Burja, the large country across the sea to the south, mostly covered in desert, also had a Queen. Queen Oraesa was not exactly a fan of her mother, but Zhafaera was friends with the Princess Liara, only a few years younger than she was. Khichora was to the southwest of Arenthia, filled with wide plains leading into tall mountains; her friend Tristain was the son of the King. Then of course her own kingdom, Arenthia, with its capital of the same name, built around the ore-rich mountains.

Every few years, all of the leaders of each country traveled to that year's host country for the Gathering, where they discussed borders, trade, and any other issues that may have arisen. And of course it was a chance to affirm alliances through arranging marriages. It was well known that the line of queens in Arenthia almost never married ("It's never a good idea to give a man any more power over you than he already thinks he has," her mother used to tell her), but it was common for them to have Consorts, usually from powerful families. Her mother had many "friends" among the other ruling families, but she rejected marriage offers from all of them, and never took a Consort.

Arenthia had hosted the last gathering two years ago, thankfully, since her mother wouldn't – or couldn't – leave her rooms, let alone the city. Zhafaera had been able to cover for her mother, saying she was ill, and she'd managed to hold her own, but she wasn't sure how much help any of them would be. Most of them seemed to expect her to fall into bed with them at the drop of a hat, which was not going to happen, and the rest acted as though she were a child. Never mind that Zhafaera had essentially been the one in charge of Arenthia by then. She had managed at the Gathering, but Zhafaera didn't think that was the kind of help she needed right now. She had to do this herself or not at all.

"I don't know if I can count on their help," she finally said carefully. "You don't understand the power he has, and it will only grow. He stole more from my mother than just her throne." She hesitated. She'd been trained from a young age not to discuss it with outsiders. Not really. "The royal family possesses a certain… artifact. A magical artifact. I suspect that he's already using it to make people more compliant – make his story more believable – but he doesn't have full control yet. Once he masters it, he'll be unstoppable." Her last words were a whisper.

50

There was a small choking sound from the other side of the room. "Are you saying he has the Sapphire?" Geon said. His face was white.

Zhafaera jumped up, eyes wide, groping at her wrists for knives. "How do you know about that?" she hissed. "Only the royal family is supposed to know!"

"I told you, your mother and I were close friends for a long time, Zhafaera. She told me many things." He paused. She had stopped reaching for knives and was simply staring open-mouthed at him. *Just how close* were *they?* She could take a guess.

"She was afraid this day would come, though we were trying hard to avoid it. We were your escape route. But the Sapphire was supposed to be with Karaena! In his hands...this is not good."

"Don't you think I *know* that?" Zhafaera cried, beginning to pace. "This was never supposed to happen! It's not like someone can just walk in and *take* it! It...it *screamed* when my mother was dying. I can feel it now, in my mind, it's angry..." Her voice cracked.

"Okay, wait, wait, back up, what are you talking about?" Delan was confused. "What sapphire?"

Zhafaera sighed. She was shaking. "I should ward the room." She took a deep breath, gritted her teeth, and a soft white fire gathered around her hands before shooting into each corner of the room. Two more streaks of light flew to the door and window, forming a glowing line around each, sealing it tight.

"We can speak freely now," she said tiredly, rubbing her temples again. Even that much magic was difficult for her now.

She looked up. "But you must tell *no one* what you hear." Her voice was harsh, but she made no attempt to moderate her tone. "Promise me."

"I promise," Delan said quickly.

Zhafaera looked into the fire. It was Geon who spoke.

"You know the stories. Each country was founded with a gem and its mages. Arenthia had the Sapphire, Burja had the Emerald, Laros the Ruby, and Khichora the Diamond. Water, Earth, Fire, Air."

"But...the Gems are just legends. Children's stories about the root of all magic," Delan said, confused.

"Not exactly," Zhafaera sighed. "The Sapphire is wielded by the rulers of Arenthia. At least two of the other Gems have been lost," she continued. "I suspect the leaders of Laros still have the Ruby, or they at least know where it is. The Emerald and Diamond, however, haven't been seen in hundreds of years. They were lost or stolen. It's why we don't talk about the Sapphire much. Mages sometimes tell stories, but very few *know*. The stones that are left are precious – they're more powerful than you can possibly imagine, although difficult to control. It takes a great deal of power and *will*. My family, we –" she stopped and cleared her throat, trying to banish the image of her mother on the floor, bleeding from the oval wound in her chest.

Avoiding Delan's gaze, she looked at Geon. "We bond the Sapphire to our flesh," she said, tapping her chest lightly between her breasts. "It cannot be taken from us while we live. And it's quite difficult to kill us while we have the Sapphire." She closed her eyes, trying not to think of her mother and failing miserably.

A hand touched her shoulder, and she jumped, her eyes shooting open. It was Delan. She relaxed and leaned into his touch, and he slid his arm around her shoulders, offering comfort. She accepted.

Delan was the first to break the silence. "So… what does the Sapphire *do* exactly?"

Zhafaera shook her head. "It's difficult to explain," she said carefully. "I suppose the easiest way – well, the Gems draw power from their respective elements. The Sapphire draws from water, as a Water mage would. Except it draws a *lot,* and it holds it. Stores it. Using the Sapphire is like… like holding the ocean in your hands. And it doesn't just store power, it amplifies that of the user." She paused. "Using the Sapphire – there's certainly a strong affinity for water-based magics, but with your power amplified and an almost unlimited well of magic to draw from, a White mage who can draw from all elements like me, or Velexar, wielding the Sapphire can practically do whatever they want."

By the slight crease between Delan's eyebrows, she wasn't sure how much he actually understood, but it was the best she could do.

"So… Velexar has the Sapphire and can pretty much do whatever he wants with it?" Delan summed up.

"Yes, and no. It's fighting him. There has never been a King of Arenthia, nor a man wielding the Sapphire." Zhafaera shrugged, struggling to find the right words. "The Sapphire isn't *alive* per say, but it's somewhat…sentient. It will choose to work with you. Or not."

"I can feel it in my mind," she continued, dropping her head into her hands. "Like someone pounding with a hammer. When I reach for my magic, it *hurts*. It woke me up when the attack started, just in time to save me. And when my mother was…was dying," her voice caught, "it was *screaming*. I can still feel its rage." She ended in a whisper and fell silent.

Delan broke the silence "Okay, so Velexar has the Sapphire, but he can't use its full potential yet because it's fighting him?" Zhafaera nodded. "Well, that's something at least. So we just need you to stay alive and get it back before he bends it to his will. Or, uh, bonds it?" He touched his chest as Zhafaera had done.

Zhafaera nodded. "Yes. If he bonds it without full control, it will destroy him." She took a breath. "I've touched it before, used it a little with my mother. It… knows me. It can sense me."

"Right, so you have to get it back. But you can't just march back up there and hope for the best," Delan said practically.

"You need allies," Geon said firmly.

"There is no one I can trust not to betray me," Zhafaera said. "I'm convinced he's using the Sapphire's power to turn the people against my mother's memory. No one even cares that she's dead." Her voice broke, but she took a deep breath and continued. "Anyone could be working for him." The image of the dragon flying over the palace flashed in her mind. "I'm sorry I dragged you into this. I'll leave in the morning."

"Gods you're stubborn!" The words that burst from Delan's mouth startled her. "You can't march back to Arenthia alone, when your death would make it that much easier for Velexar to control the Sapphire!"

"What else can I do?" She asked angrily.

"You can trust *us*," Delan said fiercely. "You can trust *me*. You came here for help, so let me help you."

"Run. Go to one of the other nations." Geon spoke quietly. "They may not be able to help you get your throne back, but they can certainly help you hide. Keep the Sapphire fighting him. Wait him out."

"I can't do that." Zhafaera shook her head. "He's powerful. Very powerful. He'll gain control of the Sapphire eventually, whether or not I'm alive. Once that happens, he'll be a *hell* of a lot harder to kill. I have to get the Sapphire back, no matter what."

They sat in silence for a long time, each lost in thought. Finally, Zhafaera leaned forward slightly, setting her teacup on the small table in front of them.

"It's late, and I'm tired," Zhafaera said finally. She couldn't face any more stressful conversations tonight.

55

Delan looked like he wanted to argue, but then he always did know when she was holding something back. Geon came to her rescue. "Of course, princess. We'll let you rest."

Zhafaera stood, and Delan and Geon followed. "No, don't," she said quickly, waving them back down. "I know the way, no need to trouble yourselves." She hurried out the door, closing it softly behind her. She leaned back against the doorframe for a moment, gathering her thoughts. There was one major thing she had left out, and that was the dragon she'd seen the night of the attack. If Velexar was working with dragons... they were in real trouble.

***

Zhafaera didn't sleep well that night. She tossed and turned until well past midnight, long after she had heard Delan and Geon walk past her room on their way to their beds. She'd had plenty of time to think on the way down from the capital, but she still wasn't prepared to make the kind of accusations she was thinking of.

Everyone knew that dragons had once ruled over humans. They'd appeared one day, hundreds of them, raining fire and magic down on the humans and shattering entire civilizations.

As the story went, they were immortal gods, and humans were their slaves. And food, though that was usually left out of the childrens' stories. But as with any group, eventually there was conflict among themselves, and war broke out.

Gods didn't need to fight their own battles. At some point, dragons passed on some of their immense power in the form of four Gems: a Sapphire, a Ruby, an Emerald, and a Diamond. The stones enabled a select few humans access to elemental magic. It gave them a way to fight dragons.

At first, a human had to be physically touching the stones to wield their power, and by all accounts it took a number of humans to control each stone, and each group worked with only one Gem...But by the end of the war, these humans found they didn't need the stones to use magic – some of the stones' power had bled into their cores, and had fundamentally changed them.

The use of human mages was a mistake – the mages rose up against the dragons, and rather than fighting themselves, the dragons found themselves fighting humans. Humans fought back, and they won. They forced the remaining dragons deep into the Livorian mountains.

Eventually, a truce was called. Dragons stayed on one side of the mountains, humans on the other. Arenthia, being the closest to the dragon lairs, had the primary responsibility of maintaining that truce. This arrangement worked for almost a thousand years, although occasionally there were scuffles along the border, usually after some *idiot* got it into his head that he's going to slay a dragon. The last one of *those* had been a nightmare for her mother to smooth over. She had met several dragons that day, and the memory made her shiver.

Zhafaera feared that Velexar had somehow convinced the dragons to work with him. If that was the case, she wasn't at all sure what she would do. What she *could* do. She sighed, rolling over to find a cool spot on her pillow. Tomorrow, she would discuss her fears with the others. They had a right to know what they were getting into.

Chapter 3

When Zhafaera woke, rain was pounding her window and the wind was whistling through cracks in the shutters. The room was chilly, but she was warm in her cocoon of blankets. She had no idea what time it was. The light coming through her window was only the gray of a storm, but she sensed that she had been asleep a long time. She laid there for some time, enjoying the comfortable bed and not wanting to move after her night of restless sleep. She could have stayed like that the whole day, but suddenly she heard footsteps, and her door slowly creaked open just a crack. Mai's face peeked in. When she saw Zhafaera was still in bed, she blushed slightly, ducked her head, and whispered, "Oh, I'm sorry, Princess, I didn't mean to wake you!" Her face pulled back from the door, and she started to close it.

"No, wait," Zhafaera called. "I was awake. I need to get up anyway."

Mai opened the door and came all the way in. "Are you sure?"

"Yes, it's fine," Zhafaera said, finally sitting up and letting the blankets fall. "What time is it?"

"An hour 'till noon, Your Highness."

"Almost noon? Again?" Zhafaera was shocked. One late morning after a near-drowning was one thing, but this was getting ridiculous.

"Yes, Princess. Master Delan sent me to check on you." Now she was really blushing. "You know, just to make sure you were all right…" she trailed off.

Zhafaera smiled. "Thank you, I feel fine." Minus the tired headache developing behind her eyes.

"Do you want something to eat?"

"Yes, please, that would be lovely."

Mai went over to the fireplace and took a moment to poke the fire back into life. Once it was crackling cheerfully, taking the edge off the chill in the room, she left to retrieve… lunch?

Zhafaera sat in the bed a few more minutes as the fire's warmth spread. Finally she dragged herself up out of her nest, sighing regretfully.

Zhafaera washed quickly, cleaned her teeth, and ran a brush through her hair. She chose a simple, light green dress from the wardrobe and dressed quickly, ready to be back near the fire's warmth.

She went back into the bedroom and found that Mai had brought bread and cheese, fruit, and even a platter of thinly sliced beef. She left Zhafaera to her lunch.

A few minutes later, there was a knock on the door. "Come in," Zhafaera called through a mouthful of bread. The door opened and Delan peeked his head in. Seeing Zhafaera eating lunch, he asked, "May I join you?"

"Of course," Zhafaera said, smiling. Delan smiled back and came to sit at the table across from her. He took an apple from the plate of fruit and bit into it. "Did you get enough of your beauty sleep?" He joked.

"I guess," she said, tossing her hair back over her shoulder. "Really, though, I feel like I'm wasting time I don't have."

"Hey, don't worry about it – the Sapphire is fighting him, you have time."

Munching on a piece of bread, Zhafaera struggled with what to say. She *didn't* have time.

Delan leaned back in his chair, filling the gap. "So what was it like? Ruling the kingdom, I mean."

Zhafaera smiled slightly and shrugged. "Meetings for *hours*. Holding court and listening to everyone's complaints and trying to solve problems the best I could, preferably non-violently. Lots of balls and parties," she made a face. "Actually, I wasn't very good at those. There were a couple of nobles at the last Gathering that were convinced I *had* to marry them. One of those almost started a war... they blamed me, but it's not my fault I broke the Prince's hand! He shouldn't have touched me..." She stopped and studied Delan's face. His blue eyes crinkled and he was turning slightly purple under his mop of curly black hair. She frowned. "What?"

Delan burst out laughing and choked out, "I'd have loved to have seen that. I'll be sure to keep my hands to myself."

Zhafaera grinned. "Well, as long as you aren't an ass that doesn't understand the meaning of the word 'no,' you're probably okay." She cleared her throat, feeling heat rise into her face. "I mean, you're a friend, so I'd probably try not to break anything." *Please, just stop.* She risked a quick glance from under her lashes. Delan's face was slightly pink, but he was still smiling.

"Don't worry, Princess. I swear on my honor not to try to take advantage of you." He was trying to be solemn, but there was a small smirk playing around his mouth. "You may not kick my ass as easily as you seem to think, but I don't really want to test you."

Zhafaera very nearly stuck her tongue out at him. Instead, she put on her blankest, most serious princess-face and said, "A wise decision, sir. I will take you at your word and spare you the embarrassment of a challenge."

He snorted. "Embarrassment, is it? Well, it is raining today, and I'd rather not get soaked *and* beaten. Maybe tomorrow." He winked.

"I'll hold you to that," Zhafaera said. She sighed. "All right, so what's on the agenda for today, then, if not dueling?"

"Not a thing. You should rest and recover your strength." Delan smiled as Zhafaera raised her eyebrows.

"I guess, but really, I'm fine. I need to start gathering supplies and getting ready to leave."

He looked at her flatly, clearly skeptical. "You haven't even decided how you're going to fight him yet, and you don't want to seek asylum with our neighbors. The most important thing is that you're at your full strength when we *do* leave."

Zhafaera gave a very un-princess-like snort. *He's right, though, damn him.* "Okay fine, yesterday I could barely light a candle, and today isn't much better. Happy now?" This time she *did* stick her tongue out at him. *What am I, four?*

"No." He stood, smiling, and walked over to her side of the table, then knelt by her chair so he had to look up slightly at her. "I'm sorry, Princess. Please forgive your humble servant and accept a quiet day in the library in front of the fire as recompense."

Zhafaera sighed heavily. "I suppose that will make up for it. I do need to figure out my next move."

Delan stood and went back to his seat. "I give up."

"I'll rest and plan at the same time." Zhafaera said simply. "It's just that... I'm afraid we're going to be too late as it is. Once Velexar gains full control over the Sapphire, it'll amplify his power more than you can imagine. We have to get it back before that happens. There's not *time* to rest. And... it's not all tiredness that's affecting my powers." She closed her eyes. "It's the Sapphire... I can still feel it in my mind. It's fighting him, but some of that anger... I guess you could say it bleeds over to me. When I reach for my magic, it gets worse... my head starts pounding, and my magic is drained faster than normal." She opened her eyes and looked at Delan. "I think that's something I'm going to have to learn to deal with for now. I don't think I'm going to be at my *full*

63

strength, but I need to at least learn to work through it enough to take on Velexar. Last time I tried… " she flinched. "It didn't go so well."

Delan reached over the table, took her hand, and squeezed it. "We'll make it work." He smiled. "We'll just have to make sure you leave armed to the teeth."

She grimaced. "That wasn't enough last time, either. But maybe combined… "

"That's the spirit!" Delan stood, releasing her hand. "Come on, let's not worry about it right now. I'm thinking we should follow lunch with some tea by the fire in the library." He looked out the window at the gloomy sky, and the rain hitting the window. "Best use for a day like this anyway."

They both stood. As they reached the door, Zhafaera stopped. "Let me just do one thing first." She paused, then raised her hand and placed her fingers against Delan's throat. He was very still as she closed her eyes and took a deep breath. Forcing herself to push through the pounding in her head, she grabbed a thread of her magic. The small cut left by her knife at his throat the other day healed instantly. She opened her eyes and brushed her fingers lightly over where the mark had been, feeling his pulse beat against her fingertips. "There. Good as new," she said quietly.

He flashed her a lopsided grin. "Thanks. You didn't have to do that, but thanks."

"Didn't I just say I need to practice using my magic like this? But you're welcome. Thanks for being test

64

subject number one." She grinned and walked towards the door.

"Um, test subject?"

"Yeah, well, my control isn't the best right now, I could have disintegrated you." She ignored his eyes bugging out of his head. "That's why I have to practice." She paused at the door and cocked her head. "Speaking of practicing control, perhaps I could help Alec with that some. He could start learning control, and I can practice using my magic this way."

"That's a great idea, you can blow stuff up together!" He laughed at her glare. "He's around, I'm surprised he wasn't waiting outside your door. He'll show up soon I bet. He has a knack for finding me." He moved past her into the hallway.

***

That evening found them all in the library again. Zhafaera and Alec were sitting in front of the fireplace, passing a small flame back and forth between themselves and the fire. Delan was sitting in an armchair nearby, reading a book and absentmindedly twirling a knife through his fingers, reflecting a spot of firelight onto the wall and greatly entertaining a few of the cats that roamed the castle.

Zhafaera could feel herself regaining control with every bit of magic she did. She was still tired, and so not at her best, but she at least felt she could reliably access her magic now. The headache was still in the way, but she was learning to push it aside, and it seemed to be lessening somewhat. Alec was still struggling, and she occasionally had to reach out and contain stray sparks, but overall he had improved greatly over the course of the afternoon. He could at least contain fire with a lot more accuracy than before. Zhafaera suspected that he would become very powerful, with the right training. She would do what she could, and he was a fast learner, but she was still worried about what would happen when she left. So she had spent all afternoon giving him a crash course in controlling fire, and fully intended to do the same every afternoon until they left. She could only hope that would be enough. But for now it was getting late, and she knew they were both getting too tired.

"That's enough for tonight," she finally said.

It was a measure of Alec's tiredness that he didn't even argue. He just nodded and slowly got to his feet. Zhafaera frowned. *I must have pushed him harder than I thought. He'll need a rest tomorrow,* she thought.

"Come, Alec," Geon called from the door. "Thank her Highness. It's time for bed."

Alec straightened and bowed slightly. "Thank you, Princess. You'll teach me more tomorrow?"

"Yes, of course I will," she said.

Alec and his father left. Zhafaera went and selected another book from the pile they had amassed through the day, most of them texts that contained legends and half-truths about the four Gems. Then she went and stretched out on the couch across from the fire. Delan had stopped playing with the knife, and the cats, now bored, came and curled up on her. She and Delan stayed in the library for some time, reading until the pages blurred before their eyes as the light from the fire started to dim. Zhafaera would occasionally stoke the fire with her magic, earning them a bit more light, but at some point she must have fallen asleep, because she suddenly woke to a hand on her shoulder. She had grabbed the hand and was preparing to flip the owner over the back of the couch before she realized it was Delan. The fire had burned down to embers.

"Easy, it's just me," he said quietly.

"Sorry, you startled me. What time is it?"

"Late. Come on. You'll be more comfortable in your room, even without the blanket of cats you were collecting." Zhafaera looked down and saw that indeed, she had half a dozen cats curled up around her.

They slowly climbed the stairs together and stopped when they reached her room. When she opened her door, she saw several dark, furry shapes race into the room ahead of them. Delan chuckled quietly. "I guess your blanket wasn't done with you yet."

***

King Velexar stood in the dark at the top of the North Tower, overlooking the city of Arenthia. He'd done it – it was all his. With his sister Karaena finally out of the way, he'd assumed his rightful place as King of Arenthia. Now all he had to do was catch her daughter.

He frowned. He had originally intended to kill Zhafaera, but now, he wasn't sure that was going to be the best option. He flexed his hand where the Sapphire had burned him the day before. He'd healed the blisters, but the pain still remained. He'd fashioned a chain to hold the Gem around his neck – there was no chance that he'd leave it anywhere but on his person – but even when it wasn't touching his skin, he could feel it, a grating presence against the inside of his skull. At first, he hadn't been able to use it at all, but he was slowly gaining some measure of control. Very slowly.

He knew it called out to his niece. When his commander had reported back that her ship had been sunk just off the coast of Crystal Point, he'd hoped that would be the end of it. But no, he could still feel her faint presence to the south, connected to him through the Sapphire's energy.

Perhaps he could use that to his advantage. He knew that bonding the Sapphire at this point would be suicide, and that certainly wasn't his end goal. But Zhafaera... Zhafaera might be able to bond it. And if he could control her like he'd controlled her mother, the Sapphire would be just as much his as if he'd done it himself, but without the risk.

Yes, keeping her alive might do nicely, he thought.

Just then, there was a *whoosh,* and a heavy thud that shook the whole tower he stood on. He looked over his shoulder. No matter how often he saw them, dragons instilled a certain level of primal fear. Not that he let it show. He would eventually deal with them.

"Targan," he said to the enormous, midnight blue dragon. "Thank you for coming."

King Velexar, Targan's voice sounded in his mind. *I am at your service.*

Velexar chose to ignore the slight twist to his words. It was the best he was going to get. "I need you to do something for me," he said.

We have already done much for you.

"I need you to find someone," Velexar continued. He pictured Zhafaera in his mind, with her pale skin, long red hair, and vibrant blue eyes. He thought for a moment, indecisive. "I need you to bring her to me. Alive," he finally said slowly.

That is no easy task.

"Are you telling me you're afraid of a young girl?" Velexar asked incredulously. "She *is* a White mage, but surely for you –"

That is not what I mean. The difficulty is bringing her back alive, Targan said with a touch of anger. It was not wise to anger a dragon, and Velexar was no fool.

"Of course, if she dies, then she dies. I simply request that she be brought back alive if at all possible."

Do you know where she is?

Velexar pictured a map of Arenthia in his mind and focused on Crystal Point. "She's there, I'm sure of it." Velexar paused. "When can you leave?"

69

Targan snorted, a rather intimidating sound made more so by the slight wisps of smoke that rose from his nostrils. *Such a task is beneath me. But I will send one of the others to fetch this girl.*

"Your help is much appreciated," Velexar said. "The sooner she can be retrieved, the better."

Targan tilted his head slightly to the side, as if studying Velexar. Then, he spread his huge wings, and dove off the tower. Velexar breathed a small sigh of relief. The dragons were useful for now, but sooner or later, they would have to be dealt with. But not today.

Today, he smiled as he looked out over his city and listened to the sound of the nearby ocean. Yes, things were going almost exactly according to his plan. As soon as he caught Zhafaera, everything would be in place.

"I will come for you," he said out loud. He could feel her through the Sapphire, and hoped she heard him.

***

I will come for you.

The voice in her dreams left Zhafaera with a feeling of deep unease when she woke the next morning with no less than five cats snuggled around her on the bed. Cats tended to like mages, everyone knew that, but this was a bit ridiculous. Nevertheless, when she got up she was careful not to disturb them – although she still received several cracked eyes frowning at her.

She washed and dressed quickly, then headed downstairs and met Delan and Geon in the dining room – Alec was still asleep. After breakfast, Geon told them he'd asked the village seamstress to come and help prepare clothes for Zhafaera. Delan promptly disappeared. By the end of the morning, Zhafaera had several sets of pants and loose shirts, coats, and a long dark cloak that she would soon need, as winter wasn't far off. She even threw in a couple of thick woolen dresses – sometimes a woman dressed in man's clothes attracted more attention than the extra range of motion was worth.

She went back downstairs for lunch to find Alec awake and as excitable as ever. She postponed their lessons until the evening, and she and Delan headed outside to the stables, where he fed his sleek black horse an apple as she chose her horse. There were only a few for Zhafaera to choose from, but she eventually selected a lithe, chestnut colored mare named Liri, who looked as if she could run forever and never tire. She spent some time talking quietly to her, feeding her an apple; she reminded Zhafaera a lot of her horse back home. It was amazing how so many things could remind her of home, and how much she missed the way things used to be. She could have stayed there all afternoon, remembering, but eventually Delan dragged her away.

Their next stop was the armory; Delan apparently hadn't been kidding when he said he wanted her armed to the teeth, which was fine by her. He had apparently spoken with the armorer yesterday morning and had a number of

71

weapons set out for her – a set of over half a dozen expertly balanced throwing knives with straps for ankles, wrists, and thighs, another slightly longer knife on a chain that could go around her neck, and a bow of smooth wood with a quiver of arrows. She half expected Delan to throw in the plate armor that she saw in the corner, just in case, but as she strapped each piece in place, she felt safer than she had in what felt like years.

That night, she worked with Alec again by the fire for a while. This time she only had to contain two stray sparks. There were others that almost went awry, but Alec caught and contained those few on his own. Zhafaera was impressed by how quickly he was learning. *He'll be a powerful mage indeed,* she thought as he practiced growing and shrinking a flame over his hand. *Thank the gods he's on my side.*

"Of course I'm on your side," Alec said earnestly. The flame flickered and vanished.

Zhafaera jumped. She hadn't known Alec could communicate mind-to-mind yet. *You and your family have been my closest friends, and I appreciate that,* she thought slowly and distinctly.

His eyes widened and he opened his mouth.

With your mind only, Zhafaera thought firmly.

Alec closed his mouth and his face scrunched up in concentration. *CAN YOU HEAR ME?*

Yes, Zhafaera thought, pulling away a little so his mind voice wasn't so loud. *Mages can communicate mind-to-mind fairly easily.*

Can I read your mind? Alec asked in wonder.

Zhafaera suppressed a laugh. *It's not polite to rifle through others' thoughts, so we try to focus on whatever is being said.*

Alec was thoughtful for a moment. *That seems fair,* he finally said.

"That's enough for tonight," Zhafaera said out loud. She glanced at Delan, who was bent over his father's desk, their heads together. "We all need some rest."

***

The next morning dawned bright and cold. Delan again met Zhafaera in the dining room, both dressed in training gear, and after breakfast they went down to the practice yard. Zhafaera claiming she wanted to get a feel for the weight of her new knives. As they practiced throwing at target dummies, Delan was amazed at her accuracy. All of her throws were concentrated in vital areas – eyes, neck, chest, and groin.

"You're good," he said, turning to face her. "Much better than the last time I saw you."

"I've had a few years of practice since you told me I was too weak to throw properly." She smiled, but there was a distinctly scary look in her eye that made Delan thankful she wasn't throwing those knives at him. "It's easier if I use my magic to find the perfect spot first – I can use it to pinpoint a man's jugular, then throw along the line

73

of my magic for an exact hit." She purposely eyed his neck and her grin widened as Delan shivered.

"Remind me not to make you angry."

"Don't anger me."

"Thanks, that was helpful."

"You're welcome." Zhafaera laughed. "You're not bad yourself, you know."

"'Not bad' is it?" Delan suddenly flung his arm out straight to the side, and a knife went flying. He could tell from Zhafaera's face that it struck the target dead in the center of the chest.

"Nice," Zhafaera said, grinning. She nodded at the sword hanging from his waist. "But how are you with that?"

"Good enough to teach you how to wield one without cutting off your own foot."

She gave him a flat stare.

"Just kidding! I'm sure you can manage a sword without losing an appendage." Delan had his sword out in an instant, meeting Zhafaera's knife as she swung it towards his ribs. Her eyes widened slightly, but he gave her no time to consider her next move. He swung low at her legs, preparing to stop his swing if she didn't block. She jumped, and as she jumped, she swung at him again with a knife already in her other hand, and he had to jerk his blade up to block. They traded blows back and forth, matching each other swing for swing. It seemed like those knives were everywhere at once. Finally, Delan began to drive her slowly back across the yard towards the stables.

Zhafaera was fast and agile, but Delan had the longer reach.

When they reached the stable, Zhafaera slipped through the open door and vanished. Delan paused, then smiled and rolled forward, spinning as he rolled so that he came up half kneeling on the floor and facing the open door, meeting Zhafaera's first knife with his sword, twisting and sending it flying, and grabbing her other arm with his free hand. He squeezed, and the knife dropped from her hand and fell with a *clunk* to the floor. Her eyes widened momentarily as he yanked her down towards him and started to bring his sword up towards her, but she managed to get her feet against his chest and tried to push off into a flip. But Delan pushed upwards, tripped her backwards over his knee, and had her pinned against the straw-covered floor with his sword at her neck before she could blink. Heart pounding, he grinned and breathed, "Give up?"

Zhafaera smiled sweetly and pushed the tip of yet another knife against the skin under his breastbone. "Do you?"

They were close, both of them panting slightly. Delan could feel their hearts pounding as adrenaline coursed through their systems. He was acutely aware of where their bodies were touching, which, since he still had her pinned, was everywhere. He couldn't tell if the look in her eyes was more excitement or anger, so he quickly stamped down his desire to lean forward just an inch and touch his lips to hers. He had a feeling he'd get a knife in the ribs for it. He forced himself to say, "Draw?"

She nodded. "Draw," she said, somewhat breathlessly.

Delan rolled off of her and got to his feet, reaching a hand down to help Zhafaera up. She took it and he pulled her up. "You're good," she said. "I've never seen anyone move that fast with a sword."

"Thanks. You're pretty impressive with those knives. Where the hell did that last knife even come from?" She raised an eyebrow. "Never mind, I don't want to know. Not to brag, but honestly, most things Velexar sends against us probably won't be as good as me with a sword, not to mention the fact that they'd have to get past your flying knives of death before they could even get close to you."

Zhafaera opened her mouth to reply, but at that moment, there was a roar and a whoosh, followed by screams. Lots of screams. They ran to the door, and saw several buildings near the gate on fire. At that moment, a huge shape, almost completely white with green wings, flew over the wall and again spewed fire down into the village, igniting more screams. Delan was frozen in a mixture of awe and horror; he'd never seen a dragon before – almost no one had – but there was no mistaking the enormous creature with a long neck and even longer tail, four powerful legs, and thick, leathery wings. Zhafaera made to run out of the stable, the air almost crackling with all the power she was drawing, but Delan grabbed her and held tight, his arms pinning hers to her sides.

"What are you doing? Let me go!" She struggled.

"You're the most valuable person here! You can't just run out there and wave a flag saying 'here I am!'"

"I can't sit here and do nothing!" She yelled angrily.

More creatures were coming over the walls. These were fat, black, scaly things that were much smaller than the dragon, but bigger than a man, flying fast towards the keep behind the dragon. From their position, they could see all of them, maybe a dozen total. As they came closer to the keep, and closer to Zhafaera, the dragon opened his mouth and breathed fire a third time, straight at the keep. Delan held his breath, trying to control his emotions and fear for those inside – it had been less than a minute since the dragon first appeared. But the fire stopped dead, roaring against a translucent blue barrier. The smaller creatures, oblivious, plowed right through the barrier and continued on to the castle, some landing on the ramparts, others still circling in the air. The handful of archers now on the walls started shooting, and several were picked out of the air. Soon after, guards came pouring out of the keep and onto the tops of the towers, slicing down several surprised creatures before they could regroup.

Delan looked down at Zhafaera, who was panting slightly. He let her go as the dragon screamed and turned towards them, sensing her magic. Again the dragon breathed fire, this time right at them, and again Zhafaera caught it in a shield, staggering this time. Two of the other creatures landed right in front of them, growling and lumbering awkwardly towards them on their thickly muscled hind legs, their thinner forelimbs reaching out towards them. They looked like miniature dragons, but misshapen and obviously powerless. Delan drew his sword, stepping forward and ducking under the swing of a huge, clawed fist, slicing one open across the belly, then falling back and beheading the other as it made its way towards Zhafaera, who was pale and resting a hand on the door to the stable. The horses behind her were screaming in terror as they smelled fire and dragon. The dragon was roaring its frustration as she held it at bay, the shield slowly growing to form half a sphere in front of the dragon. Before she could close the circle, the dragon realized the trap, threw its head back, and breathed gently on the shield, which stopped growing immediately. The dragon then tapped the shield with a huge claw, and it shattered like glass.

Zhafaera sagged like a puppet with its strings cut, but before Delan could reach her, she stiffened and straightened, fury blazing in her eyes. She raised her arms, and a wind rose with them. Palms forward, she rotated her arms, and the wind rose up into a cyclone that surrounded the dragon. The dragon started to spin slowly, raising a huge taloned paw as if to brush the wind aside, but its claws were knocked aside by several giant chunks of rock that had ripped free of the wall nearby and flew at the dragon. The dragon snarled as it spun faster and faster until the cyclone dipped back like a catapult, then flung the dragon forward and over the wall.

Delan ran back to Zhafaera and grabbed her arm to hold her up. She shook him off. "I'm fine, I'm fine, we need to get to the Keep before it comes back."

Delan looked up. A number of the strange mini-dragons were down, but about half remained, fighting the few guards left on the highest tower. The guards were clearly weakening. "Okay, quickly!" Delan said.

They started to run for the keep, which was only across the courtyard, but before they had taken more than ten steps, the dragon came soaring back over the walls, shrieking and spewing fire, and half-melting a twenty-foot-wide section of wall as it went. The archers were still firing from the roof of the Keep, but the arrows were just bouncing off the thick, tough hide. Before Zhafaera could even think to prepare a shield, the dragon opened its enormous jaws and inhaled.

But before it could breathe fire on them, a tiny fireball from the castle hit it on the side of the face. The dragon's head whipped around to where Alec was standing on one of the lower towers of the Keep. Another fireball came flying at the dragon, but it was lazily waved aside. When the next fireball was pulled out of the flaming village and came from behind and hit the dragon's tail, the dragon began to laugh, actually laugh, although the sound was deep and gravely and sent shivers down Delan's spine. The dragon roared, and the three remaining creatures on the topmost tower immediately took off and dove. One of them snatched the sagging Alec from the tower top, and headed out towards the northern stretch of wall, the other two close behind. The archers stopped firing, apparently afraid of hitting Alec if they continued. They could see Alec kick and struggle weakly for a moment; then the creature holding him shook him, and he was still.

All was quiet for a moment. Then the dragon turned back to Zhafaera and Delan, who were standing open mouthed in horror. The dragon took one final breath, still chuckling, but before he could exhale, the air around Zhafaera crackled, and the heat Delan felt wasn't from the dragon. Once again she raised her arms, but instead of wind, hot, blue lightning shot from her fingertips, splintering into a hundred tiny shards as it took the dragon full in the face, sending bright bolts into its open mouth and eyes as wave after wave of electric current surged over its hide. The dragon screamed and the lightning began to splinter further, some hitting not just the dragon, but the castle behind it. Chunks of rock flew from the Keep, hitting the dragon and raining down on what was left of the village. Just when Delan thought that if the dragon didn't destroy the keep, Zhafaera would, the lightning broke off. Zhafaera dropped to her hands and knees, as if the lightning had been the rope by which she had been holding herself up.

The dragon screeched again, as it dipped in the sky, shaking its head. Quickly righting itself, it wheeled north and took off after its remaining companions, spewing another river of fire over the village.

Delan watched as it quickly caught up to the others. The creatures carrying Alec had become black pinpricks in the sky to the north. He took a deep breath and tried to control his panic. When he felt he could speak without screaming, he knelt next to Zhafaera, who hadn't moved.

"Are you all right?" He asked. His voice was flat, even to his own ears. He put a hand on her shoulder.

She was silent for a moment. When she spoke, her voice was a whisper. "A dragon. I fought a dragon." She was trembling. When she looked at him, there were tears in her eyes. "And Alec... did they... ? I taught him, I encouraged him... ! He should have stayed hidden," she choked out.

Delan focused on his breathing again. "It wasn't your fault. He'd have tried that whether or not you taught him anything." Looking up, he saw flames roaring over the village. "Come on, can you stand? We need to get you inside."

She reached out a hand and he took it, helping her to her feet. She wavered slightly, then straightened and turned towards the sound of running footsteps. Delan looked up to see his father sprinting across the yard towards them, his face deathly white under streaks of soot.

"Are you both all right?" He called anxiously.

They nodded.

Skidding ungracefully to a halt in front of them, he said to Delan, "Come, we need to help with the bucket lines. We've got to get these fires out and save what we

81

can." Delan nodded again. "Princess, you should go inside. There might be more of them out there."

Zhafaera shook her head and stood straighter. "No, I can help. The ocean is close enough for me to draw from."

Delan was not an expert on magic, but even he knew she had already done too much. "You need to rest," he said quickly, already moving towards the fire. "If that wasn't your full strength, I don't know what is."

Zhafaera said nothing for once, turning and walking towards the keep, wobbling slightly with each step. Delan and his father ran down to where lines were already forming at the two wells in the center of the village. About a third of the small village was on fire, the blaze hot and beginning to spread. The moist ocean air kept the houses from going up like straw, but dragonfire was hot enough to burn everything thoroughly. After a few minutes, they were beginning to make a dent in the houses nearest the wells, but the fire was slowly spreading; at this rate everything would burn.

Then it began to rain. Just a drizzle at first, but it quickly started to pour. Delan tasted salt as it soaked his hair and ran down his face. He looked up and saw Zhafaera standing on the east wall, facing the ocean. She looked tiny, and she was clinging onto the battlement, but she brought wave after wave of water up from the raging ocean below and sprayed it out over the village. The soaked buildings no longer caught, and the fire stopped its spread. Slowly, the fires died, until there was nothing left but smoldering ruins, and they were able to start picking up the pieces.

Sometime later, as he pulled yet another burnt piece of wood aside, Delan realized the rain had stopped. He had no idea how much time had passed; he just knew that as long as he was moving, he wasn't thinking of what was happening to his brother. He looked around at everyone sorting through the rubble; they all knew no one could have survived in the buildings that had burned, but still they moved carefully, just in case. Up on the wall, there was no sign of Zhafaera.

Delan tossed his piece of wood into the growing pile behind him and set off for the wall. He trudged up the steps by the gate, and quickly moved down to where he'd last seen Zhafaera. He found her sitting with her back against the wall. Her eyes were closed, but as he knelt down beside her she mumbled, "I'm fine. Just tired."

"I know. Come on, let's go inside. You're soaked." He reached for her.

"I can walk," she protested, as she put her arms around his neck.

He lifted her and held her against him, "I know."

"I c-c-can," she said, shivering, her eyes still closed.

Delan ignored her and carried her back along the wall, down the stairs, through the courtyard, and back into the keep. The entry hall had been converted into a makeshift hospital, and the village herbalist was directing servants in caring for the few injured. Most were guards that had been hurt on the battlements by the mini-dragons. Delan didn't see anyone with burns; dragonfire simply melted flesh from bone, and most people didn't survive even a brush with it. They were all so busy with their own tasks, they hardly noticed him walking in.

He considered taking Zhafaera up to her own room, but the fire wouldn't be lit, and in her wet clothes, that was no good. He certainly wasn't going to remove them himself this time – a dress with a shift under it was one thing, but a shirt and pants was a whole different story. He carried her into the library, where the fire had burned down to little more than embers, and placed her on the couch. After poking the fire into a pleasant roar, he dug a warm blanket out from the basket near the fire and placed it over the princess, then drug the couch closer to the fire. He got a second blanket out for himself and sat on the floor in front of her, resting back against the couch and staring into the fire. *What are we going to do now?*

***

When Zhafaera woke, the room was dark. The fire in the grate was still burning, but the sky outside the window was purple and red, the last rays of sun just peeking through. She was alone in the room, except for the three cats that had crawled under the blanket with her. One, with silky black fur, was curled up smack on her chest, which was probably what had woken her.

She sat up slowly, feeling like she'd been beaten over every inch of her body, and waited for her head to stop spinning before standing with difficulty. She took a few deep breaths to help clear her head, then climbed the stairs to her room, where she changed out of her still-damp clothes into a heavy grey wool dress. The keep was quiet, but she could hear a few people calling to one another outside through her window. Looking out, she saw that a large portion of the damage had already been piled up. The melted wall though… that would take longer to fix.

It seemed that everyone had stopped in their cleanup and was going home for the night. At least, those who still had homes were; the rest were making their way towards the keep. She thought she could make out Geon trudging slowly up the road to the keep, but Delan wasn't with him. She thought she knew where he might be.

One floor up and two wrong turns later, she found the entrance to the low tower that Alec had been throwing fireballs from. Delan was there, standing across from the door, head bowed, gripping the edge of the wall as if the entire castle would crumble if he let go. To be fair, the keep wasn't in the best shape after its run-in with a dragon. She winced, thinking of the damage she had done herself. And that wasn't even considering what she'd done to the ocean surrounding Crystal Point. Pulling that much water would make the seas rough for *days*, and could potentially disrupt the whole tidal ecosystem. But when she'd seen how fast the fire was spreading, she had to make a choice.

Zhafaera closed the door quietly and went to stand beside Delan. She placed a gentle hand on his arm, feeling the tense muscles beneath, straining against his emotions.

After a few moments, he seemed to realize she was there, and looked up. Turning towards her, he opened his arms without a word. She didn't hesitate, stepping forward and wrapping her arms around him, burying her face against his chest as his arms enclosed her and holding him as tightly as he was holding her.

"I'm sorry," she whispered. "I'm so sorry." She couldn't force the rest of the words out. She hadn't told them about the dragon the night her mother died. She hadn't warned them. This was her fault.

"It's not your fault," Delan mumbled into her hair.

"I should never have come."

"I'm glad you did." He was trembling. "Do you… " he swallowed. "Do you think we can get him back?"

Zhafaera was silent. "Zhafaera?"

She pulled away and looked up at him. "… Delan… Maybe. Maybe. My guess is that they'll take him to Arenthia, but I don't know. Even if they do take him to the capital, it might be too late by the time we get there."

His eyes looked black in the twilight. "You think they'll kill him?"

She shook her head. "I think they'll *turn* him," she whispered. "We can try to get him back, and Delan, I swear, I'll do everything I can, but… like I said before, this is a dangerous time for him; he's not settled into his powers." She paused, trying to gauge Delan's reaction. "He's powerful. They'll want him on their side. He might resist for a while, but eventually, they'll either turn him or kill him in the attempt."

Delan's arms dropped from around her as he leaned back against the wall and slid down it, thumping heavily at the bottom. He crossed his arms over his knees and rested his head on them. After a minute, Zhafaera moved and sat next to him. Neither spoke for some time. The sun set completely, and stars started to appear in the sky above them. Eventually, Zhafaera leaned over and rested her head on his shoulder. He finally lifted his head and looked at her, then raised his arm and laid it across her shoulders, pulling her closer.

"If they turn him, could you turn him back?" he asked.

"I really don't know. I don't know how, and even if I could figure it out without killing him, I don't know if he would come back the same."

They sat quietly for a while, Delan absentmindedly stroking her hair, twirling a strand around his fingers. Finally Zhafaera took a deep breath and forced herself to speak. "There's something we need to discuss. I should have told you before… "

"You think Velexar is working with dragons?"

Zhafaera sighed. "I guess that's obvious now."

"We're not important enough for a dragon to come here otherwise." Delan stood slowly, pulling Zhafaera up with him. "We need to find my father. We need a plan."

***

"The night of the attack, there was at least one dragon in the sky. And others… like those *things* we saw today."

87

Zhafaera shuddered slightly. "I don't think this is just about Velexar's desire for power."

Geon cleared his throat and said, "I have a few remaining contacts... I heard a rumor, just before your mother's 'accident.'" He said the word with such venom that Zhafaera leaned away involuntarily. Eyes narrowing, he continued. "Supposedly some of the dragons have split off. They are no longer united. But I didn't know it was... connected."

There was silence as everyone processed what that might mean. "I'm thinking we should be concerned about that," Delan finally said sarcastically. He was pacing the library.

Zhafaera sighed. "I am. If he has dragons *and* the Sapphire... " She put her face in her hands and mumbled through her fingers. "Although it definitely does *not* like him. It's still fighting him."

"Thank the gods for that, at least," Geon said.

"Why didn't either of you *say something*?" Delan burst out angrily.

Zhafaera flinched. "I should have. I meant to. I was just afraid of what it might mean."

"What does it mean?"

"It means we could all be dead a lot faster than we anticipated." Zhafaera snapped.

Geon opened his mouth to respond, but Delan interrupted. "Maybe not."

"What?"

"The dragons." Delan had stopped pacing and looked thoughtful.

"What about them?" Zhafaera asked, confused and cautious.

"Allies. Would they be allies?" he asked. "The ones not with Velexar I mean."

Zhafaera shook her head. "Are you joking? You just watched a dragon melt half your town and abduct your brother, and you want to ask them to *help us*?"

"That dragon today... I've never seen anything like it. I was terrified," Delan acknowledged. "But what can fight dragons but other dragons? We don't have the Sapphire, but if the dragons allied with Velexar are rebels, surely that makes it their business too? If Velexar is in league with renegade dragons, then surely they'd be fighting the rest of the dragons?"

Zhafaera was incredulous. "And you want to get in the middle of a dragon fight?"

Delan paled. "No, but... look, I don't know about you, but I'd feel a lot better flying into Arenthia on the back of a dragon and demanding the Sapphire than walking in and asking nicely."

"Are you out of your mind? Dragons. Hate. Us."

"But you've seen them before? You've met with them, haven't you?" Delan asked.

"Once, on neutral ground, after an... issue."

"What 'issue?'"

"A few men went into the mountains and killed a dragon. Dragons burned their village down in retaliation. It was all we could do to settle things."

"But they spoke to you? You were able to reason with them?"

"Yes," Zhafaera said, frustrated. "But only because my mother reminded them that humans aren't helpless any more! She had the Sapphire."

Zhafaera was suddenly remembering that Delan was nearly as stubborn as she was.. "If he has dragon allies, you need allies just as powerful if we're going to get Alec back," he reasoned.

Their eyes locked, neither backing down. Geon was watching them silently, clearly staying out of it.

"I don't like this," Zhafaera finally said angrily.

"Do you have a better idea?"

"Yes!" she cried. "Stealth! I go in, grab the Sapphire, *kill* him, defend against dragons."

"And if you're caught?" Delan asked.

"Then I'm dead."

"Because there's no room for a Plan B," he said. "Look, Plan A: allies. Dragon allies. Plan B: stealth." He looked at her questioningly.

She glared at him. "Fine!" she snapped, throwing her hands up. "But if I get eaten, I'm blaming you."

"Fair enough, Princess," he said with the ghost of a grin.

***

90

They spent the whole next day in the library, pouring over maps and planning their route until Delan couldn't see straight. Dragons lived deep in the Livorian mountains, but the specific locations of their nests were secret. He'd dug out all of the books his father had on dragons, which wasn't many, and was leafing through them for anything that could help. When he finally looked up, he saw Zhafaera was almost asleep in front of the fire, curled up like a cat in her corner of the couch next to Delan. His father had gone to bed hours ago.

"All right, I think that's as good a plan as we're going to get tonight." Delan said tiredly, closing his book. "We need to prepare supplies, and you need to rest." Zhafaera made a face. "We can go north the day after tomorrow. Hopefully the dragons will see us."

"Delan," Zhafaera said hesitantly. "I know you feel you need to go after your brother, but maybe you should stay here."

Delan felt a quick flash of anger. "You think I would leave him like that?" He took a breath. "I've taken care of him my whole life."

"This is my fault, my responsibility to fix…"

"And you think you can fix it without help? It's not just about you any more. If you truly want to fix it, then you need to do it carefully and not take stupid risks. If you get killed, you won't be fixing anything."

"Quit calling me stupid." Zhafaera's voice was rising.

"Well, quit being stupid about this then!" Delan said angrily. "You'll have to get used to people risking their lives for you if you want to win this. Or did you think Velexar wouldn't tear the countryside apart looking for you?"

Zhafaera's eyes blazed for a moment, then her shoulders slumped and she looked utterly defeated. "I never wanted this, you know. I never even wanted to be Queen. I didn't want the responsibility. I can take care of myself, but other people?" Her voice trailed off.

Delan felt sorry for her, but he knew he had won. He reached over and put a hand on her shoulder. "I know you can take care of yourself. I can take care of myself. And maybe between us, we can rescue Alec and defeat Velexar *and* his dragons."

Zhafaera looked up at him. Was that relief in her eyes? "Okay, fine. Thank you." She held out her hand and they shook on it.

"Come on, I'll take you back to your room," Delan said, pulling her up by the hand as Zhafaera tried to stifle a yawn. She looked about ready to fall over.

They walked down the hall and up the steep, winding staircase in silence. They had reached the top and were walking down the fourth floor hallway that contained the bedrooms when Zhafaera said quietly, "Delan?"

"Yes?"

"Thank you. I thought I would be alone in this, and I thought I was prepared for it, but...I'm glad I'm not. I'm glad you're on my side." She squeezed his arm.

"You're welcome, Zhafaera." He hoped she hadn't felt his heart start to race.

"I do need help. I – I'm afraid. Afraid that I'll fail."

They reached her door.

"*We* won't fail." He gave her hand on his arm a squeeze. Next thing he knew, Zhafaera had thrown her arms around his neck in a tight hug.

"Good night, Delan." She quickly released him and turned away, opening her door, and disappearing inside. Delan turned and walked slowly down the hall to his room, thinking of the assurances he had given the princess, and hoping that he was right. They couldn't afford to fail.

Chapter 4

Zhafaera was lying on a cold floor, shivering, unable to move. Beneath her were giant black and white marble tiles, and the air in the room seemed to crackle. She was struggling, trying to kick free of her bindings, but it was no use. She tried to reach for her magic, but was blocked by pain through her whole body. She lay still for a moment and tried to get her bearings, and realized she was back in the throne room of the palace. She looked up and saw Velexar laughing, holding the Sapphire right in front of her face, but she was unable to move to take it. Zhafaera heard a thud and looked to her left in time to see Delan crash to the floor, sword flying from his hand, a gaping hole in his chest, eyes closed. She screamed, and the scream went on and on until she was sitting up in bed, screaming in the dark.

Zhafaera abruptly closed her mouth and the scream stopped. She was gasping, trying to catch her breath, her heart racing. In moments, she was up, throwing on pants, shirt, a coat, and her black cloak, twisting her hair into a tight braid, attaching knives and her bow, grabbing her pack, and racing out the door. Down the stairs, she slipped silently into the kitchen, shoving whatever food she could find into her pack. It would have to do. She left through the side door, and then she was running across the courtyard and into the stables. She saddled her horse and tied her pack to the back of the saddle. Then she paused, resting her head against her horse's neck for just a moment.

"I have to do this," she whispered. Her horse snorted and stamped her foot.

"Well, you're no help." Zhafaera led Liri out of the stables. Mounting up as soon as they were clear of the yard, she made her way out of the village as quietly as possible, picking her way around the rubble. With all sounds muffled by a layer of ash, she headed for the ruined gate and out into the night.

The sun rose inch by inch as she passed through the farmland surrounding the castle. Riding hard, she didn't stop until the road reached the forest that covered much of the southern half of the continent. Once under the cover of the orange and yellow leaves of the autumn trees, she finally stopped to rest, holding her breath as if waiting for something to attack.

She felt exposed, even while surrounded by tall trees that blocked much of the early-morning light. After a hurried breakfast, she continued on, and by noon she found a small trail and left the main road. As she went deeper and deeper into the forest, she finally started to relax, the quiet stirrings of the woods seeping into her and calming her nerves.

As the afternoon wore on, Zhafaera started thinking about food. She hadn't packed much in her mad dash out the door this morning, and she was getting hungry. Drawing magic to her, she spread her awareness out around her on all sides, trying to sense something to hunt. Just as she was starting to think of making camp, she felt something small and warm-blooded in the brush to her right. In one motion, she had her bow out with an arrow notched, searching for the source. A flash of motion, and she loosed.

Dismounting, she picked her way carefully through the dim forest, looking for what she'd hit. She quickly found her arrow, with a rabbit on the end of it. Holding up her prize, she turned to Liri.

"Well, at least I'll have a hot dinner."

Zhafaera looked around. Just off the trail was a clear space between three huge trees, one side blocked off by dense bushes. "Come on, we can camp here," she said quietly, taking Liri's reins.

After hobbling Liri near the largest tree and giving her a bag of feed, Zhafaera gathered wood and stones for a fire, easily finding lots of dried branches at this time of year. Once the fire was going, she dug out her bedroll and laid it in front of the saddle, so she could sit on her blankets and lean back as if it were a chair. Then she prepared the rabbit and set it cooking over the fire. By the time she was done, she was exhausted. She'd never camped alone before, and doing all the work herself made her reconsider the wisdom of leaving Delan.

When she had finished eating, Zhafaera stood and began walking a circle around the small camp, setting protective wards so no one could sneak up on her. When she was done, they wouldn't even be able to see her, and she could sleep safely.

She lay down to sleep, but her brain wouldn't quiet. She realized she felt guilty. Guilty for leaving Delan behind. It was for the best, she knew, but still. He'd be angry. Somehow that thought upset her more than anything.

***

Delan was angry – no, furious – that Zhafaera had left him behind. When he'd woken that morning, he'd known immediately that she was gone. There was something missing from her room – an energy – that he'd felt as soon as he went to knock on her door. Sure enough, her pack was gone, Liri was gone, and Zhafaera was nowhere to be found.

He had no idea how much of a head start she had on him. It was at least a few hours, but she could have left any time after they'd said goodnight. He'd nearly gone tearing out the door himself, but his father had stopped him, being the voice of reason, as usual. He'd forced Delan to stop and take a breath, pack his things, and make sure he had proper provisions. It appeared Zhafaera had taken some food, but not much. Hardly enough for one person, let alone the both of them.

It was nearly noon by the time he left the village on his horse, moving quickly through the ruined homes. He

97

had friends here – he had seen Colin digging through the wreckage yesterday, so he was at least alive, but Delan felt guilty for leaving when there was so much work left to do. He tried to remember the bigger picture.

Delan continued at a steady pace down the road. His thoughts were jumbled, torn between anger at Zhafaera and concern for his brother. Every time he thought of what might be happening to him, his chest constricted and he felt sick. Was he afraid? Or was he still trying to set them all on fire? Was he strong enough to resist being turned? Delan rode with his head down, thinking of rescue plan after rescue plan, each one wilder than the last. The sun was beginning to set by the time he shook himself out of his thoughts and remembered to watch his back.

He'd made good time on the road, and as he left it to find a decent place to camp, he felt calmer. He *would* catch up to Zhafaera. She would likely enter the woods at some point and stay off the road – she was too visible, too recognizable, even if people did think she was dead. Velexar would be looking for her, and Delan was betting she would sacrifice speed for safety. He had no such dilemma. He'd often traveled this way by himself, and even if he was recognized, it wouldn't be unusual – he lived nearby.

By the time he'd set up camp and settled down for the night, forgoing a fire, he had a plan. No, the trouble wouldn't be catching up to Zhafaera, it would be trying not to strangle her when he did.

Zhafaera traveled northwest for days without seeing any sign of another living soul. She stuck to the woods, choosing safety over speed. Then, just as she was beginning to feel as though she and Liri were the only ones left in the world, the woods stopped abruptly. A road cut straight through their path.

Zhafaera tried to recall a map of the area that she'd seen in Lord Geon's library. She was fairly certain there was a small town to the north of Crystal Point.

She debated. On the one hand, she hadn't really thought through her midnight escape, and hadn't brought nearly enough supplies. On the other, going into *any* populated area was risking exposure. She'd spent almost five days traipsing through the woods to avoid detection – she wasn't sure she could justify a trip into town now.

Finally, hunger won out. She would slip in, stock up on provisions, and get out. An hour, at most. Nudging Liri forward, she stepped out onto the small road and headed east.

She hadn't gone far when they reached the intersection with the main road. Zhafaera pulled up short. There, leaning casually against the signpost, was Delan.

"Finally," he said dryly. "I was beginning to think you'd gotten lost."

Zhafaera closed her mouth and dismounted. "How did you…?"

"I took the road and gambled that you'd stop here based on how little food you took with you when you left in the middle of the night." Delan smirked. "It took you long enough. I've been waiting here for you for nearly two days."

Delan stepped forward, and Zhafaera could see the anger flickering behind his eyes. "You left me."

"I had to."

"No, you didn't. You *chose* to."

Zhafaera looked away. "I was trying to protect you."

"I told you," Delan said, taking another step closer. "I can take care of myself."

"I had a dream." Zhafaera whispered. "It was… bad."

"It was just a dream."

Zhafaera bit her lip. She wasn't so sure.

"Look, Zhafaera, I said you weren't going without me, and I meant it." Delan reached forward and put a finger under her chin, forcing her to look at him. "It's not just about you any more. They took my brother, and it's my responsibility to get him back."

"I'm sorry," Zhafaera said, and to her horror, the corners of her eyes began to sting, and she pulled away quickly. She would *not* cry. But Delan's look of disappointment hurt.

"It's okay," Delan said, and he took the last step forward, closing the distance between them and enveloping her in a hug. "Just don't leave me again," he said with a squeeze.

Zhafaera nodded, unable to speak for fear her voice would betray her. After a moment, she stepped back, shaking her head back to toss stray strands of hair off of her face. She cleared her throat.

"So what is this town, anyway? I couldn't remember from your father's map, but I'm fairly sure I've been here before," she said, changing the subject.

"This is Green Groves," Delan said, moving towards his horse, Shadow. "I know we need supplies, since *someone* insisted on leaving two days early, but it's getting close to dusk. How would you feel about spending the night?" He flashed her a smile. "I don't know about you, but I could really use a night in a real bed."

Zhafaera peered down the road. The town was nestled in a slight dip in the terrain, and she could see the small town spread out before them. It wasn't much larger than Delan's home, but it was densely packed with buildings. Small farms dotted the sides of the hills surrounding the town proper, and a large manor house looked out over it all at the top of the hill on the opposite side from them.

"Do you know the family there?" Zhafaera asked Delan.

"Well, yeah. I mean, they're practically our neighbors. You know them too, I'm sure – it's the Cordon family."

Zhafaera thought for a moment. "I know the name. Don't they have a daughter about my age?"

Delan coughed, and when Zhafaera looked at him, she saw his cheeks were slightly red. She felt a stab of jealousy deep in her gut, but squashed it quickly. She grinned. "Ex-lover?"

His blush deepened. "There was a time when she was quite determined. But…uh…how do I say this nicely? *No, thank you.*" He glanced at Zhafaera. "Probably not a good idea to visit them though – my dad reached out already. They practically worship Velexar now. But there's an inn."

Zhafaera hesitated. A bed sounded nice. "All right, an inn it is then." She eyed Delan. "But we need a disguise."

Delan nodded. "Let's move off the road." He led the way back into the woods a ways, where they wouldn't be easily seen. "Are you up to magicking something?" he asked.

"That's what I was thinking. I suppose I could also put on a dress." Zhafaera made a face and sighed resignedly. Quickly, she unbraided her hair, shaking it out and enjoying the feeling of freedom. Taking a deep breath, she closed her eyes, tugged on a tiny current of magic, and began running her fingers through her hair. Delan's small grunt of surprise told her that the spell was working. When she opened her eyes, her hair now tumbled over her shoulder in a mass of black waves.

Looking at Delan, she asked, "how's that?"

"Beautiful," he said simply.

Zhafaera felt a slight warmth rise in her cheeks. To cover it, she asked, "what color are my eyes?"

His head tilted to the side slightly. "Brown," he finally managed.

"Good. The last time I tried that spell, I got distracted and they ended up purple. Not a very good way to avoid notice."

Delan laughed. "Definitely not."

"Here, come closer," she told Delan, reaching for him. Delan obeyed and leaned down to give her an easier reach. Zhafaera hesitated only a moment before she ran her fingers through his hair, leaving streaks of honey-blond behind. His hair was thick and soft and curled at the ends where it hung down around his ears. She continued until his hair was considerably lighter, then lightly ran her thumbs over each of his eyebrows. Finally, she pulled back reluctantly.

Delan straightened, then pulled a lock of hair forward so he could see. "Gods, I'm a *blonde*!"

"Yes, well, it's only a disguise if it's something different!" Zhafaera laughed at the look of horror on his face. "It'll wear off in a couple of days, don't worry." Delan looked mildly pacified with that. "Now, what's our story?"

***

An hour later, they rode into the yard of an inn that looked simple but well-kept. There were no drunkards stumbling out the door (yet), and it was close to the main road into town, but not right on the edge. The town itself didn't seem all that big – mostly it was a small market surrounded by homes, a couple of taverns, an inn, and the large manor for

103

the noble family – but then again, Zhafaera had grown up in the biggest city in Arenthia.

Dismounting awkwardly from her side-saddle position (*this is why I hate dresses*, she thought sourly), she and Delan handed their horses' reins over to the stable boy that came running, pulled their packs off their horses, and headed inside.

Inside was gloriously warm. Zhafaera hadn't noticed how chilly it had gotten outside until she was suddenly warm again. At one end of the room, by the stairs, was a huge roaring fire, which is where most of the dozen or so people in the room were sitting. They paid no mind to the newcomers. A serving girl moved among them, refilling drinks.

In front of them was a long wooden bar, behind which the surly-looking innkeeper stood, handing out drinks to several loud patrons. Taking Zhafaera's hand, Delan crossed the room confidently and managed to get the frowning man's attention.

"My wife and I need a room for the night," Delan said as soon as the innkeeper was close enough. Zhafaera thought he looked skeptical, so she smiled and wrapped an arm around Delan's waist. He responded easily, throwing his arm around her shoulders, and the innkeeper's frown relaxed. Zhafaera tried not to enjoy the contact too much and reminded herself it was all for show.

"Course," the innkeeper said smoothly. "I suppose we have something that will be comfortable for you." They may have been on the road, but their clothes were nice enough to mark them as having enough money not to ask questions.

Delan handed over a few coins and took the offered key.

A few minutes later, Zhafaera and her "husband" stood awkwardly in their room for the night. The light was quickly fading outside, and as the light decreased, the noise from downstairs increased. Zhafaera looked longingly at the huge brass bathtub taking up most of the right side of the room. She was surprised to see the pump at one end. So far she had only seen plumbing like this among the wealthy. Zhafaera decided she *had* to have a hot bath, and gods help the person that tried to stop her.

Zhafaera looked over at Delan and found him watching her intently. He grinned and put his hands up in surrender. "Of course you'll have the first bath, m'lady. I'll wait outside and beat away any ruffians." He bowed and made to leave the room.

"Wait..." Zhafaera bit her lip, and Delan raised an eyebrow. "Not that! I just mean – we're supposed to be husband and wife...won't it be strange if you just wait outside the door?"

Delan's lips tightened. "I'm not leaving you up here alone and..." he seemed to search for the right word "...vulnerable! What if someone sneaks up here while you're un-knived and I don't see them and they –"

Zhafaera held up a hand to stop what was quickly becoming a rant. "Okay, okay, I get it!" She paused, not looking at him. "You could just stay in here." *Don't blush,*

105

don't blush, she told herself firmly. "On the other side of the bed, of course. With your back to me. And your eyes closed. And a blanket over your head."

She snuck a peek at Delan. His face was carefully blank, but there was something in his eyes that sent a tiny shiver down Zhafaera's spine. He quickly cleared his throat, opened his mouth to speak, and shut it again. Zhafaera felt the color rising in her cheeks, somewhat pleased that she'd left him speechless, and turned around to start pumping the water, using her magic to heat it. As she pumped and watched the tub fill, she heard Delan move to the other side of the room and sit down heavily on the floor. She turned to look and could just see the back of his head over the side of the bed.

When the tub was almost full, Zhafaera moved to the bed, opened her pack, and brought it closer to the tub, setting it next to the stool where two towels and soap were already stacked. She added a couple more pumps of water to the tub and looked over her shoulder to make sure Delan was still turned around.

She took a deep breath and said, "All right, 'husband,' are your eyes closed?" Her voice didn't sound quite as steady as she'd have liked.

"Yes, my dear 'wife.'"

"Don't turn around until I tell you," Zhafaera warned, starting to unbutton her dress with fingers that shook slightly. It had been bad enough at home when servants insisted on helping her – she could wash herself thankyouverymuch – but having a man in the room was completely different.

She quickly finished undressing and climbed into the tub. The water was warm, and it felt wonderful after five days on the road. She sighed gently as she sank into the water up to her neck. Closing her eyes, she finally relaxed, slowly stretching and loosening each muscle. After a few minutes of soaking, she let herself sink fully underwater, running her fingers through her thick hair to loosen the dirt from the road. When her head broke the surface again, she reluctantly reached over to the stool, grabbed the soap, and got to work.

As she scrubbed, she glanced over at Delan. He hadn't moved, and she could still only see the back of his head. In the silent room, the sound of the water splashing as she washed seemed unnaturally loud.

"Do you think they'd notice if we took this tub with us?" Zhafaera asked jokingly, trying to fill the uncomfortable silence. Delan's head jumped, startled, and he jerked as if to glance at her, but he quickly caught himself and settled back again.

After a moment he said, "Only if you can shrink it to fit in a pack and make it light enough to carry."

Zhafaera thought for a moment. "You know, I could, but the amount of magic it would take would probably draw the attention from any mage within ten miles. Not worth it." She sighed.

"Gods, I was joking!" Delan said, laughing. "Is there anything you *can't* do?"

107

"Of course," Zhafaera said, scrubbing at a stubborn spot of dirt on her left hand.

"Name one thing."

"I can't make food appear out of thin air." She paused. "All right, actually, I can, but it wouldn't contain any nutrients, so it would be pretty useless."

"So that one doesn't count, then," Delan said, and Zhafaera could hear his smile. "What else?"

Zhafaera thought for a minute. "I can't make other people do what I want."

"Uh, somehow I doubt that," Delan said slowly.

"Magically, I mean. No mind control." Zhafaera wiggled her fingers at the back of his head to demonstrate. "It's forbidden."

"Doesn't count. Just because you *don't* doesn't mean you *can't*." Delan chuckled.

"But I *can* read minds." The chuckling stopped abruptly.

"You can *what?*" There was a definite note of panic in his voice.

Now it was Zhafaera's turn to laugh. "Well, sort of. In a way. I can communicate mind-to-mind, but only with other mages. And sometimes, if I expand my awareness and focus properly," Zhafaera closed her eyes and reached out with her mind towards Delan. "I can pick up people's emotions," she said, as she found Delan's mind. There was something there she couldn't quite catch. Something…warm? Fear maybe? Yes, definitely fear there, he didn't like the thought of her reading his mind, but there was something under the fear, something –

Stop that! Delan's voice rang clearly through her mind. Zhafaera jumped.

"W–what?" she asked, confused.

"I said 'stop that!'" Delan said, sounding mildly annoyed. "I could feel you poking around in my head." Forgetting himself, he turned around to face her fully, glaring. His eyes widened as Zhafaera quickly ducked back under the edge of the tub with a squeak, splashing water over the side. "Sorry!" Delan said quickly, turning around again. "I didn't see anything, I swear!"

Liar, Zhafaera thought.

"I'm not lying!" Delan said. Zhafaera froze. *Did he hear my thoughts?* She looked at him and could see the back of his neck was bright red. *Oh, he's* definitely *lying.*

Zhafaera couldn't help it; she giggled, then clapped a hand over her mouth. *What is* wrong *with me? Giggling? ME, giggling?* She pulled herself together and tried to sound serious. "Fine, but I'm getting out now and don't you dare peek!"

Delan faced the opposite wall as Zhafaera pulled the plug in the tub, letting the water drain then dried herself and put her dress back on. When she was done she said, "Okay, I'm decent. Your turn."

Delan stood slowly and stretched, cracking his neck loudly. As he started towards the tub, his arm darted out and poked her gently in the ribs. "No peeking!" He laughed and dodged quickly out of the reach of Zhafaera's playful smack.

Shaking her head, Zhafaera dug out her hairbrush and sat behind the bed as Delan pumped fresh water into the tub.

As Delan took his turn scrubbing the road grime from his pores and newly-blonde hair, Zhafaera carefully drew tiny strands of magic and gently dried her hair. She definitely was *not* tempted to peek as she heard him pull the plug in the tub and climb out. Instead, she focused on getting her hair to curl properly. She'd only have this one night to have her hair clean, and she intended to make the most of it, even if it was currently the wrong color.

"It looks beautiful," Delan whispered at her ear.

Zhafaera jumped, barely suppressing a squeal. Hand over her heart, she turned and found Delan fully dressed and sprawled on his stomach across the bed, his head near hers, grinning. Shoving his shoulder lightly, Zhafaera stood.

"Do you want to go down and get something to eat?" Delan asked her as she stretched. That floor really was uncomfortable.

They were quiet for a minute, listening to the rising din from the dining room below. It was full dark out now, and clearly, the evening crowd had arrived. Zhafaera shrugged uncomfortably. It wasn't that she was *scared*, she just didn't want to have to stab the first guy that tried to grab her ass. *Would you stab Delan if* he – she quickly halted that train of thought.

110

Reading her discomfort, Delan offered to go down and bring their dinner back up to the room, where they could eat in peace. Zhafaera accepted, and as he left, she gathered their dirty clothes off the floor and put them in the bathtub. Pumping yet more water into the tub, she swirled the clothes around and left them to soak.

Delan returned shortly with their dinner, and they sat cross-legged on the bed and ate. When they were done, Zhafaera returned to the clothes, grabbed the soap, and started scrubbing. After a minute, Delan came over to help, and between the two of them, they were done in no time. By the time their clothes had been wrung out and draped over the edges of the bath, they were both yawning hugely.

"Hopefully these will be dry by morning, and not frozen solid," Delan said, shivering slightly in the draft of chilly air coming through a crack in the window.

"I've got this," Zhafaera said, yawning for what felt like the hundredth time.

"It's okay, you're tired..." Delan began.

Zhafaera ignored him and drew thin strands of magic to herself. She created a heat web and carefully laid it over their clothes. Within seconds, steam was rising from their clothes. A few minutes later, the clothes were dried and folded in their packs. The only sign that they had ever been wet was the fog on the window that was quickly dissipating.

"That was pretty impressive, but I'm beat," Delan said, reaching for the bedroll strapped to his pack.

"Don't be silly," Zhafaera said, moving to the bed and pulling back the quilt. "We probably won't have another bed for a while – there's room for both of us." She looked at him in mock seriousness. "That is, if you think you can keep your hands to yourself."

"It's okay, really, I'll be fine. You take the bed." Delan looked uncomfortable, but he hadn't moved to open his bedroll.

Zhafaera raised an eyebrow. "Are you saying you *don't* think you can keep your hands to yourself?"

A blush was slowly creeping up Delan's neck. "That is *not* what I meant. I would never—I mean, not that you're not –" He stopped and took a breath, then stood and climbed into the bed next to Zhafaera fully clothed, rolling over on his side to look at her. "I'm not an animal, you know."

Zhafaera reached out and brushed a blonde lock off of his face, smiling. "I know, Delan." She rolled over and blew out the candle on her side of the bed and felt Delan do the same. Zhafaera thought it would be strange having someone else in her bed; the last time she'd slept with someone else were those nights as a child when she'd climbed in bed with her mother after a nightmare. But Delan's presence was comforting, and she quickly fell asleep listening to the sound of his even breathing.

***

112

Delan woke with a start. The room was dark and silent but for their breathing. His arms were wrapped around something soft and warm. Zhafaera. *When did that happen, I wonder?* He wasn't complaining, but was that what had woken him? From the small puddle of Zhafaera's drool he could feel on his arm, he didn't think so; they'd clearly been like this for a while. He lay there, listening, absently stroking Zhafaera's hair. She stirred momentarily, rolling over and snuggling closer until her back was pressed against his chest. Delan tightened his arms around her and rested his cheek on the massive mound of dark hair between them, trying to relax and go back to sleep.

And then he heard it.

The slow creak of a board in the hallway. A low, angry whisper.

Delan was immediately wide awake. He urgently shook Zhafaera, who sat bolt upright and stared wide-eyed around the room. Delan put a finger to his lips, gestured to the door, and silently got out of bed. His boots were on in seconds, his sword around his waist, and his pack on his back. He looked back at Zhafaera, who was likewise dressed and finishing stringing her bow. She took her own pack from him, nocked an arrow to the string, and waited in perfect stillness.

Delan could hear movement right outside their door. Someone on the other side drew a sword as Delan moved slowly towards the door. Putting his ear to the wood and his hand on the metal handle, he listened.

113

"Remember, we kill the man, but the girl lives." This from a man with a deep, gravelly voice.

"Oh, she'll live all right. That don't mean we can't have a little fun before the sun come up, now, do it?" The man who said this gave a little high-pitched giggle that turned Delan's stomach.

"Boss just said he wants her alive. Didn't say what condition she has to be in." This from a third man.

"I call her first—ain't never had me a princess before," said the second man.

"Hey, now just one minute –"

"Shut up, you morons, you're going to wake them." The first man sounded frustrated. "Move out of the way."

Delan's blood was boiling as he felt someone grab the handle on the other side of the door. He glanced back at Zhafaera and gave her a nod; she drew her bow and nodded back. Delan jerked the door open and two men came stumbling into the room. One went down immediately with a gurgling sound, Zhafaera's arrow lodged in his throat. Delan ignored him on the ground, clawing at his neck trying to get air, and quickly came up behind the second man and stabbed a knife straight through his back in between the ribs on the left side. Twisting the knife and yanking it free, he turned to the door again as the man dropped like a stone.

The third man, a greasy, skinny scrap of a human being, stood at the open door staring open-mouthed into the room, the sword in his hand seemingly forgotten. Before he could move, Delan darted forward, twisted the

114

sword easily out of his grasp, grabbed him by the hair, and yanked him forward into the room, putting his knife at the man's throat and shutting the door with his foot. Zhafaera didn't move. She stood by the window in the weak moonlight, her next arrow nocked and trained on the stringy man.

Pulling the man's head back painfully, Delan leaned down and whispered, "This was the best he could do? You three little shits?"

"There's more comin'. We wuz just here watching. Keepin' an eye out, like. Pen there," his eyes darted to the big man with Zhafaera's arrow in his throat, whose fingers still twitched weakly.

"He's a Seer. Disguises don't work on 'im. Orders were to stay here and keep an eye out for a girl like her traveling with a man and call for help if she showed." The man attempted to smile but it looked like a sick grimace. "We just had to hold 'er long enough for them dragons to get here."

Delan looked at Zhafaera. Her eyes were as wide as they'd go; he knew what she was thinking – dragons showing up was definitely bad. And aside from that, clearly *some* people knew she was still alive if Velexar had them hunting for her. Delan had only the slight tightening of her lips as warning before an arrow sprouted out of one of the man's eyes. Delan let go in disgust and the man fell with a loud thump.

"We need to get out of here. Now," Delan said quietly. "Someone might have heard all of that."

115

"Yeah, not to mention the whole 'dragons on the way' thing," Zhafaera said weakly. She turned around and looked out the window. "Come on, there's a way down here."

"Seriously?" Delan looked skeptical.

Opening the window, she threw a leg out and tested the roof below. "Yes, seriously. There might be more of them waiting downstairs!"

"I was getting to that, but *someone* shot him in the face before I could ask."

The look she gave him could have cracked stone. Delan held up his hands in surrender and followed her out the window.

He swallowed. There technically *was* a way down, but it wasn't pretty. Zhafaera quickly scrambled across the roof, heading for the side of the inn nearest the stables. Tossing her pack down first, she turned around and laid on her belly, dangling her feet over the side of the roof and edging slowly out and down until she was hanging from the roof by her hands. She let go and Delan heard a soft thump. Scurrying over and peering over the side, he saw Zhafaera on the ground, hoisting her pack over her shoulder.

"Come on," she hissed, waving at him.

It wasn't a long way down, but *Gods*, heights were not his thing. He clamped down on his fear, and quickly lowered himself over the side, landing next to Zhafaera and feeling slightly out of breath.

"Are you afraid of *nothing*?" he asked as they ran to the stables and began saddling their horses.

She didn't answer, and soon they were riding out of the town, heading straight back into the woods just as a distant roar vibrated through the air.

Chapter 5

For the next two weeks they continued northwest, growing closer and closer to the line of mountains that divided the northern half of the continent from the southern half. The Angonite Mountain range was huge, cutting across Arenthia and continuing west through Khichora. The best part? There was no other way north over land. The mountains were tall, covered in thick trees that reached up for the sky, and ending in snow-capped peaks that could only be seen on a clear day.

There were a number of passes through the mountains, but they all wound back and forth so much it was easy to get turned around and end up back on the same side that you started on by the time you reached the bottom. The entire range was riddled with mine shafts, some huge and deep. Theoretically you could get all the way through the mountains through the mines, but Zhafaera wasn't keen to try her luck finding her way through. More likely, they'd end up lost forever underground, which, given all of their possible options, did not sound like the best way to die.

Since the night they had left through the window of the inn, things had been quiet. An hour out of the village, they heard the terrible screams of a frustrated dragon, and soon after, the night sky was lit with a smoky red glow at their backs. They'd rode all that day until it was too dark to see, slept for a few hours, and then continued on when the moon rose. It was three days before they felt safe enough to have a full night's sleep.

They were still several days from the mountains, but already the air was growing colder, and the skies were covered with clouds that grew darker and darker until the skies broke and it started to rain. The first day was a slow, drizzly rain, and Zhafaera built a shield around them so that the rain ran off the sides and they stayed dry. But she tired long before the rain did, and they eventually just had to pull up the hoods of their cloaks up and hunker down in their saddles, trying to ignore the rain soaking slowly into their clothes.

As the day went on, the air got colder, the wind biting at them through their cloaks. When night fell, the rain turned to sleet, and as they left the road to find a good campsite, they heard the *tick tick tick* of ice against the trees. Most of the trees had dropped their leaves, and the forest floor was a carpet of red, gold, and brown. The horses were not impressed, and walked with their heads down as Delan and Zhafaera led the way through the woods, looking for a spot that still seemed relatively dry.

Finally they gave up and settled for a spot where three trees grew close together. Tethering the horses to a low branch, they tied a blanket between the trees to help keep the icy rain off. Between the two of them, they were able to get a fire going, Zhafaera maintaining the flames with magic until the wood they found dried out enough to catch. They took off their cloaks and laid them by the fire, hoping they would dry a bit, and sat huddled together on a bedroll with another blanket around them.

After an hour of shivering in the cold, Zhafaera had finally had enough. Throwing back the blanket, she stood and walked a tight circle around them and the horses, setting her normal wards but giving in and adding something extra.

"It's usually not a good idea to set rain – spells or heat – spells and then go to sleep," she told Delan. Talking helped keep her teeth from chattering. "When you seal out the rain, you risk sealing yourself *in* with no air. And heat...well, I'm sure you can see how that might go wrong." She sat back down next to Delan and wiggled back under the blanket. "But I'm cold, and I would really like to sleep tonight without water dripping down the back of my neck." Resting her head on Delan's shoulder, she closed her eyes.

"So...do we need to be worried about suffocating?" Delan asked.

"Do you really think I'd do it if I thought it would kill us both?" Zhafaera asked, eyebrows raised.

Delan grinned and squeezed her waist, making her jump and flush. "Obviously not. Just forgot you don't let little things like the forces of nature get the best of you." He frowned. "How do you keep it going in your sleep, though?"

"I can tie it off and anchor it now that we're not moving. I still have to keep hold of it, but if it's tied off, I won't add or take power from it. It means I won't get the greatest night's sleep, but probably better than what I'd get sitting here freezing." She was still shivering slightly, although blocking the rain was a definite improvement. Neither of them wanted to discuss the fact that it shouldn't be this cold this early in the season. Sure, they were on the edge of winter, but they shouldn't have had to worry about rain turning icy for another month at least.

As they warmed up and she stopped shivering, Zhafaera became acutely aware of Delan's hand, still resting on her waist. For once in her life, she didn't find the closeness uncomfortable. In fact, she was completely unwilling to move and break the contact.

"We should try to get some sleep," Delan eventually murmured into her hair.

"Sure, but I'm not moving. It's too cold," Zhafaera said lightly.

Delan was quiet for a beat, and she heard his heart rate accelerate. "Why, princess, are you saying you want to sleep together?"

Zhafaera lifted her head and went to smack his chest lightly, but Delan caught her wrist and held her firmly. Her breath caught, and she avoided his gaze.

Letting go of her wrist, Delan gently tucked a finger under her chin and tilted her face up to his. Zhafaera had no time to think before Delan lowered his mouth to hers and kissed her gently.

Zhafaera's mind went completely blank as she relaxed into the kiss. She rested her hand on his chest and gripped his shirt, as Delan tightened his grip around her waist, and slid his fingers into her hair, pulling her closer.

Suddenly, the rain started dripping down on them again, startling Zhafaera into pulling away, gasping in at the cold.

"I never anchored the waterproofing," she finally managed, jumping up to redo the ward. She moved quickly, shivering both from the cold and the excitement of their first kiss. When she finally turned back to Delan, he had already laid down under their shared blanket. She hesitated, but he patted the space next to him.

"Too cold, remember?" Delan said lightly, smiling at her.

Zhafaera shrugged and laid down, tucking herself close against him, trying to regain the warmth she'd had before she'd lost her focus. Delan planted another soft kiss into her hair.

Eventually, they fell asleep with Zhafaera facing the fire, Delan at her back with an arm around her waist. And for the first time since her mother had been murdered, Zhafaera had no nightmares.

***

In the morning, they quickly packed up the camp, covering their tracks before continuing on. Their days fell into a pattern – riding through the cold woods by day, hunkering down at night under Zhafaera's wards as they stole kisses and slept side by side. A few days later, around noon, their narrow trail intersected with a road running parallel to their path. They stopped a few yards back in the trees and watched as a farmer's cart passed by, heading east.

"This has to be one of the last towns before the mountains. We need some more supplies if we want to make it up and over. We weren't exactly what you'd call successful at the last place." He looked pointedly at their cloaks. It would snow any day now – two months early – and they definitely were not made for weather this cold. "I should go into town and see what I can get," Delan said.

Zhafaera raised an eyebrow. "You? Why you? Why not both of us?"

"This village will be smaller, but you might be recognized even if there's not a squad of pathetic assassins with a Seer waiting for you," Delan said. "You're the one they're looking for, and you're too important to risk over something like this."

"Gods, you're not going to start that now are you? I know what's at stake, but some risks have to be taken. You can't stop me from doing what needs to be done in the name of protecting me," Zhafaera said angrily.

"I know that, I just don't think that getting supplies in some back-woods town is worth you risking being discovered. And I don't particularly want to spend the night anywhere again – I feel safer behind your wards than I do walls at this point." Delan looked at her seriously. "This is something I can handle. But I promise, if we run into a dragon, or a mage, or hells, even an army, you can go first."

Zhafaera was still frowning, but she had to admit that what he said made sense. "Fine," she said, rather shortly. "I'll wait here in the woods, out of the way like a good little princess waiting for my prince to return."

"So you think of me as your prince?" Delan grinned. "Perhaps the handsomest prince in all the land, with unfailing courage, off to fight for his lady's honor… or warmth?" Delan asked. Zhafaera wasn't sure if she wanted to slap the stupid grin off his face or laugh.

"Oh shut up," she said, laughter winning out.

"Hmm, should I be offended now? You mean I'm not the handsomest, bravest –"

Zhafaera dismounted, picked up an acorn off of the forest floor, and with a flick of her wrist sent it flying at his head. Delan ducked and laughed.

She looked around, spotting a fallen log covered in moss a short distance away that looked like it would make for a good place to rest and wait. "Get down and give me your horse, at least. You'll draw less attention to yourself that way."

Delan dismounted, handing the reins to Zhafaera.

As she took the reins, she paused, taking his hand in hers. "Just be careful, okay?"

"I'll be fine. This is a mining town, I doubt there will be any trouble." He smiled and ducked down for a quick kiss before pulling away and heading off towards the road. "I'll be back by nightfall," he called over his shoulder.

With that, he set off down the road towards the village, and Zhafaera suddenly felt very alone.

***

Delan walked into the town about an hour later, the hood of his cloak drawn up so as not to attract attention. He had been right – this was a mining town mostly filled with the families of miners likely still up in the mountains. When they came back in a few weeks, this place would be used to sort and process the raw ore before shipping them out to the ports in the east. Luckily, no one seemed to be paying him much attention.

Delan looked closer and saw that the few people out on the street looked worried. They all hurried about their business, as if they didn't want to be on the street for very long. He looked at the sky. It was overcast and dark; there would be a storm soon, but surely that wasn't enough to worry the villagers this much. Delan was uneasy. The village was really only one main road with just a few side streets, hardly more than alleys really, leading off of it. The wind blew, icy tendrils slicing through his cloak and raising goosebumps on his arms. Right, winter gear first.

Being so close to the foot of the mountains, where winter always arrived hard and fast, Delan had no problem finding a shop that sold supplies for expeditions into the mountains. Entering the smallest shop on the street, he nodded to the older woman behind the counter. She narrowed her eyes, but said nothing. His first choices were fur-lined cloaks and thick wool coats. Some extra rope, and Delan felt he had covered all his bases for gear and moved on to the food. There wasn't a whole lot to choose from, aside from the hard mix of nuts and dried fruit.

"Planning a trip into the mountains, are ye?" the woman behind the counter croaked.

"Yes," Delan said. "Visiting family at Esport," he lied, referring to Arenthia's main port city to the east. Technically, it was one big city, but it was split in half by the mountain range, with boats being the primary mode of transportation from one side to the other. It was the quickest way around the mountains, but for them, not the safest. And not the direction they wanted to go to find dragons.

The woman reached under the counter and grabbed a rough sack, then moved from behind the counter and towards a back room. "Hold tight there – ye'll need more than nuts to get there." She vanished behind the door.

Delan waited, and soon she reappeared, the sack now full with hard cheese, apples, and some smoked ham.

"Them apples are about the only good thing fer traveling this time of year." She finished her sentence with a deep, wheezy cough.

"Thank you," Delan said, plopping the rest of his items on the wooden counter.

As she counted up his purchases, Delan felt the hair on the back of his neck tingle, and the feeling of being watched settled over him. He looked towards the door, and his blood ran cold. Out on the street, a soldier walked past the door, seemingly on patrol.

"Aye, they came the week afore last. Brought them beasts with them. 'S not safe out in the woods at night any more. That's when they hunt – great big scaly beasts. Big –" she eyed him, "taller than you even. Got wings too. Scary sumbitches." She shivered, then spit on the floor next to her.

Delan forced himself to stay calm, trying not to think of how close they were to discovery. If there were soldiers here, they were likely patrolling the area. Had they found Zhafaera? Was she far enough away to be safe? And what about him? Would they recognize him? Surely by now they knew that his family was helping the princess. That had been weighing on his mind since they left. If they attacked once, they would probably attack again, and without Zhafaera there to help...he couldn't even think it. His best bet was to try and avoid the army altogether. He just hoped Zhafaera could do the same.

Now that the woman had started talking, she didn't seem to want to stop, but Delan wasn't listening any more. He paid her what she asked for, even though it was probably too much, thanked her, and immediately headed for the door. He opened it and glanced both ways up the street...and froze.

Coming towards him from the east end of the village was a group of five soldiers. Delan tried to act casual, turning right and heading back down the road the way he came in, hoping they hadn't noticed him, but slowly loosening his sword in its scabbard.

Delan had only gone a few yards when the call rang out down the street: "Hey, you!"

Damn, Delan thought. "Stop!" They called. He could hear the sound of the soldiers trotting down the street after him. *No, no, no.* Delan turned slowly, the sack of food and gear still slung over his left shoulder, his right hand relaxed by his side, ready to reach for his sword at any moment.

The soldiers caught up with him quickly. One stepped forward, clearly the one in charge. He was tall and broad, with a rather impressive goatee. His eyes were shrewd, and he was eyeing Delan suspiciously. "You're not a local. What's your business here?" he asked Delan.

"Just passing through," Delan said evenly. "Needed some supplies." He gestured to the store he'd just left.

Goatee glanced at the sack slung over Delan's shoulder. "That's quite a lot of food for one man. Going far?"

"Not too far. I'm heading to Esport," Delan said. "I'm visiting my sister and her husband there." Delan hoped that sounded plausible.

Goatee raised an eyebrow. "Is that so?" His eyes dropped to Delan's waist. "That's an awfully nice sword."

"It was my father's, and my grandfather's before that. Family heirloom you might say."

"Uh-huh." He didn't seem convinced. "You're traveling alone, you say?"

"Yes." Delan felt strangely calm.

The soldiers were all staring at him, the leader seemingly weighing his options. "You haven't seen any other travelers on the road, have you?"

"A few farmers hauling their harvest to Esport, but that's about it."

"And you haven't seen a woman traveling with any of them? Red hair, blue eyes, rather small?"

"No."

"Like hell you haven't!" one of the soldiers in the back cried. "It's him, he's the lord's son, from Crystal Point! I was born near there, I recognize him!"

"Do you now?" Goatee said, looking at Delan with a predatory smile. "Well now that's interesting. Would you like to revise your answer, my *lord*?"

The soldiers were beginning to spread out in a semi-circle in front of Delan. His sword was out in an instant.

"Ah, well I guess that answers that," Goatee said lazily. "Take him." He waved his hand and the other soldiers started to move forward. "Try not to hurt him too much. We want him able to talk." Goatee backed up, out of the way of swords, and the others closed in on Delan.

Delan waited until they were close, then swung the sack full of food at the one farthest on his left side. It hit with a satisfying *thud* of crisp apples hitting the man's skull. He fell hard, but Delan had already moved on to the other three, slapping swords away and ducking a wild swing from his right. He stuck a leg out behind him and tripped the one trying to sneak around to take him from behind and thrust his sword out, biting deep into the flesh of one soldier. Ignoring the man's scream, he downed the last one with a blow to the thigh, then turned in time to meet the swing of the man he'd tripped. Their swords locked, but Delan was stronger. He pushed the man back, then swung his sword around, pommel first, and rammed it on the side of the man's head with a sickening crack. He hit the ground hard.

Delan turned again to face Goatee, surrounded by the other four soldiers that were now groaning and panting. Goatee was no longer smiling. He drew his own sword but didn't attack. Delan soon saw why: at least ten more soldiers were running up the street from the east end of the village. They reached him before he could even take a swing, surrounding him with swords pointed towards him. Delan held his stance for a few moments, weighing his options. Finally, his shoulders slumped, and he threw down his sword in disgust, raising his hands in surrender. The last thing he saw was Goatee's satisfied smile before someone rapped him hard on the back of the head, and everything went black.

***

Zhafaera sat in the dark, leaning against the fallen log, listening for any sound that might signal someone approaching. *He should have been back by now.* She took a deep breath, trying to calm her racing heart that was telling her something was very wrong. *It just took longer than he thought, he'll be back any moment.* She'd been

130

sitting like this since the sun had started to set two hours ago, torn between climbing a tree for a better view down the road and staying near the horses for a quick escape. But the horses would be slow through the woods at night and would risk tripping over a root or stepping over a hole and she might be better off on foot if she had to make a run for it, and some of those branches were thick enough to hide well in and...she'd been going in circles for hours.

She kept trying to reach out and sense him with her magic, but she couldn't find him in the village anywhere. *Or maybe I just can't recognize him.* But she knew that wasn't true; she knew him well enough now that she should be able to find him easily. She could sense no one on the road between her position and the village, so he had to still be there. *Or dead.*

Zhafaera made a noise somewhere between a sigh and a growl. For what felt had to be the twentieth time in the last hour, she closed her eyes and reached out with her magic, pushing through the pounding in her head and ignoring the wailing of the Sapphire. She was still vaguely aware of her body as she flowed through the forest, but it was distant, and no longer her main focus. Passing over hundreds of small woodland creatures, who had stopped being disturbed by her passing presence about ten passes ago, she quickly covered the mile or so to the village. She flowed into the village, spreading her awareness out, oozing along walls, feeling for a familiar presence. Again, nothing. Drawing more of her magic, she pushed herself farther, expanding her awareness outside the perimeter of

131

the village. *Surely he didn't get lost.* She shook her head, preparing to pull back, deciding to climb a tree, when something caught her attention to the east of the village, right on the edge of her range. Drawing herself in, she focused her attention on that one spot. A person. Not Delan, but male. She pulled more magic, forcing an image to form.

Her eyes snapped open and she was instantly back with the horses, who were still munching slowly on the tiny brown stalks of grass poking up through the forest floor. A soldier. Gods, a soldier. They were here.

Zhafaera put her head down on her knees, heart pounding, breath coming in gasps. *Captured, then.* She shook herself, pushing the panic to the side long enough to draw magic to her again, and quickly pushed her awareness out again, looking for the soldier. This time she passed by him, pushing farther to the east, spreading out north and south so as not to miss anything.

There. To the northeast of the village, she found it: the army camp. Well, sort of an army. She could sense fifty or so soldiers, and... something else. Bile rose in her throat as she pulled an image into focus and saw the hulking black beasts, those tiny, fat dragons. They sat around a huge campfire, grunting and snarling and eating something that Zhafaera sincerely hoped was a deer. Shaking herself, she moved her awareness forward, narrowing her range and drawing into a ball. She doubted there was a dragon with them, but, well, it was just safer this way. She held the image so she could see where she was going; it took

132

more magic this way, but she wanted to see what was going on, not just feel her way blindly.

It didn't take her long to find Delan, tied to a single sturdy post in the center of their camp, apparently there for just this purpose. His eyes were closed and dried blood covered one side of his face. She was beside him in an instant. She gently brushed a tendril of her awareness against his face, feeling the life within. *Delan*, she called, hoping he'd hear her. *Wake up.*

His eyelids fluttered.

Delan, come on, open your eyes.

He groaned, his head twisting away from her.

DELAN!

His head jerked back to her, eyes fully open, his eyes almost seeming to focus on her for a moment before he looked around.

"Zhafaera?" He whispered. "Where are you? Zhafaera, you need to run, hide, they're here looking for you, you need to –"

Delan, it's okay, I'm still back in the forest. They haven't found me.

He nodded, and then groaned again.

Zhafaera wished she could heal him, but from this distance, it was all she could do to communicate, and even then she wasn't sure how he could hear her.

Delan was twisting his wrists, trying to free them from the rope that bound him to the post. "I don't suppose you can magic me out of these, could you?"

No, I'm at the edge of my range, it's all I can do to be here. I couldn't light a candle this far out.

"Okay, I'll think of something. But you need to go. Take the horses and make a run for it before they find you. They're searching the woods now, I'm sure."

Delan, I—

"Well, look who's awake." Zhafaera looked up into the face of a man with the pointiest goatee she had ever seen in her life. She suspected that if she touched it, it would probably slice right through her finger. "Did you enjoy your little nap?"

Delan looked up and smiled at him. "Yes, in fact, I did. Thank you for keeping watch for me. You can untie me now, and I'll just be on my way."

"Of course, *my lord.*" The man sneered and signaled to several soldiers. "Just as soon as you tell us where we can find the girl."

"I don't know what you're talking about." Delan's face was blank and calm.

"Oh, come now, let's not play this game," Goatee said smoothly "You tell me where we can find her, and I'll let you go – it's as simple as that."

"There's nothing to tell; I don't have any idea who you're talking about."

"Princess Zhafaera. Where is she? I know you're traveling together." Goatee sounded irritated.

"Princess Zhafaera? What, do you think I'm traveling with a ghost?" Zhafaera found this rather ironic, considering the form she was currently in next to him.

134

"She was killed weeks ago... unless you're calling our new king a liar?"

Goatee's face paled in the dim light from the fires. He waved to a soldier, who brought forward a long, narrow whip with a tiny, wicked-looking spike on the end. He slowly unrolled it, Delan watching his every move. Zhafaera felt his body tense next to her an instant before the whip cracked against his chest. She recoiled from the sound, drawing away involuntarily. When she looked back at Delan, she saw a line of red slowly appearing on his shirt.

"Now, would you like to reconsider your answer, my lord?" Goatee asked silkily.

"I don't know what you're talking about, I'm not a lord, I've been traveling al –" *Crack!*

Zhafaera watched in horror as the whip was drawn back for a third time. She threw herself in front of Delan as it came down, but of course it passed right through her. Delan was panting slightly.

"Spoiled little lordlings aren't cut out for whippings, you know." Zhafaera hated this man. She wanted nothing more than to strike him down where he stood, burning him out of existence... but she was too far away, her magic growing fainter and fainter with each passing moment.

Wait, that can't be right, Zhafaera thought as the whip came down yet again. She was tired, yes, but... she felt almost as if her magic was draining away from her. That was impossible, she was in control, she—

The rest of her magic left her in a rush, and she snapped back to her body as the whip cracked again. Zhafaera had time for only one thought: *What in the twelve circles of hell just happened?* Then she collapsed, rolling half under the log as she hit the ground in a dead faint.

***

Delan barely felt the next crack of the whip. Zhafaera was gone. He was hot. Too hot. He felt as though his bones were melting from the inside. And still the heat grew.

Goatee was laughing, watching Delan writhe, hitting him again and again. He was speaking, probably asking again where Zhafaera was, but Delan couldn't make out his words through the pain. He would die before he betrayed her. He hoped she'd gone back to her body and started running as fast as she could in the opposite direction.

He could hardly think, could barely breathe, the pain of the lashes across his chest forgotten as the heat rose in him like dragonfire. Was this some kind of trick? Some new way to make him crack? If so, it was working. He opened his mouth, starting to scream… and then he felt sure he was breathing fire because the heat was pouring out of him, rushing through his body and pushing outward. Delan felt he would explode, his skin too small to hold him, sure he was going to die, hearing screams and roars and crashes. Then there was a great *whoosh*… crackling…

136

more screaming… and then Delan was lying face down on the ground, cold as ice, shaking and shivering.

He lay there for days, or perhaps only minutes, before he raised his head and looked around. The dark camp was in ruins. Tendrils of smoke rose like a thick fog all around him. Tents had been reduced to piles of ashes, and the ground was littered with lumps of molten metal. The screaming had stopped.

He sat up, slowly pushing himself up to his knees, feeling sick. The post he had been tied to was gone, another pile of ashes behind him. He looked at his arms; there were no burn marks, so it wasn't a dragon. *Did Zhafaera do this?* Delan thought. *She said she was too far away, but… what other explanation is there?*

He sat like that for several minutes, watching several small fires burn at the edges of camp. There was no one to put them out. He tried to breathe through his mouth to try and block the scent of burned flesh, but he couldn't stop shaking. *All those people.*

Finally he took a deep breath and forced himself to his feet. He stumbled through the camp, barely able to keep his eyes open. As he got about halfway to the edge, his eye caught on something shiny poking out from the ashes. A sword. He moved closer. *His* sword. "Wha—How?" he said aloud. "How is this possible?" No one answered. Nearby he spotted the sack he'd bought from the village what felt like days ago. He picked up his sword and shoved it back into the scabbard at his waist that they hadn't bothered to remove. Moving slowly, he walked to the sack,

137

bent, and picked it up. Everything in it seemed untouched, the ash nowhere to be seen. There wasn't even a smudge on the outside of the sack. With difficulty, Delan hefted the sack back over his shoulder, leaning under its weight. Confused and disoriented, Delan continued through the camp, found the road, and headed away from the carnage and into the night.

When he reached the village, he stopped. He considered going around, but eventually decided that faster was better, and cut straight through the middle, sticking to the road, but trying to stay in the shadows of buildings. He thought he saw curtains flicker in windows, but no one stopped him, and he couldn't spare the energy to look closer.

Hours later, Delan stumbled back into the forest, hoping he'd picked the right trail. In the dark, the forest all looked the same, and it didn't help that his eyes kept trying to close. He knew the spot Zhafaera had chosen to wait wasn't far off the road, but if she'd put up her wards, he might walk right by and never find her. If she was still there. He *had* told her to run after all; she might be long gone. But somehow he doubted she'd listened to him.

He heard movement ahead and to the left. Not bothering to move quietly, he crashed through the brush towards the sound. Moments later he found himself standing in front of their two horses, the log behind them. His horse snorted and stamped, putting his head against Delan's raised hand.

"It's okay, I'm fine," he whispered. "Where's Zhafaera?"

Looking closer, he saw her: crumpled and folded against the log, eyes closed, completely still. Delan surged forward and fell to his knees beside her, his shaking hand going to her throat. A lump rose in his throat as he felt the steady beat of her heart under his fingers. *Stop being ridiculous, of course she's alive, she's just asleep.* But she hadn't just gone to sleep. She hadn't gotten the blankets out, despite the cold, and the way she was crumpled… *She said she was at the edge of her range… she must have exhausted herself with that explosion.* Suppressing a groan, he crawled over to where Zhafaera had laid the packs and dug out a blanket. Hauling himself back over to Zhafaera, he pulled her to him, wrapped the blanket around them both, and was asleep before his head touched the ground.

Chapter 6

Zhafaera woke slowly the next morning. She was warm, and snuggled deeper into her bed. It was soft, yet firm. She inhaled deeply, smelling… smoke? Her eyes snapped open. She was curled against Delan's still-sleeping form. His face was pale, and there were dark purple circles under his eyes. In the grey light of dawn, he looked like a ghost. The events of the night before came crashing back to her and she stifled a gasp. *How did he get free?* Zhafaera tried to sit up slowly, gently pulling out of the arms wrapped around her, trying not to disturb him. Delan's eyes immediately sprung open and he jerked upright, hand on his sword. *How in the world does he still have that?* Zhafaera thought. His eyes darted around the clearing, then came to rest on Zhafaera.

"You're awake," he croaked. "Are you all right?"

She couldn't help herself. She threw her arms around his neck and clung on for dear life.

"I thought they were going to kill you," she whispered.

"Yeah, me too. But they didn't, I'm fine." He said, holding her tightly. They sat in silence for a few moments, his hand gently stroking her hair.

"I should have gone with you." Zhafaera finally pulled away and looked at him, her hands still gripping his shoulders. "How did you get away?"

Delan frowned. "What do you mean 'how did I get away?' The explosion worked, everything was ashes when I left." He looked down, breathed deep, then looked back at her and tried to smile. "Thanks for not blowing me up too, by the way."

"I—what? What are you talking about? What explosion?" Zhafaera stood, swaying slightly. She was so confused. She remembered her magic draining away and passing out. Had she lost control? But she hadn't had any magic left to lose control *of,* and magic didn't just get up and walk off on its own.

"That wasn't you?" Delan stood too, looking just as unsteady and sounding as lost as Zhafaera felt.

"What explosion?"

"Well, I couldn't feel you any more, and they were whipping me, and then I felt really hot," he cringed. "It was like I was melting from the inside. I thought they must have had a mage with them, and he was... getting creative."

Zhafaera could feel the blood draining from her face. She thought she might faint again.

"And then, when I thought it would kill me, I – I started screaming, and the next thing I knew I was cold and everything around me was in ashes. Everyone was – they were gone. I assumed that their own mage wouldn't do that, so I thought it had to be... Zhafaera? What's wrong?"

He took her arm as the world tilted; she stumbled and sat back down heavily, pulling Delan down with her.

She rested her head on her knees, breathing deep. *Surely not... it's impossible... well,* practically *impossible.* She shook herself. "Nothing, I'm fine, I'm just tired."

She used the log to pull herself to a standing position, and was thankful when her legs held her. She was still so damn tired. She took Delan's hand and helped him up. He looked wary, and she could tell he knew something was wrong. She ignored it. "Come on, we need to get the hell away from here."

Delan didn't look convinced, but he clearly wanted to be as far away as she did. Slowly, he started saddling the horses as she stuffed the blanket back in the pack. She found the sack of food he'd bought yesterday on the ground where he'd dropped it. Digging through it, she brought out two apples and tossed one to him. Both horses immediately converged on him. Delan laughed.

Pulling out his knife, he sliced the apple in half and offered a piece to Zhafaera's horse, Liri. His horse, Shadow, tossed his head and stamped impatiently. "Ladies first," Delan admonished him, handing him the other half. Zhafaera tossed him a second apple, for him this time, and they mounted, eating as they rode through the forest.

When they reached the road to the village, they decided that putting as much distance between themselves and the village was more important than stealth. They took the main road and moved quickly away from the village. This road was well maintained, and they covered a lot of ground, trotting the horses in a ground-eating stride. It was a quiet ride. Zhafaera's mind was racing with possibilities.

An explosion – but how? Endless theories chased each other around and around her head, bouncing off of the inside of her skull until her head was pounding. Her brain was so busy trying to come up with another explanation, *any* other explanation, that she rode with her head down, hardly paying any attention to where they were going. Up ahead, she could see that Delan was jumpy. He rode with one hand hovering near his sword, head constantly swinging left, right, behind, and up.

Finally, Zhafaera pulled herself together enough to help keep watch. She was still tired, but she didn't feel like she was going to fall over at any second. She drew a little magic to her and pushed out with her awareness. She didn't go far, and was still aware of her body, but just enough so they would have some warning of anyone coming down the road. They only saw two other people around midday, traveling in the opposite direction. Miners by the looks of them. Delan led them off the road when Zhafaera sensed them coming, and they watched them pass from deep in the trees. They didn't stop or even speak again until night began to fall and they started looking for a good place to camp. Eventually, they just left the road and made their own trail through the woods, pushing through the undergrowth until they found a relatively clear spot.

As she gathered dry wood for a fire, Zhafaera finally had to acknowledge the only logical conclusion for the explosion, but she couldn't for the life of her think of how to tell Delan. She looked over at him as he cared for the horses, wanting to doubt herself but knowing she was right.

She had the fire going quickly, using just a spark of power and setting it blazing in minutes. Delan had laid out their bedrolls and brought their saddles over to set up their "chairs." He was resting against one of them, looking pale and grimacing. His shirt was covered in dark, rust-colored stains.

Zhafaera hissed through her teeth. "Let me see," she said, reaching up and pulling him down next to her. He sat, and she knelt next to him, helping him out of his coat and peeling his shirt away from his chest and over his head.

"Gods, Delan, I'm so sorry, you should have made me heal this before we left this morning," Zhafaera said, her fingers hovering above the oozing gashes in his chest. They were deep, red, and swollen after being left unattended all day.

"You were tired, and we needed to move." Delan grimaced as she touched the edge of a cut, checking for debris. His skin was hot and clammy. "It's really not as bad as it looks."

Zhafaera gave him a flat stare. "Who's the healer here? It's exactly as bad as it looks." She shook her head. "I can heal it, but you'll likely have scars now."

"You don't have to—" He wisely stopped mid-sentence when he saw the look on her face.

Zhafaera took a deep breath, drawing magic to her and gently weaving it into Delan's flesh. The gashes obediently closed, leaving behind lines of blood, both dried and fresh. Zhafaera retrieved a water skin, poured a bit on the end of his already-bloodstained shirt, and gently wiped away the blood. She certainly didn't linger, enjoying the view, because now was so *not* the time. She blushed as she saw the small smile on Delan's face.

"What?" she demanded.

"Nothing," he said, putting his hands up defensively. Then he looked at her seriously. "Thank you."

"You're welcome," she said, grinning. "Good as new." She tapped on his chest.

Before she could move away, he grabbed her wrist and pulled her close, staring at her intently. Not taking his eyes from hers, he slowly reached out and brushed his hand over her cheek, moving a lock of her hair out of the way and tucking it behind her ear. Their faces were only inches apart, and Zhafaera couldn't think straight. Nothing seemed to matter except for him and that slight smile on his full lips –

A gentle presence brushed against her mind. Hesitant, searching. She jumped up as if she'd been electrocuted.

"No, Zhafaera, I'm sorry, I –" Delan stuttered as she darted over to his pack and retrieved a clean shirt. She could feel his confusion.

Avoiding his eyes as she handed it to him, she said, "It's not that." Finding the bag he had brought back from the village yesterday, she dug inside and found the fur-

145

lined cloaks. Handing one to Delan, she watched the ground as he pulled the new shirt over his head and wrapped the cloak around himself. Zhafaera was struggling. Gods, she should have figured it out when they were able to communicate mind-to-mind. She had *never* been able to do anything like that with someone who wasn't a mage. Unease churned in her belly. "Delan, I – I have to tell you... I mean... you really don't know?"

He just stared at her, clearly confused. "Know what?"

Zhafaera finally looked at him and took a deep breath. Let it out. Took another. *Just spit it out!* The words came out slowly, as if they were being forcibly pulled from her. "That you're a Black mage?" She couldn't help turning it into a question. Judging by the look on his face, that would be a no.

"Are you kidding?" Delan asked, his eyebrows raised so high they were disappearing in his hair. "I'm not any kind of mage, I've never been able to use magic."

Zhafaera shook her head. "No, Delan. You can use magic just fine. You just can't draw it to you in its raw form, straight from the elements." She paused, looking him in the eye. "But you *can* draw it from another mage. It wasn't me that caused the explosion last night – it was you."

***

Delan couldn't believe what he was hearing. "Zhafaera, that's insane. I've never even heard of a Black mage. Are

146

you sure you're feeling okay?" Perhaps she was ill, or still exhausted from exerting herself the night before. He reached for her.

"Yes, I'm fine," she said impatiently, shaking her head and brushing him off. "Last night, when they were whipping you, my magic drained out of me. Quickly. That's when I disappeared – I had drawn as much magic as I could, but suddenly it was draining out of me and I snapped back to my body. And then you... you said you felt hot. Really hot. The heat you felt, that was the magic that you drew through me, and I was holding a lot." Something flickered in her eyes, but Delan couldn't read her expression. "You drew enough that it could have killed you, being untrained. You could have killed *me*. But instead, it exploded out of you and burned everything around you." Delan was silent. He'd been trying not to think of that. All those soldiers... His stomach churned.

"How else can you explain how you escaped last night? I wasn't there, and even if I *had* still been there, I could never have caused an explosion while projecting. Think back. You've probably been doing it for a while. It explains why Alec was able to go untrained for so long without burning down the entire keep – you've probably been siphoning magic off of him whenever he pulled too much or started losing control."

Delan stared at her incredulously. There was no way. But, almost against his will, he did as he was told and thought back. The accidental fires that Alec had managed to start *had* all been small and were easily put out, very

147

unusual for an untrained Fire mage with as much potential as he had. But… it didn't make any sense. How could he use magic without realizing he was doing it? You had to learn to control magic. Without control, the wild, elemental magic would destroy you, and usually anything else nearby. He opened his mouth to say so, but then something occurred to him. A memory of a feeling, similar to the one he had felt last night, but not as strong. Heat rising up in him, and him intentionally willing it to pass from him and into Zhafaera's cold, unconscious body as he carried her up the cliff the day he found her. He cocked his head. Surely that had just been his own body heat warming her. Zhafaera was watching him closely.

"Maybe," he said slowly, not really convinced.

She looked triumphant, but also… angry, maybe? Surely that wasn't fear?

Zhafaera stood and began to walk her normal circle around the camp, warding them. Delan could feel the breeze on his skin again. But was it a breeze? It didn't ruffle his hair or his clothes, but he could feel it moving along his skin. He closed his eyes and realized that he could still feel exactly where Zhafaera was in the circle.

He leaned back against Zhafaera's saddle, closing his eyes and trying to stay calm. After a moment, he felt Zhafaera sit down beside him again. She rested a hand on his shoulder and waited.

"So if I told you I think maybe I could feel you setting the wards just now… " he trailed off.

"It would make sense," Zhafaera said quickly. "Black mages can do whatever the mage they're drawing from can do; they can sense magic and use it. They just can't draw it to them in the normal way. They have to draw it from other mages, but they can draw from *any* other mage – they can use all types of magic." There was a ghost of a smile on her face. "So congratulations, you're probably the only living person who could be my equal in power, really."

Delan snorted. Even if what she said about Black mages were true, there was no way he was as powerful as she was. "And I've never heard of Black mages before because... ?"

"They're even rarer than White mages," Zhafaera said. Her eyes were clouded.

Delan frowned. "Aren't there only three of you now?"

"Yeah. And you're probably the only Black mage alive." She considered that for a moment. "Although, who knows? You guys might actually be more common and just don't know about your abilities. There might be more just like you – siphoning off little bits at a time if you're around a mage, not enough for anyone to notice... but you just happened to get desperate enough to draw a lot, and really use it."

Delan couldn't quite wrap his head around the idea that he could be a mage. "This is crazy."

"Well, that's putting it mildly, I think." She laughed, but it was forced and shaky.

He put a finger under her chin and forced her to look at him. "Are you afraid of me?"

149

"No," she said. Delan held her gaze. "I mean, not really. You're you." He let her go and looked down. "It's just that, it's a scary idea, okay? You have the power to drain me at any moment. Pull too much through me and it's all over. Best case scenario you leave me defenseless. Last night, I was out cold... and that was lucky." She hesitated.

"I'm sorry," Delan said quietly. His chest was tight.

Zhafaera shook her head. "Don't apologize; it's not your fault."

"I—all those soldiers." Delan choked out. He barely felt the hand that Zhafaera put on his shoulder. If this was true... a whole campful of soldiers... burned alive, and it was his fault.

"They would have killed us. Or captured us, which would have been just as bad, if not worse," she said softly.

They were both silent for a long time, Delan still trying to process and control his emotions. His guilt. Finally, he said, "So what do we do now?"

"Some people... um... well, mages, really...they think Black mages are dangerous. A lot of Black mages... well... it's probably best to keep it quiet." Zhafaera took his hand and looked him in the eye. "But you have to practice."

"You're kidding, right?" Delan asked incredulously. "Didn't you just say that it's dangerous? Zhafaera, *I'm* dangerous!"

"I didn't say that!" He raised his eyebrows. "Fine, but you're only dangerous if you can't control it!" Zhafaera said earnestly.

"Well, now, that just makes me feel loads better."

"You have to learn how to pull magic at will, control how much you pull at a time, and learn to direct it properly." Her face was full of determination. "This could be a good thing. I can only do so many things at one time, and seeing as how there's only the two of us against the rest of the world right now, we need all the extra help we can get." Zhafaera stopped suddenly and cocked her head.

"What is it now?" Delan asked cautiously.

"I... I just thought... Velexar is a White mage, you know."

"Yes, and?"

"Well, he would have no idea that you're a Black mage." Her eyes were alight like blue fire, and she fixed Delan with such an intense stare he very nearly leaned back. "We'll have to fight him eventually... but with you, we'll have an advantage. You could drain him and –" She stopped suddenly, her face going dead white.

"What's wrong?" Delan asked quickly.

Zhafaera's eyes focused on his. "No," she whispered. "It's nothing. I mean, we can't risk you fighting Velexar, you're too valuable... "

Delan was confused. He knew that wasn't it. "Zhafaera, what?"

Her eyes were bright in the light from the fire. "My dream."

151

"What dream?" Delan asked, trying to put the puzzle together, but knowing he was still missing pieces.

Zhafaera sighed. "The night I left, I had a dream. Velexar had me trapped in the throne room, and you were trying to fight him, but you… " She put her head in her hands. "You died."

Delan was quiet for a long time, watching sparks fly up from the fire and disappear into the chill night air. "Zhafaera, it was a dream. What if you're wrong? We don't even know if I can do anything."

"I'm not wrong." She turned and sat cross-legged facing him. "Look, let's just try a little bit." Delan was still skeptical. "No, really, just for a little while, I'm still tired, you're still tired, and we need to eat, but… let's just see."

"Fine," Delan said. "What do you want me to do?"

"Okay, let's just start with getting you used to sensing magic." She inhaled deeply and stretched her hand out in front of her, palm up. A moment later, a small flame appeared, hovering above the center of her palm. She watched him carefully. "Close your eyes." He obeyed. "Tell me what you feel."

Delan didn't answer. For a long time he felt nothing, and then… there was something. Something… soft. Delicate. He frowned slightly and focused on the feeling. It felt like…

That's me. Zhafaera's voice whispered in his mind.

Delan gasped slightly and opened his eyes. "What?"

Zhafaera's mouth didn't move. *It's me; you're sensing my presence, my mind.*

152

Delan cocked his head, then closed his eyes again. The feeling solidified slightly. It felt warm, and… blue? And then it reached out to him, brushing gently against his mind. He smiled. Definitely Zhafaera. *Hi*, he thought to her, wondering if this would work.

Hi, yourself. Her voice again, and this time he could hear her smile.

I still can't feel the fire.

That's okay, just clear your mind. Ignore me and look for the magic.

Like he could ignore her for even a second. Still, he took several deep breaths, trying to block her from his mind. Slowly, so faint he was hardly sure it was there at all… something new: warmth. He tried to focus. He could feel the heat from her flame radiating out to him. Except her flame should have been way too small to feel and the heat was concentrated in his hand. Just a tiny fraction of the heat he had felt the night before, but it was there; almost as if there was an echo of Zhafaera's flame. Raising his hand in front of him, palm up, he brought the echo to life, visualizing a flame identical to hers forming above his hand. He heard Zhafaera gasp softly and opened his eyes.

A tiny, perfect flame hovered in the air an inch above his palm.

"I'm impressed," Delan finally said, still staring at the flame in his hand, wavering like a tiny heartbeat. "I guess it's not as hard as it looks… "

Zhafaera was just shaking her head, a small smile on her face. "Is now a good time to say 'I told you so?'"

"Ha, ha," Delan said wryly. They sat silently for a minute. "Okay, but really, how do I make this go away?"

"Well... " Zhafaera appeared slightly confused. "Usually in the beginning, it'll vanish as soon as you lose your focus – like if you start talking." She paused. "Then by the time you have more control, it's just sort of... second nature? I never really thought about it before."

"Yeah, well I guess I'm pretty great at multi-tasking," Delan said, attempting a smile. He had a feeling it came out more as a grimace, as Zhafaera immediately made calming motions with her hands.

"Don't worry, it's fine—just... uhh... *focus* on letting it go?"

Delan stared at the flame in his hand for a moment, then closed his eyes and pictured it vanishing, dispersing its energy into the cool night air. When he opened his eyes again, the flame was gone.

"Very good," Zhafaera said, sounding almost cheerful for the first time. "I mean, really, that was great!" She looked thoughtful. "I'm thinking maybe fire magic will be easier for you. Like I said, you've been siphoning off of Alec mostly, so that's probably what you're most familiar with."

"Okay, number one, I'm not familiar with fire magic, and number two, I'm not familiar with *any* magic." Delan said.

Zhafaera looked rather like he was speaking a foreign language. "But you have to know *some* – not only is your brother a mage, but clearly you've been managing your

154

own capabilities enough to not kill yourself and everyone around you."

"Gee thanks. Way to make me feel better and not at all terrifying."

Zhafaera just rolled her eyes. "Okay, okay, start from the beginning. Tell me all that you *do* know."

"Uh, well, I know that it's elemental magic." Delan paused and Zhafaera motioned impatiently for him to continue. "You know, there's fire magic, water magic, earth magic, and air magic." Zhafaera did not look impressed at the extent of his knowledge. "OH, and it's inherited!" Delan threw his hands up. "That's all I've got." At Zhafaera's frown, he said, "it's not like there were a ton of mages nearby – Alec was usually the only one. Well, except for when you and your mother visited," he corrected.

"Ugh, okay," Zhafaera said, getting up and scrounging through their packs for food. As she prepared their meager meal, she continued. "So mages are divided into four elemental categories, but magic itself isn't only based in the elements." She paused, thinking. "Magic is more just... energy. And magical energy flows through everything – rocks, plants, air, us." She tapped the center of her chest. "We all have a core of energy, it's just that mages can expand and control theirs." Tossing him an apple, she sat next to him. "We can add to our cores by pulling energy from the different elements – water, earth, fire, and air. They all have energy, but each one's energy is unique. Depending on where you pull the energy from,

155

the magic you can do with it is slightly different. We can control the elements that we draw from, but as the strength and skill of the mage increases, you learn to manipulate the energy more precisely and can do more with it." The confusion must have shown on Delan's face, because Zhafaera continued, "Look at it like this – when I use fire energy for magic, I can start fires," she gestured towards their campfire, "but I can also do things like warm the air around us, like I've been doing sometimes at night. And there's definitely some overlap with what the energies can do, like the wards that I set – wards can be made from any kind of elemental energy, but the resulting ward is slightly different depending on the energy used."

"Okay, but what about me? You said I don't pull energy from the elements," Delan said slowly.

"Exactly, you pull directly from another mage's core." That look was back in her eyes – the one that Delan would have called fear in anyone other than Zhafaera. "Most mages learn to store elemental energy in their cores, sort of a reserve – a buffer between your own self and the rest of the magical world. Once you pull the energy to you, it becomes a part of you, but it retains most of its elemental properties. That's something you have to get used to when you're first training as a mage – the feel of different energies in your core. They're part of you, but not you. It's a bit weird at first."

Delan was silent for a while. "So when I draw magic from you, I'm pulling energy from your core?"

"Yes, exactly," Zhafaera said.

"And what happens if I pull all of your reserves?"

"Don't do that," Zhafaera tried to laugh, but her hands were wound tightly together, the knuckles white.

"Right, I got that part, but what if I *do*?"

She looked at him seriously. "If you get to the point where you've drained all of my reserves, you would likely start drawing on my own life force. You know that sometimes, when I use too much magic too quickly and I exhaust myself? If you're using magic faster than you can draw it in, you start using your reserves. If you keep that up for too long, you'll start drawing on your own life energy. And if you use all of that, then you die."

Although that was about the answer he was expecting, Delan still felt slightly sick. "I'd rather just not draw from you."

But Zhafaera was shaking her head. "There's no way around it – you have to learn control and there's no one else here for you to draw from. We'll just start small and practice taking little bits at a time. Then maybe we can try and work your way up to bigger stuff."

Zhafaera reached out and took one of his hands in hers. "Look, it's going to be fine. You're a quick learner, and you have an excellent teacher." She smiled and elbowed him gently in the ribs, and Delan gave a weak smile in return. Slowly her face got serious again. She squeezed his hand tightly, not loosening her grip until he met her eyes.

"I promise, I'm not afraid of you."

Delan mostly believed her. He just hoped she stayed this confident.

Chapter 7

Five days later, the mountains were finally closer than a distant blue haze. Zhafaera rode through the icy rain, head down, every bone in her body aching, her head pounding. She was wet through, and her thick wool coat and new cloak weren't as effective at keeping out the cold when sopping wet. She had held the rain shield again the night before, and clearly had not gotten enough sleep... but that shouldn't make her feel like this. She had tried to heal some of the ache away, but it hadn't helped. Her very skin felt as if it were being rubbed raw with every movement of her sodden clothes. She tried to ignore it the best she could, but she had a distinct feeling that something was very wrong.

By noon, they rode in the shadow of the Angonite Mountains and the ground was already beginning to rise in earnest. They had yet to decide the best route over them. Was taking the main road, which followed the biggest pass over the mountains, foolish or brilliant? Would Velexar's spies assume they'd leave the road and take one of the smaller passes after discovering the soldiers waiting in the last village? Probably, but they'd almost certainly be watching the main road as well. They probably couldn't watch all of the smaller passes, although at this point in the year, taking a smaller pass ran a real risk of getting trapped by a snowstorm. Zhafaera looked up. The sky overhead was dark with thick clouds. It was likely already snowing in the mountains.

Zhafaera felt more miserable with every passing hour. The rain had soaked through her cloak and was running in icy tendrils down her back. There was still an hour or so left before true dark by the time they reached the foot of the mountains, where the road turned steeply up and to the right as it began to wind its way up the side of the mountains. Aching and shivering, she reined in her horse next to Delan, staring at where the road disappeared into the thick trees.

Delan glanced at her and said, "So which way?" He did a double take. "Gods Zhafaera, are you all right?"

"What?" she asked, somewhat defensively.

"You look like death warmed over," he said, frowning and reaching for her.

"Yes, well I've been riding in the rain all day," she said, jerking away from his hand, not wanting him to touch her sensitive skin. She felt his presence brush against her mind; he had quickly gotten the hang of communicating mind-to-mind with her. *Zhafaera, you feel... rough. What's wrong?* Delan's voice in her mind was worried.

It's nothing. I just need to get out of the rain. As if to prove her point, she shivered.

Delan held up his hands in his gesture of surrender, but still looked worried.

159

Zhafaera looked away, up the slope of the mountain ahead. "We can't follow the main road any more; they're going to be waiting for us there. I'm surprised we haven't been attacked already. Come on," she said, turning and heading to the left, opposite the road. "Maybe we can find a nice dry cave to camp in tonight."

"I don't know that I remember what it feels like to be properly dry," Delan said, following behind her.

As they traveled deeper into the woods, the ground rose steadily and the light started to fade. Zhafaera kept an eye out for any sign of a cave, or even just any kind of overhang that might keep the rain off without magic. But as they rode, her headache just got worse, and she slumped lower and lower in her saddle, until finally she heard Delan ride up beside her. She looked over at him and saw him trying to crane his neck to see her face. Straightening, he said, "You're not all right, are you? Are you ill?" There was real concern in his voice.

"Yes... I mean, no... I mean... maybe? I'm not sure."

"What's wrong?" he asked, as they both halted again.

"I don't know," Zhafaera said, shivering violently now. "I ache all over, and my head feels as if someone buried an axe in it."

"Can't you heal yourself?"

"That's just it—I've tried, but it hasn't worked. So I don't think I'm ill exactly, but something is definitely... wrong." Through sheer force of will, she sat up straighter and looked around. "Let's keep moving."

Ignoring Delan's frown and his worried presence at the edge of her mind, she continued on, climbing higher up the slope and continuing west.

Just as the sun was truly setting, Zhafaera felt a slight tingle on the edge of her awareness. Her head jerked up and she looked around. Not twenty yards ahead of them was a piece of rock jutting out from the mountainside. It was hard to tell from this angle, but she thought it was big enough to cover them all. *Finally*, she thought. She wasn't sure how much farther she could go.

Reaching the outcrop, she realized it was an opening to a cave. Hardly believing their luck, she dismounted gingerly and peeked inside. It was tall enough for them and their horses to stand in, but she couldn't see the back. At this point, she ached so much that she didn't care what sort of vicious creature lived in the back; she was sleeping in this cave. As Delan dismounted behind her, she moved forward into the cave. Taking a deep breath, she drew on her magic and made a flame hover over her palm for light. The tingling on her skin intensified tenfold. She gasped, and looked over her shoulder at Delan, who was rolling his shoulders and looking uneasily towards the back of the cave. He transferred the reins of their horses to one hand and loosened his sword with the other.

Do you feel it too? she asked silently.

I'm not sure. I feel... something, he answered hesitantly.

Lifting her hand high and ignoring Delan's protests, Zhafaera moved slowly towards the back of the cave, sensing that something was there. The cave seemed to go back forever, but finally her light hit the back wall. Something stirred in a corner at the base of the wall, half-hidden behind a chunk of rock sticking up from the floor of the cave. It was a snow leopard, a huge, white, spotted creature. Zhafaera froze, staring at the animal as it scrambled to its feet, snarling and showing its teeth, the hair on the back of its neck standing straight up. It was thin, hardly more than skin and bones, and its fur was dull in the light she cast. Zhafaera was rooted to the spot, hardly believing her eyes, sensing the magic pulsing from it.

"Zhafaera, move!" she heard Delan call, but she ignored him until she heard his sword leave its sheath.

"No, Delan, stop!" she called back, throwing her hand behind her. The big cat had backed up as far as it could and jumped when its back hit the wall. Deep growls echoed through the cave, and its claws scraped the floor of the cave, leaving deep gouges, as it began pacing back and forth.

"Zhafaera… "

She ignored him. She held her hands out, palms out, maintaining her light in the air beside her head. To the cat, she said, "It's all right, I'm not here to hurt you."

The cat continued to pace, lurching and stumbling against the back wall of the cave. Zhafaera stood still and waited. Eventually, the cat stopped, stared at Zhafaera, and sat heavily. Zhafaera took a tiny step forward. The cat immediately lunged forward, taking a swipe at her with a huge paw. Zhafaera quickly backed up several steps, narrowly avoiding the long claws.

"I am not your enemy! Whatever has happened to you, let me help!" Zhafaera pleaded.

The cat sat again, panting, slumping slightly.

"Are you stuck?" Zhafaera asked carefully.

The mountain lion looked her directly in the eyes, staring at her with a look that was a mixture of calculation and panic. Minutes passed, and still Zhafaera waited.

Finally, the big cat took a deep breath. Its whole body expanded... and kept expanding. The neck and snout elongated, ridges appearing above bright yellow eyes and huge white teeth growing from the muzzle. Its toes grew into three-inch long claws; the tail lengthened, and spikes appeared along the spine, going from the back of the head to the tip of the tail. As the body continued to swell, the fur retreated, as if it were being sucked into the body, and was replaced by shining, multi-hued scales. Delicate, black wings unfolded from the body, spreading to either side to fill the cave before folding back against the body.

I wasn't stuck, the small dragon said in her mind.

Zhafaera could hardly believe what she was seeing. She could feel Delan's wordless fear in her mind, but she wasn't afraid. This dragon was tiny, barely bigger than their horses. That meant she couldn't be very old, no more than twenty. So why was she out here on her own? Why was she out here at all? The dragons lived in the western mountains, much farther north and west than they were now, although technically connected to this same mountain range.

Delan cleared his throat behind her, and the dragon's luminous eyes immediately fixed on him.

"Hello," he said to the dragon. *Zhafaera*, he whispered in her mind, *when I say run, run.* She looked at him. His hands were in the air, palms facing forward like her own, his sword back in its sheath.

Delan, no, it's okay. She won't hurt me. Zhafaera quickly thought back.

Yes I will! By the way Delan's eyes went wide, Zhafaera knew he had heard it too. He looked rooted to the spot. She turned back to the dragon.

"I'm not afraid of you. I want to help. I know you're injured." Her head was still throbbing and her skin crawled and prickled under her clothes. She knew now that this was probably the reason she had felt terrible all day – she could sense the injured dragon, feel her injuries. Zhafaera's pain wasn't her own, it was simply bleeding out of the dragon's energy, and Zhafaera was the nearest mage to feel it. She glanced at Delan. Well, trained mage, she amended.

And the dragon must be *very* injured to not be able to shield her energy from mages – that was practically the first bit of magic that young dragons learned. The pain was radiating off her in waves. Zhafaera looked closer at the small dragon. Her scales were dull, lacking the luster typical of her kind, and there were places where they looked almost dented. It was hard to tell, but Zhafaera thought her left wing was at a funny angle, not completely against her body as the other one was.

The dragon was panting slightly, looking from Zhafaera to Delan and back again. *I don't need your help,* she said. But she swayed as she said it.

Zhafaera took another small step forward. The dragon bristled, shaking her head, but not lashing out again. "Please, let me heal you." Zhafaera begged, taking another step.

"Zhafaera," Delan's urgent voice was behind her, but he didn't move to stop her.

Dragon allies were your *idea,* Zhafaera thought to him.

I'm reconsidering. His thoughts were jumbled and fear overrode every other emotion.

Zhafaera ignored him and took another step. The dragon backed up, hit the wall, and sat heavily. She was eying Zhafaera warily, the fear plain in her eyes. Her fear made Zhafaera's throat close up. She had never seen a scared dragon before in her life, and she truly hoped she'd never see one again. Another step. Zhafaera reached out, slowly easing her hand toward the beautiful creature in front of her. The dragon tensed, but she didn't protest as Zhafaera's hand gently touched her shoulder. She was cold. Very cold. Zhafaera shivered. Dragons were supposed to be almost too hot to touch. She closed her eyes, breathing deeply and drawing power to her despite the pain coursing through her body. As she breathed out, she let the magic flow through her hand and into the dragon. As she explored the young dragon's injuries, she wanted to cry. Scales broken and torn out, ribs broken, several tears in her membranous wings. Her left side was essentially one giant bruise, and her breathing was shallow and pained. She was hungry… *so hungry.*

Who did this to you? Zhafaera couldn't keep the pity out of her thoughts.

At first, she didn't think the dragon would answer. Then, so quietly that Zhafaera wasn't entirely certain she'd heard it, *my father.*

Zhafaera couldn't respond. She was afraid if she did that she would start crying, and that certainly wouldn't help anything. She focused on the dragon's body, smoothing each injury away, pushing bones and scales back into alignment, knitting muscle, warming her body. Finally, she felt the breathing of the dragon ease. Her hand felt warm. Opening her eyes, she found herself looking into two great green orbs.

The dragon tilted her head. *Thank you,* she said. Realizing the pain was gone, Zhafaera smiled slightly, then fell to her knees. The dragon stopped her fall with a forepaw around her waist before her face met the floor.

"Zhafaera!" Delan called, and she heard his fast footsteps rushing towards them.

The dragon pulled her around and held her close to her body, letting out a low hiss. Zhafaera saw thin lines of smoke trail out in front of her. Delan froze ten paces away, his hand stretched towards Zhafaera, the forgotten horses huddled by the entrance to the cave, clearly afraid, but unwilling to go back out into the icy rain.

"It's okay," she managed to croak. "He's a friend." She steadied herself with a hand on the scaly leg, pushing herself up and reaching for Delan. The dragon loosened her grip and allowed Delan closer, but she didn't let go until he had taken Zhafaera's hand.

Zhafaera closed her eyes as he pulled her against him. "Are you all right?"

"Fine," she mumbled. "Just tired. Healing dragons takes a lot of energy." At least the pain was gone.

She heard the dragon shift behind her. Opening her eyes, she turned around slowly, still holding onto Delan for support. "What's your name?" she asked.

The much improved dragon tilted her head. There was a long pause. *...I know you, don't I?* the dragon asked.

Zhafaera frowned. She'd only met dragons once in her life, and she had never been allowed near the young ones. "I don't think –" she started.

But the dragon interrupted her. *You're the Queen's daughter.*

"How do you –" Zhafaera started.

She was cut off again by the musical voice. *My mother. She met with you when she flew east. I've seen you in her mind.*

Zhafaera frowned, trying to remember all the dragons she'd met. It was a pretty short list. "Who's your mother? And *where* is she?"

The dragon's head dipped, and she seemed to deflate. Zhafaera's heart sank. She already knew. There was only one reason a dragon this young would be alone.

The silence stretched out. Zhafaera couldn't find the words to comfort the dragon. She knew that there were no words of comfort she could offer that would make the slightest bit of difference. When the dragon spoke, it was reluctantly, as if she could keep them from being true.

She's gone. My father killed her when the man came. They fought. Many died. And the rest… they went with him.

Zhafaera's grip on Delan's arm tightened. She knew she must be hurting him, but she felt as if without him as an anchor, she would simply float away. They were finished. Allying with the dragons had been a long shot to begin with, but if *all* the remaining dragons had allied themselves with Velexar… Zhafaera remained on her feet through sheer force of will.

"I lost my mother, too," she said quietly.

The dragon quickly looked up at her, her wide eyes meeting her gaze and reflecting back Zhafaera's own pain. She fought the lump in her throat and won. Barely. Slowly, she reached out to the dragon.

"What's your name?" she asked again.

Evamoira.

"Are you hungry?"

Yes. Her eyes burned, and Zhafaera wondered how long it had been since she'd eaten. Grown dragons could go quite a long time without eating, but who knew with young ones.

"Right, well, I'm on it." Delan's shaky voice didn't *quite* startle Zhafaera, but it was close. She turned to him. He looked mildly uncomfortable under the stare of both women. "You two rest," he gave Zhafaera a look that clearly said he might not be brave enough to tell a dragon she looked like hell, but that wouldn't stop him from tying *her* down if she argued. "I'll go find us some dinner." He looked at the dragon, who was staring at him with her head tilted to the side as if she'd never seen anything quite like him. "Evey, any preferences?"

Her head tilted more; Zhafaera almost laughed at the sight, as she was now almost looking at them upside down. *Evey?*

Delan blushed and mumbled, "sorry" before bowing and making a quick exit from the cave, grabbing Zhafaera's bow from her saddle on her way out.

Evamoria looked at Zhafaera. *Evey?*

Zhafaera grinned. "It's a nickname."

Oh. Evamoria looked thoughtful. *So my human name is Evey?*

Zhafaera actually chuckled a bit, something she wouldn't have thought possible given the circumstances. Maybe she was cracking. Probably. But she liked this young dragon. "I suppose, if you'd like."

She was quiet for a moment, then, *Evey.* She said the name as if tasting it.

Zhafaera went to the horses, calming them and coaxing them farther back into the cave. They weren't pleased being this close to a dragon, but now that it wasn't

169

an *angry* dragon, they were much more willing to share a dry cave with her. Moving slowly, she unsaddled them and set the saddles up to make their usual chairs side-by-side. Evey watched as she spread the bedrolls on the ground in front of the saddles, and then pulled out blankets, laying them over the saddles. Quickly, before Delan returned, she stripped out of her wet clothes and put on her spare pants and shirt, which were at least dri*er* after spending the day in the pack. Wrapping a blanket around herself, she walked the cave until she found a few stones that they could use for a fire ring.

With the camp set up, Zhafaera flopped down onto her bedroll, leaning back against her saddle and undoing her long braid. Sighing as her hair fell across her shoulders, she closed her eyes. She had no idea how long she sat like that, close to falling asleep if only she could stop shivering, listening to the *tick tick tick* at the mouth of the cave as the rain turned to sleet again with the setting of the sun. After a time, she heard Evey shift against the back of the cave, then felt her presence move closer and settle nearby. She could feel slight warmth from the dragon radiating out to her, making her smile. Opening her eyes, she saw Evey curled up nearby, almost cat-like, just watching her.

Zhafaera closed her eyes again, taking a deep breath and reaching out with her mind to sense Delan. After all their practicing this week, she could easily find him nearby now. She found him less than fifty yards from the cave entrance. She gently brushed a tendril of her awareness to his mind and immediately felt his answering acknowledgement.

How's it going? She thought.

Fine, he replied. *I'll come back soon. Just want to have enough to feed a starving dragon.* There was both wry humor and mild concern in his voice. Zhafaera was just grateful that he seemed willing to accept a dragon's presence. Intellectually, going to look for dragon allies was one thing, but after what had happened to Delan's home, Zhafaera was frankly surprised he wasn't more upset.

Zhafaera cracked an eye open and peeked at Evey again. Her eyes had closed. Up close again, the dragon looked like nothing but skin and bones. Zhafaera's heart went out to her. She looked vulnerable, and Zhafaera couldn't suppress the urge to take care of her.

One great dragon eye cracked open and met Zhafaera's gaze. *Tell him whatever he finds will help,* she said. *And the faster, the better.*

In that case, tell her I'll be back momentarily, Delan said.

Um... why exactly are you both asking me to be your messenger when clearly you can both hear each other? Zhafaera smiled and shook her head.

Evey's head jerked up. Can *he hear me? But... he's not a mage! How are you doing that?* The last thought was clearly directed to Delan.

He's listening through me. Zhafaera explained.

Oh. Evey was tilting her head again, clearly confused. *He's your… friend?*

Yes. I trust him completely, Zhafaera told her.

Aw, thanks, Delan joined the conversation. *We've come a long way from you holding a knife to my throat.*

Zhafaera wished she could mentally stick her tongue out at him.

Now that wouldn't be very ladylike. Zhafaera could hear the smile in Delan's mind-voice.

She was smiling herself. *Yeah, well, I was never a very good princess.* She focused on Evey again and could tell they'd left her behind. Her head was turned almost upside down again.

You tried to kill him? Evey asked, confused, as Delan appeared in the mouth of the cave, shivering and stomping his feet. He carried an armload of wet firewood and had three rabbits hanging from his belt.

"No!" Zhafaera said quickly. Delan looked at her with a raised eyebrow. Zhafaera winced at the frozen drops of rain clinging to his hair and got up to help him. "I just… roughed him up a bit." They looked at each other… and burst out laughing.

When they finally composed themselves, Zhafaera tried to take the wood from his arms, but he brushed her off, shaking his head. "Sit. Rest. You still look terrible."

"Thanks a lot," Zhafaera said, but did as he told her. Sitting and resting felt good right now.

Delan followed her and put the damp wood next to the fire ring Zhafaera had made. "I'll let you get this lit," he said. Zhafaera fixed him with a flat stare but started arranging the wood to make a fire. She tried to pick the driest pieces to go in the fire ring and set the wetter ones close by for them to dry out. But really, they were all wet. Delan took a seat next to her, took out his knife, and started skinning the rabbits. Evey was watching him with a hunger that clearly made him mildly uncomfortable.

Zhafaera drew just a spark of power to her and flicked it out to the damp wood in the fire ring. There was a tiny wisp of smoke that quickly vanished. She drew a bit more power to her, pushing past her growing headache, and tried again. Nothing. She turned to Evey.

"So, how's your fire breathing? We might need you to cook dinner for us tonight." She was only half joking.

Evey shook her head. *No fire yet,* she said. Then she stood, opening her mouth in what Zhafaera sincerely hoped was a dragon grin. The dragon shook her entire body, stretching her wings before inhaling deeply. Then she started to gag.

Zhafaera looked at Delan, whose face mirrored her own concern. The dragon moved closer to the wood pile, coughing and making a terrible sound. Zhafaera was reminded strongly of a cat with a hairball.

"Evey," she began.

Just then, Evey gave one final cough, paused, and then spit onto the fire. Looking closer, Zhafaera saw a wad of some kind of jelly-like substance stuck to the wood. She couldn't decide if she was interested or repulsed.

You should be able to light that, Evey said.

"Impressive," Delan said. "I could get used to traveling with a dragon."

Traveling? Evey asked, her wide eyes fixating on Delan. *Does that mean you'll be leaving?* Zhafaera's heart wrenched at the disappointment in her voice. She was so young.

"Well, yes, eventually," Delan said awkwardly. "We can't hide in a cave forever, no matter how much we might want to."

Why not? Evey asked.

"Because… " Delan looked at Zhafaera, his eyes pleading for help.

"Because we have to stop the man who killed my mother," Zhafaera said.

Evey's gaze turned to Zhafaera. She was quiet for a time, as if trying to put the pieces together. Finally she asked, *What happened to your mother?*

***

Delan watched as Zhafaera's face closed off. Her eyes darkened, her lips clamped together, and she barely seemed to breathe. No one moved for several minutes. Then Zhafaera started to tell her story.

Delan continued preparing the rabbits as she spoke. He soon had them over the fire, fat sizzling as they cooked. As she told of how Alec had been captured, Delan got up and walked out of the firelight, over to the horses, on the pretense of changing out of his wet clothes. He didn't want

174

to remember how Alec had been taken, and he didn't want to hear the guilt dripping from her voice. When he returned, somewhat drier, she had finished her story and was hugging her knees, gaze fixed on the ground. Delan sat next to her on her bedroll and draped an arm over her shoulders. She lifted her head and looked at him, her eyes over-bright, then leaned against him and rested her head on his shoulder. He had to consciously stop himself from reaching out to her mind, not wanting to intrude. It was amazing how quickly touching her mind had become second nature to him.

They sat like that for some time, listening to their dinner cooking, Delan absently twirling a strand of Zhafaera's silky hair around his finger. Evey spoke first.

I don't understand how, but... it can't just be coincidence.

Delan and Zhafaera both looked at her. Delan wasn't sure Zhafaera was capable of speaking yet, so he asked the question they were both thinking. "What happened to you?"

Evey looked at him, and he could swear her scales had darkened. Finally, she spoke again.

Essentially, exactly what happened to Princess Zhafaera. She tossed her head, as if trying to shake off the reality of her memories. *Things in our home had been... odd, lately. Some of the others were restless. Then the man came to visit. I wasn't allowed near him, of course, but I know he made my mother angry.* She paused for so long that Delan wasn't sure she'd start again. He reached

175

forward and checked the rabbits, giving her time to collect her thoughts.

Finally, she continued. *It was less than two weeks later that my father betrayed my mother.* Her voice was completely expressionless, no trace of the normal musical quality. *He killed her and everyone who tried to help her. I only just got away. Most of the others joined him. And the rest... everyone scattered.* Delan could feel Zhafaera trembling against him, and tightened his grip around her, as if he could help hold her together. *After the initial fight, I hid in one of my mother's secret tunnels and watched. My father looked for me for days, but he couldn't find me. I'm good at hiding,* she added proudly. *Eventually the man came back, and my father and some others left with him. It was soon after that that I managed to escape. I fled down the mountain.* Evey hung her head. *I couldn't fly, so I stuck to the caves. If any other dragons see me, I'm sure they'll kill me.*

Zhafaera finally found her voice. "Why? Why would they want to kill you?"

My mother was powerful, Evey answered. *Dragons do not have Queens, but she was one of our leaders. I tried to help her, but they hurt me.* The dragon looked up at them, and the confusion was written plainly across her face, right alongside the anger. *I don't understand why though!*

Delan pulled the rabbits off the fire and offered one to Evey. It was gone before he could blink, despite how hot it was. He held out a second one for her, and this one she took delicately in one paw. She pulled it off the stick, sniffing it, clearly trying to savor this one. He turned to Zhafaera and they began pulling apart the last rabbit as Evey began to crunch bone.

In no time, there was absolutely no trace of their meal. Between the meal and the fire and the warmth coming from the dragon, Delan was able to feel his fingers and toes again. The heat was starting to settle into his bones, but it did nothing to settle his unease.

Their one faint hope was to find their own dragon allies, and what do they find? A half-starved dragon child that had already been beaten within an inch of her life. In fact, he had a strong feeling that they had just picked up a permanent traveling companion to care for.

Zhafaera interrupted his train of thought. "This man you saw, Evey... what did he look like?"

Evey answered immediately. *Dark. Long black hair, deep voice. Tall for a human, but thinner than most. He felt... wrong.* A picture formed in her mind, showing them, and Delan felt Zhafaera tense. If Delan didn't know better, he would say that Evey shivered in fear. But anything that could scare a dragon was something that Delan did *not* want to think about.

Zhafaera looked at Delan. "Velexar. He would never entrust that deal to someone else." She sighed and seemed to deflate. "Evey, our plan had been to go to the dragons and ask for help, but you said the ones that didn't support Velexar died or fled?"

Evey nodded her head. *Those that escaped... I don't know where they are. I'm sorry.*

Zhafaera tilted her head back against her saddle. "It's not your fault," she said. "It's *him*. Why? Why did he have to do this?" Before Delan could react, Zhafaera had picked up a stone next to her and hurled it across the cave. It shattered on the far wall, making all of them jump. Zhafaera took several deep breaths, wiping angrily at a tear that coursed down her cheek. Finally, she opened her eyes and looked at Evey. "I'm sorry about your mother. We want to help you."

And I want to help you, Evey said earnestly. She sounded like a small child.

"We'll go to the capital, together." Zhafaera said. "I'm going to punch a hole straight through Velexar's ugly, stupid face. I'm going to rescue Delan's brother. Then we'll take the Sapphire and fix this. Somehow." The last word was a whisper. She looked intently at Evey. "I want you to come with us. The three of us will be better off if we stay together." Her voice softened. "I don't want to leave you here."

Evey nodded. *I can disguise myself if I need to. I'll come with you.*

"All right, it's settled then." Zhafaera nodded once, sniffed, and tossed her hair, clearly composing herself. Then she got up and went to the mouth of the cave, where the rain had turned to snow that was just barely sticking and dusting the ground white. Delan could sense her begin her nightly wards, sealing the entrance of the cave against intruders. Delan was already planning their next course. It would probably be best to stay here for a bit and prepare for the journey across the mountains. They could hunt, maybe find a water source they could follow over the mountains.

You... take care of her? Evey's quiet voice interrupted Delan's thoughts.

"What? Well, yeah. I mean, we take care of each other. And we'll take care of you." He added.

You're afraid of losing her. Evey frowned at Zhafaera near the cave entrance, where she was still engrossed in her spells. *And she, you.*

"Yes." Delan didn't know what else to say.

Luckily, Evey didn't seem to expect any more of an answer. She curled up on the other side of the fire. As she moved, Delan scooted the few feet to his own bedroll, lying down and pulling his blanket over him, putting the saddle with his sword still attached to it between him and the mouth of the cave. Since the rain started, he and Zhafaera had mostly slept curled up together for warmth, and it suddenly felt strange to bed down alone. He listened as Zhafaera walked back to the fire and climbed into her own blankets. *At least we're dry*, Delan thought as he drifted off to sleep.

***

Zhafaera huddled in the dark, shaking from head to toe as her breath came in short gasps. She tried to quiet her racing heart, sure that it would give her away. She could hear slow, soft footsteps coming closer to the door behind which she hid. She pressed herself further into the corner of the closet, as far from the door as she could get. The footsteps stopped near her door (which suddenly seemed flimsy and insignificant against the horror on the other side) and Zhafaera automatically reached to pull magic to her, not willing to go down without a fight. But... something was blocking her. She pushed against the barrier in her mind, stretching it with all of her willpower, but it was fluid and just flowed with her. Just as she started to panic, the footsteps started again, moving away now.

When the footsteps had faded out of earshot, Zhafaera tried to calm herself. *Breathe... just breathe.* She pushed tentatively at the barrier in her mind again. Again, it flexed with her. Panic flared in the pit of her stomach, and she started to feel trapped, surrounded in her own mind –

The door slammed open, swinging just in front of her nose and slamming back against the wall. An unseen force wrapped around her ankles and jerked her forward, out of the closet and out into... her bedroom? Zhafaera screamed, digging her fingers into the floor, trying to find anything to give her purchase to stop her flight, but the well worn-wood offered no help.

The invisible force crept up her legs like a snake, binding them so she couldn't move an inch, pulling her into the center of the room and jerking her upright. She closed her eyes against the motion sickness she felt at this sudden change of perspective. *Breathe.* But she found that breathing was suddenly much more difficult for some reason. *Oh Gods.* The unseen force holding her in the air had slowly crept up her body until she could no longer move from the neck down.

Gasping for breath that would barely come, she thrashed her head back and forth, fighting against the barrier in her mind, desperate to reach her magic and free herself.

"Now, now, my dear, calm down. You don't want to hurt yourself before our big day." Zhafaera froze at the sound of the voice echoing through her. She squeezed her eyes closed even tighter, fighting the tears that were already forming behind the lids.

A hand lightly touched her cheek, and she jerked as if she had been scalded.

"Why were you hiding, my darling?" Another hand wound itself into her hair, its grip tightening painfully until she was truly bound in place, unable to move an inch.

Zhafaera slowly forced herself to open her eyes, knowing what she would see. Velexar stood directly in front of her, his smile chilling her to the bone as she let out a scream that was part anger, part frustration, but mostly pure terror...

Zhafaera woke suddenly, barely able to breathe with her face buried in her blanket, muffling her scream. She immediately sat up, fighting her way out of her blankets that felt as though they were wound tightly around her body, squeezing the air out...

Breathe. She sat on the floor of the cave, shaking from head to toe, breath coming in short gasps and panic churning in her belly. It wasn't a vision. It couldn't be. But it felt real enough. *Breathe.*

There was a noise from her right. Barely stifling a scream, she jerked in that direction, only to see Evey's huge, round eyes glowing back at her from the darkness, reflecting the meager light cast from the dying embers of the fire.

Are you all right? Evey asked, her mind-voice sounding worried.

Zhafaera shook her head and ran her fingers roughly through her hair, drawing her knees up and resting her forehead on them.

Do you need help? Clearly she was frightening the young dragon.

Trying to get ahold of herself, she took as deep a breath as she could manage and lifted her head. *No, really, it's okay. Just a nightmare. Go back to sleep, Evey.*

Zhafaera saw her rest her huge head back on her forepaws, but those bright eyes didn't close.

Looking away, Zhafaera's eyes fell on Delan, still sound asleep across what was left of the fire. As she watched, Delan frowned in his sleep, muttered something, and then was still again. Zhafaera hesitated barely a second – she hopped up and darted over to his bedroll, lifting the blanket and sliding under. As she got settled, trying not to wake him, he suddenly rolled over, wrapping one arm around her and drawing her tight against him. She pressed her forehead to his chest and could feel her body start to relax just slightly as his warmth seeped into her.

"Sorry, I didn't mean to wake you," she whispered quietly, hoping he wasn't awake enough to hear the tremor in her voice.

Eyes still closed, he leaned forward and pressed a gentle kiss to the top of her head, sliding his other arm under her head and holding her tight. That simple action was enough to break her control, and Zhafaera felt hot tears roll down her cheeks. The thought of being at Velexar's mercy terrified her to the core. She'd be better off dead. That made her think of her mother, how he had murdered her, and she cried even harder.

Delan didn't let go, holding her and slowly stroking her hair as she cried and shook like a leaf. He didn't hush her or tell her everything would be all right, for which Zhafaera was grateful. Little by little, she calmed. The tears quit flowing and she slowly stopped shaking, her grief and fear replaced by a vast emptiness. Finally, she lifted her head from Delan's chest, looking up at his shadowy face. She started to speak, but Delan cut her off.

"Don't apologize," he whispered seriously, placing the tip of one finger on her lips. He gently tucked her head under his chin, and Zhafaera closed her eyes, suddenly dead tired. "Just sleep." Zhafaera slept.

***

Delan woke the next morning very warm. He glanced down. Zhafaera was still asleep, curled up next to him and using his arm as a pillow, her red curls half covering her face. It was nice to see her face so peaceful and unmarred by worry. He would never admit it to her, but last night had terrified him. Seeing her that upset had chilled him to the core. He'd never seen her cry. Ever.

Pushing those thoughts aside and trying not to disturb her, he carefully looked around, trying to see what could be making him so hot. He didn't have to look far – as soon as he moved, a dragon head appeared in his field of vision, startling him slightly. He tipped his head back to see her better and saw that she was curled up in a half-circle between him and the mouth of the cave. He could only assume that she was feeling better; her eyes were practically glowing, and he could have sworn her scales were brighter.

"Good morning," he whispered, grinning at her.

In response, Evey opened her jaw wide and yawned. At least he hoped it was a yawn and not a not-so-subtle threat. Heat radiated off of her, keeping them warm despite the frost Delan could see outside when he looked towards the mouth of the cave. He was suddenly hopeful that maybe they wouldn't freeze to death crossing the mountains.

You're welcome, she said silently. Delan felt something else bleeding through her connection to his mind. Almost pain, with a slightly desperate feeling to it… hunger? Delan suddenly remembered the only thing she'd had to eat since who knows when was a couple of rabbits no bigger than her snout. Somehow he had a feeling that a dragon the size of a horse needed a bit more than that.

Looking down at Zhafaera regretfully, he reached out and gently brushed the hair off of her face. She stirred, breathing deeply and snuggling closer. Delan seriously considered just going back to sleep. *She just couldn't make it easy, could she?* He thought. He stroked her cheek, fingers lingering on the silky skin. "Wake up, Princess," he whispered.

Zhafaera cracked open one eye, peeking up at him and frowning. "Nnnnn," she groaned. "Warm." Then she grabbed the blanket, and all in one motion rolled over and wrapped the blanket over her head so that it looked like she was enclosed in a cocoon.

Delan bit back a laugh with some difficulty. "Does this mean you're good with my plan to rest here for a couple of days and stock up on food to take over the mountains with us?"

"Mmmmm," was the reply.

"I'm taking that as a yes." Delan slowly sat up and extracted himself from the tangle of blankets. Standing slowly and stretching, he dug through their supplies and found the last hunk of smoked ham he'd bought from the village.

"Here," he told Evey, holding it out to her. "Hopefully this'll at least take the edge off until we can do some hunting."

Evey delicately took the ham in a forepaw, and Delan went over to feed the horses. They seemed quite content; the dragon's heat had warmed the whole cave, and the horses were clearly happy to have spent a night warm and dry.

"Don't get too comfortable," Delan told Shadow. Shadow nuzzled his hand. They had been together for nearly ten years now, and they understood each other pretty well. Zhafaera's horse couldn't allow Shadow to get attention without her, and before Delan knew it his hands were occupied scratching the necks of both horses as they sniffed and nibbled on his clothes searching for treats. He fed them each half an apple, then left them to their feed bags.

When he turned back to Evey, the ham was gone and Zhafaera was sitting up and poking the fire back to life. She looked better than she had last night after the healing, but the dark circles under her eyes told him how hard she was pushing herself. Grabbing another two apples from the pack, Delan sat back next to Zhafaera and handed one to her.

"So we're staying here?" she asked.

Delan nodded. "It's a sheltered place we can spend a couple of days in and decide on our path over the mountains. And we can do some hunting here, maybe not starve on our way over. Hopefully." He looked at Evey. "How much do you need to eat, exactly?"

Evey's pupils dilated slightly, ready to hunt. *I can go a week or so without food, but as you saw, the result is not ideal.* She looked down at her paws. *I've never hunted before.* She looked up at them, somewhat defensively. *I mean, I went on a couple of hunts, but mostly the other*

186

dragons brought us food. I was too young, she practically spit the words out, *to go very far outside the caves.*

Zhafaera reached out a hand to rest on Evey's shoulder. Her scales twitched slightly, but she didn't pull away. "Evey, we'll take care of you."

"And we can probably teach you some of the basics," Delan added. "But for now – amounts. How much do you need each day? Are we talking one deer a day, two, what?"

Evey snorted in what was clearly a dragon laugh. *Normally, if I've been eating regularly, I'd be fine on what you just gave me. But I've only had a few small meals in the last month, so for today...just as much as you can find.*

"Right then," Delan said, finishing his apple and standing. "We'd better get started then. We'll get you fed first, and then see if we can't smoke some for the trip." He looked down at Zhafaera. "Feel up to coming?" he asked. When she nodded, he extended a hand and helped pull her to her feet. Evey stood and stretched, looking exactly like a giant, scaly cat. Delan blinked. Or maybe not so scaly. Before him stood the snow leopard they had seen the night before, although it didn't look nearly so bedraggled.

Will this form do for hunting? Evey's voice was back in their minds.

"How did you –" Delan began, then stopped himself. "Never mind. Magic. It'll be great." They moved towards the mouth of the cave, stopping for Delan to pick up the bow and arrows as Zhafaera quickly checked that all of her knives were in place. As they stepped out into the frosty

187

morning, a thought suddenly occurred to him. He looked at Zhafaera. "Could you do that? Could I?"

Zhafaera smiled. "Technically, yes. Practically, it's not ideal. It's a lot easier to transform from human to animal than animal to human form, so it's easy to get stuck." She paused. "And don't try a dragon form."

"Why not?"

"Human bodies can't withstand the change to immortal."

"I'll keep that in mind." Something she had said last night clicked for Delan. "So when you asked her if she was stuck last night, you thought she was another mage?"

Zhafaera nodded. "I knew she had to be another mage of some kind, but based on how I'd been picking up on her presence all day, I guessed dragon. Human mages usually don't just leak out power like that."

Sorry, Evey said. *I didn't mean to.*

Evey was quiet, her huge paws making no sound as she padded across the icy ground. The storm yesterday had left a glaze of ice over most surfaces. If it was this bad down here now, at the very beginning of the season, Delan hated to think what it would be like at higher altitudes.

"Well, maybe you can share some of your knowledge with me." Delan said.

The leopard's head tilted, as it seemed to do whenever there was something she didn't quite understand. *You're a mage? But... I can't sense it, and you're not using magic now to feel the environment around you, you're relying only on your physical senses.* Clearly in her world, this was unheard of.

"Zhafaera says I'm a Black mage," Delan told Evey.

Evey stopped, turning to Delan and tilting her head to the side in question. Delan shrugged and looked at Zhafaera, who was staring intently at a nearby pine tree but clearly not seeing it.

"Well," Zhafaera said slowly, "I don't suppose the dragons have anything like it." She blinked and looked at Delan. "Dragons are essentially White mages – they can draw magic from any element. Remember that human magic started out as sort of a – a watered down version of dragon magic."

Very *watered down*, Evey chimed in.

Zhafaera looked at the snow leopard dragon flatly, and Delan had the distinct impression that it was all she could do to not roll her eyes. "Yes, thank you, Evey. Anyway. Almost all dragons are White mages –"

No they're not, they're dragons. Evey sounded confused.

"No – yes – I know, Evey, I'm just making a comparison that everyone can understand here." Zhafaera paused, waiting for Evey to object. When the young dragon was quiet, she continued, speaking directly to Evey. "A Black mage is a human mage who can't draw magic from the environment, but *can* draw their magic from another mage. They're very rare." She glanced at Delan. "I mean, at least we *think* they're rare. We didn't

189

figure out Delan was a Black mage until he blew up a legion of soldiers on our way up here… "

"I didn't 'blow them up,'" Delan protested. "It was just a bit of fire!" Zhafaera just stared at him. "Okay fine, so maybe I blew them up a little bit." The familiar guilt flared up.

Who did he pull magic from to blow up those soldiers? Evey didn't look convinced.

"Me," Zhafaera said simply.

Evey was quiet for a moment. *Isn't that dangerous for you?* She sounded genuinely concerned. *What if he had pulled too much from you? Without knowing your limit, he could easily have killed you.* Her voice sounded more like a growl, and the look she gave Delan was not friendly. He shifted uncomfortably, trying to look non-threatening.

"Well, he didn't kill me, and I've been teaching him control since then." Zhafaera smiled at him. "He's a quick learner. Watch."

Delan immediately felt her power grow, and he gently reached out, drawing a small amount of power through her and bringing it into his core. Once he felt he had a firm hold on it, he cut the thin thread of magic connecting him to Zhafaera and let the magic from his core flow down his arm and into his palm. He lifted his hand so that Evey could see the tiny, perfect flame hovering just above his palm, the light and heat remaining constant for several seconds before he closed his palm and released the magic gently. The night after she'd told him what he was, they'd practiced that for hours until Zhafaera felt relatively safe –

190

or at least confident that he could control the amount of power he drew from her enough not to kill her.

Evey stared at them both for a long moment, her head now tilted nearly upside down, looking at Delan as though trying to see straight through him. Her tail twitched back and forth a few times, as if she were making up her mind.

Impressive, she said finally. *I've never seen anything like that before.*

She suddenly stood, shook out her pelt, and turned to continue the way they had been heading before their stop. Delan looked at Zhafaera, who shrugged.

"Soooo, she's not going to eat me?" Delan asked jokingly. Mostly.

Not right now, Evey butted in. *But I might if we don't start hunting soon.*

"Dragons… " Delan muttered under his breath, shaking his head. The elbow in his ribs let him know it wasn't quite quiet enough.

"Watch it," Zhafaera said, following Evey.

He grinned and bowed. "Apologies, Princess." He lifted his head in time to see her eyes roll as she struggled not to laugh.

As amusing as this is, I am still hungry, Evey interrupted.

Delan bowed again, this time to Evey. "Apologies, my lady."

When he straightened, Evey had stopped and was looking at him with her head tilted almost upside down again. He really hoped she didn't get stuck that way.

***

Six hours, two deer, and one content dragon later, Zhafaera was huddled under her blanket in front of the fire, still trying to thaw her frozen toes.

Delan sat across the fire with Evey, explaining to the very fascinated dragon exactly how the little compass from his pack worked. Apparently, dragons were like birds in that they were born able to sense the direction of magnetic north. According to Evey, Delan's compass was "pretty close." The two of them seemed relaxed together – Delan had taken it upon himself to help Evey improve her hunting skills that day, and apparently feeding a dragon is a good way to gain their trust.

As the sun began to set, Evey's eyes started to droop. Her full belly was clearly catching up to her. Delan noticed.

"It's Okay to sleep, you know," he said to her. Her eyes shot open, and she shook her head as if clearing it.

I'm not a baby, she said. Then she ruined it by opening her jaw in a huge yawn, showing a mouth full of pointed teeth each almost six inches long. Zhafaera had to admit, the sight was mildly terrifying. As she watched, Delan laid a careful hand on Evey's long neck, and the dragon jumped, her mouth snapping closed as she turned to face him. *Not the best idea to startle a dragon, but hey, maybe that's just me,* she thought to Delan. Delan sat perfectly still, not moving his hand as Evey regarded him carefully.

Finally, she gave up and rested her head on her forelegs, closing her eyes completely and breathing out a contented sigh. *Maybe I'll just rest for a little while... that feels nice*, she added, as Delan began gently scratching behind one of her ears as if she were a cat. Zhafaera expected her to start purring any minute now. Although Zhafaera had to admit, that *did* look like it felt good. What she wouldn't give for a massage right about now. She could practically feel Delan's strong hands on her neck, gently working out the knots in her shoulders as he rained light kisses down her neck...

Zhafaera's eyes shot open and her eyes darted guiltily around the cave. Delan still sat next to Evey, now stroking her long neck as he examined her multi-hued scales. Zhafaera shook herself slightly and stretched, trying to forget the pleasant shiver that had run down her spine... *okay, enough already!* She told herself firmly. She wasn't some silly, simpering court lady who couldn't think of anything beyond catching a man. *Get a grip!*

Delan finally stopped petting the young dragon and moved around the fire to plop next to Zhafaera.

"So, lessons tonight?" he asked. "Or are you still worn out?" He was eyeing her critically, clearly making his own assessment despite what she would say.

"No lessons," she said. "Healing a half-dead dragon wasn't exactly as easy as it looked." Between that, her nightmare, and the long day out in the cold, Zhafaera was beginning to think Evey had the right idea. "Still, you should practice some." She sat, watching Delan, tapping her finger on her chin as she thought.

"OH, I KNOW!" she said, making Delan nearly jump out of his skin. "Sorry, I – no, you can put the knife away," she said, resting a hand on his shoulder and trying not to laugh.

"Gods, Zhafaera, don't *do* that," he said, putting a hand over his heart as he slid his knife back into his boot. "You scared me half to death!"

"Sorry, sorry, I just got excited!" She quickly leaned back against the saddle behind her and rested her feet in Delan's lap. "Warm my feet." She wiggled her toes at Delan.

He grinned and raised an eyebrow at her. "Of course, Princess. But next time you want a royal foot rub, you can just ask – no need to give me a heart attack to soften me up first."

"Oh, ha ha, very funny," she said, rolling her eyes as his smile widened. "It's not a foot rub, it's a magical exercise." She reached down and pulled her socks off, then wiggled her cold toes some more. "Use magic to heat my toes. You want to use enough heat to warm them, but not enough to burn my skin off."

Delan's smile was gone, and he suddenly looked nervous. "Uhhh… "

"You'll be fine," Zhafaera said, leaning back again. "Just go slow and work your way up."

Delan made a slight choking sound.

"What?" she asked.

Delan just shook his head, not meeting her eyes.

She thought over what she'd said. *Oh, well, that's just great. Good job, Zhafaera.* It took all of her willpower not to blush, and she still wasn't sure she completely succeeded.

She cleared her throat. "Okay, ready?" she asked Delan.

"I guess. Not really," Delan didn't sound thrilled.

Zhafaera ignored him and drew a little extra power to her, holding it out for Delan to take. She quickly sensed him as he took the power from her very slowly, carefully. Closing her eyes, she waited. Within a minute, she felt his large hands encircle one foot, deliciously warm against her icy toes. She smiled and relaxed as the heat seeped into her skin and warmed every inch of her foot down to the bone. Just as the heat began to feel like too much, Delan released her foot and took hold of the other one. Soon, both feet were toasty warm and Zhafaera was nearly asleep. Delan let go of her other foot, and Zhafaera made to move.

"Ah, nope, not done," Delan said firmly.

"What do you mean? I only have two—ahhhhhh… " Delan's hands were back on her feet, massaging the soreness of the day's hike away. The heat in his hands had receded, but that didn't make it feel any less wonderful. Zhafaera forced herself to say, "you – you really don't have to give me a royal foot rub, you know."

"Ah, but why else would I have come on this grand adventure if not to serve my lady's every whim?" Zhafaera could hear the smile in his voice.

195

"You make a compelling argument," she said, cracking one eye open and grinning at him.

"There's also this one bit of burnt skin hanging off here that I'm trying to remove before you notice it..." Delan laughed and easily ducked the small stone Zhafaera sent flying at him.

By the time he finished, Zhafaera was half asleep and more relaxed than she'd been in weeks. She slowly sat up, trying to wake up enough to find her bedroll.

"Thank you," she said, somewhat groggily. "Top marks in feet warming."

"At last, my life's ambition fulfilled," Delan said, climbing under his blankets.

Zhafaera started to crawl past him to her own blankets, but stopped, unsure of what to say. It was one thing to sleep together out in the cold rain, but they were safe and comfortable here.

"Delan –" Before she could even form her request, Delan had already lifted his blankets, inviting her under. She hesitated only a moment before crawling under and curling up next to him.

"I'm not a *little girl*, afraid of the dark or the monsters under my bed, or something else stupid like that, I just –"

"I know," Delan interrupted her, tucking an arm around her and pulling her close. "The nightmares. It's okay."

She looked up at him, trying to hide her fear. "I know it's silly –"

"No it's not," he said seriously. "You've been through a trauma." Then he grinned. "Besides, we wouldn't want your royal toes getting cold again."

She smiled and shoved him lightly. "My 'royal toes' managed just fine before you came along, thank you."

"Yeah, but that was before the snow started. They wouldn't make it much longer without me."

Zhafaera rolled over, still smiling, and pulled the blankets over her head. "Goodnight, Delan."

Delan pressed his lips to the back of her head in a gentle kiss. "Goodnight, Zhafaera."

Chapter 8

Zhafaera had always thought that snow was beautiful –
falling like sparkly feathers from heavy silver clouds,
specially made by the gods for the enjoyment of children
everywhere. After days of trudging uphill through the
ever-deepening snow, her opinion had changed drastically.
They weren't anywhere near the top, and already she was
wishing for warm, tropical beaches.

They had decided their best chance at making it over
the mountains undetected was to head west until they
found the small pass that Evey had used to cross.
Supposedly, it came out right near the Angonite River,
which they could then follow down the other side of the
mountains and straight out to the capital, where it sat on
the banks of the river, maybe a ten day journey
downstream, by boat. Good plan, as long as they could find
the damn path. And as long as it wasn't completely
blocked by snow. *Hells, at this point, I'll just blast the
cursed snow out of my way and be done with it, and damn
the consequences.*

When they had first left the cave – *that wondrous,
warm cave,* Zhafaera thought – Zhafaera had tried to clear
the snow out of their path to make their hike easier. Parting
the snow into piles on either side of them had lasted for

about an hour, until she realized there was no way she would be able to keep that up the whole way. Melting the snow lasted for all of ten minutes, when they all agreed that snow was better than mud. The best she could do now was hold heat shields around them and the horses and occasionally clear a path through dips in the ground where the snow was just too deep. It was starting to make her a little crazy.

It was nearly dusk, and Zhafaera started to look for a good campsite before she realized it didn't matter – they had left the last of the trees behind that morning. Everything around them looked the same – empty and white. They stood out like a sore thumb against the endless expanse of snow; if anyone came looking, there was nowhere to hide. Zhafaera tried to put that out of her mind before she started looking over her shoulder every two seconds.

She had just opened her mouth to suggest they stop for the night before it got too dark when Evey, in her snow leopard form, darted off up the slope to their right. *This is it!* she called excitedly, stopping perhaps thirty yards ahead of them under a tiny rock outcropping. At first, it looked nothing like a road, but as she drew closer, Zhafaera could see that there was quite a large fissure in the rock. It blended so well with the rock and snow surrounding it that Zhafaera could have walked right by it and never seen it. Through the opening, there was a clear path that sloped gently upwards before disappearing. At first, the road seemed to be completely covered overhead, but as she moved inside and looked closer, she could see gaps in the rock above that showed the first stars of the night beginning to appear.

"I must admit, I'm impressed," Delan said from behind her. "How did you see that, Evey?"

Evey looked as if the question made no sense. *I told you I came through this way before.* When this didn't produce immediate understanding, she continued. *It's hard to miss your own scent.*

"Ah, of course," Delan said seriously. He turned to Zhafaera. "Well, what do you think? Camp here or move in a ways?"

Zhafaera thought for a moment, peering ahead into the quickly darkening crevice. "Let's move in a little. Not too far, just enough to get out of the wind," she finally said, leading the way forward. "If nothing else, there's not much snow in here, so we can at least sleep dry tonight. Without magic."

They had walked for only a few minutes when suddenly the path widened on their right, making a small hollow that looked just large enough for a small party to rest in off the road. Looking closer, Zhafaera saw there was even a small fire pit in the center, confirming her suspicions that this was made specifically for travelers. These mountains were known to be rich with copper ore, and mines covered the entire range. Over time, once the vein of silver was discovered at the eastern end of the range, the mines at this end were abandoned. As new mines moved closer to the coast, tiny fishing villages grew into major ports, and this pass would have been abandoned in favor of the larger one closer to the sea.

"Well, this should do nicely," Delan said eagerly, clapping his hands together. The sound echoed up and down the quasi-tunnel and Zhafaera gave him a look. He shrugged and moved forward into the hollow, leading Shadow over to the far wall and starting to remove their gear. Liri looked at her as if for permission, and Zhafaera dropped the reins and waved her hand, indicating that Liri should join the boys. She immediately trotted over, leaning close to Delan, maybe hoping to sneak an apple while he was busy.

By the time everyone was fed, it was all Zhafaera could do to stay awake. They had set up camp so that the humans' blankets were against the back wall of the hollow, with the dragon on the opposite side of the fire to help trap the heat in the hollow. Evey had settled for the night and was curled into a large, warm ball, and Zhafaera sat leaning against Delan's saddle, her eyes drooping. Delan sat next to her, his arm around her shoulders, holding a blanket around them both. His thumb was absently tracing slow circles on her arm, and the soothing motion was lulling her into sleep.

"Time for bed," Delan said quietly as Zhafaera's head started to fall on his arm. With her eyes mostly closed, Zhafaera followed Delan and curled up under the covers, quickly molding against him and tucking her head under his chin. His arms went around her automatically, enveloping her in furnace-like warmth.

"Zhafaera…" Delan whispered.

Zhafaera sleepily tilted her head back so she could look at him. "Yes?" she whispered back. She suddenly realized they were very close, their noses only a scant inch apart. Her heart rate ticked up rapidly. *Don't be silly*, she thought. *You've been sleeping like this for days…weeks even!* But they hadn't kissed since the incident with the soldiers, since learning Delan was a Black mage. Not because she was scared of him, more just because they had been focused on other things, and then they'd met Evey…

Delan didn't say anything, only looked at her. This close, she could see the dimming light from the fire dancing in his eyes; she noticed his pupils were slightly dilated, and it was suddenly like she was looking through a window into his soul. What she saw there made her breath catch slightly, and a slight shiver ran down her spine.

Throwing caution into the wind, Zhafaera stretched her neck and brushed a light kiss against Delan's lips. She could feel his smile against her lips as he responded, deepening their connection.

It was some time before they broke apart, slightly breathless. Zhafaera, at least, was warmer than she'd been in days. Tucking her head back against his chest, she could hear his heart – beating as if in a race with her own rapid pulse. Then she felt him take a deep breath and let it out slowly.

"I was worried," he whispered.

"About what?" Zhafaera asked, just as quiet. She glanced behind her at Evey on the opposite side of the fire. She appeared to be asleep.

Delan hesitated. "I thought maybe you didn't...feel the same way about me, after learning about...what I can do."

Zhafaera shook her head firmly. "I'm not afraid of you, Delan."

"Good, because I'm trying really hard to keep you safe."

"I know I'm safe with you."

Delan pulled her close. "Goodnight, Zhafaera," he whispered softly against her hair. She simply snuggled closer, breathing in his scent as his hand stroked her hair, finally lulling her to sleep.

***

"Well, at least it's not rain," Zhafaera was not thrilled as she trudged along the narrow path. It had been snowing non-stop for the last three days, slowing their progress through the pass and making it an overall miserable experience. Considering it was still only early fall, Zhafaera was convinced that the constant snow was Velexar's doing. Delan had tried to gently suggest that perhaps she was being a tad paranoid, but one look from her had silenced him on that topic forever.

Natural or unnatural, the icy flakes were slowly burying the mountain as they climbed higher and higher.

For a while, the pass overhang protected them from the worst of the weather, with just the occasional clump of snow falling on their heads. But that morning their luck had finally run out when the mostly covered path opened up into a slowly narrowing, bare expanse of rock that wound its way along the side of the mountain. So not only were they being buffeted against the mountain by the swirling winds, but their only path looked and felt like a narrow, icy ribbon.

It was only now, as the edge of the path to the right got closer and closer to the solid wall of rock on their left, that they realized just how high they had climbed. Delan and Zhafaera both staunchly ignored the enormous drop just a few feet to their right, but it wasn't easy.

The path was beginning to slope gently downward, headed towards a sparsely wooded valley three hundred meters below. They had decided to try and make their way down to the valley before stopping for the night, but their progress was slow thanks to the ever-strengthening wind periodically blowing swirls of snow into their eyes. To make matters worse, it was mid-afternoon and already the light was fading as the sun began to drop behind the mountains, its descent made even faster as they moved lower towards the valley floor. Between the mountains and storm clouds blocking the sun, it wasn't long before they were walking in almost complete darkness, slipping on unseen icy patches as the temperatures dropped.

"What do you think?" Zhafaera finally asked Delan. "Keep going, or turn back?"

Delan turned around to look at her following behind him. "We've got to be more than halfway."

Gods I hope so. Zhafaera thought, peeking over the edge of the precipice. It still looked like a *very* long way down. Looking up, she realized that she could no longer see where they had come out of the mountain, as the tops of the mountains were covered in a solid grey blanket of clouds. They kept going.

Eventually, the path had narrowed so much that they all walked in single file, with Evey leading the way, followed closely by Delan, and then Zhafaera leading the horses, one tied to a lead behind the other as Zhafaera concentrated on keeping them relatively calm by sending as much warm, tranquil energy through the lead as she could. It was the only way they had been able to keep the horses moving along such a terrifyingly narrow ledge; hell, she could barely keep *herself* moving at this point. Zhafaera was just grateful to have something to focus on besides how cold she was. Oh, and the obscenely dangerous drop to her right, but she barely noticed *that*, nope, not at all. Judging by the way that Delan looked almost glued to the side of the mountain, Zhafaera guessed that he also wasn't paying any attention to the death trap to their right.

"If this path gets much narrower, we're going to have to find another way down." Delan called back to her, sounding distinctly uncomfortable.

"There is no other –"

Uh oh, Evey interrupted.

205

What 'uh oh?' Delan and Zhafaera thought together as they all came to a sudden stop.

Peering forward through the gloom and snow, they saw exactly what the "uh oh" was. The path, already narrow, had apparently had a little accident at some point. In the next twenty meters of the path, chunks of rock had fallen, leaving gaping wounds in the ledge, looking almost like a large, jagged bite mark.

"Damn," Zhafaera whispered.

"Not arguing with you there," Delan replied. "But how the hell do we get across?"

"I have no idea," Zhafaera said, sitting heavily in the snow and resting her head in her hands to think.

After a few minutes of silence, Delan asked, "Hey, you know, we do have a dragon, and she has wings – Evey, could you fly us over?"

Zhafaera was shaking her head even before Evey answered. *I could maybe fly one of you at a time, but not the horses.* The snow leopard eyed the horses that were currently twice its size. *They're just too heavy.*

Zhafaera stood and examined the broken ledge. There was enough of the path left that they could scooch across it carefully, but the horses would never fit. Zhafaera moved to the front of the group. Could she make the ledge any wider? Maybe she could extend a platform of air over the holes. She couldn't support herself with her own magic, but if she stayed on what was left of the ledge, she might be able to get Shadow and Liri over. She shared her plan with Delan.

"Are you out of your mind?" Delan was less than pleased with the suggestion.

"Do you have any better ideas? Because I would be more than happy to hear them." Zhafaera asked sharply, already probing the edges of the section and beginning to attach a platform to it. Delan made no response, which was answer enough for her. When it was complete and she felt confident that it was relatively stable, she went back to the horses, digging through their packs and pulling out two shirts to cover the horses' eyes. The platform should *feel* sturdy, but it would look as though they were walking on thin air. Zhafaera felt slightly ill at the thought.

Evey and Delan flattened themselves against the mountain side, letting Zhafaera lead the horses past them and towards the platform. The horses were clearly unsettled, knowing something was different, but Zhafaera managed to get them moving forward on her platform, focusing on holding it steady while she walked along the broken stone ledge next to them.

Zhafaera sensed Delan and Evey following them closely, but she was too focused on maintaining her footing and the platform and the fact that one misstep or lapse in concentration would lead to an utterly horrifying death to pay them much attention. She was about halfway across when her foot slipped on a loose rock. A tiny scream slipped out of her as she grabbed for the rock face behind her, but she managed to regain her footing. Leaning back against the solid rock, she ignored Delan and Evey's cries of alarm, trying to control her racing heart and focus on holding the platform steady. Shaking slightly, she started to edge forward along the rock ledge again with tiny, steady steps.

And then the rock under her feet simply broke away. She slipped and landed on all fours next to the horses in the center of her platform. She had only a heartbeat to realize that the ledge was crumbling in both directions before the platform gave way and she was falling. Her stomach dropped as she plummeted towards the valley floor, listening to the horses screaming as they fell next to her.

She couldn't hear Delan or Evey, but as she grabbed for all of the magic that she could reach, she realized she could sense them, already a long way above her, falling much slower than she was. She hoped Evey had taken her dragon form. Wings would be useful right about now. Theoretically she could try and shape-shift, but she wasn't at all sure that she could do it fast enough. Plus, that would only save her – she didn't have it in her to just let the horses die. She could feel their utter panic as they fell next to her.

Only moments had passed since the ledge crumbled, but it could have been hours. Zhafaera felt as though she would burst with all of the magic she was holding. She had to try something fast – if the fall didn't kill her, holding this much magic for much longer certainly would. Looking down at the ground that was rapidly getting closer (*oh Gods*), she pushed *down* against the ground, resisting the motion of their fall. She immediately began to slow, but it wasn't enough; the horses flew past her. She began pulling more magic from her core and kept pushing. There was a solid *crunch* and the horses' screaming cut off abruptly. *Delan, I'm sorry, I've failed.* Finally, when the ground was frighteningly close, she couldn't help it – she closed her eyes and with the last of her reserves, she pushed with all her might.

And she stopped. Zhafaera didn't dare breathe. She hovered less than a meter from the rocky ground.

Slowly, shakily, Zhafaera let the air cushion fade, and she lowered gently to the ground, finally dropping only the last few inches.

Zhafaera lay on the cold ground, feeling the show melt into her back despite her fur cloak, too shocked to move, barely able to remember how to breathe. Through sheer force of will, she wasn't dead. She couldn't quite wrap her head around that, so she just laid there and waited, snowflakes drifting into her eyes and blurring her vision. Slowly, she became aware of a rather large shadow descending from the sky towards her with jerky, lopsided motions. It had large wings, and was making some kind of noise, but Zhafaera couldn't make any sense of it.

It wasn't until the creature landed close by with a huge thud that Zhafaera realized that the "creature" was actually Delan and Evey. Evey must have caught him when the ledge collapsed and flown them both down, if only barely. Zhafaera knew she should feel relieved, but she still couldn't feel much of anything, and her body wasn't responding to her instructions to get up.

In seconds, Delan's face came into view above Zhafaera as he fell to his knees next to her. She finally recognized the noise she was hearing was her own name; Delan was calling her name, leaning over and quickly searching her face with eyes filled with complete panic. His hands fluttered over her body checking for injuries, but afraid to touch her.

Zhafaera was finally able to blink. And blink again. It was a few more seconds before she was able to turn her head slightly, enough to look straight at Delan.

"I'm all right," she whispered.

"Gods, Zhafaera, *how*...I thought you were dead," Delan's voice broke slightly, and his eyes were overbright. She thought again about sitting up, but Delan didn't give her the chance. As soon as she moved, he grabbed her shoulders and pulled her hard against his chest, wrapping his arms tightly around her, cradling her head and rocking slightly. Zhafaera couldn't tell who was shaking more, her or Delan. She tried to tell him again that she was fine, but the connection between her brain and mouth wasn't working quite right, and it was all she could do to remember to breathe before everything went black.

**

Velexar paced his study, trying to focus. Something had happened. Something he couldn't explain.

He could still feel Zhafaera through the Sapphire's energy, felt it calling to her as each day she moved closer

210

and closer to the city. But today… today she'd drawn a huge amount of power. And she'd drawn it from the Sapphire.

Velexar had felt the power of the Sapphire rise and crest, draining out quickly and flowing into Zhafaera. At least, he assumed it had been Zhafaera. It certainly wasn't him, and she was the only other person connected to the Sapphire, let alone powerful enough to use it. But she was still much too far away.

It's not possible, he thought.

But it happened.

He'd been arguing with himself all day. The only benefit was that now he had a better idea of where they were – Zhafaera was definitely in the mountains, crossing over somewhere in the western part of the range. He was surprised – they'd gone significantly out of their way, rather than coming straight up from Crystal Point. He didn't know what their game was.

He could use this to his advantage. Now that he knew roughly where she was, he could start planning her capture. He could send more dragons… but not into the mountains, where it was easy to hide. No, he'd have to wait until she came out the other side.

She's more powerful than me. The thought came unbidden, and Velexar squashed it quickly. The Sapphire was *his*, and every day he grew stronger as he learned to control it. The pain was still there, and still intense, but he found he could work past it.

Yes, soon he would have full control. And Zhafaera would be his.

**

Delan sat next to Zhafaera, watching her face as she slept and occasionally brushing a stray strand of her flaming hair back from her pale face. Evey had examined her and assured him she would be fine, that she had simply drained herself magically and just needed to rest, but he couldn't get the image of her body lying still in the snow out of his head.

After Zhafaera fainted, Evey had been the one to take charge. She had forced Delan to get up carrying Zhafaera, and led him to an entrance to one of the old mines that had been mostly hidden by fallen rocks. Delan hadn't even had it in him to be surprised by the dragon's ability to find caves – a side effect of being born and raised in the most massive network of caves on the planet, he assumed. She had started a fire and set the wards. Then it had taken her a full ten minutes to convince Delan that Zhafaera was fine, and that he could set her down and make her comfortable in her bedroll.

They sat around the fire as night fell, no one speaking, still in shock over what had happened. Delan couldn't wrap his mind around how Zhafaera wasn't dead. When the ledge collapsed, he thought that was it, they were all done for. And then Evey had grabbed him in her talons, which was *not* comfortable, and their plummeting had at least slowed. Evey had barely had the strength and coordination to fly with a full-grown man hanging from her feet and dragging them down. But Zhafaera... Zhafaera had fallen like a stone, becoming a speck far below them before Delan had even had time to register that he did not appear to be about to go splat on the rocky ground far below. And then he had heard her say his name in his mind – and then silence. The loudest silence he had ever heard in his life, silence that he was sure meant that Zhafaera had died, silence that had grown until it permeated his entire being, like the entire world had paused as he and Evey half flew, half fell to the valley floor. He knew he should be grateful to Evey for saving him, but all he felt was guilt.

He glanced at the mouth of the cave again, remembering what it was like as he'd gotten close to the ground and saw Zhafaera in the center of a small crater, with cracks spreading out from either side. Looking back on it now, he thought it was lucky she hadn't triggered an avalanche with the way she'd cracked the rock. Then again, maybe it wasn't so lucky. As Delan looked around their hiding spot, he could see spider web cracks in several places on the walls. Hopefully the mountain wasn't going to fall in around them.

He'd done his best with the horses' bodies, stripping them of their packs and covering them with snow. The ground was too rocky and frozen to truly bury them, as much as it pained Delan to leave them like that. Shadow had been his horse for ten years. It felt like losing a friend.

213

Zhafaera was the important one; he had come along to help *her* – she should have been the priority. But there she was, lying still in her bedroll, so pale that Delan couldn't keep from watching her breathe, afraid that if he looked away, she would stop. He knew she was one of the most powerful mages alive, but still…mages can't just make themselves fly on a whim. However she did it, the amount of power it must have taken…he couldn't even imagine. From the look in Evey's eyes as she examined Zhafaera, he guessed that drawing that much power alone could easily have killed her before she even hit the ground. This thought made him take her wrist and check her pulse for the hundredth time – it was still strong and steady.

Putting his head in his hands, Delan tried to breathe. Too much loss was taking its toll. His village, his brother, now even his horse. What would be next? He tried not to imagine what was likely happening to Alec at this very moment. How was a mage turned? Torture? Magic? Most likely both, he eventually decided. He was nearly ten years older than Alec, and had always felt the need to protect him. *Alec needs protecting more than most,* Delan thought, remembering the pirates last summer. Alec had sent fireballs from the top of a tower just like he had done against the dragon. It's why he didn't blame Zhafaera for his brother's capture – Alec couldn't help drawing attention to himself.

Looking up at Evey, he realized that the young dragon appeared to have finally fallen asleep, curled up in her normal position with her back to the mouth of the cave, using her body heat to keep the cold out as the wind howled outside. Delan decided that he might as well try to rest, although he doubted he'd sleep with his thoughts still racing. Slowly, he crawled under the blankets and into the bedroll next to Zhafaera, drawing the blankets up to her chin and draping one arm over her, tucking her close to him. He lay awake for some time, watching the dying embers of the fire flicker red light across Zhafaera's pale face until exhaustion finally took over and he slept.

***

The first thing Zhafaera felt was warmth. Like a golden glow washing over her body, filling her with a deep sense of well-being. She lay still, enjoying the peaceful feeling. As her memory slowly returned, it occurred to her that she probably hadn't actually lived through the fall today – it was probably the magic that had killed her; she had used more than she ever had before, and she was pretty sure that it had been *way* beyond too much. Somehow the strongest feeling she could muster up over being dead was a mild disappointment.

Time passed. Eventually, she heard a whisper, so soft she wasn't sure if it was really there. She opened her eyes to a world of swirling white mist. Sitting up slowly, she looked around and saw nothing but white in all directions. She wasn't concerned – she could still feel that glowing warmth, like the sun shining on her face.

Eventually, she stood and began walking in the direction of the warmth through the unchanging landscape. She had no way to tell how long she walked – everything was just white.

At last, the mist seemed to thin and Zhafaera could make out the shadow of a man. She heard the whisper again – *Zhafaera* – and picked up her pace, swiping her hands out in front of her to push away the mist.

And then she saw him – Delan, standing with his back to her. Looking closely, she could see the fresh holes in his black coat where Evey must have grabbed him earlier. She hoped that his being here didn't mean he had died, too. That would *really* make it all for nothing.

She crossed her arms and smiled, taking a few moments to admire his tall form for what could be the last time. His hair had grown longer and somewhat shaggy in the weeks they'd been traveling – she wondered if she could get away with running her fingers through it. Hells, if she was dead, she may as well do it. Moving silently, easy on such a barren surface (*seriously, are those clouds?*), she snuck up behind Delan until she was almost touching him, then she pounced forward, quickly clapping her hands over his eyes and standing on tip-toe to whisper in his ear, "Guess who?"

Zhafaera wasn't prepared for his reaction. Delan whirled around faster than she would have ever believed humanly possible, grabbed her shoulders, and kissed her. Hard. Hard enough that she couldn't think, couldn't move, couldn't breathe (*do dead people breathe?*). And she was kissing him back, her hands fisting in his shirt and holding on like he was a lifeboat in the middle of a churning ocean. When Delan pulled away momentarily, Zhafaera opened her eyes, meeting his heated gaze before drawing him back to her. He was only too happy to comply, snaking one hand around her back and the other behind her head to crush her mouth against his.

Just when Zhafaera was about ready to crawl out of her own skin and into his, Delan wrenched his mouth away and pulled her tightly against his chest, both of them gasping for breath.

They stood like that for some time, catching their breath and just taking comfort in one another. Finally, when she could finally think in a relatively straight line again, Zhafaera remembered a very important question. Slowly, she pulled back and looked at Delan.

"Did you die, too?" she asked quietly, a small, sad smile on her face.

Delan's eyes went wide, and his hands tightened painfully on her arms. "What?"

"Today, when we fell…and I died…" she waved a hand to indicate their surroundings, because what else could this place be? "Did you make it?"

Delan's mouth worked, but no sound came out, so Zhafaera kept talking – she didn't know how long she had. "Look, you have to keep going, you and Evey. It's up to you to get the Sapphire now – just take it and run, hide it somewhere as far away as you –"

"WHAT?" Delan had finally found his voice. "I – you – why – you're not…"

She reached up and stroked the side of his face. "I love you, Delan."

And then he vanished.

Zhafaera stood there, feeling sad and alone for the first time in weeks. Just as she started to wonder what she should do next (*shouldn't there be a 'light' or some such to walk to?*), the world began to shake. Cracks in the white fog began to appear as the very ground she stood on rocked with enough force to make her lose her balance. She hit the ground on all fours and –

Everything was black, but the world was still moving. There was some kind of red glow to her right, outlining the dark shadow hulking just inches from her face.

She blinked.

The violent shaking stopped.

Delan's face swam into focus above her, cast in deep shadows thrown by the light of the dying fire.

"*Zhafaera?*" His voice was a strangled whisper.

She looked around slowly. She was lying on the floor of what appeared to be a cave. Or at least, she was almost on the floor. Delan's hands gripped her shoulders painfully tight as he held her slightly off the ground – he must have been shaking her. *Well, that makes a lot more sense,* she thought. Evey lay on the other side of the fire, apparently sound asleep; she doubted the dragon could have slept through an *actual* earthquake.

She looked back to Delan. "Sooooo, I'm not dead then?"

There was a choked sound, possibly maybe almost a laugh? She could feel his warm breath brush her lips as he spoke. "No, you are not. But I swear by all the gods and the twelve hells that if you ever scare me like that again, I will kill you myself." And then he kissed her again. His fingers loosened their grip on her shoulders and his arms wrapped around her, cradling her against his body as his lips moved fiercely over hers.

Delan must have sensed her confusion, because he abruptly pulled away. Frowning, he searched her face. "Sorry, I – I think… was that a dream?"

"You mean the part where you kissed me and then I thought I was dead and then you kissed me again?" Zhafaera asked, sounding slightly breathless to her own ears. "Because I'm pretty sure that last part I was awake for."

"Yeah, but that middle part," he said quietly, "the part where you thought you were dead." He cleared his throat. "Was that real? Were we talking in our dreams?"

"Maybe. It can be done," Zhafaera said, trying hard to bring her fuzzy thoughts into focus and think of things besides kissing him again. "But really – how am I *not* dead?"

"Umm, you're a ridiculously powerful mage who can…do really amazing magic?"

She smiled slightly, although she could feel her eyes drooping with exhaustion again. "Well, that explains a lot." She felt, rather than heard, Delan's chuckle. "Truly, that much power should have killed any mage," she whispered.

Delan brushed back a stray curl from her forehead. "You're not 'any mage,' Zhafaera."

She tried to focus on his face and give him a stern look. "You're just saying that so I'll let you kiss me again." *Please kiss me again.*

Delan kissed her gently, first on her forehead, then her nose, and finally just the barest brush on her lips. Then he eased her gently back to the floor and settled down next to her.

Just as she closed her eyes, Delan whispered, "Did you mean what you said?"

Zhafaera winced. She had hoped he'd vanished *before* he heard that. But she wasn't going to lie. "I did," she said quietly, turning her face into his chest to hide her blush.

Delan brushed his hands softly over her hair. "Excellent, because I've been in love with you since I was seventeen."

Zhafaera smiled and looked up at him. "That's lucky."

Delan laughed under his breath. "Go back to sleep, princess."

And Zhafaera slept.

Chapter 9

Zhafaera slept on and off for the next two days, waking only long enough to eat and drink a little before curling back up in her nest of blankets. It was just as well, as the storm outside had become a raging blizzard. They were very nearly trapped in the cave, with huge snow drifts piling up at the already tiny entrance. At least they weren't in danger of freezing to death – between the fire they kept going and the body heat of a dragon, the small space was almost balmy.

On the third morning after their little "shortcut" down into the valley, Zhafaera awoke to low, urgent voices close by.

"I still say we should try it."

I don't think you fully comprehend the dangers inherent in such an experiment. It could go very, VERY wrong. For either of us.

"Yes, you've *said* that." There was a sigh. "But I think it's worth the risk."

What do you know of the risk? You're a...a child in this – barely walking and thinking you're ready to fly.

"Ouch, Evey. Ouch."

I don't understand.

Zhafaera, more awake now, almost smiled at the impatience in Delan's voice. "I'm just saying, we should *try*. I don't even know if I can do it. Zhafaera – she's easy to sense. I always know where she is now. But you...does this even work cross-species?"

I don't know, I'm not in the habit of letting anyone *try and draw magic through me, let alone a* human!

"But—"

At this point, Zhafaera groaned and sat up slowly, completely breaking through the haze of sleep for the first time in days. Delan was by her side in an instant, moving to steady her as she stood and stretched. Flopping back on her bedroll, Zhafaera sat cross-legged and accepted an apple from Delan.

"Can't I leave you two alone for a couple of days without you bickering?" she said with a smile as she crunched her apple.

We weren't 'bickering.'" Evey said with all the dignity she could muster. *We were discussing something.*

"So I heard," Zhafaera said, barely refraining from rolling her eyes. Looking at Delan as he sat beside her and passed her more food, she continued. "I see both sides. I assume you were asking Evey to let you try and draw magic from her?" At Delan's nod, she continued. "Yes, it could be dangerous, but it was also dangerous to let you draw from me. In the beginning at least," Zhafaera added hastily at Delan's look. She looked to Evey. "But I can see how it could come in handy in an emergency. It would be good to know if it can be done." Zhafaera looked down at her empty hands, and then to either side of her, wondering where her breakfast had gone. Delan passed her cheese and another apple. "But it doesn't have to be right now," she continued, reaching out and laying a hand on Delan's knee. "Evey, I won't lie – it can be scary, relinquishing even a little bit of your control over your own power," she ignored Delan's wince. "But...maybe just consider it?" She shrugged. "That's all I've got."

Evey's head was tilted in the way it did when she was processing new information. *I'll think about it. But dragon magic is much more powerful than human magic; it could be dangerous. Once he's more advanced in his training... maybe.* Evey scooted closer and rested her huge, scaly head on Zhafaera's lap. The young dragon let out a deep breath and closed her eyes. *I'm just glad you're all right.*

Zhafaera absently rubbed behind the dragon's spiky ruff, watching the firelight play on the electric blue scales of her face. *Thank you for saving him,* she thought quietly to Evey, being sure to block out Delan's presence on the edge of her awareness so he wouldn't hear.

It was the only thing I could do, Evey replied. *It happened so fast...*

Zhafaera leaned down and rested her cheek on the young dragon's snout, offering comfort and receiving it in return. Finally, she sat up and clapped her hands, startling both Evey and Delan.

"So, guys, what's our next move?" She waved her hand to indicate the storm outside. "I don't think we're going to be able to go that way." Now that she was finally awake, she was filled with nervous energy. Unable to sit still any longer, she stood and began pacing the small corridor. "Velexar must know our general location, even if he doesn't know which pass we took. This storm – Delan, I *told* you it wasn't natural. This is his work – probably hoping that we'll freeze to death…or you know, *fall off the side of a mountain.* That would certainly solve some of his problems." She knew she was rambling but couldn't stop. "We've been in the mountains for how long? More than a week, certainly, and we're barely halfway through. Even with all the extra hunting we did and those preservation spells I put on the meat, we could run out of food – I mean, we have no idea how long this storm will last…it could go on quite a while. Honestly, the fact that he's been able to keep it going this long means that he's probably been able to exert *some* control over the Sapphire – not full control obviously because if he had then he would know exactly where we were – he'd be able to feel us through the ground you see, and—"

Delan caught her by the shoulders before she could wear a path in the floor. "Zhafaera, breathe. We have a plan." He guided her back to her seat as she tried to calm herself down.

She felt somewhat silly – of course, they had made plans while she recovered; did she really think they had just sat there watching her sleep? She was just used to being the one in charge, the strong one – even before the coup. Her mother had always been somewhat… flighty. Powerful, yes. And strong willed. But always distracted, on the move, never able to focus on one task for long. And then suddenly, she stopped. They hadn't left the city for *years* before the coup; Zhafaera had barely even left the palace. Her mother had been gone long before she'd actually died, and Zhafaera had been alone.

Jerking herself away from that line of thought, Zhafaera gave herself a shake. "Okay, let's hear this master plan of yours."

Delan hung an arm around her shoulders and attempted to smile, but he was clearly worried about her. "Well, really, it's simple – we keep following the route Evey took through the mountains the first time."

Looking from Delan to Evey, Zhafaera was confused. "Okay, so where to next?"

I spent a good part of my journey in the old mines. Evey sounded confident. *I can find my way back through.* She paused. *This isn't the* exact *way I came, but I grew up in caves like this. I'll be able to tell which way is out.*

"Yes, but—" Zhafaera could feel panic bubbling up from her belly. When they had decided to take Evey's route, Zhafaera had conveniently ignored the fact that much of Evey's journey had been through the mines. The thought of being stuck underground in a dark, confined space made Zhafaera want to scream. "How long would it take us? Do we have enough supplies? What if we take a wrong turn?" She took a deep breath.

Delan squeezed her shoulders briefly. "Evey says she can find the way through. It couldn't take as long as it would to try and fight our way through this storm." He

225

gestured towards the back of their cave. "This is an entrance. We don't even have to go outside."

She understood the logic, really, she did. But she *hated* the dark. And confined spaces. And spiders. Ugh.

This was going to suck. But as much as she hated it, she didn't have a better idea, and if there was one thing she couldn't stand, it was people whining about a plan without having a suggestion of their own.

"Fine," she said, trying to sound confident but knowing she failed. "But if we die in those mines, I'm coming back to haunt the both of you."

That night, Zhafaera couldn't sleep. After spending two solid days sleeping, her mind just wasn't having it, and her thoughts raced. Delan lay next to her, breathing evenly, his solid presence comforting to her.

Sighing quietly, she rolled over yet again, turning her back to Delan, and tried to snuggle closer to him without waking him. She knew he needed the sleep – based on the dark circles under his eyes, she guessed that he hadn't slept well while she'd been recovering from her magical exhaustion. It was sweet that he worried about her, but she felt guilty for causing him such distress.

As if sensing her thoughts, Delan's arm wrapped around her waist and squeezed her gently, while his head dipped to her neck and he took a deep breath, inhaling her scent.

"Relax," he whispered softly, planting a soft kiss behind her ear.

She turned her head slightly so she could see him out of the corner of her eye. "Sorry, I didn't mean to wake you," she whispered back.

He shook his head and nuzzled her neck softly, his fingers beginning to trace slow circles on her bare hand. The move, while comforting, had the opposite effect of lulling her to sleep – her heart immediately started to race. His hands were rough and calloused, and the contrast of his rough fingers against her smooth skin gave her chills. Slowly, his hand moved up her arm, gently massaging the tension from her muscles as he worked his way up to her shoulder and brushed her hair gently away from her face and neck. From there, he trailed his fingers lightly down her back, her thin undershirt providing only scant protection from the scorching heat of his skin. Down over her shoulder blade, lower and lower until his hot touch grazed her hip and she gasped.

At that moment, Evey snuffled in her sleep, and they both jumped. Delan jerked his hand back to a more appropriate height, and they held their breath, waiting to see if Evey would wake. After a minute, they relaxed, but Zhafaera was torn between wanting to laugh and a sense of shame. She loved her mother, but how often had Zhafaera criticized her for sleeping with any man she could? It was one of their most contentious arguments. And yet here she was about to do the same. She sighed and tried to reason with herself. *She* actually loved Delan; surely that made a difference.

***

Zhafaera and Evey took turns creating the light to guide them through the old mining tunnels. Delan occasionally took a turn – Zhafaera was impressed at how quickly Delan was learning – despite the lack of regular lessons, he at least got the basic idea. Controlling your magic was all about your will – and Delan was smart enough, and persistent enough, to make it do what he wanted. Come to think of it, that was probably why she liked him. She wasn't used to being around someone who could keep up with her. It was…refreshing.

They hadn't spoken about last night, and Zhafaera had been afraid it would be awkward, but it wasn't. After sleeping on her feelings, Zhafaera thought now was probably a good time to let go of her old resentments and move forward. She was in an odd limbo, both slightly nervous and completely comfortable with Delan. Nothing had changed, except they seemed to touch more. Just little touches – hardly noticeable really – but Zhafaera found herself smiling anyway.

Until she walked through *yet another* gods cursed spider web. Her squeal echoed down the empty shaft as she flailed her arms, frantically brushing away the sticky strands as she felt for the giant hairy spider that she knew was crawling over her somewhere. She turned to Delan, who knew the drill by now. Bringing his light close, he inspected her closely (perhaps a little *too* closely based on the way his gaze lingered), brushing his fingers lightly

228

over her braid before declaring her spider-free. Zhafaera shuddered as they moved on.

"I still don't get it," Delan said, shaking his head. "You can face down angry dragons no problem, but when it comes to tiny arachnids you completely lose your mind." He chuckled as he dodged her shove.

"It freaks me out that they could be *anywhere* and I wouldn't know it – sneaky bastards." She made a face.

Suddenly, Delan leaned in close and clamped his hand on her shoulder, and then quickly removed it, looking at his palm in mild distaste.

Zhafaera was confused. *What the…?* She jumped and beat at her shoulder. "There was a spider on me, wasn't there?"

Delan quickly hid his hand behind his back. "Nope. I checked. No spiders."

"*I know you're lying!*" Zhafaera's voice was much too high.

He slung an arm around her shoulders as they kept walking. "Why, Princess, I would never!"

She shoved him away. "Don't hug me with your spider-guts hand!"

"Don't worry, I already wiped it on your cloak."

Zhafaera whacked him on the arm. "You're disgusting."

With insanely fast reflexes, Delan stopped, grabbed her around the waist and yanked her close. "That's not what you said last night," he murmured softly into her ear.

229

Before she could respond, he kissed her swiftly on the temple, winked, and carried on down the dark corridor, leaving Zhafaera to scurry behind him, trying to stay within his circle of light while she debated giving him a swift kick in his (rather fine-looking) rear.

I can feel you ogling me, Delan's mind-voice was heavily amused.

Just as Zhafaera opened her mouth to make a smart comment, Evey's voice cut in. The dragon was leading the column, a faint blue light emanating from her scales as she led them through the tunnels.

Human mating rituals are strange.

Zhafaera closed her mouth.

Quickly catching up to Delan, they glanced sideways at one another, then back at Evey. Delan opened his mouth, paused, then closed it again. He looked at Zhafaera and shrugged. She smothered a giggle.

Evey stopped, and Zhafaera nearly tripped over her long tail.

"Oof! Sorry Evey –"

What's funny? Her head was tilted to the side.

"Nothing," Delan managed to choke out, clearly trying hard to compose himself.

Okay, well, we're at a fork, so try and pay attention and not get lost. Zhafaera fully expected the dragon to roll her eyes.

"Yes, Evey," Delan said obediently.

"Which way?" Zhafaera asked, getting herself under control. Zhafaera could barely make out the diverging tunnels. Their lights helped, but they barely penetrated more than a few feet in the clinging darkness. For her part, Zhafaera was mostly just following the glowing dragon.

Evey moved off to the left. *It's this way.*

Zhafaera had stopped questioning how the dragon knew the way about ten forks ago. Something about the smell of the rock...? Earth magic had never really come easily to her. They continued on.

Spending the day in pitch darkness was disorienting. There was no way to tell time, and they quickly started to lose track. They hadn't really stopped, preferring to eat and walk, and they were finally starting to feel the pace. It wasn't long before Zhafaera finally called a stop for what felt like the end of the day. They didn't bother setting up much of a camp, simply spreading out their bedrolls and eating a cold supper. A fire wouldn't work – there was nowhere for the smoke to go in these mines.

Zhafaera decided to take advantage of their isolated position and take the time to give Delan lessons. Now that he had some degree of control and was learning to refill and manage his reserves, she could start teaching him the next steps. He was quick to pick up anything fire-based, but they hadn't really tried any other elements. Seeing as how they were surrounded by rock, Zhafaera thought it was the perfect time to start getting him to work with Earth.

Drawing in energy from the surrounding rock, she opened herself and let Delan draw magic through her. Zhafaera reached out and grabbed a stone about the size of her two fists and set it in front of them. "Okay," she said, "let's start with 'move a rock.'"

Delan looked at the rock, raising an eyebrow at it. "Sure. No problem."

Evey watched intently as Delan focused. He glanced at Zhafaera a few times but didn't speak. He knew that he could ask for more direction but that Zhafaera liked to let him try to figure it out for himself first.

Evey wasn't quite so patient. *Stop trying to* tell *the rock to move and just* move *it already.*

Delan shot her a glare that had Zhafaera struggling not to smile. Just when she decided she should probably move in and give some pointers, the rock shot across the narrow mine shaft and *pinged* off the opposite wall. Evey flattened herself to the floor as the rock flew over her head.

"OH crap, Evey – sorry, are you okay?" Delan asked, flinching. "I swear, that's not what I was trying to do."

Evey looked only mildly offended, which, granted, on a dragon, was still pretty terrifying. *Well what* were *you trying to do?*

"Well, you *said* just move it, so I imagined just sort of… flicking it? I guess I flicked it a little harder than I thought."

Hmph, Evey said, but Zhafaera thought there was a distinct note of pride in her mind-voice. *I suppose it's to be expected. But you'll have more control if you feel for the individual parts, rather than the whole.* A long talon twitched and the rock flicked back over and came to rest in front of Delan. *This rock is not one cohesive piece. Do*

you see the different colored flecks within the stone here?
She was pointing delicately with one sharp claw while
Delan leaned closer and nodded. *They each have their own
feel and will respond differently. Once you can focus on
the individuals, you can make them do what you want,
independent of what the whole currently is.*

Delan looked at Zhafaera for confirmation. "Hey,
she's the resident rock expert," Zhafaera said, waving a
hand to indicate Evey. "But, yes, that's essentially how it
was explained to me at one point. I'm just not great at
feeling the 'individuals.'"

Delan put a hand to his chest in mock surprise. "Do
you mean to say there's actually something you *can't* do?"

"I didn't say that – I can *do* it, it just takes more effort.
So you know, I tend to just let other people punch holes in
the sides of buildings for me."

"I'll get right on that, Princess," Delan said, slinging
an arm around her shoulders.

It was amazing how quickly he could distract her. Her
heart rate immediately sped up at his touch, and she
instinctively leaned in closer to him. He tightened his grip,
but Evey had already taken charge of the lesson.

*Again, you two are very, um... cute? Is that the word?
But can we finish this first?*

Zhafaera looked up at Delan and grinned, then pulled
away, making shooing motions with her hands as she
scooted further away to avoid temptation.

Delan sighed and said, "Sorry Mistress Evey, please
continue your lesson."

And there's the head tilt, Zhafaera thought, stifling a giggle. Gods, she had never been a giggler before, and now was so not the time to start. But really, Evey's classic confused look was adorable.

By the time they had finished, Delan had managed to mold the little rock into a number of different shapes, finally ending by shaping it into a perfect sphere. Evey looked quite pleased with her student, but Delan just looked worn out. Zhafaera was a bit tired from being the conduit for the magic, but she at least hadn't needed the concentration that Delan had maintained for the last hour. As soon as Evey declared Delan talented and the lesson done for the night, the three of them finally bedded down for the night.

Zhafaera couldn't resist. She slid in close to Delan, and was rewarded when he wrapped his arms tightly around her and kissed first the top of her head, then her forehead, then her nose, and finally her lips. This kiss was slow and gentle; tender, but playful. She loved it. And then it stopped. Zhafaera opened her eyes and looked up at Delan questioningly. It was pitch dark in the mines, but a faint blue glow coated Delan's face. Zhafaera looked over her shoulder and found Evey still awake, watching them curiously, and still glowing faintly. Zhafaera could feel herself blushing. Flirting in front of the dragon was one thing, but… anything else was quite another. She was a very young dragon, after all. Not quite a child, but still.

"Sorry, Evey," Zhafaera whispered. "Didn't mean to keep you awake." Rolling back over, she bit her lip to keep from laughing as she buried her face against Delan's chest. She knew Evey was only curious, but that didn't make it less awkward.

Delan gently stroked her back and ran his fingers through her hair, slowly relaxing her until finally, after some time, she drifted off to sleep.

***

By their third day in the mines, Delan had forgotten what sunlight looked like. He was starting to feel like they were going to be stuck here in the dark forever until they eventually just turned into little mole people that *couldn't* go out in sunlight.

The only bright side (if anything could be considered "bright" down here) was that Delan had discovered he had quite a talent for Earth magic. It had taken him no time at all to learn to sense the individual pieces that made up the giant slabs of rock surrounding them. The mines they traveled were still rich in copper ore, the veins crossing their path at regular intervals and glowing brightly to Delan's eyes, once he learned how to look. And now today, he thought he was beginning to understand how Evey knew the way through the mines. It wasn't really something he could put his finger on, just a feeling really. But so far, he had known the direction that Evey was going to take them at each turn that day, without really knowing why. It was almost like a gentle tug, an affinity for one direction over the others. Honestly, it was weird. Zhafaera was the one that was supposed to be good at this stuff, but she was jumpy and on edge underground. While Delan longed for sunshine, he was starting to find the feeling of being surrounded by rock somewhat comforting.

He looked at Zhafaera, walking on his left. She looked pale in the combination of light cast by the orb she currently held and the blue glow cast by Evey leading the way.

Delan reached out and took Zhafaera's hand lightly in his own, smiling at her when she looked at him. He worried about her. He knew she could take care of herself, but she was so used to doing things on her own, he worried that she wouldn't know to ask for help when she needed it. He worried that she didn't know that he would do anything, *everything*, for her, the instant that she asked, and he wasn't sure how to tell her.

He thought she meant it when she told him she loved him in the dream, but she kept a tight hold on her feelings. Usually when they were connected, the only clear emotion he could pick out from the jumble of feelings that made up Zhafaera was grief. Grief for her mother, for her country, for everything that should have been. Even the other night, when they had almost been… intimate… he hadn't been able to sense much beyond desire, both his and hers. And desire was different from love. Delan wanted both.

As if sensing his thoughts, Zhafaera squeezed his hand and nudged him. "What are you thinking about so seriously?"

His first instinct was to laugh it off, make some stupid joke and carry on walking. But instead, he stopped and pulled her close, searching her face intently for reassurance that she felt the same as he did, reaching out with his own magic to connect with hers. Her eyes widened as he caressed her, stroking his thumb down her cheek and gently touching her lips while his magic entwined with her own, searching, searching…

There was grief, yes, but fainter now. Anger, loyalty, fear, a fierce protectiveness and… there. What was that? Down deep, close to the core that made her Zhafaera, was something bright, almost like her magic but not. It was warmth and happiness and peace and trust all mixed together. Love? Maybe. He tried to delve deeper, to explore that seemingly endless well of brightness, but suddenly he was kicked back, and found himself still looking into Zhafaera's eyes. She looked both amused and… fearful?

"Stop that," she said, sternly. At his confused look, her gaze softened into amusement. "Didn't your mother ever teach you not to go poking around in other people's emotions? It's quite rude, you know."

Delan was embarrassed – that really should have been common sense, but he'd been so focused on finding the truth that he hadn't thought about what it would feel like to her as he rifled through her emotions. "Sorry, Princess," he said quietly, releasing her and looking away. He made to move forward – Evey's glowing blue form had moved

237

quite a ways ahead of them – but Zhafaera stopped him with a hand on his arm.

"Apology accepted," she said with a smile. Then she stood on her tiptoes and quickly kissed him on the mouth. "Perhaps as punishment, I should go searching through *your* head," she said with a wicked grin.

Delan made to grab her and pull her back to him for a proper kiss, but she danced out of reach with a laugh. He stepped forward towards her, intending to pin her against the wall if he had to, and Zhafaera took another step back and to the side –

Delan blinked. Zhafaera was gone. Vanished into thin air. Then he heard it – a faint scream that was getting fainter by the second. Rushing forward, he started to yell for her, and then the air was sucked out of him as he fell. Straight down through a hole in the floor barely big enough for a man. He bumped against the walls on either side – rough rock that scraped at his clothes as he fell, trying to grab him and hold him there forever. His heart was in his throat, choking his yell as he plummeted towards who-knew-what. Hopefully a few thick feather mattresses. Or water. Yes, he'd take water over hard, unyielding stone any day. He fell for what felt like ages, until suddenly he realized the shaft was narrowing, his descent slowing as the angle shifted until finally his sword wedged against a rock and he stopped.

Oh gods, this is worse than falling. I'm going to die here.

As panic rose in him like hot bile, Delan tried to think. *Okay, come on, you're a mage now, you can fix this.* He reached into his core, feeling for his reserves and hoping that maybe there was enough in there to do something that might help. It took him several tries, his heart feeling like it would pound out of his chest, but finally, *finally* he got a hold on his magic. Spreading tendrils into the rock surrounding him, he tried to force the shaft wider. Nothing happened. The surrounding rock was too thick – there was nowhere for it to move to. Fighting a panic like he'd never felt before, he tried again, this time trying to feel for the individual pieces in the rock, and the minute spaces between them, trying to mold the rock into something denser, molding it so that every nook and cranny of empty space within his magical reach were packed with rock until he felt the now-smooth shaft widen. Suddenly, he was falling again, but this time it was a short trip. Within seconds, he felt the shaft disappear altogether, followed by pain as he hit a rock floor.

Gasping, trying to refill his lungs with air, he laid still. Off to his right a light flared, and he heard Zhafaera whisper, "Delan?"

He listened as she scrambled over and fell to her knees next to him. As she reached him, he was finally able to get a breath, sucking air into his lungs as he reached for Zhafaera. They didn't speak, just reached for each other both physically and magically, feeling for injuries. By the time they were each satisfied that the other was unhurt, Delan had caught his breath and found himself clinging to

Zhafaera as though his life depended on it, trembling uncontrollably.

Or was that her? It was hard to tell, they were so intertwined. Zhafaera was on his lap, her hands finally coming to rest on either side of his head, turning his face up to hers as she bent down and kissed him with a ferocity that would have stunned him, had he not been kissing her back just as hard. The shock of being alive had left him numb, but here was something he could cling to. Something to ground him and take his mind away from the feeling of being trapped between thousands of pounds of rocks.

Eventually, as the adrenaline from the fall wore off, they parted enough to breathe. Delan was almost panting, his heart still pounding entirely too fast. He leaned back, looking up at Zhafaera and running his fingers through her hair.

"I don't remember you being such a klutz," he breathed.

Zhafaera pulled back, frowning. "...what?"

"Well, you realize that's the second time you've fallen off this mountain. I guess this time you fell *into* it rather than *off* of it, but still. Seems a bit klutzy to me."

Zhafaera rolled her eyes and tried to push off of him, but he held tight.

"You have some nerve, you know that?" she asked.

"Comes from getting stuck in the shoot on the way down. I think my brain got a little squished."

"Please, you've always been this way." But Zhafaera looked at him more closely. "You got stuck?" He thought she paled, but it was hard to tell in the glow from her magical light.

He couldn't help shivering slightly, remembering the feel of the rock pressing in on him from all sides. "Yeah. For the record: not fun." He looked around at the tunnel they were in. "And I had to um…compress the rock a little to get out? So I'm kind of hoping that the mountain is still structurally sound and isn't about to crash down around our ears."

Zhafaera looked around, eyeing the walls and ceiling warily. "That's what that was? I thought I felt you pulling from me. I wasn't sure – I was too busy recovering from catching myself. Again." She paused and looked thoughtful. "I really do need to quit falling, don't I?"

"Told you."

Zhafaera looked like she was about to reply with a witty comment about how she was totally *not* a klutz, but she froze, her mouth open.

"Do you hear that?" she asked, looking around.

Delan listened. And heard a small, lost voice calling for Zhafaera.

Evey? Delan heard her think.

Zhafaera! Came the dragon's frantic thought. She sounded distant and muffled. *What happened to you? Is Delan with you? Are you all right? You just vanished!*

Guilt flooded Delan. They had ditched the young dragon. Unintentionally, but still.

Yes, we're all right, she replied. She finally stood and looked around, strengthening and lifting her light higher to give them a better view. Delan followed. They were in another tunnel that looked identical to the one they fell from. He looked up and found the hole in the ceiling where they had fallen.

It looks like we fell through some kind of ventilation shaft, Delan added.

You mean this tiny hole in the floor? Evey sounded horrified. *How did you even fit?*

I almost didn't, Delan thought. He felt Zhafaera shiver slightly beside him. *I don't recommend trying it.*

Yes, thank you, I think I'll stay up here. But what are we going to do?

Zhafaera was quiet, clearly thinking. But there was no way they could climb back up. "Delan, can you sense the way out from here? I know you were getting good by watching Evey."

Delan froze, and he looked at her like she was crazy. "I honestly have no idea. Maybe. Or maybe we'd get stuck down here forever."

Zhafaera nodded. *Evey, we're going to have to split up for now. We have our packs – that's going to have to get us through until we can get back together.*

"Zhafaera, I appreciate your confidence in me, but I really don't know if I can –"

"You can," she cut Delan off. "We'll figure it out." She took his hand and squeezed. Delan tried to find the same confidence.

242

Look, Evey, if we get separated – I mean, if we can't sense each other any more – just find the river when you get out. Follow it down the mountain. There's a lake at the bottom, with a village. We'll meet at the lake if we can't feel each other before then. Stay on the opposite side of the lake from the village, and we'll find you. Zhafaera sounded completely sure of herself.

How hard could it be to find a dragon? Delan thought. Assuming they weren't all trapped down here forever.

All right. Evey sounded nervous, and Delan was reminded again just how young the dragon was. *We'll meet there if we lose touch.*

See you soon, Zhafaera thought.

Within the hour, neither of them could sense Evey any more. Delan could tell Zhafaera was worried about Evey, but he figured the dragon had a better chance of finding her way out of this warren than they did and tried to focus on their own problems. The path they walked seemed to slope down, which really didn't seem like the direction they wanted to go, but so far they hadn't had a choice.

"Can you feel anything?" Zhafaera finally asked. She looked anxious, and watched the walls like they might start closing in on them at any moment.

Delan paused and closed his eyes, drawing on Zhafaera's magic. Finally he shrugged and opened his eyes. "A lot of these tunnels. A fork up ahead."

Within minutes, they came to the fork Delan had felt. They stopped, and Delan closed his eyes again. He was quiet for a long time, trying to focus. Each path

243

felt…different, but sorting through them all took time. Finally, he pointed to the right. "That way," he said.

Zhafaera frowned. "Delan, that way is still sloping down. The others look more level."

Delan opened his eyes and looked closely. "I don't know – I just feel like down is the way to go." He looked at Zhafaera worriedly. "It's like a maze that I can only see certain parts of at a time. I can feel which general direction is out, and I can see a few turns ahead, but not all the way to the end."

Zhafaera put on a smile, though she was starting to feel trapped, like the walls themselves were watching them. "One turn at a time then, yeah?"

"Yeah," Delan said, taking her hand and squeezing.

Chapter 10

By the time they were ready to stop for the day (or night –
who knew what time it was in the outside world), Zhafaera
was relatively certain that she wouldn't be able to find her
way back to where they had fallen even if her life
depended on it. Earth magic was *really* not her strong suit.
She didn't want to say she'd be lost without Delan,
but…she would have been lost. His confidence had
seemed to grow as the day went on, and she had enjoyed
watching him start to use his magic without thought, as an
extension of himself like she'd been teaching him.
Unfortunately for her, his use of magic required pulling it
from her first, and with that on top of the pale sphere of
light she had been holding for them all day, she was
exhausted.

Checking for any more bottomless holes first,
Zhafaera plopped down on the cave floor and leaned back
against the wall, ignoring the small bit of rock poking into
her back. Delan sat down only slightly more gracefully
next to her and began looking through their pack, as
Zhafaera leaned her head back against the cool rock and
closed her eyes.

"We're going to have to really be careful with our
food and water down here. I don't know how long it will

take us to get through." Delan was speaking almost to himself, but Zhafaera's heart still tightened at the thought of spending an unknown amount of time in the belly of the mountain. She felt something brush over her lap and started, her eyes flying open and hands reaching for knives before she realized it was just a blanket. As her heart rate returned to normal, she gave Delan a weary smile. They had been warm enough while walking, but now that she had stopped moving, she felt the cold, stale air of the caves creeping into her skin.

"Here," Delan said, handing her some food from their pack, while keeping some for himself. Zhafaera *was* hungry, she realized. She hadn't eaten since that… morning? She wasn't sure how long ago that was exactly, but it was long enough.

They ate their small meals quickly and in silence, both too tired for their normal banter. When they had both finished, Zhafaera scooted closer to Delan, lifting the blanket and spreading it to cover his lap as well. She leaned over and rested her head on Delan's shoulder, closing her eyes. After a moment, she felt his cheek touch the top of her head, and she took a deep breath, trying to relax. After several minutes of sitting this way, Zhafaera finally worked up the nerve to ask the question she'd been wondering all day.

"Delan?" She whispered.

"Mhmm," he muttered sleepily.

"Why… why did you jump in after me?" Zhafaera asked quietly. "The fall could have killed me – why did you follow?"

Delan was quiet for a moment. "I didn't think. I just… I saw you disappear, and I just… followed." He shrugged and lifted his head off of hers. "I didn't actually know you'd fallen down a mine shaft until I was falling, too." Looking up, Zhafaera rolled her eyes and smiled at him.

"Well, that explains a lot," she teased, shaking her head slightly.

Delan smiled slightly and reached up to brush a strand of hair from her face. Tucking the errant strand behind her ear he said softly, "Even if I had known, I still would have gone after you."

"Why?" Zhafaera whispered.

"Because without you… I… well, I'd rather take my chances diving headfirst into a bottomless pit."

Zhafaera blushed, but didn't look away from his intense gaze. After a moment, Delan leaned down, pausing just briefly before brushing a light kiss over her lips. Though it was nothing like their earlier kiss, caught up in the heat of being alive, it still made Zhafaera's heart race and her breath catch in her throat. When she didn't pull away, Delan reached a hand to her face, brushing across her cheek and around to the back of her neck, where his fingers stretched up into her hair as he deepened the kiss. Zhafaera leaned into the kiss, reaching one hand around his waist and pulling him closer, while her other hand slid up his chest, coming to rest over his heart, which was beating just as hard as her own. Wrapping both arms tightly around her, Delan eased her gently to the floor, neither of them noticing when the light she'd held all day flickered out.

Zhafaera relaxed into Delan's arms as he began to unbutton her shirt. It was easier now; her resolution to move forward helped spur her on. Reaching up, she wound her fingers into his hair as he released her mouth and bent to drop light kisses along her throat. With no one to interrupt them this time, Zhafaera let herself drift, lost in sensations as coherent thought fled.

***

Delan awoke slowly the next morning, disoriented by the pitch black surrounding him. Finally he remembered – they were deep in the mountain caves, where the only light would come from whatever Zhafaera conjured.

He could feel Zhafaera next to him but couldn't see her. Rolling over carefully so as not to wake her, he slipped an arm around her waist, feeling her soft skin against his palm and smiling at the memory of the previous night. He wasn't sure how long they lay like that before she started to stir. Gently brushing her hair out of the way, he placed a light kiss on the back of her neck. At his touch, she rolled over onto her back and stretched, and he could feel her smile.

"What time is it?" she asked groggily.

Delan raised his eyebrows, though she couldn't see it. "Hells if I know down here."

"Oh, right," Zhafaera said, coming more fully awake. She rolled towards him and tucked her head against his chest. "Five more minutes."

Kissing the top of her head, Delan trailed his hand up and down her back, taking just a few more minutes of relaxation before he knew they had to start hunting their way through this maze again. Pulling just a bit of magic through Zhafaera, he reached out and tried to feel his way along the tunnels again. There was another fork not far ahead. Focusing, he thought they'd need to go right. Zhafaera sighed against him.

"I guess we should get moving," she said.

"Probably, if we ever want to get out of this place," Delan said, pulling her close and holding her tight for a moment before releasing her. He sat up and looked around – or at least tried to – everything was still pitch black. Feeling around, he couldn't find what he was looking for.

"Uh, Zhafaera?"

"Yes?" She sounded amused.

"I'm going to need a light to get dressed."

Instantly, the cave filled with the dim light of Zhafaera's orb. Momentarily blinded by the sudden light after the complete darkness, Delan threw his arm up to cover his eyes. As he did, he felt fabric hit the back of his head, and heard Zhafaera's laughter.

***

Six days had passed – or at least, they had stopped to sleep six times – since they fell, and Zhafaera was really starting to consider the idea that they might die down here. The food had run out yesterday, and they were low on water. Delan said they were getting close to an exit, but it all felt the same to Zhafaera – like she was buried alive in rock and was slowly suffocating. Everything was starting to blur together, and she felt worn down. They hadn't spoken much that day, Delan focused on finding the way out and Zhafaera on her own misery. By the time that they stopped for the "night," Zhafaera was about ready to crawl out of her skin – like her desire for light and the warmth of the sun would cause her to combust at any moment. She flopped on the ground in the middle of the tunnel, not wanting to touch the walls, and laid spread eagle, trying to imagine that she was in a wide-open meadow with blue skies above her. It wasn't working.

"Are you all right?" Delan asked.

Zhafaera sat up suddenly. "No. No, I'm really not. I'm trapped underground and my skin is crawling as the walls close in around us and my bones ache like they're already being crushed by the gazillion tons of rock on top of us. We're never going to get out of here, we'll never find Evey, or Alec, or the Sapphire, and Velexar is going to break the world while our bodies lay down here and rot!" The last part came out as a choked yell.

Delan reached for her but she threw out a hand. "Don't touch me!" she yelled at him, and he drew back as if burned. She didn't dare look at his face, but she could sense she'd hurt him, leaving her feeling even worse than before. Great.

Moving a few feet away, Delan sat with his back against the wall of the tunnel, giving her space. Zhafaera curled up as small as she could, wrapping her arms around her knees and trying not to cry.

Zhafaera, Delan's mind-voice brushed gently against her own. *You feel like you did just before we found Evey. Listen – are* you *actually upset or is something wrong magically?* Each word was spoken carefully and clearly, as if he wanted her to understand but didn't want to upset her further.

Zhafaera's initial thought was more anger – couldn't she even be allowed to just feel sorry for herself now? – but the more rational part of her brain considered it. She tried to extend herself into their surroundings, and found that she couldn't. The trapped feeling was coming from her mind, not just the walls of the (*gods-cursed*) tunnel. As she reached deeper for her magic, she met pain – blinding pain threatening to split her head in two as the screaming of the Sapphire was pushed to the forefront of her mind for the first time in months. Gripping her head in both hands, she gritted her teeth and tried to see through the pain, deeper into her magic until – *pop*!

The pain was gone, and power was flowing through her. Opening her eyes, she found that she was sitting on a black-and-white tiled floor. Looking up, she found that the room was mostly dark, with only a bit of moonlight

251

shining through the tall windows along one side of the room. After her time in the mines, it was plenty of light to make out a tall man standing only feet from her, the moonlight glinting off of his sleek black robe as he turned to face her.

"Ah, my dear niece," the figure said. "I thought I felt you. I was wondering if you'd be able to recognize my magic."

Zhafaera just looked at Velexar, unable to move, unable to comprehend what had happened.

Velexar continued, "It's the Sapphire – it keeps reaching for you. We're connected through it. Yes, it feels quite awful when it's angry. Makes it very difficult to control a nation, you know. The feeling that your bones are going to snap out of your skin at any moment is a bit distracting." She thought he might have shivered. "But we'll come to an… arrangement soon enough." The moonlight glinted off of his perfect teeth as he smiled down at her. "You're much quieter than I remember. Finally learned to hold your tongue, did you? Well, that's certainly an improvement."

Zhafaera stood, willing herself to stand straight. "I hate you," she hissed.

He shook his head sadly. "As I expected. But your mother brought this on herself. Hardly my fault that she decided to fight me. If she had just done what she was told, all of this could have been avoided." He clapped his hands together, making Zhafaera jump. "You and your friend are still in the mines, yes?" Zhafaera didn't answer, but

Velexar nodded all the same. "Yes, that'll be perfect for this spell – there's only so many exits on this side of the mountains." He waved his hand at her. "Run along, my dear. You won't want to miss this."

Zhafaera dove for him, ready to strangle him with her bare hands, but suddenly the tiled room dissolved into the rock of the *damn-them-to-hell*s mines, and Delan was scurrying backwards from her as fast as he could as she flew towards him.

"Zhafaera, stop, it's me!" Delan cried.

Zhafaera managed to halt her forward charge and found herself trembling. Delan slowly edged back to her, approaching her as one might approach an injured wild animal – afraid, but concerned.

"Delan, we have to get out of here *right now!*" Her voice sounded on the edge of hysteria even to her ears. "Velexar knows we're here, and he's using the Sapphire to do something."

"Do what?" Delan asked carefully.

"I don't *know*," Zhafaera was close to full-blown panic now. She grabbed Delan and ran down the tunnel, just as a low rumble sounded behind them.

"Oh gods, he's going to bring the mountain down on us," Zhafaera panted as she ran.

"Can he do that?" Delan called to her over the rumbling.

"PROBABLY!"

Zhafaera and Delan ran, but the rumbling was now closer on their right. Suddenly they came to a fork. The

253

darkness in the right-hand tunnel seemed to be moving, boiling almost. Then, from the blackness, came one long, hairy leg. Then another, and another, until an enormous, hairy spider stood before them. Zhafaera froze as it reached one of its long legs out and wrapped it around her leg, preparing her to yank her into the giant pincers looming in front of her. The feeling of its leg on her made her want to curl up and die right there. Instead, she did what she usually did in situations like this: threw a fireball right at its big ugly face. Then turned and ran.

"Left!" Delan yelled, grabbing her arm to keep her from going back deeper into the mines. They darted down the left-hand fork just as the giant spider roared. *Spiders can make a noise?* Zhafaera thought as more spiders of all sizes burst forth – the smallest the size of a pin, the largest twice the size of a horse.

How far? Zhafaera thought to Delan, unable to waste precious oxygen screaming when there was a horde of spiders chasing them.

Not very. Keep straight.

They passed two more forks and took the middle path each time, Zhafaera throwing fireballs behind them every so often. Zhafaera's lungs burned, but she didn't care – she did *not* sign up for death by spider.

Finally, her nose caught a whiff of fresh air, and she forced her legs to move faster. As the exit grew closer, the air grew warmer and more humid. She could see the light at the end of the tunnel, probably only moonlight, but it seemed so bright to her after more than a week in the dark mines. Beyond that, she could make out a lake, and then square shapes that could only be houses.

As they burst out from the side of the mountain, Zhafaera stopped, breathing hard. *Can't let man-eating spiders into a village,* she thought, drawing as much magic to her as she could. It felt good pulling from something other than rock. She could feel the placid waters of the lake, energy swirling through its depths; she could feel the energy of the living trees around her, the wind whipping through their leaves and across her face; the glow of the moon bathed her in light. She pulled as much magic to her as she could and spun towards the cave, preparing to throw it all into a shield that covered the entire exit of the mine shaft.

She froze. There were no spiders. There was nothing but darkness. No long, hairy legs or giant pincers reaching towards her.

Zhafaera dropped the shields and doubled over with her hands on her knees, trying to catch her breath. *What the hell?* She resisted the urge (barely) to rip all her clothes off and burn them, just in case they had tiny spiders in them – it had seemed so *real*. She sensed Delan next to her, as tired as she was, and reached out her hand to touch his arm.

He jumped and turned, fists up as if to fight, before he realized what had touched him.

"Gods, Zhafaera," he panted. He looked like he wanted to say more but didn't have the breath to finish his sentence.

"What... were you going... to do?... *Punch* the giant spider... in the face?" She took a few more deep breaths.

Delan looked at the mine entrance for the first time and frowned. "What the – what happened to the spiders?"

"Velexar is an asshole."

"What does that have to do with vanishing spiders?"

Zhafaera shuddered. "We saw what he wanted us to see."

"Are you telling me they weren't real?" Delan sounded incredulous.

"Oh they were plenty real – in our minds. He knew generally where we were. It's not hard to put images like that in someone's mind." Zhafaera felt her anger rising. "Illegal, but not difficult."

She took a deep breath and tried to focus. "We have to get away from here." She gestured to the trees behind them. "I'm betting that was a way to flush us out. He knew I'd run from spiders faster than I could think, and now we're out in the open. He probably has patrols sweeping the nearby exits."

Turning, she ran – okay, walked briskly – to the tree line, scanning the sky for any sign of movement as Delan followed. They'd apparently come out at the base of the mountain, right at the lake. They needed to find Evey.

When they reached the trees, they hid, leaning against the trunk of a large tree, watching, waiting for any of Velexar's servants that might be looking for them. Nothing moved. The forest sounded normal. Zhafaera drew up a concealment spell, just in case, covering them so they wouldn't be seen, and hunkered down to hide.

They waited for over an hour, watching the moon begin its descent towards the horizon. Just as they had decided nothing was coming, several large figures appeared over the village, flying from the east.

Zhafaera held her breath as the dragon and his mutated followers flew closer and closer towards their hiding spot. She didn't dare move, afraid of breaking her spells and drawing attention to herself. The dragon descended slightly as they got close to the woods, but they did not stop as they passed over.

They waited for what felt like forever, expecting the dragon to circle back around, but it never came. Finally, as dawn neared, they turned and made their way deeper into the trees, Zhafaera reaching out with her magic as quietly as possible.

Before long, they heard the rustle of leaves, just before a large mountain lion appeared from between two large trees just ahead. Zhafaera rushed to Evey and threw her arms around the young dragon/lion's neck, burying her fingers in her thick fur.

I'm so sorry, Evey, she thought. *We didn't mean to leave you.*

It's all right, Evey's mind-voice chimed. She sounded happy, but tired. *I could sense you most of the way – you just couldn't hear me. I waited as close to your exit as I dared, but there were humans searching the area. I hid.*

"Have you been waiting for us long?" Delan asked.

The mountain lion shook her head. *I left the mines two days after we were separated, but I only got here yesterday.*

Zhafaera almost groaned. Her fall had cost them an extra four days in the dark, not to mention the spider-fest that it had ended with. Although, she had to admit, the first few days alone in the dark with Delan had been fun… well, parts of it at least. She tried to push that thought out of her head and focus.

We need to find a place to hide. There's a dragon searching the area, and some of those small, mutated dragons –

Drakis? Evey interrupted.

I don't know what those are, Zhafaera answered, picturing them in her mind.

Drakis, Evey said confidently. *They're strong, but stupid. Not like dragons at all, really.*

Either way, we need to be gone before they get back here. She felt the now-familiar panic rising in her chest again. *I might know a place to lay low for a few days, but we need to get there* now.

Delan rested a hand on her shoulder. "Zhafaera, if this place is more than about five minutes away, I'm going to need to sleep first. Couldn't we just hunker down in a deep, dark corner of the forest for the day and rest?" He waved his open palms, indicating the dense undergrowth surrounding them. "Like right here for instance?" He stifled a yawn.

Zhafaera looked around. It actually wasn't a bad spot for hiding, and she could anchor her concealment spell. The trees here were old and thick, their branches blocking out the sky almost completely. They were far enough away from the village that it was unlikely someone would wander out here, and they hadn't seen any trails on their way in. Much of the brush in this area appeared to be of the thick and thorny variety, a fact that the scratches on their hands earned as they made their way here could attest to. And Delan was right – they needed to rest. She could feel her eyes drooping just thinking about it.

I'll help you set the wards, Evey said, and Zhafaera nodded.

Chapter 11

BOOM. Zhafaera jolted awake to the ground shaking beneath her. Delan, sitting up next to her, grabbed her arm.

"What the hells was *that*?" he asked.

Zhafaera sat up and shook her head. By the height of the sun shining brightly through the tree cover, she assumed it wasn't long past noon. "It sounded like it came from the town," she said, standing quickly. She started walking towards the sound.

"Evey, stay here," Delan called back, following Zhafaera out of the tangle of branches surrounding their makeshift camp.

They moved quickly and quietly through the woods, Zhafaera's fingers touching her knives, counting to make sure they were all still there – a bit of a nervous habit. Soon, the trees began to thin out, and they could see the lake peeking through the branches, the sunlight reflecting off of rough waters. That's when they heard it. Screaming.

Zhafaera took off towards the edge of the treeline, Delan close on her heels. As they reached the last of the trees, Zhafaera stopped dead in her tracks, covering her mouth.

The town across the lake, the small square homes they had seen last night, was falling into a giant crack that had opened in the earth. The water level of the lake appeared to be going down, exposing slimy rocks covered in algae at the edge. A great cloud of dust hung in the air over it all.

CRACK. The chasm opened wider, sending smaller cracks out in all directions, almost as if something heavy were forcing it apart from the inside. As they watched, more buildings crumbled and disappeared from view, the screams carrying over the rapidly diminishing lake.

Zhafaera took several steps forward, not knowing what she intended to do, but unable to stand still and watch. Delan grabbed her before she stepped out of the trees.

"You can't. You know you can't," he said quietly.

Zhafaera turned to look at him. "But the town – all those people!" She could feel tears welling in her eyes, whether from anger or grief she wasn't sure.

"Zhafaera, you can't go out there. You know it's what he wants." Delan's voice was dull, emotionless.

She looked back at the town. There were only a few buildings left standing, and the lake was merely half the size of what it was the night before.

Before she could do or say anything else, there was a new sound – a screeching sound like metal being ground through a mill. Zhafaera and Delan covered their ears and watched as the chasm began to close before their eyes. In minutes, the edges met, most of the smaller cracks sealed, and everything stopped. It was eerily silent as the dust slowly began to settle over what remained of the town, which wasn't much. From what they could see from their

261

vantage point among the trees, there were only a handful of buildings left standing, and even they looked crooked, like they might come tumbling down at any moment. The lake had stopped draining, but looking down at the river that drained from the lake and led to the capital city, it was barely a trickle.

Zhafaera was shaking as she turned to Delan. He still had not let go of her arm, and his face was deathly pale. He met her gaze with his shocked one.

"I thought the Sapphire let him control... water?"

Zhafaera shook her head, dazed. "It... it doesn't work like that. The Sapphire will only pull magical energy from water. But once you have it... well, energy is energy for a White Mage like Velexar. We're not limited like elemental mages are. The Sapphire will amplify whatever power you have."

Delan seemed to pale slightly. She could see the true urgency to get the Sapphire back suddenly click in his mind.

"He's learning to control it," Zhafaera continued in a whisper. "He knows this is where we came out. I guess maybe – maybe he thought – that's where we would go," she choked out. "He destroyed a whole town to *maybe* kill us."

Delan tugged on her arm and pulled her close, wrapping his arms around her and holding her tightly. Zhafaera wasn't sure if he was trying to comfort her or himself. Probably both. Finally releasing her, he rested his hands on her shoulders and met her eyes.

"We need to get out of here. *Right now*," he said seriously.

***

It was almost dusk of the next day when they reached the place Zhafaera had wanted to take them. It was slightly off of their route – to the west of the now shrunken Angonite River – but according to Zhafaera, it was safe.

As soon as Delan stepped over the low stone wall and entered the ruins, he could feel a change in the air. The sounds of the forest surrounding them became muffled, as though it were a great distance away. Looking around, Delan could see the outlines of what used to be buildings, long abandoned. Here and there a stone wall remained standing, even the outlines of rooms in some places, but for the most part, there were only piles of weathered stone to mark where structures once stood.

"This place used to be a monastery," Zhafaera called out, picking her way through the stones ahead.

"A monastery?" Delan frowned. It didn't look like any monastery he had seen, even in ruins. He looked to Evey walking on his right – her head was tilted to the side in the way that meant she was confused.

"Yes, a monastery." Zhafaera appeared to be heading for the largest building, with the most walls still standing. There appeared to have been one long, large room, with several smaller rooms in various stages of deconstruction off to the sides. "Monasteries and Cathedrals didn't used to be used for training mages," she continued. "They used to be places of worship, back when people believed in a single, omniscient god." She stopped in front of what appeared to be the main building and gestured. "The monks who lived here would have worshiped that god – but that was before dragons, and magic of course." She turned to them and shrugged. "Now people worship the spirits of the land – the rocks, the trees, the rivers –" she spread her arms to indicate the forest around them. "They worship magic. And so monasteries became the places where we train our mages."

Delan stepped closer, squinting into the main hallway as the sun began to dip behind the trees. "But this place…" he began. "It has magic. It's… protected."

Zhafaera led the way into the ruins of the main building. "Magic is just energy that we've learned to harness. Back then, there would have been hundreds of people that lived or visited here over the years, all praying for the same thing – sanctuary, protection, guidance – that focused energy is still here, and provides a protection stronger than any ward I could generate. Some might say this place is still sacred. And for all intents and purposes, it is."

Delan thought this over as they moved to the end of the hall and began making camp in a corner just in front of the entrance to a somewhat intact room. A large tree had grown up through the center of the room, mingling its branches with others outside of the walls and replacing the missing roof with a thick, natural canopy over the room.

Delan imagined they'd stay relatively dry if it rained, but so far the evening was clear.

Zhafaera began gathering dry wood for a fire. Although, now that he thought about it, they didn't particularly need one – at least not for warmth. It was early winter now, or at least it should have been, but there was no chill to the air. In fact, now that he thought about it, he hadn't even worn his cloak that day.

"Zhafaera?" he called, walking towards the side room and depositing their packs under the base of the tree.

"Yes?" He heard her voice somewhere behind him and down the hall.

"Does it seem warm to you?" he asked, moving out of the room and back to the main hall with Evey and the horses.

Silence. Then he heard her light footsteps moving back towards them, and she appeared from behind a stone pillar with an armload of wood. "Yes," she said slowly, dropping her wood in front of him and kneeling to begin arranging it for a fire. "But I thought we could use the light and extra warmth. Especially after those caves." She shivered slightly.

"Fair enough," Delan said, shrugging and taking a seat. But he couldn't shake the feeling that something wasn't right.

Something's not *right,* Evey's mind-voice interrupted his thoughts. Delan looked to her, but she was watching Zhafaera. *It's the Sapphire, isn't it? He's using it somehow.*

Zhafaera straightened from her task, biting her lip. "Most likely," she said with a sigh. "He's likely keeping the capital warm for the winter. But all magic has consequences, and the bigger the magic, the bigger the reaction." She rubbed her temples. "On this side of the mountains, it's unseasonably warm. But on the other side, we ran into early snows. To warm the capital, he's drawing warmth from other places." She paused as Evey spit on the fire, making it easier for the wood to catch. Flicking her finger at the pile of wood, Zhafaera watched as flames appeared and quickly moved along the logs. "Some consequences are unintentional. Like the lake." She shivered at the memory, but pushed forward. "Velexar opened that chasm to erase the town, but in doing so, he drained half the lake. That lake feeds the river which flows to the capital. That river is now low, which will affect irrigation, trade, and... everything. I doubt Velexar even thought of that before he pulled his little stunt." She practically spat the last words.

They were all silent as Delan handed out what was left of their food from the packs that had remained with Evey while they were in the mines. By the time they had finished, the sun had truly set, and their only light was the fire.

"How far are we?" Delan finally asked.

Zhafaera started out of her thoughts. "From the capital? It depends on if you want to take the long way or the short way."

"What's the short way?"

266

"We cut back over to the river and follow it along the bank until we get as close to the city as we can."

And the long way? Evey asked.

"We pick our way through the forest. Except at some point, we'd have to cross the Livorian Gorge, where *that* river comes down from the western mountains, and that could be problematic." She glanced over where the horses were resting, their eyes closed. "But walking down the river, out in the open – well, that's where he'll be looking for us." Zhafaera went silent, as if something had just occurred to her.

"What is it?" Delan asked when she didn't speak.

"Well… we might be able to… it might work…"

"*What* might we be able to do?"

Zhafaera finally looked at him, a sparkle in her eyes. "The Angonite River is low because of the lake. Usually we wouldn't be able to cross anywhere near here, but now… who knows? If we can get to the other side and into the forest there, we might be able to stay hidden *and* cut time off our trip." She was speaking very fast by the end.

Delan thought for a moment, trying to picture a map of Arenthia in his head.

"Well, what do you think?" Zhafaera pressed.

Delan ran a hand through his hair. "Look, I'm all for whichever way you think is best, but personally, I like the plan that gets us to Alec the fastest. Let's try to cross the river."

"It's settled then." Zhafaera jumped up and looked around, as if she were ready to leave that moment.

Zhafaera? Evey asked. Zhafaera looked down at her questioningly. *I may not know humans very well, but I don't think he meant right now.*

Zhafaera looked up at the sky as if realizing for the first time that it was dark. "Oh. Right." She sat back down next to Delan and gave him a somewhat sheepish grin. He nudged her leg with his knee.

"Don't worry, like you said, this will be the fast way." Delan paused, thinking. "Really, we should probably stay here another day or so anyway." Zhafaera opened her mouth to protest, but Delan stopped her. "Look, we need to hunt and replenish our supplies. And rest. We're safe here – let's take advantage of that and get a couple of good nights of sleep."

Yes, please, Evey said. She immediately stretched, then curled up, resting her head on her front paws. The firelight glinted off of her multicolored scales, casting strange reflections on the wall behind her.

Delan caught Zhafaera's eye and gave a tiny jerk of his head towards the side room next to them. She fought back a grin.

"Evey, we're going to sleep in the next room – maybe find a softer patch of ground under the tree. Are you coming?" Zhafaera asked.

No, I'm quite comfortable here by the fire. She opened one cat-like eye and looked at them. *You go.* She closed the eye, dismissing them.

Delan stood, turning to help Zhafaera up behind him. Her eyes still sparkled with excitement. Holding hands, they picked their way carefully past Evey, across the uneven stones and into the side room. As soon as they crossed the threshold, Zhafaera gave his hand a quick tug, and before he knew it, she had spun him around, pressed him against the wall separating their room from the fire, and was kissing him ferociously. Delan didn't argue, wrapping his arms around her and kissing her back. When they finally broke apart, they were both a little breathless. Raising his hand to her face, Delan pushed aside a lock of Zhafaera's hair, already unbraided for the night, and whispered into her ear.

"If you push any harder against that wall, it's liable to come down around poor Evey's ears."

Zhafaera pulled back, meeting his gaze and grinning. "Don't worry, I won't push on the wall," she said quietly, pulling him towards her.

Later, after they had made their bed under the tree, Delan was relaxed, Zhafaera's head resting on his chest as they watched the fire beginning to burn low in the hall. He could just see the tip of Evey's nose from where they lay.

"You know what I dream about?" Delan whispered after a while.

"What?" she asked, turning her face up towards him.

"Sleeping in a real bed again." He kissed her forehead. "Preferably with you."

Zhafaera blushed, but smiled. "That would be nice. Although I imagine that an actual mattress might feel odd after all these nights on the ground."

"True. But it will be worth it just for a real pillow."

269

"You're not wrong," Zhafaera said, pulling the blanket up to her chin and closing her eyes again. Delan ran his hand along her back.

"Zhafaera?" Delan's voice was even quieter now, but he forced the word out.

"Yes?" she whispered back, not opening her eyes.

"When this is all over... I mean, when you defeat Velexar and get the Sapphire, and rescue Alec –"

"Oh is that all I have to do?" she murmured against him.

"Yes, well. You know what I mean. Once this is over, you'll be Queen. I just wondered... would you – well, do you want me to stay?" Delan held his breath. He desperately wanted to know, but was afraid of the answer.

Zhafaera's eyes popped open, and she quickly propped herself up on her elbow, looking at Delan. He met her gaze seriously.

"What do you mean?" She frowned. "Of course I want you to stay."

Delan licked his lips and pressed on. "I just – I know you'll be busy fixing things, and I wasn't sure if you'd want people to know about us, or if you'd want me to back off, or –"

Stop. Her mind-voice was firm. *We're in this together, aren't we?* She paused. *Unless you don't want to?* Delan felt her hesitate.

No, not at all, Delan thought quickly. *I want to be with you.*

270

Good, Zhafaera smiled down at him. *I want to be with you, too.* She snuggled back down under the blankets. *Who knows, if I do manage to become Queen, maybe I'll take a Consort.* Delan's brain froze in shock. Zhafaera must have sensed it, because she flinched. *Sorry, too soon?*

No, I just didn't expect – I mean, I didn't think – I mean – your mother never took a Consort, he finally blurted out.

"My mother was a slut," Zhafaera said suddenly. She gasped, and covered her mouth. "I didn't mean that," she whispered out loud, her eyes filling with tears. Delan was surprised. He'd never heard her say anything bad about Karaena.

"I know you didn't." Delan pulled her close and ran a hand over her hair. He waited until she had calmed some. "Do you want to talk about it?"

"I – she –" Zhafaera took a deep breath and wiped the tears from her eyes. *She was a good diplomat.*

Yes, you've said that before.

Because she was. But she also knew how to use men to get what she wanted. She never stayed with a man for longer than a few weeks. I don't even know who my father is, and I don't think she did, either. None of them really mattered to her. Oh, plenty of them tried to win a place as Consort, but she wouldn't have it – she just never cared enough. And when all the leaders met for Gatherings, well, let's just say the men usually voted with her. She used to say that men have two brains but can't use both at the same time.

271

Honestly, that's probably true. Delan's voice was light, but he was concerned.

I just never wanted to be like that.

Delan was quiet for a moment, trying to sort through his feelings. *Do you regret this?* He finally asked.

Regret what? Zhafaera was confused.

Us? he asked anxiously.

Good gods no, Zhafaera said quickly. She rested a hand on his chest. *This is different. I care about you.* She hoped he could feel that she meant it.

You mean you still respect me in the morning? Delan tried to sound amused now, but mostly he was just relieved.

Something like that, she said with a smile. *Now hush, I'm trying to sleep.*

Yes, Princess.

***

Ultimately they stayed in the ruins of the monastery two more days. Zhafaera felt like she slept more in those two days than she had during their entire time on the road put together. Delan spent most of the time hunting, Zhafaera occasionally joining him, but mostly she handled the preserving part. On their second day, she discovered an area behind a small square foundation that might possibly have been a garden at one time. Of course, it was mostly just part of the forest now, but there were still some roots and berries to be found. Enough that she was able to fill a pack with them and still have some left over for a venison, potato, and carrot stew that night. It was quite possibly the best thing she had ever eaten – it was so delicious that she barely even noticed Evey crunching on the rest of the deer carcass while they ate. She swore the young dragon grew before her eyes in those two days.

When they rose at dawn on the third day and began packing camp, everyone was in much better spirits than they had been when they arrived. The loss of the horses meant they were on foot now, but Zhafaera tried not to focus on how much that would slow them down.

Her good mood and sense of hopefulness held even after they left the protective bubble of the monastery. The weather had been clear since they had reached this side of the Angonite Mountains, and despite knowing the mild weather was unnatural, Zhafaera couldn't help but be grateful for the warm days. The forest was dense, making riding impossible as they picked their way around tangles of creeping vines, but at least they weren't trudging through knee-deep snow.

Evey took it upon herself to be their forward scout, often slinking through the trees a ways ahead of them in her mountain lion form. Zhafaera even caught her practicing her hunting skills – hunkered down and blending in with her surroundings, eyes fixed on the slightest movement of small animals. Each time she missed, Zhafaera would go through the hunt with her, giving tips and tricks on how better to catch her prey. After a while, it became almost a game. And when Evey caught her very first rabbit, she trotted proudly back to them, carrying her kill gingerly in her mouth, waiting to eat it until after she had shown them her prize. Watching as she tossed the rabbit in the air, caught it, and began munching happily on her snack, Zhafaera had never felt so proud. Delan was so excited for her that he reached out and rubbed her head roughly as you would a dog that had done well; Zhafaera couldn't stop laughing at the look of confusion on Evey's face at what had just happened, and Delan's embarrassed face as he realized what he'd done. They then spent the next good portion of their hike explaining to Evey the concept of humans owning animals as pets.

Their trek back to the Angonite river took longer than Zhafaera had hoped – they didn't reach its banks until almost dark the next day. Zhafaera, Delan, and Evey stepped out onto the river's muddy banks, surveying the obstacle before them.

Delan whistled in amazement. "Wow."

"I know," Zhafaera could hardly believe it. "This is less of a river, and more of a – I don't know, a big stream?" She shook her head. "That *idiot*." Delan didn't have to ask who she meant.

"Well, the good news is, I think we'll be able to make it across," he said, eyeing the long, muddy expanse down to the water moving lazily downstream.

"Yeah, you think?" Zhafaera's irritation was spilling out.

Delan rested a hand on her shoulder. "You'll put it right soon enough."

She looked at him and sighed. "I appreciate your confidence, and I'll certainly try, but… this is really not good."

They camped that night at the edge of the trees, keeping their fire small and extinguishing it quickly after they ate. After the dense tree cover, Zhafaera felt exposed sitting on the riverbank, able to see clearly in all directions up and down the river. She'd be glad to be on the other side and back under the cover of trees, even if it was slow going. Theoretically, they could pick up the road before too long if they kept heading east, but the closer to Arenthia they got, the more people she expected to see, and the greater the risk of being caught. Again, it was going to come down to speed versus safety. Zhafaera was beginning to think that speed might be the way to go — slogging through the woods was getting old.

***

Anxious to get across, they were all up before dawn the next morning, and by the time the sun had fully risen, they were packed and ready to go.

"We should be able to cross, but the center is still fairly deep," Zhafaera was saying, standing at the line of mud that marked where the river used to come up to. Delan reached out with a small tendril of magic, feeling for the currents of the water. They were slow but… unsteady. It was as though the river was unused to its new arrangement, and it hadn't quite settled into a routine yet.

"I'm thinking Evey should go across first, with our packs to keep everything dry." Zhafaera paused, clearly thinking it through. "And maybe lay a rope across the water, just in case."

"Couldn't you just –" Delan wiggled his fingers to indicate magic – "send them across?"

Zhafaera frowned. "We're getting close," she said sharply. "I think it's best if we use as little magic as possible – I don't want to draw attention to us." She rubbed her temples. "Besides, this headache is *killing* me."

I can do it, Evey said, as Delan, eager to make himself useful, began rummaging through his pack for a long enough piece of rope. Evey was back in her dragon form now, and she stretched her leathery wings out, flexing them and giving them a couple of flaps, sending Zhafaera and Delan stumbling back a few steps with the force of the air.

"Maybe if we just attach the packs like we would to a horse –" he broke off, trying not to think of Shadow and the guilt that came with the memory. He refocused.

Evey was eyeing him with disdain. *Do I look like a horse to you?*

"Just to get them across the river," Delan said quickly. "You should be able to slip out of them on the other side."

Evey's intense gaze bored into him, but he didn't flinch. *Fine,* she finally agreed. *But mind my wings.*

276

Delan delicately placed the first pack along her spine and began fastening it in place. He'd only touched her a couple of times in this form. He was amazed at how smooth her scales were – almost silky, but hard, like diamonds. And their iridescence was stunning. From a distance, he could tell that her scales were different colors, but up close, he could see that each individual scale actually rippled with colors, rather than being fixed.

Adult dragons are generally just one or two colors, Evey's mind voice interrupted his thoughts, and he started. Jolted back to what he was doing, he took the second pack from Zhafaera and continued working.

"So… these are like… baby scales?" Delan asked somewhat awkwardly. Just how young *was* she?

I'm not a baby, Evey snapped, tossing her head.

Delan grinned and took a step back, just in case she decided to stamp her foot, as Alec sometimes did. Thinking of Alec sent another surge of guilt through his gut. "Of course not," he said. "I just meant… will you shed them one day?"

Not precisely, but they will change, she said.

"All right, let's get this moving," Zhafaera said. Evey nodded and spread her wings again. She gave them another couple of flaps before pushing off with all four legs and leaping into the air, catching herself with her wings. Prepared for the gust of air this time, Zhafaera and Delan held their ground and watched as the dragon rose several meters up in the air in just moments. Her wings looked delicate, but even immature, they were powerful. Delan

277

noticed she dipped a little, as if she were slightly off balance, and Delan worried that he'd placed his pack too close to her wings. Just before she reached the water, she recovered and was on the other side of the river in less than a minute.

From where they stood, she appeared to have some trouble getting the packs off. It looked like she was trying to slide them off over her hindquarters, but it wasn't quite working.

"I guess dragons don't have thumbs," Delan murmured to Zhafaera.

She snorted, covering her mouth quickly to hold back her laughter. She flashed a grin at Delan, watching Evey still struggling with the packs. Now she appeared to be rolling on them.

"Technically their thumbs are claws, and while they might not get points for dexterity, they could probably still rip out your intestines before you could blink."

Delan winced. "Fair point." He was just about to call out to Evey when suddenly her form shifted. It was just a quick blur, but the next thing he knew, she was slipping easily out of the saddle and hauling the rope over a fallen tree.

Your turn, she called to them.

"Don't mention the thumbs," Delan hissed under his breath. Zhafaera just laughed.

***

That night, Evey had been the one to set the wards. Zhafaera's headache had only gotten worse as the day went on, to the point where it just *hurt* to use magic, and she was more than a little grumpy by the time the sun went down.

They had stopped for the night in a small clearing, which suited Zhafaera just fine. After spending the day fighting through woods so dense they could hardly see the sky, sleeping under the stars seemed ideal. The thick undergrowth combined with the huge trees looming overhead had made her feel like she was back in the mines again. She wondered if she'd ever get over that claustrophobic feeling. Delan may have sensed her unease, because he made up their bed smack in the middle of the clearing without a word from her.

Even so, Zhafaera was restless. She was exhausted and in pain, but she simply couldn't fall asleep. She tossed and turned, every so often reaching under the bedroll to remove a miniscule rock from under her spot, hoping that *one rock* was the cause of her wakefulness. No such luck.

Finally, at some point in the night, just as she was rolling over for the thousandth time, Delan caught her and pulled her close. She stopped moving and felt herself blush.

"I thought you were asleep," she whispered.

"With you rolling all over the place *and* hogging the blanket? Not quite."

"Sorry." She tried to pull back, thinking of getting up and walking for a bit so at least one of them could get some sleep, but Delan's arms didn't budge.

"*Sleep*," he murmured into her ear.

She opened her mouth to tell him that's what she'd been trying to do, when she found her eyelids drooping. She wanted to ask him if he had used magic, or more accurately if he had *intended* to, but before the thought had even fully formed, she was asleep.

***

Screaming. So much screaming. She could hear the sounds of men, women, children, animals – everyone screaming as though they were dying. The acrid scent of smoke burned her nostrils, choking her. And still, the screams –

Zhafaera sat bolt upright, and found herself once again in the room with the black and white checkered floor. *The Throne Room*, she thought. It felt different somehow. Not how she remembered it.

"It seems this is the place for us to meet," came a smooth voice behind her.

She spun around and scrambled to her feet as Velexar entered through the door that led to the antechamber to the left of the throne.

"You're a fool," Zhafaera spat at him.

He paused, and she could see moonlight reflecting off of his smile. "Do you mean the lake?" He sighed dramatically. "Yes, well, that earthquake was a tragedy."

He touched something hanging from a heavy silver chain around his neck. "Luckily, I was able to step in and help when I did, or the lake would have been entirely consumed. At least now they can still rebuild their little town." His voice ended very near to a growl.

Zhafaera wanted to recoil as he came closer to her, but she held her ground. "You couldn't possibly have thought I'd actually be there," she said with as much disdain as she could muster.

"Of course, not," Velexar said, waving his hand impatiently. "Although, considering the idiocy of some of your mother's plans, I thought it best to make certain. Besides—" he stepped into her personal space – "it made for a good demonstration, did it not?"

Zhafaera felt sick. Something flashed at the corner of her vision, and her eyes flicked towards his chest.

"I see you're *wearing* it," she said disdainfully. "What's the matter? Too scared to bond it yet?"

Velexar's hand shot out so fast Zhafaera didn't have time to react before she felt the slap across her face. She let out a scream that was pure rage, and made to grab for the Sapphire, but her hand went straight through him. As her ghost-hand moved through the Sapphire, its screams pierced her mind, forcing itself out of the corner she had tucked it in and back to the forefront. She grabbed her head and closed her eyes, afraid she might topple to the floor.

Velexar's cool fingers grabbed her by the chin, forcing her head up to face him. She wrenched her eyes open to see his wide smile looming above her.

281

"Don't fret, my dear niece." His voice was like oil sliding over her skin. "You'll be here before you know it. After all," he paused for effect. "You know the closer you get to me, the better I can sense you coming." His last words were a hiss in her ear. Her whole body was tense, ready to run but unable to move.

"I'm going to kill you," she whispered through clenched teeth.

"I'd like to see you *try*," he said, shoving her face away from him so hard that she fell to the floor. As she went down, she tucked and rolled, reaching for her knives, ready to throw them on principle, regardless of whether they could hit him or not. Getting her feet under her, she pushed off the floor as hard as she could, springing up and –

She blinked. She was standing in the middle of a clearing in the woods. She blinked again. She could hear birds chirping somewhere in the distance, and smell wildflowers on the light breeze.

"Zhafaera?"

She spun to see Delan's shocked face staring at her from where he sat with Evey, eating breakfast. She shook her head and looked down at the hands that still held the points of her knives. Turning slowly away from them, she stood very still. Then, with a frustrated yell, she cocked back her arm and hurled a knife as hard as she could at the spot where she had expected Velexar to be.

***

282

"AND THEN – do you know what he said *THEN?*"

"No," Delan said, but he didn't think Zhafaera could hear him.

"I'd like. To see. You. *TRY.*" Her last word was punctuated by a *THUNK* as yet another knife buried itself in the tree upon which Zhafaera was currently taking out her anger.

The poor tree will never be the same, Evey said.

Better it than me.

She would never throw a knife at you.

Don't be so sure – she did hold a knife to my throat once.

There was another *THUNK.*

Should we do something? Evey asked. Her head was tilted just slightly to the side.

Like what? Take her knives? Good luck with that. At this point, Delan wasn't even sure where she had pulled all of these knives from. He counted six in the tree, and two more in her hands. *No wonder she couldn't sleep.*

"I'll show him *TRY.*"

THUNK.

"I'll try to put my *FIST* through his bloody ugly *FACE.*"

THUNK.

"And *HOW COME* he could touch me, but I couldn't touch him, hm? It's not *FAIR!*"

THUNK.

283

Zhafaera sat down hard on the ground, her face in her hands.

Exchanging a glance with Evey, Delan got up and slowly moved towards Zhafaera, not wanting to startle her. When he got close, he knelt next to her, but didn't touch her.

"Are you okay?" he asked softly, speaking to her as one might to an injured animal.

She looked up and met his eyes, her gaze sparking with rage and unshed tears. "I'm out of knives," she said thickly.

Delan reached out and tucked a loose hair behind her ear. "Come on," he said, taking her hand. "Let's go pull them out of the tree."

***

Zhafaera felt as though something had snapped inside of her after her last dream encounter with Velexar. They rose each morning before dawn and didn't stop moving until well into the night, moving quickly through the dense woods thanks to Zhafaera's intense focus and her subtle use of magic to clear a path. While she *really* wanted to just start throwing fireballs, she had settled for convincing the vines and brambles of the thick underbrush to simply… move out of the way. She still hadn't decided if she wanted to risk the road yet, but at least this way, they could actually walk through the forest without tripping.

The closer they got, the more her headache intensified. Every time she used her magic, it felt like her brain was straining to escape the confines of her skull, but ultimately it just egged on her anger. By the end of the week, her rage had settled into a cold, hard ball lodged in her core.

She sensed that Delan was worried about her – hells, if she was honest, she was a little worried about herself – but something about seeing the Sapphire hanging from his neck… the memory made her see red.

Their first stroke of good luck was when they came across a small stream. Zhafaera assumed it must eventually become some kind of tributary into the Angonite river, based on the direction of its flow. By sticking to the strip of dried sand at the top of the bank thanks to the lack of rain, they were able to maintain their good pace without Zhafaera's magic, for which her head was thankful. As long as the stream kept on its current course, she was hopeful they'd be able to follow it all the way to where the river curved back around to meet the capital before flowing out to sea. Their path had become essentially a straight line connecting the two arms of the Angonite River, cutting off the section farther north where it met the Livorian River before the combined rivers cut hard to the east.

Their second stroke of good luck had been Evey's growing ability to move among the trees unseen. She had begun to scout further and further ahead, and was particularly useful after the sun went down, when she could guide them in the dark through the safest route. She was by no means an expert in survival skills yet, but she was certainly a lot more savvy than she had been when they'd found her. Zhafaera couldn't help but be proud.

Their third bit of good luck came when, after following the stream for several days as it progressively got wider, they came out at a small waterfall, and at its base a pool. At this point, it was actually warm, and Zhafaera longed to bathe in the lightly swirling waters.

"I think we can get down from here," Delan called from a few feet away. "It doesn't look too steep if we edge into the woods a bit."

Zhafaera sighed. It was only just past noon, and they really didn't have time to stop.

She followed Delan into the woods and down the slight incline. When they reached the bottom, they moved back towards the stream, coming out just at the other end of the pool. Delan dropped his pack.

"What are you doing?" Zhafaera asked.

"Oh, come on, this is a perfect place to stop," he said, somewhat pleadingly.

"Delan, we really don't have time –"

"You know as well as I do that a few hours won't make a difference. Besides, I really need a rest." He rolled his shoulders and cracked his neck, wincing.

Zhafaera wanted nothing more than to dive into the crystal clear waters of the pool and start soaking off the grime of the road. But still, she hesitated, looking at the position of the sun.

Delan came and put an arm around her shoulders, turning her head to meet his grin.

"Come on, you know you want to take a swim."

There was a splash, startling them both and making Zhafaera reach for her knives. Looking over at the pool, they saw Evey, in her dragon form now, gliding under the water like a glittering fish. A moment later, her head popped above the surface.

I was hot, she said.

***

The cool water on her skin was better than Zhafaera had even imagined. For the last week, she had thought of nothing besides getting to Velexar; but floating in the pool, dressed only in her undergarments, her hair spread out like a sunburst around her head, she realized just how worn down she was. The water was just deep enough that she couldn't *quite* touch the bottom in the middle, and so she lay there, soaking in the energy from the water, and the woods, and the sun beating down on her skin.

She wasn't sure how long she had been in the water when she felt something brush against her back. Startled, she opened her eyes and tried to sit up, splashing water everywhere and gasping.

"Sorry! I didn't mean to scare you," Delan's voice was next to her, and tinged with laughter. "I just wasn't sure if you'd fallen asleep, and I didn't want to have come all this way just for you to drown." He planted a quick kiss on her temple in apology.

"Fair enough," Zhafaera said, leaning back into the water, Delan's arms supporting her back and legs. He could clearly touch the bottom. "I was just relaxing."

"Well, if you relax in the water much longer, you're going to turn into a prune," he said teasingly. "Come on, why don't we lay on the rock? Then you can nap in the sun without drowning."

"What am I, a cat?" Zhafaera murmured, but she didn't protest. She allowed Delan to carry/float her towards the rock that jutted out like a peninsula at the end of the pool, where they had laid their clothes (and weapons) out to dry. With a groan, Zhafaera climbed up onto the rock, picking up the blue dress that she had dug out of the bottom of her pack for just this purpose. It was somewhat looser on her after their time on the road, and she was able to slip it over her head while wiggling out of her wet underclothes, laying them next to her shirt and pants to dry in the afternoon sun.

"So modest now," Delan said with a mischievous grin as she started squeezing the water out of her hair.

"I'm always modest!" Zhafaera tried to look offended and failed. "Well. It's different out in the open, in daylight."

"You weren't very modest when you were floating in the water in your undergarments either."

288

"Swimming is different," Zhafaera said, flipping her hair so that Delan got splashed with the dregs of water now dripping slowly from the ends.

"I see. So should I dress too, now that I'm out of the water?"

Zhafaera turned and looked over at Delan, who was now seated leaning back on his hands, wearing only his undershorts. She admired the view for a moment, tapping her chin with a finger as if thinking. "That won't be necessary," she said finally, moving to sit next to him on the rock. "It's different for men." Leaning over, she kissed him, then laid back on the rock and stretched out, arranging her hair in a fan around her head so it could start to dry and closed her eyes.

"I'm not sure how I feel about this double standard," Delan said, as he lay back against the warm rock next to her.

Zhafaera opened one eye and looked at him. "… I also have three knives stashed in this dress."

Delan laughed and rolled over to face her. "I should have known." He planted a quick kiss on her lips. "Should I be concerned about the number of knives you own?"

"Only if you make me angry," Zhafaera said, smiling sweetly.

"Point taken," he said, now kissing her nose.

Zhafaera grabbed him before he could move away and kissed him again, deeper this time. Delan didn't resist. He slipped a hand behind her head, weaving his fingers into her hair, holding her to him.

I think I found a cave! Evey's excited mind-voice interrupted.

Delan gave a tiny groan and pulled away, resting his forehead on the rock next to her head. Zhafaera let her arm drape across his shoulders.

That's great, Evey! she thought. *Where?*

Behind the waterfall.

I think that's called a grotto, Delan chimed in, rolling over onto his back and closing his eyes.

Zhafaera followed suit, closing her eyes as she listened to Evey's commentary as she explored the hidden space behind the waterfall.

She was just drifting off to sleep when she sat bolt upright. She wasn't sure what had startled her, but suddenly all she could feel was panic.

Delan sat next to her, looking at her quizzically. "What is it?"

Zhafaera shook her head. "I—I'm not—"

She was cut off by an unholy shriek as one of the *drakis* dropped from the sky, coming straight at them, claws first.

Zhafaera was up in a flash, Delan in front of her with his sword out, ready to defend, as she drew on her magic and knocked the first one out of the air, sending it crashing into the trees across from them. But there were more behind it. The next two came in slower, dodging her attempts to throw them into the trees, swooping closer and closer to their heads, but just out of reach of Delan's sword. It was like they were toying with them. Suddenly, the two creatures darted off in opposite directions.

It wasn't until the net dropped down on her that Zhafaera understood that the odd mutated dragons had only been a distraction. Panic rose up fast and hot in her chest as the net restricted her movement. Feeling along the net with only her fingers, looking for the edge, Zhafaera stomped down on her emotions and tried to focus on getting out. A net was annoying, but hardly enough to actually capture her. Frustrated, she tried to slice through the net with her magic. Nothing happened. *Oh hells,* she thought. *It's warded.*

Looking up, she saw the dragon – a real, full-size, black and blue dragon – hovering over them just above the tree line, waiting to be noticed. Baring its teeth, it suddenly dove down towards them, reaching out with its hind legs like an eagle catching a fish.

Delan stepped forward, to do what, Zhafaera wasn't sure, but before she could tell him to *move*, the dragon was on them. Zhafaera saw it all happen in slow motion. Delan made to swing with his sword, aiming for the dragon's underbelly, but the dragon had the greater reach. It grabbed Delan around his upper body, its talons sinking deep into his back and chest before throwing him forwards into the water. Zhafaera could see the deep slash marks on his back as he hit the water; she could hear someone – maybe herself? – screaming, but it was far away, dimmed through the roaring in her ears.

The next moment she was yanked off of her feet and into the air. The dragon had grabbed the net and was now climbing back into the sky, Zhafaera bound both physically and magically inside. As they rose above the trees, all she could see was the red stain spreading through the once clear waters of the pool, and she suddenly found her voice.

"DELAN!"

She hadn't seen him come up.

"NO! DELAN!"

QUIET, roared a deep voice in her head. The dragon shook the net roughly, and Zhafaera's world went black.

Chapter 12

Evey peeked her head ever so slightly out from the – *what had he called it?* – grotto, just at the edge of the falling water. She wasn't sure what had happened exactly, but she knew there had been some kind of attack – she had felt the small, twisted *drakis* just moments before she heard them, which was of no use at all. Like her. She could smell blood, and she couldn't sense Zhafaera.

Oh no.

She stuck her head farther out from behind the waterfall. She could feel Delan nearby still, but she couldn't see him. And his presence felt... dim. As if he were far away.

The smell of blood was getting stronger, and she realized a red cloud was slowly creeping closer to her through the water. She jumped, thinking it might be some sort of spell... but no, that wasn't right.

Blood. It was blood. Delan's blood, she could smell now.

Taking a quick breath and sealing her nostrils, she dove, shooting through the now murky water to the other end of the pool in seconds.

There.

Delan was suspended in the water, not quite touching the bottom, but neither was he at the surface. His eyes were closed, his arms and legs floating out to either side. The blood was coming from the deep gashes in his back and chest.

With a flick of her tail, Evey was at his side. She nudged him, but he made no response. She knew he wasn't dead – she could still feel him, but his life force was muted and fading fast.

No!

She knew she had to get him out of the water. Humans couldn't hold their breath nearly as long as a dragon. Diving lower, she positioned herself so that his body draped along her spine, taking up nearly the full length of her back. Opening her wings, she *pushed* up as hard as she could, quickly breaking the surface, but feeling Delan starting to slip off. Flicking her head quickly to the side and behind her, she managed to catch his forearm in her jaws and stop his slide. She tasted blood, but didn't dare let go.

Carefully, she stretched her wings out again, using them to push them forward towards shore as quickly as she could until her claws scraped the bottom. Getting her legs under her with Delan draped over her back was a strain. In the water, he was light enough, but on land his dead weight was almost too much for her.

Don't be a baby, she thought angrily at herself as she scrambled out of the water. Moving as quickly as she could without dropping him, she made for the tree line a little bit back from the pool. She let go of Delan's arm and tried to ease him to the ground, but he still landed on his back with a solid thud.

His body convulsed, and water came pouring out of his mouth in a great stream. Then suddenly, a ragged, gasping breath, followed by deep coughs and more water. Finally, he lay still. Evey nuzzled his arm, trying to get him to rouse, but there was no movement aside from his rough breathing.

Evey stepped back and looked him over. Small rivulets of blood were forming along his chest and dripping onto the ground around him. The cuts she could see on his chest were deep – too deep. His life force was getting dimmer by the moment, and beginning to flicker.

Fear gripped her. He couldn't die. He was her friend, and Zhafaera was already gone – without him, she'd be alone again. But dragons her age were *never* taught complex magic like healing, let alone on a human. The raw, untempered magic of dragons was not meant to be used on humans, not if they were to live.

My magic hasn't reached its full potential yet. At least, that's what the Elders were forever telling her. *Maybe if I just –*

She reached out as delicately as she could with her magic, using as little as possible and letting it spread out over Delan's skin. She felt his life force flicker again – she refused to think about it. She focused on his injuries, the deep gashes allowing his life's blood to flow out onto the sandy soil underneath. She wove her magic into the

295

rivulets of blood and *willed* them to stop. To her surprise, they did.

Pausing, she tried to feel for the next step. Maybe she could push the blood back in? Slowly the blood began to move in the opposite direction, flowing into the cuts instead of out. His body stiffened, and she stopped. It didn't feel right. She just needed to close the gashes.

Stopping the bleeding was one thing – controlling blood was a lot like controlling water – but getting muscle and skin to knit back together was entirely different. She tried to imagine it closing like they had seen the cracks in the earth back at the lake village close. Nothing happened.

Steeling herself, she let her magic seep into his skin, tracing the edges of each cut gingerly, bathing them in warmth and light. Starting at the deepest points, she tried to pull the divided flesh back together, stretching the strands of muscle towards each other and using her magic almost as a bridge between them until they finally met, and she felt them seal precariously.

It took immense concentration, the pieces almost slippery in her magical grasp, but slowly, they began to heal. She could feel the muscles knitting slowly back together, their connections brittle, but holding. His life force hadn't flickered again.

It wasn't until she had closed the muscles and hit the thin layer of fat on top that she began to feel the problem. His skin was warm, much too warm for a human. The edges of the cuts, where her magic was focused, were hot and slick, and she realized the skin around them was smoking faintly. Quickly, she pulled back, watching anxiously, waiting for the smoking to get worse, or the bleeding to start again... but it didn't. As soon as she pulled her magic away, Delan's skin began to cool back to a normal temperature – cold to her hot touch.

Looking him over, she saw that the bleeding had stopped and his breathing was much more even. The gashes weren't as deep as they had been, but they weren't fully healed either. It was the best she could do – she was afraid if she tried any more, she'd just make it worse.

At least he hasn't died. Yet.

***

It was dark when Zhafaera and her "escort" reached the city of Arenthia. The city was almost completely dead, and the sound of rushing water seemed loud in the darkness – first the river, as it made its way through the center of the city, dividing the upper echelons from the peasants below before it emptied into the sea. Then, faintly at first, but quickly growing louder, the deep *whooshing* sound of waves hitting the cliffs. Taking a deep breath of the ocean air, Zhafaera almost relaxed. It smelled like home.

Except home wasn't exactly the best place to be right now. Though it should have been full winter in the capital, the air was warm and sticky as though it were the night of the midsummer festival. Even high up in the air, Zhafaera was hot, although that could have been because of how cramped she was. Every muscle in her body screamed to

297

be stretched, but that wasn't really feasible while trapped in a *gods forsaken* net being carried through the sky by a full grown dragon. Not to mention her headache. She felt as if her skull were about to split in two, the screaming of the Sapphire back at the forefront of her mind. Even if the net hadn't been a magical shield, she doubted she could have used her magic much, if at all.

The moon was almost full, and she could see the castle looming ahead of them, its tall towers an ominous silhouette. As they got closer, the dragon began to slowly lose altitude and drift towards the ground. Zhafaera prepared herself, pulling a knife from one of the hidden pockets in her dress. It may not have worked on the stupid magical net, but it would sure as hell work on whoever the dragon delivered her to.

Right, because I can absolutely take out Velexar with a dagger, she thought grimly. Well, she was damn well going to try at least.

They cleared the Middle Wall separating the Temple District from the rest of the city, followed quickly by the Inner Wall, Zhafaera holding her breath as she just barely cleared the ramparts. She was home.

The dragon was quickly diving towards the open area in front of the sweeping castle steps. Zhafaera braced for the impact – the last thing she needed on top of everything else was a broken bone – as the dragon let go of the net and let her drop the last few feet to the ground. She tried to roll as she normally would when falling, but the net didn't allow for much movement, and she still ended up flat on her back staring at the stars.

I hope those are actual stars and not an indication of how hard I just hit my head. Ow.

As she caught her breath, she saw that she had come to rest at the feet of three hooded figures, two tall flanking one shorter. Mages. Only they would wear robes like that in the stiflingly warm night, let alone face a dragon.

Knife in hand, she twisted and pushed up quickly onto her feet, lunging towards them. Or trying to. Her feet tangled in the net, and instead of moving forward, she fell flat on her face. The mage closest to her took a hasty step back, but the others seemed unphased.

"We'll take her from here," one of them said calmly.

I suppose His Majesty *is too busy now to meet me himself?* The dragon's deep, rumbling mind-voice did not sound pleased. If Zhafaera could have run, she would have.

"Obviously," snapped one of the figures, clearly a man with more nerve than sense. He motioned to the other figures, and they hurried to grab handfuls of her net.

The short mage suddenly turned on his heel and took off through the night without so much as a "thank you" to the dragon. His companions followed, dragging Zhafaera unceremoniously through the dirt behind him. The dragon let out a long, low hiss, and for a moment Zhafaera was sure they were all about to be roasted, but ultimately the dragon simply spread his wings, kicked off hard from the ground, and disappeared into the night.

Zhafaera took a deep breath. "You know, offending dragons is not the secret to living a long life," she said loudly, trying to sound bored.

"Quiet!" one of them barked.

"Why? Afraid someone might hear me and come to see why three men – sorry, I'm assuming you're all men, because a woman wouldn't be so idiotic as to be rude to a dragon – are dragging a helpless woman trapped in a net to gods only know where in the middle of the night?"

The one on her right kicked out, catching her arm and making her drop the knife she was holding. No problem, she had more. They just weren't easy to get to while being dragged.

An idea struck her. "HELP!" She screamed as loud as she could. "HELP! HELP ME!" She waited, but there were no sudden lights flickering on in the guard barracks across the yard near the wall; no one came running to help her.

She tried again. "FIRE! HELP! FIRE!"

One of her captors let out a harsh laugh. "Scream all you want, little girl – no one can hear you. We're priests of the Fire Temple – we *do* know how to set a ward."

Zhafaera cursed, but stopped screaming and focused on digging out another knife.

They passed by the barracks and turned left, skirting along the edge of the castle itself, and Zhafaera suddenly knew where they were taking her.

"Well, I guess I should have known, if he's too busy for a dragon, he's too busy for me," she said sarcastically.

"What's his plan? Throw me in the dungeon to rot?" No response. "I guess he knows he can't beat me outright."

The short mage in the lead stopped and faced her. His head tilted and his hood fell back off of his head. Zhafaera felt like she'd been punched in the gut.

"You're just not that important, Princess," Alec said coldly. He turned and continued towards the small barred door hidden at the base of the castle, digging out a key and opening it to let the others and Zhafaera through.

Zhafaera was numb with shock, her body completely disengaged from her brain. She hardly noticed the moans of the other prisoners as they dragged her through the dungeon. Finally, she found her voice.

"Alec?" she squeaked. Maybe her mind was playing tricks on her. Yes, that had to be it. Even if Velexar *had* turned Alec, there was no way he'd already be this high up in the ranks. It had only been... she tried to count... two months? Three? He was powerful, but training took *time*.

"Alec?" she repeated, slightly louder. He had stopped to open the next locked door, the one that led to where they kept the *real* criminals. Again, he stood aside, letting the other two drag Zhafaera in before he turned and relocked the door. It was pitch black now.

Suddenly, a light flared. Zhafaera quickly shut her eyes and turned her head, the brightness piercing through her head like an arrow. They began moving again, and from here the path sloped steeply down, deep into the bowels of the castle where no light could penetrate. She wasn't sure how long they walked, but she could feel her

301

chances of escape slipping with every step. Alec – *no, not Alec* – was walking behind her, holding the light as though challenging her to look.

It took some time for her eyes to adjust to the new brightness. At least, that's what she told herself. Finally, shaking, she looked up into his face.

"Nooo," she moaned, closing her eyes again. *Please, no.*

Alec laughed, his boyish giggle replaced by a hard, cold sound.

"What, Princess?" She could hardly stand to hear his voice. "Not what you expected?" He laughed again, pushing past her to stop the two dragging her net. She heard a heavy iron door squeal, and her eyes popped open. This was it – she had to do something *now*.

She twisted, trying to get her legs under her, gripping her last knife tight. But she was moving again, she was being lifted, and she lashed out wildly, shoving her arm through the net and making a blind stab. She connected with something and heard a yelp – and then her knife was gone and she was thrown unceremoniously into the dark cell, net and all. She flailed, quickly trying to find her way out of the tangle, and she heard the door slam, the key screeching in the lock as it turned.

"NO!" she screamed, finally freeing herself and flying against the door.

"That *whore*! She stabbed me!" Their voices were muffled through the thick door.

"ALEC!"

302

"Stop whining, you'll live," Alec said, and their voices began moving away. "You're lucky she missed. I *told* you she'd have knives."

"NO! ALEC! PLEASE!" Zhafaera beat her fist on the door.

"You call this missing…" His voice was faint.

"ALEC!"

***

The first thing that Delan was aware of was pain. Horrible, deep, pounding pain permeated his upper body, and his lungs burned with every breath. He moaned, forcing his eyes to open and finding himself staring up at a vivid blue sky through a canopy of trees. He heard running water nearby, but it wasn't the familiar, comforting sound of the ocean lapping the shore.

Where am I? And why do I feel like I've been trampled and gnawed on by lions?

A large, iridescent head with a long snout appeared in his line of vision. He jumped, and every muscle in his body protested the sudden motion. Blinking to clear his vision, he finally recognized the shape.

"Evey?"

You're awake! The young dragon sounded immensely relieved.

"What happened?" He tried to look around, but he found he could barely lift his head. "Where's –" His brain finally caught up. "Oh gods, *Zhafaera*," he moaned, closing his eyes again against the memory of the dragon coming at them. The last thing he remembered was seeing the net land on her and the huge talons of a dragon coming at him.

She's gone, Evey said. *I don't know where. I imagine they took her to* him.

Delan could feel the panic rising up in his throat like bile. He had one job, *one job* – to get her safely to the capital – and he had failed. Again. They'd taken her like they'd taken Alec, and he'd been powerless to stop it. She was probably already – *no.* He stopped the thought. He had to believe she was still alive.

"How long have I been out?" Delan asked, turning his head to face Evey, who was now seated next to him.

Not quite two full days.

Delan tried to sit up, but his muscles just wouldn't cooperate. He felt as weak as a newborn kitten. "Help me up," he said, reaching one arm out to Evey.

A moment later, she stretched her long neck out over his body, close enough that he was able to lift his arms and wrap them around, and she slowly pulled him up. They were still at the forest pool. Once in a sitting position, he leaned heavily over his lap, panting slightly and fighting the intense pain screaming from his chest and back. He looked down at his bare chest and saw two huge raw, open slashes. He imagined his back wasn't much better, judging from the pain. He turned his head and looked at Evey in confusion.

"How am I even alive right now?"

You lost a lot of blood. He could hear the anxiety in her voice and knew it must have been bad. *But I managed to close the deepest parts before my magic started to burn your skin.*

Delan gingerly reached up and touched the edge of a cut. He hissed and jerked his hand away.

"I think you cauterized these top edges," he said, shaking his head in amazement. "Thank you, Evey. I – you saved my life."

Yes, very likely. She looked faintly uncomfortable. *I'd never healed anything before, and dragon magic really isn't meant for humans, and I was afraid I would kill you, but I –*

"Evey," Delan stopped her. "You did a great job."

She seemed to relax some and began inspecting the gashes more closely. *I'm sorry, they'll probably scar pretty badly.*

"Please, women love a man with scars. And it'll be a great opening to tell the story of how I fought a dragon."

I think you lost that fight.

"Yeah, well, it *was* a dragon."

They sat in silence for a moment. Looking around, Delan realized he had been laying on his bedroll, and there was even a blanket in his lap. Both had plenty of dried blood on them.

"Evey, how…?"

I may not have thumbs, she said, sounding somewhat irritated, *but I do have magic.*

"Right."

To his right, there was a large pool of dark brown that had soaked into the sandy soil and marked the small plants nearby. His blood. A lot of it. He swallowed and found he was parched.

"Evey, could you –" The water skin was already floating towards him. He reached out to take it and winced. Not only was his upper body on fire, he found his wrist hurt pretty good too. Inspecting it as he drank deeply, he realized there were small, shallow puncture wounds surrounding his left wrist.

That was me, I'm afraid. Evey said nervously. *It wasn't easy getting you out of the water. Those wounds weren't the priority.*

Delan glanced at the bloodstained ground again. "I imagine not. Thank you, Evey."

His thirst now quenched somewhat, Delan rested one arm gingerly on the ground and tried to twist to get up. He almost collapsed.

What are you trying to do? Evey's head was tilted, but her voice was concerned. *What do you need? I'll get it, you must rest.*

"We need to go after Zhafaera," Delan said, panting slightly from the pain and just the slightest exertion. He couldn't believe how weak he was. "Here, help me up." He reached out to Evey again, but this time she backed away and sat firmly out of reach.

You're joking. Her head was almost all the way to the side.

306

"What? No? Zhafaera could still be – she *is* still alive, and Velexar has her. We have to help her."

Evey shook her head. *This is not a very funny joke.*

"It's not a joke!" Delan said, feeling angry now. "She's still alive! She has to be." He trailed off.

I believe she is, too, and I agree we have to find her, but you are in NO condition to go anywhere. Your wounds are held together by barely a thread. They would almost certainly come open before we'd gone a mile.

"We've already lost too much time! They're probably already in the city, and we're still weeks out!" There was a desperation in his voice that he couldn't suppress.

And how exactly will you help her after you bleed to death?

Delan glared at Evey. "If we could find a horse –"

Where would we find a horse out here? She said shortly. *I had no idea humans could be so stubborn.*

"So what, we just sit here and do nothing?"

Not nothing – heal. She sounded like a mother scolding her child. *I barely put you back together the first time. I doubt I could do it again.*

Delan felt a twinge of guilt. He eyed the pool. It couldn't have been more than twenty yards away, but it seemed like miles. Considering he couldn't even sit up on his own, there was no way he could make that trip by himself yet.

Evey's voice softened. *If Zhafaera is still alive now, she is likely to remain so, and we have time. If not..."* She trailed off, and Delan's heart clenched. He couldn't think about that. He had to believe she was alive.

"How long?" Delan asked.

Until you'll be well enough to travel? Evey gave a half shrug, and it occurred to Delan that the young dragon was picking up human habits traveling with them. *It depends.*

"On what?"

When you can walk unaided, then *we can think about leaving here.*

"Fair enough." Delan said. He reached out once more, and Evey looked suspicious. He shook his head. "You win, Evey. But can you help me over to the pool? I'd really like to wash some of this blood off." The dried blood was pulling at his skin with every movement.

Evey stretched out her long neck, letting him wrap his arms around her again before lifting her head and pulling him up slowly. He gasped at the pain that shot through his chest and back as he tried to get his feet under him.

Go slowly, Evey warned.

He stood still for a moment, leaning heavily on Evey as his legs shook with the effort.

"Okay," he said firmly, and jerked his head towards the pool.

Evey took a step forward, and Delan half walked, half let himself be dragged to the water. By the time they reached the edge, he was panting heavily with the exertion. Evey lowered her head, easing him to the ground, and he fell on all fours, catching his breath. When he felt he could move again, he crawled forward the last couple of feet and into the shallow water.

With Evey's help, he managed to quickly rinse the blood and grit off and dry himself. He even managed to get out of his wet undershorts and into some clean, dry clothes before collapsing on the second bedroll that Evey had pulled out. As his eyes began to droop, he could see Evey carrying his old, bloodsoaked bedroll and blankets to the water, presumably to wash. He felt a pang of guilt at how she'd suddenly become the caretaker, but he didn't have long to ponder it before he was sound asleep.

Chapter 13

Zhafaera had been in the pitch-black cell for twenty two days. At least, they had fed her twenty two times, and she thought they fed her once a day, so that was her best guess. There was no sunlight, no interaction with anyone else, nothing. Each day, they pushed a hunk of stale bread and cold broth in through a flap in the door, and she tried to save it – make it last as long as she could – but somehow it always left her even hungrier than before. Although lately the hunger was tinged heavily with nausea, probably from the ever-worsening smell.

In the first days, the dark, contained space had almost sent her mad. She had beaten her hands bloody on the heavy door and she thought she might have sprained her wrist at one point, but it seemed to be all right now. How long did it take a sprain to heal? She couldn't remember.

She had quickly realized that the cell was warded somehow, just like the *gods cursed* net. It damped her magic completely, making her feel even more isolated. She had tried not to depend solely on her magic in life, but she got the feeling that she had failed miserably at that goal. But at least she couldn't hear the Sapphire screaming from here.

That left her nothing to do but think, and her thoughts were no better than the dark cell she was in. She wasn't sure which was worse – the image of Delan's blood spreading quickly through the small pool, or of Alec's young face laughing through the darkness as he had her thrown into the dungeon.

She sometimes dreamt that Delan was still alive – injured, but alive – and coming to rescue her. In her dreams, she imagined he and Evey moving slowly through the forest, and then later down a road, headed towards the city where they would help her get the hells out of here. That's what she wanted to believe. Occasionally she *did* believe it. Deep down, she hadn't given up hope, but that hope was hard to hang on to stuck in this bloody place. She imagined Delan was dead, and Evey was lost and alone again, and that was almost harder to bear than any of the rest of it.

She thought a lot about her mother. Of how they'd ended up like this. She didn't blame her – not totally – but she couldn't figure out exactly what had gone wrong. Her mother had once been the strongest, smartest person she knew, and somehow in the last few years, she had faded so much that it felt like she had already died. She had moments of clarity, but they grew farther and farther apart over the last four years until she was a complete recluse, never leaving her rooms and speaking to almost no one besides her daughter.

Zhafaera went around and around, trying to answer the core questions her mother had drilled into her when

311

processing any situation. The Who, What, When, Where, and Whys of the last few months wouldn't stop chasing each other through her head. It wasn't supposed to be a literal process of answering the questions, but Zhafaera was finding it helpful to organize her thoughts. At first pass, the answers were simple, and the simple answers were what Zhafaera had been focusing on. Velexar had murdered her mother four months ago in her own rooms here in the castle in order to gain power. But three weeks locked in a dark cell had Zhafaera reevaluating all the answers to such seemingly simple questions.

Who? Velexar wouldn't have been able to pull this off by himself. He obviously had mages on his side, willingly or not, but did he have other allies? Obviously at least some of the dragons, but who else stood to gain from his taking power? And what was with the dragons seeming to serve him? They would *never* serve humans, but the dragon that had brought her here certainly seemed to.

What? He had killed her mother, but had that been the primary objective? Possibly not – the Sapphire was likely more important than her mother, given that her mother wasn't *really* ruling any more. Zhafaera had done that, for all intents and purposes. But to get the Sapphire, he *had* to kill her mother. Velexar had tried to kill her too, but he failed. Or had he even really tried? He hadn't even sent mages to her rooms, just your run-of-the-mill assassins. He should have known she'd be able to deal with them easily – she'd caught him watching her practice often enough.

When? This hadn't just started four months ago. As her mother became more and more withdrawn, Zhafaera had picked up her duties, and Velexar had started appearing in court much more often. In fact, he was almost always there whenever her mother *wasn't.* But he'd seemed content enough to let Zhafaera lead; at least, he'd never overtly offered his help to her, which she might have even accepted, being expected to slowly take over a kingdom at the age of fifteen. Her best guess was that something had happened nearly four years ago, or even more, that had weakened her mother. Was it Velexar's doing? And speaking of *when,* when was he going to pay her a visit? Or was he just going to leave her here to rot? She didn't think that was his plan.

Where? Her mother was killed in her chambers, and the blast had clearly been targeted there. Zhafaera's room was just down the hall, and she had been up and out and into her mother's room relatively quickly after the Sapphire had started its protest. So if Velexar had been the one to actually kill her mother, and there weren't many people who could, where was he when Zhafaera got there? And why hadn't he come for her himself if he wanted her so badly? He hadn't killed her when she ran into him in the throne room, either. And if he didn't want her dead, then *why* did he want her?

Why? That was the big question. Velexar had done it to gain power, but was that it? If so, why hadn't he done it four years ago, when her mother had started to withdraw? Why now? What had changed to push him into action?

313

Why did he have dragons working with him? And why did he want power anyway? Leadership came with responsibilities, particularly to the people you led, and Velexar had never cared about the people. Everything he'd ever done he'd always done for himself. His whole life, he'd had the freedom to go and do whatever, wherever he wanted. To her view, that was the ultimate power. So why change? He *was* the oldest child, but he was a son, and so the throne had passed to Karaena upon the death of their mother, but he likely felt the throne was his by right. But that line of thinking took her back to the *when.* Why was he doing all this *now?*

The scrape of metal on metal startled Zhafaera out of her thoughts as the guard pushed in a "fresh" tray of food. Leaping forward and ignoring the jolt of nausea that shot through her, she quickly drank all of the broth before grabbing the bread and retreating to her "bed" (honestly, it was more like a nest) in the far corner of the cell.

Picking off crumbs from the bread and savoring them as slowly as she could, she took a deep breath and tried to pick up her train of thought again, but she found she couldn't. Her thoughts were too jumbled, disorganized and racing. She took another deep breath, and tried to stretch, but as soon as she made to turn her head, the room spun around her. Her nausea immediately intensified. She tried to put a hand to her head, but it felt as heavy as lead, and she couldn't move it more than a few inches. *Damn it, they drugged me,* she thought, just as her head tilted back against the hard stone and she lost consciousness

***

Zhafaera awoke to an intense bright light. *What the…?* It was sunlight.

Hope sparked within her – Delan and Evey had rescued her, they'd gotten her out! But she could feel a soft mattress under her back, and that was unlikely if she had been with Delan and Evey. And there was something heavy around her neck.

Squinting and blinking rapidly, she managed to open her eyes enough to get a glimpse of her surroundings. Grey stone walls surrounded the bed she laid on. Light blue gauzy drapes hung around the edges of a dark wood canopy.

This can't be right. She was in her own room. *I'm dreaming.*

Even dreaming, her first instinct was to get up and go for her hidden knives. But she couldn't move. She found that her head could move, but the rest of her body refused to comply with her orders beyond the barest twitch. *Still drugged. So… not dreaming then?*

But why would Velexar put her back in her own room? Surely he knew she'd have hidden weapons here. This was *her* territory – not very smart to fight someone in their own home. *Yeah, because you're going to be fighting while paralyzed.* Right. Her thoughts were slow, like moving through syrup. Hopefully whatever they'd given her would wear off soon. At least she had been bathed and dressed in something other than her ragged dress. She tried not to think of who had done it.

In the meantime, she tried to remember all of the places she'd hidden knives in the room. She was sure they had searched it thoroughly – Velexar wasn't *that* stupid unfortunately – but there were a couple of spots she thought might have been missed. The hidden compartment in the underside of her two-hundred pound oak dresser across from the bed seemed a likely spot. It was a nightmare to move, but her small arm, even thinner now after three weeks in the dungeon, could slip through the gap between the floor and the dresser easily.

By the time Zhafaera was able to move her limbs, the light streaming in through the tall windows was dimming into the pink tones of dusk. The first thing she did was reach up and touch her neck. Her hair had been cut, and her fingers met a thick metal collar that was cold to the touch. No wonder she still couldn't feel any magic; she was shielded. She felt around the collar all the way to the back of her neck, but she couldn't feel a lock or any kind of catch. *Doesn't matter,* she thought, swallowing her fear. *I don't need magic to kill Velexar.*

Her arms and legs felt like jelly, but they moved, if barely. Using all of her strength, she pulled herself into a sitting position on the edge of the bed, facing the dresser. She took a deep breath. *Stand. Walk to the dresser. Get the knife.* Easy.

The second she put her weight on her feet, she knew it was not easy. She lurched forward, but her legs refused to support her, and she landed heavily on her hands and knees on the hard wooden floor. *Ouch.*

Okay, crawling it is, then. Moving one limb at a time, she made her way slowly over to the dresser and slipped her arm underneath, feeling for the catch that would open the secret compartment. It opened with a quick *pop*, and a knife fell hilt-first into her hand. She clutched it tightly, feeling relief spread through her body like warm honey.

She thought about checking her other hidden stashes, but as most of them required standing, she decided against it.

Instead, she backed up back towards her bed, managing to position herself next to her nightstand, her back against the wall and facing the door directly across the room, her knees drawn up, hiding the knife in her lap.

She wasn't sure how much time had passed, perhaps an hour, when she heard footsteps in the hall, followed by the clink of a key turning the lock on her door. She gripped her knife tighter.

The door opened, and there was Velexar, in the flesh, smiling at her as he walked confidently into her room, the Sapphire around his neck. She couldn't feel its presence thanks to the collar around her neck, but it seemed to glow in the dim light of the room. She could see at least two guards outside, one on either side of the door. Had they been there all day? She was still woozy, and she wasn't at all sure she could take them *and* Velexar.

So she waited. She didn't throw her knife. She stayed put, back against the wall, knife hidden in her lap, as

Velexar closed the door gently behind him, and turned back to face her.

"Well, my dear niece, here we are at last," he said brightly. "I apologize for not coming to see you sooner. I've been quite busy."

"You threw me in a dungeon to rot." She spat at him.

He waved a hand, brushing off her comment. "Please, don't be so dramatic. You were fed. I thought you needed some time alone to think."

"Oh, I did a lot of thinking," she hissed. "What did you do to my mother?"

"I killed her."

Rage stirred in Zhafaera's belly, but she clamped down on it. "You know what I mean."

A slow smile spread across his face. "You mean when she shut down and hid in her rooms? Hmm, well, it wasn't exactly pleasant, but it had to be done." He stepped closer, his eyes flashing. "It's what I'm going to do to you."

"Why not just kill me?" she asked as he took another step. Just a little closer.

"You're far too powerful for that, my darling. It would be such a waste." He tutted. "This way, bound to me, you'll be much more useful." He touched the Sapphire around his neck and strode towards her.

With a yell, Zhafaera flung her knife at him. Even dizzy and stiff, her aim was true, and she watched as it sailed directly towards his heart. Hope surged in her heart – if she killed him and grabbed the Sapphire, she could deal with anything else.

The knife stopped abruptly, the point just barely touching his silk shirt. Velexar looked slowly down at the knife and then back at her, smiling his lazy smile.

"I thought we might have missed one," he said. He grabbed the knife from the air by the hilt and threw it away behind him. "Thank you for finding it for us."

Zhafaera struggled to her feet, using the wall behind her as leverage. She forced a laugh. "You're afraid of me," she panted, touching the collar at her neck. "You know that, unshielded, I could crush you like a bug."

Velexar was across the room in a flash, his hands around her neck, his magic forcing her hard against the wall so she couldn't move.

"You think so?" he asked in almost a growl. His body relaxed, but the magic didn't let up. "Perhaps," he said lightly. "And perhaps not."

His hands weren't so tight that Zhafaera couldn't breathe, but they were tight enough that she was seeing spots.

Suddenly, his grip loosened slightly and one hand released her, trailing slowly down to her collarbone. She tensed and tried to move away, but he had her pinned, both physically and magically. His other hand still at her throat, he forced her to meet his eyes.

"You want to know what I did to your mother?" His face was only inches from hers, and she could feel his warm breath on her face.

"I bound her to me." His hand moved lower, sliding between her breasts. She wanted to vomit as panic squeezed her chest.

"It wasn't easy." The hand trailed across her chest and moved to her side, cupping her body.

"She fought me the whole way." Her anxiety was so intense she was seeing spots again. This couldn't be happening. He was her uncle. Her mother was his *sister.*

"But it was when I told her what I had planned for *you* that she almost broke free. I had no choice but to kill her." The hand moved down to her waist, the fingers digging painfully into her hip.

A tear slipped down Zhafaera's cheek, but she couldn't look away from his black eyes. Equal parts anger and fear roiled inside her. She couldn't move, couldn't fight. She was trapped against him.

"Besides, the ritual is much more effective with… those who are pure. And you're more beautiful than your mother ever was." He moved his hand back over her lower belly, towards her other hip… and froze.

The sharp intake of breath between his teeth was a hiss. His hand tightened on her throat, but his other hand didn't move for what felt like minutes. She could see the Sapphire glowing around his neck from the corner of her eyes, but she couldn't lift her arm to reach it.

"You little *slut,*" he growled, slamming her against the wall hard on the last word, then quickly releasing her. She fell to her hands and knees, feeling a flood of relief breaking through her intense disgust and fear. She was thankful for Delan in a whole new way.

"Just like your mother." He backhanded her across the face, knocking her to the side. "I should have known you wouldn't be able to travel with a man for more than an hour without letting him mount you." He turned away from her.

Zhafaera spat blood on the floor and managed to smile at his back. "Sorry to ruin your big plans," she said, with a sarcastic bravado that she didn't feel. She was proud she managed to keep her shaking from her voice.

He whipped around to face her, his eyes blazing with anger. His hand curled into a fist, and she braced herself for another blow, but Velexar seemed to suddenly regain control of himself. He closed his eyes, breathing deep before opening them again, much calmer now.

"No matter. The blood of an innocent will work just as well. Temporarily at least." He turned away, heading for the door.

"I've killed people," she hissed. "I'm not innocent by *any* definition."

"No," he said lightly. He glanced over his shoulder at her, his hand on the doorknob. "But your child is."

Chapter 14

Delan and Evey were in the city of Arenthia. Finally.

It had been a week before Delan was well enough to move, and even then, it wasn't pretty. Picking their way through the woods had proved to be too difficult for Delan, with every stumble threatening to tear open his wounds again, not to mention the issue of speed. Ultimately they decided that with Zhafaera gone, it was less likely for people – or dragons – to be hunting them, and the road became the better choice.

Once they made the road, their progress sped up considerably. Delan convinced Evey to take a smaller form, and she had chosen a sleek black cat, trotting beside Delan as they moved quickly down the road. When asked why she tended to favor feline forms, she tilted her head to one side. *Cats are very like dragons, temperament-wise anyway. It's an easier transition, and I can act more or less like myself, only smaller and furrier.*

Based on the cats he had met, Delan thought this was a fair assessment.

They checked into a small inn just over the bridge into the main city, in an area low enough that it was far from the castle, but not so low that it would be odd for him to leave the area. Delan was anxious to move, to get close

322

and inspect the palace itself for any sign of Zhafaera, but they decided to wait until dusk before leaving the inn.

As the sun set, Delan and Evey set out, Evey riding on Delan's shoulder so as not to get separated, heading for the main thoroughfare that cut through the upper market from the bridge to the castle gates. Wending their way through the crowded streets, they passed tightly packed stalls selling everything imaginable. At first glance, it was chaos, but upon close inspection, there did seem to be some sort of order. Closest to the bridge, near the docks, were the fishmongers, closely followed by butchers, tanners, blacksmiths, and other more unsavory necessities. Smaller side roads led off between stalls, and Delan could see other vendors tucked away, stretching as far as he could see.

As they got closer to the Temple District surrounding the castle, the quality of the market changed. Stalls became actual shops, and these were filled with much more refined items. Here you had bakeries, florists, tailors with silk gowns in pride of place in the windows. The change was gradual, but eventually it was easy to see they were in the *very* nice part of town.

It wasn't until they reached the middle wall, separating the temple district from the rest of the city, that Delan began to reconsider. He'd been to the city once before, when he was much younger, and he remembered that the Temple Gate stayed open at all hours, and anyone could enter any temple and pray at any time. But most people didn't pray in the dark, and it was true dark by the time they reached the gate. Sure, there were still people out and about, but not nearly as many as Delan would have liked.

You go look for Alec, Evey said. *I'll go to the castle and see if I can sense Zhafaera.*

Delan opened his mouth to protest and closed it again. Velexar knew by this point who she'd been traveling with – he was just counting on the fact that few people knew his face. Walking into the castle, however, was probably not a good idea until they knew more. Like where Zhafaera was being held. Besides, the castle gates were closed and locked at nightfall, and even in daylight, you couldn't just walk in without a good reason. But Evey might be able to slip through in her current form.

"Fine," Delan murmured out of the corner of his mouth. "We'll meet back here in an hour. This is recon only."

What's recon?

"Just check things out."

With that, Evey jumped down off of his shoulder, landing gracefully and trotting off, following the smaller road to the right that led to the castle.

Delan headed left, making his way through the temple district, which hugged the inner wall that surrounded the castle. The city was arranged for defense. The three walls alone – outer, middle, and inner – would stop, or at least significantly slow, most enemies, and each one was magically reinforced and manned by well-trained guards. *Probably loyal to the wrong person,* Delan thought.

324

As Delan moved through the temple district, aiming for the Cathedral tucked behind the far side of the castle where they trained young mages, he couldn't help but admire the temples. Each one was different – dedicated to every kind of god. Gods of summer, gods of winter. Gods of trees and streams and skies. The temples were generally clumped together in groups by element, with a larger temple devoted to said element somewhere in among the rest. The Water Temple was close to the Temple Gate, as that's where the healers lived. Anyone could come for help at any time, and no one was ever turned away. Earth came after Water, and here Delan could feel flickers of magic, like echoes. It was somehow comforting; being away from Zhafaera, he hadn't been able to draw any magic, and he found he missed the… rush? That wasn't the right word, but it was the best he had. He'd realized that he enjoyed the feeling, even if he couldn't really control it.

He passed through the Air temples more quickly, although the architecture was somewhat distracting. The light, delicate arches seemed ready to fall at any moment, as if they were held up by… magic.

Last, and closest to the Cathedral, were the Fire Temples. He imagined it was set up intentionally this way, as fire mages tended to be the most useful in a battle, and this way they could guard the Cathedral and the young mages who lived there. Mages weren't so common that they could afford to lose any – they protected the young as if they were their own. Which, in a way, they were.

As he passed the large Fire Temple, he slowed and stopped. He couldn't put his finger on it exactly, but… there was a feeling. *What if?*

Moving purposefully, he headed for the door, thinking he may as well stop and pray *somewhere* so as not to look completely out of place if anyone had been watching. But as he grew closer, a feeling of unease took root in his belly, and he slowed. There were voices coming from inside. Quickly, he diverted his path to the window several feet from the door and crouched down behind a statue of a man holding a large sun in his hands. He ignored the slash of pain as his injuries protested the cramped position. The voices were coming closer, and he was beginning to make out words.

"… your hand…"

"Fine… healers…"

"She… knives…"

"If you… told you so… time…"

There was a laugh. A familiar laugh. Delan's breath stopped. They were much closer to the door now.

"You heard they moved her?"

"Yes. Not what I would have done." Delan thought he might be sick. He knew that voice.

"They should have left her there to rot." This voice was grumbling, almost whining.

"Probably. But she's certainly more useful this way."

Delan tried to push down his panic and pay attention to the rest of the conversation, but it was impossible. He couldn't breathe. He couldn't think. Tears stung the corners of his eyes and he was entirely too hot. He felt lightheaded and fought not to pass out. They would be coming out of that door at any minute. He had to move. Taking a deep breath, he scurried in a half run, half crawl around to the side of the Temple.

He made it around the corner just as the door creaked open. Flattening himself against the stone wall, he waited. He couldn't hear them any more. Slowly, he turned his head just enough to see around the corner. There were three men – well, people – walking down the paved path, headed towards the Cathedral. Delan took a deep breath, his first in what felt like hours, and felt a small jolt of magic surge into him. He jumped at the sensation, but held onto it, trying to store it like Zhafaera had taught him. The shortest one of the trio turned abruptly, looking back towards the Temple, and Delan jerked his head back.

Alec. It was Alec. Alec had turned. No, he'd *been* turned.

Zhafaera had warned him. She'd told him this could – no, probably *would* – happen, but he'd done his best to ignore the thought over the time they'd been traveling north.

The guilt was intense. He'd focused on Zhafaera's goal – get the Sapphire, kill Velexar – instead of finding his own brother. *That was part of her goal too,* a small voice in the back of his mind reasoned.

Logically he knew he hadn't forgotten about his brother – he'd thought about him everyday since he was taken – but somehow, seeing him, *hearing him* like this was almost too much to bear.

What's wrong? Evey's voice was urgent, and very close, startling him. *Did you find him?*

Delan nodded, but didn't trust himself to speak. He was holding on to his emotions by the barest thread, and he was legitimately afraid that if he opened his mouth, he would scream. He could still feel the warm glow of magic inside of him, but it didn't help his mood. He didn't need it. He didn't *want* it. He didn't want any of this.

You don't mean that, Evey said gently. But Delan thought she sounded worried. Perhaps a little hurt? He shook his head.

No, I didn't mean it. He said. *I just...* Even his mind voice choked.

Evey didn't resume her perch on his shoulder, but she did come close to him and lean against his leg, in an extremely cat-like gesture.

Let's go back to the inn. We can talk there. They turned and headed back the way they had come earlier that evening. The streets were now much more deserted, and the journey went a lot faster.

Did you find her? He asked.

Yes. Delan's heart leapt. *She's alive, and...* somewhere *in the castle.*

Delan bit back his frustration, cramming it down on top of all of his other emotions and forcing as much calm as he could manage. She was alive. He clung to that.

We knew that already.

328

I should be more clear. When I say she's in the castle, I mean she's in the castle proper, not the dungeons. Not any more at least.

Any more?

Yes. When I got into the courtyard, I could feel her presence like a trail. It was weak, but I followed it and found the dungeons, and then the cell where I believe she was kept. She was gone, but I can still feel her. It's just... muffled.

The net? Delan remembered the look on her face when the net had fallen over her. He'd never seen that look of complete panic on Zhafaera before.

I doubt they still have her in the net, but there are other ways to shield someone.

They had reached the courtyard of the inn, and Evey jumped down from his shoulder. They didn't speak even when they reached the room. Delan took off his boots and stripped down to his undergarments, ignoring the black cat with slightly iridescent fur watching with her head tilted to one side. He climbed into bed, completely exhausted, but still fighting to keep his emotions in the box he'd stuffed them in. Evey curled up at the foot of his bed as he blew out the last candle.

This is actually quite comfortable. I see why you and Zhafaera spoke so highly of beds.

Delan smiled slightly in the dark. It faded quickly.

"Do you think you can find her?" he whispered.

Possibly. It'll take time to narrow it down.

"We may not have a lot of time."

I know. I'll try, Delan. I promise I will.

The hint of desperation in her voice broke him. He rolled over, burying his face in his pillow as the tears flowed silently. The last thing he was aware of was Evey's small form moving closer, her head coming to rest gently on his feet.

***

The moment Velexar entered his rooms, he picked up the first thing he found and hurled it across the room. The delicate crystal goblet shattered on the opposite wall, and he slammed the door behind him.

"That *slut,*" he yelled. "Just like her whore mother." He kicked a chair as he walked past, knocking it to the side.

"I should have known," he murmured. Alec had told him that his brother was in love with Zhafaera, but Velexar hadn't counted on the time it had taken them to get here. Time that they'd spent alone together.

But still, nine months was a long time to wait to fulfill his plans. Panic began to rise up in him. This time he was determined to do the thing properly, not halfway as he'd done with Karaena, but Zhafaera already being pregnant was not something he'd planned for. He didn't like things he hadn't planned for.

Perhaps they wouldn't have to wait quite that long. After all, he didn't need the child – just its blood. He'd speak to a healer tomorrow, he decided.

A small knock on the door jerked him out of his reverie. "Enter," he called angrily.

Alec appeared in the doorway. As young and small as he was, Velexar couldn't believe his power. Then again, maybe it made sense.

"My brother is in the city," Alec said as he bowed.

Velexar smiled slowly. "Is he? You're sure?"

"Positive." Alec's small voice was firm. "I felt him this evening. He was in the Temple District."

So he's not dead then, no matter what Targan said. And he's trying to find a way to free his brother and *his lover,* Velexar thought. "Thank you, Alec," he said aloud. "You've been a great help."

"Should I try to find him in the city?" Alec asked.

"No. Your brother will come to us soon enough. Is there anything else?"

"No, your Majesty."

"Then you may go." Velexar waved his hand, and Alec scurried out the door.

Velexar smiled slowly, moving to fill a goblet – one that he *hadn't* shattered – with wine. This would make things easier. Not only would Zhafaera be more compliant once they had the threat of her lover's death to hold over her, but having the father of her child would be useful for the ritual. Blood magic was complex, and one could never be too careful.

Sipping his wine, Velexar stepped out onto his balcony, breathing deep, calming breaths. Everything

331

would still work out the way he intended, just a little different than expected.

***

Zhafaera was still sitting on the floor, her back pressed against the cold stone, when the sun rose the next morning. Her body protested the uncomfortable position, but she couldn't bring herself to move. A guard had brought in supper, but she had ignored it. Her brain was stuck, replaying the events of the previous evening over and over. What had happened to her mother had been far worse than anything she could have imagined. And he wanted to do that to *her*. To bind her to him. Every time she thought of his touch she wanted to vomit. Or was that the pregnancy?

She was still trying to wrap her head around it. Could she really be pregnant? Well, obviously she *could*. She had spent at least an hour trying to remember the last time she had bled, but the last she could come up with was before they'd entered the mountains. She could have bled while in the dungeons, but she thought that unlikely – her monthly visits were usually heavy and painful, and therefore hard to miss, no matter how dark it was.

She spent the next several hours going back and forth between cursing herself for being so careless and feeling like this was the luckiest thing that had ever happened to her. After all, it had stopped Velexar from… well, it had stopped him. Right now, her main emotion was just relief.

If he wanted the blood of an innocent – *my child* – he'd have less than eight months left to wait, as near as she could figure. That gave her time. She was a prisoner, yes, but Zhafaera knew that he didn't want to kill her, and he couldn't bind her until after her child was born. That meant she had eight months with nothing to do but plot her escape.

And what's your great escape plan? What if you can't escape? What then?

He kills my baby and binds me to him. She had to get out of here. There was no other choice. Her arms, already crossed over her belly, tightened protectively.

She smiled. A mother's instinct she supposed.

Just like her own mother.

Her mother who had died trying to protect her from her own fate.

And the cycle started over again.

Sometime around mid-morning, she heard the sound of footsteps again. She had heard the guards change sometime around dawn, but these steps were different. Not the clump of soldier's boots, but a lighter, confident tread.

Her door opened and Velexar entered once again, this time followed by a man in the deep blue robes of a Water mage. The silver collar marked him as a healer. Of course. *Now* Velexar cared about her well being.

"Zhafaera, my dear, have you been there all night?" He said, feigned surprise in his voice. "I take it you didn't know." He waved a hand. "No matter. Come now, my dear, move to the bed and let the healer examine you."

Zhafaera glared at him and didn't move. She didn't want any healer in service to Velexar laying so much as a finger on her.

"I'd be perfectly capable of examining myself if you'd just take this collar off," she said, smiling sweetly and touching the collar shielding her from magic.

"Yes, well, as we both know, that isn't possible, so get on the bed. Now." The last words were low and dangerous, and she knew that he'd force her if she tried to resist. Better to go of her own accord.

Slowly, her joints stiff and protesting every movement, she stood up. The room spun slightly, and she grabbed her night table for support. Someone grabbed her elbow. Jerking roughly away, she brought her left fist flying across her body, hitting someone hard in the sternum from the sound of the grunt.

It was Velexar, his jaw tight as he breathed deep, clearly trying to catch his breath. She didn't have time to gloat at her *very* nicely aimed punch before he shoved her roughly onto the bed, making her head jerk hard enough that she bit her lip and tasted blood. The "healer" said nothing.

Suddenly she felt as if each of her limbs weighed a ton. She tried to struggle, but she couldn't move. The smirk on Velexar's face told her why – he had her pinned again with his magic. Bile rose in her throat, but she forced it down and met his gaze steadily, determined not to show her fear. But the feeling of helplessness made her want to scream.

Slowly, her body lifted slightly from the bed, moving until she was spread out in the center, her arms by her sides, and her legs parted slightly and facing the end of the bed. She struggled, harder this time, but found she could only move her head.

"I'm going to kill you," she hissed at Velexar, but he just smiled wider.

"Good luck to you," he said. "She's all yours." He waved the healer closer, while he stayed put at the side of the bed.

The healer cleared his throat and stepped forward, gathering a pale blue magic around his hands. *Ameteur,* Zhafaera thought. Colors and gestures were for weaker mages.

Sitting on the end of the bed to one side of her, he spread both hands out and gently placed them on her lower abdomen. He closed his eyes, moving his hands slowly back and forth across her belly, even reaching underneath her body to feel her back. Zhafaera closed her eyes and gritted her teeth, trying to ignore what was happening to her body and imagining herself somewhere else. It was professional and quick, but watching the magic play across her belly and being unable to sense it unsettled her. Finally the glow faded, and she realized she could move again. Scrambling up, she scooted back across her bed to put as much distance between her and the two men as possible.

"Well?" Velexar asked.

"She's definitely pregnant," the healer said briskly, speaking for the first time. "Around six weeks along. I can't feel a heartbeat yet, but I suspect that won't be long. The embryo appears to be solidly implanted, despite the condition of the mother."

"'The condition of the mother?'" Velexar asked coldly.

"I only meant, she's quite underweight," the mage said hurriedly. "She needs to eat. Preferably lots of protein, and fruits and vegetables if you want the pregnancy to survive." He paused. "Unless… you'd like me to take care of it?"

Zhafaera's heart stopped. This was not part of the plan. "NO!" she shouted, her arms once again wrapped around her core.

Velexar held up a hand, silencing her. "That won't be necessary. It needs to be stronger for what I have planned. How long until it's large enough?"

The healer didn't even blink. "Full term is best, of course, but really the fetus is fully formed by about six months. At least enough that it should be able to provide the required blood."

Zhafaera was a hair's breadth away from full out panic. She wasn't sure if it was because they were cutting a good three months off of her escape time, or if she couldn't stand the thought of losing the baby. It was surprising how protective she felt already. The middle of a war was certainly no time for a baby, it was completely idiotic of her to let this happen in the first place, and she was not at all sure that she was mother material, but dammit, it was *hers,* and they couldn't have it.

"Very well," Velexar was saying. "I suppose we can reassess as we go."

He waved a hand and dismissed the healer. The man was out the door in seconds.

Velexar took a seat on the end of her bed. They were alone. The Sapphire shone on the chain around his neck. Before she could process what she was doing, Zhafaera dove forward, one arm outstretched, aiming for the Sapphire. If she could just grab it...

Velexar caught her hand in a vise-like grip and twisted. She gasped, but didn't stop her forward momentum, throwing her other fist towards the side of his head. He ducked and she tried to get her legs under her and into a better position. She sent out a sweeping kick, catching him in the ribs and eliciting a pained grunt. Bracing her foot against his hip, she managed to grab hold of his other shoulder and twisted, leveraging her weight to flip him off the bed...

And nothing happened. She realized with horror that she didn't have the strength any more. In a matter of weeks, her body had completely given out on her.

Her moment of shock was all Velexar needed, and he yanked her wrist, bringing his knee up to break her foothold and sending her flying facedown into the bed. Grabbing the back of her neck just above the collar, he climbed on top of her and straddled her legs. Zhafaera bucked hard, trying to throw him off, but he leaned forward, using his heavy body to pin her completely.

"Is this what you want?" His hot breath was in her ear. "You're a dirty whore like your mother."

337

Zhafaera tried to thrust an elbow behind her, but flat against the bed, she couldn't get the momentum. Panic rose in her throat. *Please no.*

"Do you know what I'm going to do to you? Do you know the strongest bond?" He snorted a derisive laugh. "Of course not. You were always quite shielded. Naive. It's not just sex." She could feel his slow grin against her ear and her whole body revolted. She struggled anew, flailing whatever bits of her limbs she could move, yanking her head around trying to find something to sink her teeth into. Suddenly all movement stopped. She was pinned again by his magic.

She breathed hard, a frustrated tear slipping down her cheek. "You can't even best me while I'm pinned and unarmed without magic. Uncollar me, and–"

"It's a child," Velexar continued as if she'd never interrupted. "Not this child." He slipped a hand under her belly. "This one will be a temporary fix. Enough to bind you until *our* child is born." He paused. "That's where I failed with your mother, you know. By the time I tried to bind her, she was already barren. I didn't get as strong of a bond, and she fought me. But you..." She could hear the satisfaction in his voice. "You're young and strong. You'll bear my child. And then you'll be truly mine." His last words were a sickening whisper.

He shoved her face hard into the mattress and got up, moving quickly off the bed and away from her. He left her room without another word, leaving Zhafaera to cry silently into the blankets.

Chapter 15

I found her, Evey said triumphantly as she came trotting towards Delan.

He'd been sitting in a small Water garden in the Temple District for the last hour. The gardens here were extensive, and there were plenty of places to hide in plain sight. They might not be actively looking for him, but there were plenty of reasons for him to wander the city as little as possible.

He kept himself from jumping up, but only just. This was Evey's third day of searching. Unfortunately, it hadn't been as easy as following a magical trail. Evey suspected Zhafaera had been unconscious when they moved her, which made Delan even more anxious.

"Where? Where is she?" he asked, his voice urgent but quiet.

One of the upper floors of the east wing. Once I figured out the general area of the castle she's in, it was easy for me to slip inside and search more precisely until I found where her presence is strongest.

"Do you know which room?"

I assumed it's the one with the two guards outside, Evey said dryly.

"Probably. Did they see you?"

I think so, but they thought I was just another palace cat. Her head tilted. *I caught a mouse just to be sure.*

"Good job, Evey."

I thought so too. The mouse was fast. What do we do now?

Delan checked their surroundings again. His spot on a bench tucked behind some shrubbery beside a small pond was secluded, but it was still too public. He had a feeling of being watched, but he didn't see anyone.

"Come on, let's go back. We can talk there."

Evey hopped on his shoulder as they headed back to the inn. As soon as they entered their room, she jumped down onto the bed, her new favorite spot, and sat, looking at him with her head tilted.

"Did her room have a window?" Delan asked, taking a seat across from her in the room's single chair.

I can't say for certain, but I would assume so. There were plenty of windows that I could see from the outside.

"Could you fly us up?"

Evey's eyes narrowed. *I could barely pull you out of a pool of water. What makes you think I can fly you up a castle?*

"Point taken."

We can go in the way I did today – there's a side entrance near the kitchens.

"I'm sure we could take the two guards, but getting all the way up to her room through a palace full of people without being caught will be the trick." Delan was thinking

340

out loud. "I might be able to steal a guard or servants' uniform. After that, it's a matter of acting like we belong."

Won't someone think it's odd if they see a guard following a cat through the castle?

"You can stay a ways ahead of me. We need to figure out how far away I can hear you."

We can do that now. No one will pay any attention to a cat wandering around.

He nodded his agreement, then frowned.

"Wait, will the other mages be able to hear you? Or sense your magic?"

What other mages?

"Didn't you see any today? I assumed the castle would be swarming with them."

No, I didn't see any. And to answer your question, they wouldn't hear or sense me unless I wanted them to.

"Why wouldn't there be mages?" Delan wondered out loud. A thought occurred to him. "If he's turned them against their will… maybe he doesn't trust them?" Delan shrugged. All that mattered was that they weren't there. "I need you to steal a uniform for me. From the barracks maybe."

Am I going to have to do everything? Evey's voice was almost teasing, a first from her.

"You can actually get through the inner gate – I can't. Not without good reason."

You didn't ask if I can carry them in this form.

"Can you?"

Of course.

341

"All right, then let's do it."

One thing.

"What?"

How do we get her back out? We might get away with sneaking in, but there's no way someone won't notice Zhafaera leaving.

Damn. Delan had been too focused on just getting *to* Zhafaera. He just had this feeling in the pit of his stomach, growing stronger every day, that something was very wrong.

"What about her? Can you fly *her* out?"

Evey was quiet, thinking. *Possibly,* she said slowly. *But not very far.*

"To the beach?" The castle was perched on a cliff face that led straight down to a rocky beach. If they could get down there, they might be able to escape the city without notice. At least, there were no guards down there. That he knew of. They should probably scope that out too. This whole thing was going to take longer than he had hoped. *If Zhafaera is alive now, she'll still be alive in a few more days,* he reminded himself.

It's pretty much straight down, Evey was saying. *I think I can manage that. But what about you?*

"I'll figure something out."

They spent the next few hours determining the range in which Delan could hear Evey. Ultimately they estimated it was about a quarter mile – plenty of space in which Delan could follow Evey through the castle. As Delan lay in bed that night, he felt hopeful for the first time since

342

Zhafaera had been taken. They could do this. He drifted off to sleep easily, for once not having to toss and turn for a position comfortable enough for his wounds.

He opened his eyes to a soft white light. Blinking, he looked around. He was standing in an expanse of pure white, like fog surrounding him. He had a moment of panic before he realized he'd been here before – he'd spoken to Zhafaera in this place, dreaming after her fall from the mountain. Was she here? His heart rate sped up.

Holding perfectly still, he listened for any sound. He heard nothing. But… there. A slight pull at his navel was tugging him to the right. He followed, and the feeling got stronger.

Suddenly he slammed face first into a solid barrier. He couldn't see anything, but as he backed up, rubbing his nose, he reached out one hand and felt for what he'd hit. His hand touched a cool, smooth surface, like perfectly clear glass. He squinted through the fog on the other side. There was a darker shape, and it looked familiar.

He pounded on the barrier. "Zhafaera!" He called. He pounded again, trying to get her attention.

The form came closer, and Zhafaera's face appeared, her hands pressed flat against the invisible glass.

"Help me!" Her voice was muffled by the barrier, and he could barely hear her. "Please, we have to get out of here, help me!" Tears streamed down her face, and Delan's heart clenched.

"I will, I swear!" He yelled through the barrier. "We're coming for you. Just hold on."

"You don't understand, I –"

A sudden electric shock through the glass sent them both flying back. Delan braced for impact, tensing his muscles and preparing to roll back up –

He sat bolt upright in bed, his heart racing, breathing hard and drenched in sweat. A dream. It had been a dream. But in their dream like that before, it had been virtually *real* – they'd spoken. Was this real too?

What's wrong? Evey's voice was concerned. He couldn't speak for a minute. He was shaking. *Delan?*

"Zhafaera's in serious trouble."

***

After the dream the night before, when Delan had found her, Zhafaera had a renewed energy. She wanted to believe it was real, and that he was alive, but she was terrified it was her own imagination projecting her deepest hopes into her dreams, no matter how real it felt. She wanted to believe Delan was coming for her, but she knew she couldn't rely on it.

Zhafaera had searched every one of her hiding spots with no luck – no more knives. The window, while not barred, was impassable thanks to what she could only assume was a magical barrier. Not having access to her magic was starting to seriously grate on her nerves.

The only way out was going to be through the door, and that was locked, warded, and guarded twenty four hours a day. The only times she'd seen it open were when

Velexar had entered, and that was not something she wanted a repeat of. For all the time she'd spent trying to get here, to get to Velexar, the thought of seeing him made her ill. She'd made more than one trip to her attached washroom to be sick when the memory of his body pinning hers overwhelmed her. She'd known there would be risk in coming back to the capital, but nothing could have prepared her for the reality. She tried not to think about it. She was beginning to feel that she should have run and hidden when Delan's father had told her to. But she'd wanted the Sapphire. Was it worth it? She wasn't sure any more.

Her meals still came through a flap that had been cut out of her door that only opened from the outside. No cutlery of course. Not that she had expected them to be that stupid, but still, it was disappointing. One more option off the table. The food was at least better than what she'd had in the dungeons, but she'd quickly realized that it wasn't what it seemed. Sure, it was all the things the *healer* had ordered, but it was also drugged. Not as heavily as the broth had been in the dungeons, not enough to knock her out cold, but enough that she was perpetually groggy and slow, no matter how little she ate.

She slept as much as she could, which was usually easy with the drugs. She was lonely and quickly growing claustrophobic. Sleep was her only escape from the reality that she was trapped, and pregnant, and... scared. It pained her to admit it even to herself. Usually she could mask her fear with anger, but alone in her room, there was no one for her to be angry at but herself.

Some days she paced the room. Other days she sat in her corner by her nightstand, her head resting on her knees, her mind blank.

Every day she was locked in this room was one day closer to the inevitable. She'd known mages could bond another person to them against their will, to control them. She'd known sex could be used in blood magic rituals to complete said bonding. It wasn't the *only* way, but it was one of the strongest. It had never occurred to her that the sex was only a means to an end. But then, she hadn't known that any of that would ever apply to her. It was forbidden for a reason. Bonding was different from simply turning someone. When you turned someone, you forced them to see things from your perspective, agree with you, and act accordingly. Bonding someone forged a much deeper connection. Bound by blood, the person had no free will. They were completely in the power of the one who had bonded them, with no ability to resist.

Velexar had done that to her mother. The thought made Zhafaera's chest constrict until she could barely breathe, the thought of what he would do to her racing through her mind over and over again. Except her mother had tried to resist, and apparently succeeded somewhat. She might have been a hermit, but at least she wasn't Velexar's puppet. Zhafaera supposed the more powerful you were, the harder it was to control you completely, even through a blood bond, and her mother had had the

Sapphire. Zhafaera tried to tell herself that she was powerful enough, strong enough to resist him like her mother had done. But even so, what kind of life would she lead? Shut away in this damn tower, forever fighting a battle inside her own mind that she could never win. She'd rather be dead.

But that wasn't an option either. Even if she'd wanted to (and she'd thought about it), she discovered that the sheets didn't come off the bed, nor the drapes off the canopy. That had scrapped another escape plan – one which involved strangling the guards with the gauzy drapes before making a run for it.

If she could just get the Sapphire...

She knew that if she escaped, Velexar would hunt her down. He wanted her for a purpose, and she was beginning to suspect she knew what that was. The fact that he was still wearing the Sapphire instead of bonding it told her it was still fighting him, making bonding it entirely too dangerous. If he couldn't bond it, he'd need to be able to control someone who could.

So she sat, and waited. She wasn't a patient person, and the feeling of utter helplessness made her antsy and frustrated. She wanted to believe that Delan would come for her, but she couldn't be sure that her dream hadn't been just that – a dream, born of desperation and an inability to accept that he was likely dead. But either way, the best she could do at this point was wait, and watch for the opportune moment to escape. She had to believe it would come.

***

Getting inside the castle was a lot easier than Delan had anticipated.

Evey had stolen a guard's uniform, then gone into the Keep ahead of him. Walking purposefully, he'd entered through the side door near the kitchens, working his way up through the belly of the castle under Evey's guidance.

No one questioned him. The guards posted sporadically through the castle were satisfied with a quick nod of the head, and as Evey had said, they didn't see any mages. In fact, the halls were almost empty. He was able to walk through the middle of the castle fully armed and no one so much as blinked.

It didn't take long for them to reach the east wing where Evey said Zhafaera was being held. The Throne Room was there, on the ground floor, with its ornate gilded doors cracked open enough that Delan could see the stark black and white tiles on the floor. Delan moved past the room and its guards quickly, heading for the small servants' stairs at the far end of the corridor.

Evey was waiting for him there. He resisted the urge to run up the stairs, or take them two or three at a time, not wanting to tip off any guards upstairs that something was off. Hopefully they would think he was just another guard, as everyone else had. But the ease with which they'd made it this far was making him nervous.

It's up ahead here, Evey said, as the fourth floor landing materialized above them on the stairs.

Delan didn't pause for breath. When he reached the landing, he opened the door that led from the stairs and emerged into a large hallway with rooms on either side. One room, halfway down, had two guards posted outside, both of whom were staring at them. Delan lifted a hand and waved, not slowing his forward motion.

"What're you –" the closest guard's words were interrupted by Delan's fist in his face. By the crunch it made, Delan was pretty sure he'd broken the man's nose. He fell to his knees, clutching his face.

The second guard had let out a short yell of surprise at the sudden turn of events, but had quickly composed himself enough to draw his sword. Delan ducked under a swing, half drawing his own sword and using his forward momentum to jam his fist holding the pommel into the guard's solar plexus, knocking the wind and the fight out of him instantly as he fell on all fours.

Knowing he had a minute before *that* guy could breathe again, he spun back to the first guard, his sword back in place but a knife in his hand. The hallway was entirely too narrow for swords to really be useful. To his surprise, the man was still on the ground, now sprawled out and face down, with Evey standing on his back.

"Is he…?" Delan had hoped to do this quietly, without actually killing anyone if he didn't have to. The memory of the burned camp of soldiers shot through his mind, quickly followed by the familiar wave of guilt. It wasn't

349

their fault they served the wrong ruler. Velexar had absolute control.

He's fine, just sleeping. Evey jumped over his still body and moved to the second guard, still holding his stomach and coughing hard.

Delan watched in awe as Evey stood on her hind legs, placed both paws on the man's hip, then quickly stepped back as he dropped to the stone floor face-first. Delan winced. That was going to hurt when he woke up.

"I should have just let you do this alone," Delan said, grinning at Evey as he moved towards the door.

Your distraction was helpful.

Delan wasn't sure how he felt about being the "distraction." He reached for the door handle.

Don't touch that! Delan froze as Evey moved closer, inspecting the door.

"What?"

It's warded.

"Of course it is." His anxiety was through the roof, knowing Zhafaera was on the other side of that door and unable to get to her. "What'll happen if I touch it?"

I have no idea. I would guess at the very least it would set off alarms.

Delan took a deep breath. "Can you break it?"

Evey's head tilted. After a few moments, she opened her mouth and *breathed* on the door. A low blue flame began to crawl across the face of the door, slowly at first but picking up speed. Like fire moving over oil, the flame seemed to be devouring something on *top* of the door, while the wood underneath remained untouched. When it reached the top, the fire burned out immediately.

It's safe now.

Delan didn't hesitate. He shoved his knife into the lock on the door and jerked upwards, feeling the mechanism break under his hand. Turning the handle, he threw the door open.

And there she was. Zhafaera was sitting on the floor directly opposite the door, her head resting on a wooden nightstand next to her bed. She was pale, her dull red hair hanging limply at her shoulders. Someone had cut it, and it just barely brushed the tops of her shoulders.

But it wasn't her hair that terrified him as he darted across the room, skidding to a halt on his knees next to her. Zhafaera had always been slender, but now… she'd lost so much weight she looked almost skeletal. Her eyes were still closed, despite the small ruckus they had caused outside.

"Zhafaera," he said urgently, placing one hand on her exposed neck, just above a hard metal collar, feeling for a pulse. There. Her pulse was strong and steady, and Delan relaxed marginally. She was just asleep.

"*Zhafaera,*" he repeated, a little louder this time as he slipped his other hand around the other side of her face, lifting her head from the nightstand. Her eyelids fluttered. "Zhafaera, *wake up.*" He wanted to shake her, but she looked entirely too fragile for that. He stroked her hair instead. "Come on, open your eyes."

Slowly, her eyes opened, but he could tell she wasn't all there. "Zhafaera?"

Finally, she focused her gaze on him. As her eyes met his, a fog seemed to clear, and she smiled. "I'm dreaming," she whispered.

"You're not, I'm here," Delan said, leaning forward and kissing her hard on the forehead. "And we have to get you out." Pulling back, he could see the confusion in her face. This was already taking too long.

"You're really here?" she asked.

"Yes."

"You're not dead?"

"No, I'm fine."

Zhafaera made a small noise and launched forward, wrapping her arms tightly around his neck and grabbing fistfuls of his stolen guard's shirt. His half-healed wounds protested the contact, but he held her to him as hard as he dared, one arm around her waist and the other moving gently up and down her back, trying to calm her shaking. He could feel her spine protruding under her thin green dress.

Finally, she pulled back, wiping tears from her face. Her blue eyes sparkled as she glanced around the room, taking in the open door and the black cat standing guard there.

"Evey?" she asked, surprised.

Zhafaera. Evey sounded relieved, and she glanced over her shoulder. *What's that on your neck?* The dragon sounded horrified.

352

Zhafaera reached up and touched the collar, flinching. Delan could see the skin underneath was red and raw. He reached up, holding the collar gently and feeling around it for a latch.

"It's shielding me from my magic. It doesn't open." She added to Delan.

"It *has* to open *somehow*," he said.

Evey left the door and trotted over to them. Stretching out and placing her paws on Zhafaera's chest, she inspected the collar. She *breathed* on it as she did the door, but there was no blue fire this time. She tilted her head, reaching up a paw to touch the metal in a very cat-like gesture.

The spell is bound in the metal. The young dragon sounded nervous.

"What is it, Evey?" Delan asked.

I... I don't like this magic. It's wrong.

"Okay, but can you break it?"

Evey climbed on Zhafaera's lap, placing both paws on the collar. For a long moment, Evey simply stared at the collar, unmoving, her attention completely fixed. There was a loud crack, making Delan jump, and the collar fell away. Evey quickly moved away, her fur standing on end and her back twitching.

"Are you all right?" Delan asked Evey, as Zhafaera reached up her hands and massaged her neck. She closed her eyes, and suddenly Delan could feel her presence. Not as strongly as he was used to, but he knew she had been able to draw at least *some* magic.

353

I'm fine, Evey said. *Let's just go.*

He looked to Zhafaera. "Can you stand?"

She nodded, and he pulled her to her feet. She stumbled, using his arm to steady herself.

"I'm all right," she said quickly, in answer to his worried look. "I just got thirsty." She waved her hand over to a tray near the door. The food looked almost untouched, but there was an empty cup on the tray. Something clicked in his brain.

"He's been drugging you?" he asked as Zhafaera regained her balance. She nodded.

"Why? He already had you collared. Literally." He eyed the band of metal on the ground with disgust.

Zhafaera ran a hand through her short hair but didn't let go of him. "He knows I'd win a fair fight," she spat out. "Delan, we can't go yet, we have to find Velexar."

Delan looked at her incredulously. "No way. Forget about him. Forget about the Sapphire. Just run, please, let's just go."

"I can't do that," her voice was quiet but hard. She met his eyes, and there was an unfamiliar emotion there. "No matter where I go, how fast and far I run, he'll find me. And I'd rather jump out that window than let him…" she stopped. "We can't leave him alive."

Delan just looked at her. Something had happened. Something bad enough to scare the toughest woman he knew.

"Besides," she looked away, unable to meet his gaze. "Alec is here. He's –"

354

"I know," Delan whispered. "I saw him. I didn't know what to do. It's not like I could hold him without you."

Zhafaera reached up and touched his face. "The only thing we *can* do is try to kill Velexar. Killing him might break his spells." She paused. "I hope."

Delan ran a hand through his hair in frustration. He'd never been so conflicted in his life. On the one hand, his little brother was in deep trouble. On the other hand, he couldn't do anything about it without Zhafaera, and she was severely weakened. He wanted to get her away from here.

"What if we left now, and came back when you've regained your strength?" He asked. Definitely not begging.

"I already tried that once. I'm fine."

Anger flared in Delan. "Don't lie to me. Argue all you want, but don't lie to me."

Zhafaera met his anger with some of her own. "Fine, I'm not fine. But if I leave this city, I'm not coming back. I'm not leaving while Velexar is still alive. And the Sapphire is *mine.*"

She has us, Delan. Evey chimed in. *We can help her.*

Delan sighed in defeat. "How will we even find him? He could be anywhere."

"I know where he is," Zhafaera said grimly.

Chapter 16

Zhafaera could feel the pull of the Sapphire. Its presence was almost overwhelming, not screaming now, but calling to her, drawing her in. Zhafaera led the way, slipping quietly down the hall and into her mother's chambers. Making her way quickly through the main living quarters, she made for the bedroom, but as soon as she stepped over the threshold, she froze. Much of the damage from the night of the attack had been repaired, but a large brown stain still darkened the wood. From where her mother had lain as she bled out in Zhafaera's arms.

"Zhafaera…" Delan gently touched her arm, and she flinched, jerking her arm away.

"*Don't*," she hissed, her eyes still on the floor.

Her heart was pounding, but a cold rage had settled somewhere in her navel, and was slowly spreading its icy tendrils through her body.

Turning abruptly, she stepped over the bloodstain and headed to the bed, shoving her hand under the mattress and pulling out a long, viciously sharp dagger, then moved to the closet, where she began strapping on her mother's knives. Feeling better now that she was armed again, she turned to leave, and stopped. She looked to the left side of the room to the large vanity, framed by three mirrors.

Memories of sitting here, next to her mother, watching her brush her hair washed over her and her throat tightened.

Setting her shoulders, she moved quickly to the vanity and yanked open the only drawer. There in front of her, completely undisturbed, was a thin silver circlet. Her mother's crown, delicately shaped to look like ocean waves and highlighted with a handful of small sapphires.

She took a deep breath and closed her eyes, hesitating.

Delan stepped up beside her, and her eyes shot open. Reaching into the shallow drawer, he pulled out the crown, wiping away a thin layer of dust as he did.

"Let me," he said quietly. And he laid the crown gently on top of her head, setting it to rest in her hair just back from her forehead.

She met his eyes, just as he dropped to his knees.

"My Queen," he said, inclining his head.

For a moment, Zhafaera couldn't speak around the lump in her throat. "Don't be ridiculous," she admonished, rather more forcefully than she had intended. She softened her tone. "You never have to bow to me."

Leaning down, she grabbed Delan under the armpit and made to pull him up... but the room spun, and she stumbled. Delan was on his feet with an arm tightly around her shoulder before she could blink.

"I'm fine, I'm fine." She wasn't sure if she was saying it to him or herself. She took a breath and shook her hair back off her face, straightening her shoulders and stepping forward. Delan's arm fell away, but she reached back and grabbed his hand, not looking at him to avoid the worry she knew was written across his face.

What he didn't know was that she intended to either kill Velexar or force him to kill her. No more locked rooms. No more blood magic. One way or another.

She led him back out to the hallway where Evey had waited. Together, the three of them made their way down the back stairwell, moving as quickly as they dared.

At the bottom of the stairs, they paused, Zhafaera reaching out with her magic. She tried not to think about how much effort it took.

"A few guards inside the throne room. Two more at the end of the hall at the entrance to the east wing." Evey took off down the hall like a streak of shadow.

"Is Velexar in there?"

"Yes."

"Plan?"

"You take the guards, I've got Velexar. Try not to get killed."

Delan ground his teeth, clearly not happy. "Can I at least drain his magic, like we talked about?"

Zhafaera paused. "Only if you're very, very fast. And be careful of the Sapphire."

There were several soft "*omphs*" from down the hall. Delan fell in behind her as Zhafaera turned the corner to see Evey trotting back from the end of the hall, having knocked out the guards, and looking rather pleased with herself. They converged at the side entrance to the throne room, reserved for the royal family's use.

Without slowing, Zhafaera raised her arms, and blew the doors inward off their hinges.

Stepping over the threshold onto the black and white tiles, she drew power through the air, feeling the electric crackle of lightning heating between her fingers.

Velexar stood just ahead of her, standing in front of the large silver throne, smiling as he met her eyes.

She let loose everything she had, and white hot lightning shot forward towards him. He spread his arms, sending the lightning to either side, not letting it hit him... but she hadn't expected it to. It was the gap he'd left that she needed.

Ignoring the sounds of a fight beginning behind her, presumably between Delan and the handful of guards just now reaching them, she pressed forward, reaching directly for the Sapphire hanging around Velexar's neck. She stretched out both physically and magically, and she felt it reaching back for her. She knew the instant her magic touched the surface – she could feel the power emanating from it, meeting her own and washing over it like waves. She *pulled* as hard as she could, drawing the power towards her.

Velexar stopped smiling.

Good.

The waves of power began to swirl until they were like a tempest, drawing her own magic into their depths and leaving her struggling to stay afloat. She fought, hard. She could feel Velexar's own presence woven through those waves like the thin, deadly tentacles of a jellyfish.

Everywhere she turned, there was a new sting. But she could feel the Sapphire, calling to her louder than ever before, and there was sweat beading on Velexar's forehead.

Zhafaera gritted her teeth and focused on pushing those stinging threads back. She could hear the sounds of a scuffle behind her, the ring of steel on steel, but she couldn't spare even a glance. She was too focused on controlling this ocean of power, riding the waves while trying to get a foothold in the deep, dangerous depths. She'd worked closely with her mother, even using the Sapphire on occasion, and she'd felt its raw power. It clearly wanted *her*, not him, no matter how hard he tried to bend it to his will. She *pulled* again, and she could see the Sapphire lift slightly off of Velexar's chest.

Suddenly there was a *pop*, and her magic was gone, like someone had pulled a plug. Or put a shield in place. She fell to her hands and knees, unable to support herself against the sudden emptiness. Gasping for breath, she watched as Velexar's fine boots walked slowly towards her.

Looking up into his face, she noted that while his mouth was quirked up in a smirk, his eyes were blazing, and he looked just slightly disheveled. She couldn't suppress a wild grin. That fight had taken more out of him than he'd anticipated, and she was nowhere near her full strength.

Knife in hand, she pushed up hard from the ground with all the strength she could muster, aiming below the Sapphire on its chain, straight for Velexar's heart.

Velexar clenched a fist and she froze mid-air, the knife falling from suddenly numb fingers as her body went rigid. She was eye to eye with him and unable to move more than her head.

He reached up and caressed her face. She tried to jerk away but couldn't. "This looks lovely, on you my dear," he said quietly, touching one finger to the crown on her head. "Perhaps I'll let you keep it."

"You're dead," she hissed at him, struggling against her invisible bonds.

"Please, dear, be reasonable. You're weak, still half drugged I believe, and now bound and contained in more ways than one. What was your plan, exactly?"

Before she could reply, the sound of clanging metal died suddenly, and her heart stopped as she listened for who the winner of that fight was.

"Let her go!" Delan's voice was low and furious, with just a hint of breathlessness.

Velexar's smile widened, and he turned, moving Zhafaera to the side to better see the new challenge. He turned her so that she could see Delan and Evey – Evey in full dragon form with one taloned paw pinning two unconscious guards to the ground. Delan looked overall no worse for wear, holding his bloody sword in both hands. It looked like they'd managed to close and block the door behind them, keeping their backs to it while they'd dealt

361

with the guards. Now it was just Velexar, and he had her in his grip once again.

"Or what, Delan?" called a voice from behind her.

Her heart turned to ice. She couldn't turn to look, but she knew who it was. Clearly Velexar *wasn't* the only one left.

Delan looked like he'd been punched in the face. It was one thing to know, logically, that Alec had turned. It was quite another to hear his voice, so unlike the young, carefree boy he had been just a few months ago. Zhafaera felt Alec move up to stand next to her, and she turned her head to look at him. He was dressed in a floor length black robe, the sleeves hanging down over his hands. Seeing him in the daylight, he looked older. Taller, more angular, his dark blond hair longer and framing his face. She'd been so focused on Velexar, she'd had no idea he was even in the room. Now she was suspended in the air between them.

She struggled against the shield blocking her magic, but Velexar wasn't the only one that had expended effort fighting for the Sapphire. She could only *just* feel the shield surrounding her core, but she could sense it enough to use her own life force to press hard against it. The shield stretched. And stretched. Zhafaera pushed harder. Suddenly the shield snapped back in place, causing her to recoil as though she'd been slapped. Which she supposed she had, in a way.

"Stop that," Alec snapped.

She gaped at him. "But you're not –" she blurted.

"Not what? Strong enough to shield you?" Alec grinned widely, his eyes alight. "Guess again."

"He's stronger than you ever thought, darling," Velexar said lightly.

Zhafaera was too shocked to form words. There was no way he'd become this powerful in the space of a few months. *No. Way.*

"Ah, I see you didn't know either." Velexar tsked. "Lord Delan," he said suddenly, and Delan jumped slightly, startled out of his focus on Alec. Evey took a protective step closer to him.

"Yes, yes, I know who you are," Velexar said. "Alec has told me all about you. And," he added, "he felt your presence the moment you entered the city. Quite good luck, actually." He lifted one hand and tapped a finger against his lips. "The ritual will work much better with you here as well. Blood magic can be a bit particular. With you alive, it should go much smoother. It's why we let you into the castle in the first place."

Delan looked confused, and Zhafaera's heart clenched. *Please don't let him find out this way,* she thought.

"Now, Delan, tell me," Velexar was saying. "What happened to your mother?"

What? Delan's surprise must have mirrored her own. Their eyes locked.

"What the hells does that have to do with anything?" Delan growled, adjusting his grip on his sword.

"Why, Alec, of course," he said, as if it were obvious. "Now. Your mother."

Delan spoke as if the words were being pulled out of him. Which, they very well may have been. "She died in childbirth."

"Whose?" Velexar asked.

"What?"

"Whose birth?"

Delan frowned deeply. He appeared to be struggling with something. "Alec's?" he finally said. But it came out as a question. Zhafaera was confused.

"Was it?" Velexar's voice was light, with a hint of amusement.

"I–" Delan paused, shaking his head. "It was – it was me. Mine. My birth."

"Hmm, I see. Then tell me, who is Alec's mother?"

Delan's eyes flickered from Zhafaera to Velexar, and finally to Alec. He took a step forward.

"Alec, please, you're my brother, please just let go." He held out a hand.

Alec laughed. "I'm not your brother."

Delan's face was a terrible mix of confusion, anger, and fear. "Of course you –"

"To be fair," Velexar interrupted, holding up a hand as he turned to look at Alec. "He could be." He turned back to Delan. "But you did not have the same mother."

A feeling of dread was uncurling in the pit of Zhafaera's stomach that had nothing to do with her current predicament. A memory was flitting on the edges of her mind, but she couldn't bring it into focus.

"Yes," Velexar said, smiling widely at her. "There it is. My sister Karaena, the slut, had more than one child, apparently." Velexar reached out a hand to Alec, and Alec took it, moving over to his side and letting Velexar place an arm around his shoulders. Delan looked sick.

"People would have known," Zhafaera whispered. "*I* would have known." Her denial sounded weak, even to herself. The memory was fuzzy, but she could see her mother sitting on the edge of a bed, holding a baby. *She held plenty of babies,* she argued to herself.

"And I suppose you yourself have never used an illusion spell, is that right?"

"I –" Zhafaera took a breath, trying to quell the panic beginning to rise. "She couldn't have. All of the people she would have had to convince." She jerked her head at Delan. "So many, for so long… it's impossible."

Velexar touched the Sapphire around his neck. "I've managed to make half the country all but forget her. Forget *you.*" He waved a hand dismissively. "One village is nothing to those like us. And it was only one small lie, really. She just had to make them forget *when* the woman had died. Beyond that, everything was the truth."

Zhafaera's thoughts had stopped. She remembered how they always stayed at Crystal Point longer than anywhere else when they had Toured. Tours that had started when she was seven or eight. Not long after Alec had been born.

"Trust me, our family's magic is distinctive," Velexar was saying. "I'm surprised you didn't see it for yourself. But then again, I suppose we only see what we want to see."

"But why?" she asked. Delan still hadn't spoken a word.

"Why what? Why would she hide him?" Velexar held up a hand and began ticking items off his fingers. "For one, having a male in the line of succession has historically been detrimental. Just look at me." He sounded amused, but there was an undercurrent of bitterness. "Two, I believe that at that time she'd already begun to suspect I was plotting against her, although I was rarely in the capital then. And three... perhaps she simply didn't want him." He raised a hand to stroke Alec's hair, and Zhafaera wanted to scream. "But I do. He'll make an excellent Heir." He smiled down indulgently at Alec, and Alec beamed.

There was a strangled yell, and Zhafaera turned her head in time to see Delan charging forward, sword raised, Evey close behind. Together, Alec and Velexar raised their hands. Fire shot out of Alec's palm, and Evey leapt in front of Delan, breaking their forward momentum as she blocked the fire blast, breaking it and sending it rushing to either side of them. Velexar swept his hand to the side, and Delan flew across the room, hitting the wall behind the throne with a loud *crunch*. Evey hadn't moved.

"Delan!" Zhafaera screamed. He hit the floor and didn't get up. She struggled again against her bonds, straining with all of her might, determined to get free.

Velexar whipped around and seized her by the throat, cutting off most of her air. "Enough," he demanded, giving her a rough shake. "Alec, take the dragon," he called over his shoulder.

"With pleasure." Zhafaera could see Alec rush forward towards Evey, quickly moving out of her field of vision. She heard Evey roar, and Zhafaera went cold. Evey was a dragon, yes, but a very, very young one. She could perform *some* magic, but she was far from fully trained. She couldn't even breathe fire yet. Zhafaera was not at all confident that she could win a fight against a mage of Alec's power. And he *was* powerful, Zhafaera had to admit.

She scrabbled against the shield blocking her magic, and strained against Velexar's grip, both the physical one and the magical one.

"I said *enough*," Velexar yelled, tightening his grip on her throat until she saw stars. She didn't stop, she couldn't. One way or another, she was going to get free, even if that meant the freedom of death. Her eyes fell on Delan at the base of the wall over Velexar's shoulder, facedown and still. Her heart clenched and she fought a wave of despair. She'd had him back for so short a time.

She heard Evey and Alec, somewhere to her left, out of her line of sight. There was a heavy crash, a whoosh of fire, and a roar of pain. Her heart sank further. Then she suddenly felt herself buffeted by air, and she knew Evey had taken flight. She felt a kernel of hope. If Evey could stay airborne, she might have a chance. She wanted to call out to her, tell her to just leave – fly away out of one of the large windows lining the opposite side of the room, but she couldn't speak. She couldn't even breathe. Darkness was creeping in from the edges of her vision, and her struggles were weakening. She was going to die. Strangely, that thought didn't scare her. She felt only disappointment.

And then suddenly, Velexar's hand released her throat. He had stepped back, shaking his head and looking at his hands.

"What the –" he stumbled, and the magical grip surrounding her vanished abruptly, dropping her face first to the floor, gasping for air. Lifting her head, she saw the look of horror on Velexar's ashen face.

He met her eyes. "What are you doing to me?" he screamed wildly.

Behind him, Zhafaera saw movement. Delan was rising to his hands and knees, shaking his head, and she understood.

Delan was drawing power from Velexar. A *lot* of power.

She pushed herself up, grabbing her dagger from the floor where it had fallen earlier, just as Velexar fell to his knees in front of her. They both looked down at the knife in her hand, then their heads shot up and their gazes locked.

Zhafaera shot one hand forward, grabbing the Sapphire hanging around his neck along with a fistful of the silk shirt beneath it. Its presence washed over her like a balm, shattering the shield, and giving her the strength to jerk her other arm up as hard as she could, driving her knife home under his ribs and into his heart, twisting viscously as she pulled it back out. His hands came up, weakly trying to cover the wound as blood poured out from between his fingers. With an almighty jerk, Zhafaera broke the chain holding the Sapphire and yanked it from his neck.

Velexar fell backwards and hit the marble tiled floor with a heavy thunk, his hands falling to either side of his still body.

Zhafaera released a breath she hadn't realized she'd been holding. She felt the power of the Sapphire rising up, rushing through her, threatening to overwhelm her. She used the last of her strength to force it down and regain control. Left unchecked, the Sapphire could kill anyone not powerful enough to control it. And just now, it took every ounce of power Zhafaera had left to rein it in. She stayed on her knees, cradling it in both hands, breathing deeply as she felt its power recede to a small warmth in the back of her mind. The light radiating from its deep blue depths subsided into a faint glow.

Delan was stumbling toward her. "Alec!" he called. "It's over! Stop!"

She turned to look behind her at the destruction caused by the battle between mage and dragon. Evey was still in the air, but at Delan's call, she landed on the side of a tall pillar, digging her claws in and sending small stones flying to the floor beneath. There were scorch marks all over, and several columns looked as though they were ready to tumble over. Stones littered the floor, mostly from the ceiling from the look of it. Several of the large windows were broken out, open to the darkening sky beyond. Alec stood in the middle of the room, panting slightly.

"Over?" he said. "You think it's over because you killed *him*?" Alec laughed. "You have *no idea* what's coming."

"Alec, please, you're my brother," Delan pleaded, stretching out his hand as he reached Zhafaera. She could hear his rough breathing. "It doesn't matter –"

"Oh, it matters," Alec said forcefully. "It matters because my *real* master is on his way."

Evey hit the ground behind him just as Alec began to change. Zhafaera couldn't look away as his form blurred and twisted. His arms and legs lengthened and widened, bubbling as blood red scales replaced his robe. Talons formed at the end of each finger, elongating into curved blades as he hit the floor. His neck lengthened, sharp spines growing out of the back as his hair vanished and his face elongated into a snout filled with razor sharp teeth. His body grew… and grew and grew, his robe ripping as black, leathery wings sprouted from between his shoulders and a tail extended from his hindquarters.

Standing before them, shaking his body as though settling everything into place, was a red and black dragon.

Not full grown like the one that had brought Zhafaera here, but double the size of Evey. She wanted to scream with frustration and grief.

"Alec," she whispered. "What have you done?" Tears spilled from her eyes, and she could do nothing to stop them.

The dragon that had been Alec drew his lips back, revealing all of his gleaming white teeth in what she thought might have once been a smile.

I've taken our magic to the next level, he said. *And unlike this* baby – he swung his tail at Evey, who had been creeping up behind him, and she dodged behind a column – I *can breathe fire.*

He opened his mouth and Zhafaera braced herself, reaching up and finding Delan's hand and gripping it tight. She reached for the Sapphire, trying to pull magic to her, but found she couldn't. She was utterly spent. In her present state, she doubted she could do so much as light a candle. They were going to die in a hail of dragonfire, made a thousand times worse by the fact that it was Alec. Her brother. Their brother? *Oh, Alec.*

The red dragon inhaled.

Zhafaera could see Evey flying towards them, but she wouldn't reach them in time. Good. Maybe she would survive.

The red dragon breathed, and a jet of fire shot forward. And froze.

The fire hovered in the air, its motion completely frozen, as Zhafaera watched in shock.

Everything happened in slow motion as the fire began to reverse its course. Roiling, churning, forming into a loose sphere, it moved back towards the red dragon, whose jaws were still open.

All of a sudden, the ball of flames released, and white hot dragon fire shot back down the dragon's throat.

The red dragon – *Alec,* she thought, her heart twisting – clawed at his throat, ripping off chunks of flesh and spraying blood across the black and white tiles. His sides seemed to be emanating smoke, and he leaned his long neck towards the floor and began to retch. Slowly, he fell to his knees, rolling over onto his side just as fire began pouring out from his belly.

Delan rushed forward, but Zhafaera grabbed his arm, using all of her strength to hold him back as the red dragon lay panting on the floor. The fire leaking from his belly had turned to blood.

It doesn't matter, Alec's voice sounded in their minds, and Zhafaera felt her heart break. *They're here.*

The dragon gave one last, shuddering breath, and was still.

Zhafaera looked up at Delan, who was frozen to the spot, his eyes glued to the scaled form on the floor. *Alec.*

"Delan, I –"

Delan ignored her and moved slowly towards the red and black body. Zhafaera followed closely. Dropping to his knees, he reached out a shaking hand to touch the large scaly head. He took in a deep, shuddering breath.

"Why? Why did you –" His voice choked off.

Zhafaera was numb. She reached out a hand and gently touched Delan's shoulder. He flinched and she pulled away, but he immediately reached out and grabbed her hand, looking up at her with tears streaming down his face.

"I killed him."

Zhafaera's mind couldn't process what had happened.

"I saw the fire coming at us, and I just –"

"I know," she said, kneeling next to him and pulling him to her. "You reacted on instinct. You were holding so much power, and… you saved us." But her heart broke for him. He'd killed the brother he'd sworn to protect. That she'd promised to get back.

Delan let out an anguished cry, burying his face in her shoulder and clinging to her. She glanced at the body next to them. *Why?*

"Delan," she whispered. "It's not your fault. He would have died anyway. Mortals can't hold the change to immortal. It tears us apart." She took a breath, trying to sound soothing, but her voice sounded dead to her ears. "Even if it hadn't, the other dragons would –"

She was interrupted by an almighty crash that shook the whole castle. More stone came loose from the ceiling, showering them with dust and small rocks. A shrieking roar shook the floor under their feet, shattering what remained of the glass windows facing the ocean. There was another *BOOM,* followed by the crunch of breaking rock, and what looked like part of the East tower went flying past the windows, landing in the keep below.

Screams, very human screams, began – both from inside the castle and the city outside.

"What the hells was that?" Delan asked, his head shooting up.

We have to go. Evey was running towards them. *We have to leave right now.*

Two more crashes, as if something huge had hit the castle. Something like –

Dragons! Evey said. Her mind-voice was frantic. *We have to GO.* She darted to one of the broken windows, flinching back as more rock flew by. Zhafaera heard the deep *whoosh* of a large fire somewhere nearby, and the screaming intensified. *They're going to destroy the city!*

Delan stood abruptly, scrubbing his arm across his face and pulling Zhafaera up with him. Together they stumbled over to the window next to Evey. A deep roar echoed through the night, and terror gripped Zhafaera.

"Evey, take her," Delan said, lifting Zhafaera and placing her on the young dragon's back, behind the wings. Zhafaera swayed, but held on one-handed, her other hand still gripping the Sapphire so tight it was painful. Evey stepped up onto the wide ledge of the window, and Zhafaera could see straight down. This part of the castle was directly at the top of the cliff, with the rocky beach far below them.

Delan, get on, Evey's mind voice was grim, but urgent.

"Evey, you can't carry us both –" Another *whoosh* of fire and the sound of huge wings flapping made them all flinch.

Zhafaera weighs almost nothing now. GET. ON.

Zhafaera tugged on Delan's shirt, and he clambered onto the horse-sized dragon behind her. Evey sagged a little, but regained her footing quickly.

Good enough, she said, and she leapt.

Their flight was more like a controlled fall. Zhafaera was thankful for Delan's arm around her waist, pinning her in place, or she was fairly certain she would have slipped right off. She gripped Evey's sides as tightly as she could with her knees, feeling the muscles of her wings flex as she fought to keep them airborne. Evey may have been the size of a horse, but dragons were like birds – their bones were hollow, and therefore they were much lighter than they looked. A full grown dragon may have no problem ripping a castle apart, as the ones behind them were doing from the sound of it, but a young one of Evey's size… Zhafaera was amazed they weren't plummeting like a stone.

They hit the ground hard, Zhafaera and Delan jerking forward and tumbling off over Evey's head, rolling over the hard round stones on the beach. For a moment, Zhafaera could only lie there, staring up at the dark sky, now lit with a faint orange glow. The city.

She groaned and rolled just as Delan reached her, pulling her to her feet again.

"Are you all right?" He asked, his hands running across her body, checking her quickly. "Evey, are you all right?" he called.

I am fine. Even Evey's mind-voice sounded tired.

"I'm good." Zhafaera panted. She stopped and squinted. In the flickering light from the fires beginning to rage above them, she could see blood seeping through his shirt. "You're bleeding!" She made to undo the buttons, but he grabbed her hand.

"It's nothing, I'm okay." Delan said, wincing. "It's just the wounds from the dragon at the pool. I think one's split open a bit." He placed one hand over his chest, on the bloodstain, then pulled it back to inspect. "It's not bleeding much. Come on, we need to find somewhere to hide. There's a cave down the beach a bit."

Zhafaera wanted to say more, but she couldn't form the words. Delan scooped her up in his arms and took off down the beach, Evey following close behind. Looking over Delan's shoulder, she could see the castle, lit from below by the orange glow of fire. Several dragons were moving over the castle like they were climbing a tree, shredding towers and flinging stones as they went. Half the castle was already in ruins.

Zhafaera counted five more dragons flying over the city, weaving back and forth and spewing flames down into the streets below. The sound of the city screaming would haunt her nightmares forever.

Epilogue

They sat huddled in the cave. Delan held a sleeping Zhafaera in his lap, with Evey pressed up against his side. He was shaking, and he couldn't stop.

Evey had managed to shield them from magical detection, hopefully masking the energy of the Sapphire still clutched in Zhafaera's hand. Evey assured him they'd be safe. One thing a young dragon *could* do was avoid detection. He thought back to when they had first found her in the mountains. At least, they usually could, when they weren't half dead.

They'd been silent for some time when Evey finally broke it.

I think we figured out why the dragons were "working" with Velexar.

"What?"

He was a means to an end.

Delan was silent. At this point, he couldn't even muster up the energy to be afraid. He stroked Zhafaera's hair, brushing it out of her pale face. *She'll wake up soon,* he told himself.

The screams outside were dying down, but the crackling of flame could still be heard, almost drowning out the sound of the waves lapping the shore of the cove.

He wasn't sure how long they'd been sitting here, but he had a feeling dawn wasn't far off.

What are we going to do? Evey asked worriedly.

"We'll go home. Get as far from here as we can."

Delan, these dragons won't stop at Arenthia, the city or *the country itself. They want to see humans back in what they think is their proper place – as slaves. And a good portion of the country's mages were just burned alive in the city.*

"We'll figure out something."

And if we don't? We won't be able to run forever.

"Then we're screwed," Delan snapped.

Zhafaera stirred in his lap. She turned her face into his chest, and white-hot pain shot across his body. His wounds had definitely split open, but they didn't seem to be bleeding too much. But gods, did they hurt. He tried to shift her without waking her fully, but her eyes flew open and she sat bolt upright, rolling off his lap and landing on her knees in the dirt.

Delan held up his hands in a calming gesture. "You're okay, we're safe." His voice sounded hollow even to his ears.

Zhafaera took in her surroundings and relaxed a fraction. "How long did I sleep?"

"I'm not sure. A few hours at least."

She turned her face to the opening of the cave and her face twisted in pain. "The city…"

"I know."

378

"All those people," she choked on the last word. The scent of ash and char was heavy in the air.

"I know."

Zhafaera finally looked at Delan. Her eyes filled with tears as she reached for him. "Delan, I'm so–"

"Don't," he held up a hand and cut her off abruptly. She recoiled as if he'd slapped her.

He instantly regretted it. "Don't say it," he whispered. He could feel the deep, black pit of grief inside his chest, hovering just under the surface, ready to break through at any moment. If she touched him, he would break. Zhafaera turned away, moving towards the opening of the cave and leaning against the opposite side to watch the carnage, her face carefully blank. Delan could see the fire from the city reflected in her eyes. Evey looked back and forth between them, unsure what to do.

They sat in silence for some time, until the darkness outside the cave began to lighten into the faint grey light of pre-dawn.

"I'm sorry," Delan finally croaked out.

Zhafaera didn't look at him. Her gaze never left the burning city. "You have every right to blame me," she said softly. "It's my fault."

"That's not what I meant, I don't blame you at all," Delan said in horror. "You're not the one who –" his throat closed, guilt warring with grief.

Zhafaera didn't respond. When she finally spoke, it was to Evey.

"Is this cave secure?"

379

Yes. They will not sense us.

"Good." She finally broke her gaze away from the ruined city, and looked at her lap. Slowly, she opened the fist that was clutching the Sapphire. It was the size of her palm, and glowing faintly with an inner light. Zhafaera stared at it for a long time, as dawn broke and the cave slowly lightened.

Suddenly she reached up and slipped the sleeves of her thin gown off of her shoulders, letting it hang low so that it only just covered her breasts.

"Zhafaera, what are you –"

I'm not sure that's a good idea, Evey said.

But before either of them had finished speaking, Zhafaera had lifted the Sapphire in both hands, folded them over each other and pressed the Sapphire to her chest just above her heart.

She gasped, and her head snapped back against the stone.

And she began to glow.

The glow started as a faint blue fuzziness rippling over her skin from her chest outwards. It quickly consumed her entire body, growing larger and larger as it went until it extended to at least six inches off of her body. Her mouth and eyes were open, and the glow that emanated from them was a hot blue-white that shot straight to the roof of the cave.

Delan shifted towards her, unsure what to do.

Don't touch her! Evey's voice was alarmed.

What's she doing?

380

She's bonding *it.*

Is that safe? Fear shot through Delan. He remembered Zhafaera telling him that the Sapphire required precise control. She wasn't exactly at her strongest.

No, but she's doing it anyway. She can't stop now. She will either succeed or die.

Delan felt sick as he watched helplessly.

Finally, after what felt like an eternity, the glow began to recede. Slowly at first, then more quickly, until her eyes closed and the glow was gone. She was panting, but Delan let out a huge breath. If she was panting, then she was alive.

"Zhafaera?" he said tentatively.

Her eyes opened and her gaze met his. She gave a small smile and slowly removed her hands from her chest. The Sapphire remained in place, sunken part way into the skin between her breasts. She quickly pulled up her sleeves again, and the Sapphire disappeared under the cloth. No one would ever know it was there.

"Can I touch you now?" Delan asked.

Her smile twisted and turned sad. "Do you want to?"

In answer, Delan launched himself across the cave and pulled her into his arms, holding her tightly. He could feel her heart racing, and the new hard, hot oval of the Sapphire pressed against his chest.

"I told you, it's not your fault."

"It's not yours either," Zhafaera said softly, pulling back to look at him. Her gaze dropped to his chest and she frowned. "You're still bleeding."

"It's nothing," he began, but she was already slipping off his coat and lifting his shirt over his head. When she saw the slashes, she gasped and hissed through her teeth.

"Delan, these are – you must be in incredible pain!"

He was, but less so from the physical wounds. Zhafaera placed her palms flat on his chest and he winced. Then he felt the familiar tingle of magic wash over him, soothing away the pain.

"Zhafaera, don't, you're still weak…"

"Hush." She was biting her lip in concentration. Delan couldn't argue. He could feel the skin on his chest and back knitting back together. It didn't hurt, but it wasn't exactly a pleasant sensation; it felt like his skin was crawling. But the pain was almost gone.

Delan didn't look until she pulled away, and when he did, he was amazed. His wounds were healed, finally closed, leaving him only with two thick red scars across his chest. He imagined his back looked the same.

"There's not much I can do about the scars," Zhafaera said. "They were half-healed, and the scar tissue was already forming. But at least you're not bleeding."

He reached up and took her head in his hands, kissing her lightly on the forehead. "Thank you."

"You're welcome. Can't have you bleeding to death on me." She looked at him seriously. "I need you."

His breath caught. "I need you too," he said, resting his forehead against hers.

Zhafaera opened her mouth and took a breath.

I think we should move, Evey interrupted.

Zhafaera's mouth snapped closed and she pulled away, letting go of Delan and looking at Evey.

"You're right," she said briskly, giving her head a small shake and tossing her hair back. "We should go while they're still busy with the – with the city." She stood, dusting off her dress, and looked around. "At least we don't have to pack up camp."

Delan could feel her anxiety despite her light tone. They had nothing but the clothes on their backs, and a long journey ahead of them. But he tried to match her energy, getting up and stretching. "Which way?"

Zhafaera was already moving. "Our best bet is out of the cove and down the beach. Hopefully we can find a ship going south."

Evey trotted ahead, and Delan hurried to bring up the rear. It didn't matter to him. He'd follow her anywhere.